Written by: Holland Cutrell

For my grandmothers, aunts, uncles, cousins, brother,

and Daddy most of all

Prologue: Bad Night

I was running, screaming in pain. I ran even as the wind threatened to tear me off my bloody feet. My long blonde hair whipped at my eyes, stinging them, blinding me further. Nothing could possibly be worse than this.

I was going to die. Every haggard breath I took felt like it would be my last. Buildings fell just feet away from my body, flinging sand everywhere. I put my foot down on what I thought was a stone, but it was soft, fleshy. It was a person, a dead body.

I shrieked as loud as my throat could bear and then fell into nothing...

Ch. 1 Finds

I awoke yelling at a handsome face. My mind was still in turmoil so I grabbed this person and squeezed hard, straining my thin fingers. He yelped then took hold of me in a grip far stronger than mine. "Lyn, stop! It's me."

I loosened my grip then as reality hit me.

"Oh, Glen, it was awful!" I was surprised at how my voice rasped thinking I must have kept everyone up again.

"Was it the dream?" he asked, concern wrinkling his perfect brow.

I nodded, eyes downcast and cheeks burning. It was the fourth time this week I'd had the same dream.

"Is she awake?" a timid voice asked. Raine, I thought, thank goodness she's okay. A curly brown head peaked over Glen's broad shoulder and smiled. "Hi, sleeping screamer."

I managed a slight smile. "Raine... How'd it go last night?"

"Fine," a voice that was not Raine's answered. "You should know since you set it up."

"Caine, I see you're still as arrogant as ever."

A narrow face came into my sight as Caine walked over, chuckling. "And I see you're still as demanding as always."

I smirked at his cut.

"Here, look," said Raine, shoving a sack on to our makeshift pallet.

I picked it up gingerly, feeling its weight, then untied the string that bound it and peered in. What I saw made my breath hitch. Jewels, gold, silver, and bronze lined the bag.

"Where did you find this?" Were the only words I could sputter out.

"It's a secret," said Caine, smiling slyly.

"Glen!" I spat, "I though you were watching what they picked up."

"Hey, listen, Glen had nothing to do with it."

"Yeah," Raine added, "He didn't even come."

"Oh." I suddenly felt guilty for going off like that, "Why not?"

Glen colored a bit and replied, "I was... worried about you."

"Well, it was sweet of you to stay."

I looked at our array of stolen wealth, frowning, and sighed. "Look, guys, we can't accept this. It's too much."

Caine scowled and protested, "What are you talking about? This could feed us for weeks and we'd still have some left over! You can't just expect us to *give* it away."

Raine frowned and looked like she was about to bawl. She hated it when we argued.

"You think people won't notice we stole all this? They'll start sending trackers after us!"

Caine opened his mouth to say something else, but was silenced when we all heard a loud "Ka-boom!"

Raine let out a terrified shriek and Glen clamped his hand over her mouth. I scanned the beaten-down shack wildly, searching for whatever had made that sound. Bandits and looters were common in this area, but I never thought they would target a ruined building.

"Quick, we have to hide!" I whispered since I didn't know how close the attackers were.

"Hide? We need to fight or else they'll blow us outta here!"

"Caine, would you just listen for once! We need to-"

I was cut off and thrust backward by another resounding blast. I hit wall, hard. It knocked the breath out of me and I landed on the ground with a "thud." I groaned, seeing blood drip off my forehead and started to panic. I wanted to shout for help, give a signal, but was too paralyzed with fear to do so.

Footsteps started close-by. I held my breath, hoping the owners wouldn't gaze around the corner. My heart was pounding in my chest seeming loud enough to lure them right to me.

Suddenly, a gloved hand shot out from behind my cover and grabbed me with a hand around my middle and another clasped over my mouth. I let out a muffled scream as I was drug around the rock wall, kicking and flailing in the stranger's grip, oblivious to my surroundings.

While I was struggling, my foot connected with a solid person that darted out in front of me. It jarred my leg from foot to hip and I felt my captor loosen his hold, apparently caught off guard. This was my chance. I slammed the back of my head into the man's face and saw blood fly. He released me with a grunt and fell backward.

I managed to keep my footing, even ~~know~~ Though the dizziness threatened to take me down with the stranger. I tried to race forward, but tripped on the body of the person I had kicked earlier. I landed on top of it only to find myself staring into eyes much bluer than my own. "Glen! I-I'm so sorry."

"Up."

"Wh-what?"

"Get up!"

I shuffled hurriedly to my feet, careful to avoid his chest. I extended my hand and he took it with both of his. With effort I was able to haul him to his feet.

"Pow!" A bullet whistled past my ear, so close, I could feel the wind as it went.

"Lyn, run!" Glen propelled me forward as another bullet flew past our heads. We ducked simultaneously to make ourselves smaller targets.

"Keep your head down and don't stop running! I'll draw them off you."

"No! I'm not letting you get hurt because of me. I'm coming-"

"Caine and Raine are waiting in the woods. Now go!"

He broke out to the right in a sprint. I almost followed him, but the woods were just a few paces away and I didn't think my heart could take any more excitement so I put my remaining strength into those last steps to the trees.

Spying movement in my peripherals, I braced for more bandits. I wasn't sure if tightening up would help against guns, though. I caught a glimpse of Caine and Raine poised and ready for an onslaught before they finally realized it was me.

As Raine flung herself into my arms, crying, I thought of how menacing our world had become. Children her age should not be battling hoodlums and then running into woods that were even more sinister. I felt a tear slide down my cheek and clung to Raine tighter than before. We had to get through this. I swallowed the lump in my throat and told her, "It's going to be okay. Those men won't follow us any more."

I heard a sob beneath me and suddenly wished I had someone that would whisper reassurances to me, too. I closed my eyes and felt a hand on my shoulder. I turned my head to see Caine nod; it was his way of saying let's move on.

Blinking away tears, I gave Raine a pat on her back and she stepped away biting her lip, trying not to cry. I took her dainty hand in mine and we began to run on shaking legs.

We finally paused to catch our breath in a small clearing. Clutching my side, I scanned the perimeter of it searching for movement. I ambled over to Caine to give him my report. "I can't see anything, but we still need to keep our eyes open for something suspicious."

"I have things under control here. You just might want to take care of that head wound you've got there." He gestured toward my head and smiled like he was about to make a joke but dropped the thought.

I nearly asked him what he was talking about, but then recalled the blood and put my dirty hand on my forehead. It came away wet and colored with crimson. My eyes widened at the sight. There was no telling how much blood I had lost while we were running. Furious at Caine for not bringing it to my attention earlier, I spat, "Why didn't you tell me I was bleeding?"

"How was I supposed to know? I just saw it now!"

I gave him a look of irritation and started tearing my already ripped shirt into long strips to bind the wound with. Probably feeling to blame, Caine came over and stilled my shaking hands. I let him finish the wrapping and fasten it at the end. I heard him sigh. "Look, I'm sorry, alright. I guess I should have been paying better attention."

"I apologize, too. I know you were looking out for us. I should have noticed myself."

I watched Raine wander over to us. She giggled at my bandages. "Lyn."

"Yeah?"

She grabbed her stomach and said, "I'm hungry."

Numerous thoughts crossed my mind, then, none of them good. It all came down to one thing. I had left the sack. "Oh no."

Caine gave me a questioning look and asked, "Lyn, are you okay?"

"The money," I breathed. He appeared even more puzzled, and then froze. I saw fury flicker in his dark eyes and knew I wasn't going to win this dispute.

"You didn't leave the money, did you, Lyn?" I could hear the tightly controlled anger in his voice. I ~~shook~~ nodded my head yes. Caine gave out a ferocious wail and yelled; "We ain't gonna make it!"

A frightened Raine asked me, "L-Lyn, are we really going to die?" her voice rising with every word. I gazed into her hazel eyes, my jaw set, steeling myself. "No, of course not."

Caine was pacing, and I saw perspiration forming on his forehead. I went to confront him. "Caine, stop it! You don't know what you're talking about."

He skidded to a stop and glared at me with rage-filled eyes. I honestly thought he was going to jump me, but a crashing sound to our right made heads turn. My body tensed as the shape of the person came into view. They were upright on two long legs with a very muscled build. I squinted through the dim light and made out a dirty blonde head. My face lit up at once seeing Glen wasn't dead. That thought alone made me feel much improved.

I started toward him and noticed he was shaking. Quickening my pace, I wondered if he had been injured, but as I advanced, I noticed he was not trembling with anguish, but with laughter.

"Glen?" I inquired, "Are you alright?"

He looked at me with those startling blue eyes and beamed. "Been better, but I made sure those fools won't be coming back. The question is, are you?"

He brushed my blood stained bandages with the back of his hand, concern dissolving his smile. I felt the blush creeping up my neck.

"I-I'm fine, really. It's just a cut."

"Glen, we missed you *so* much!" Raine came and wrapped her arms around his waist and he encircled her in a hug. Caine stood off to the side, arms folded, looking rather gruff. I recalled the bag and asked, "Glen, you didn't happen to go back for the sack, did you?"

"No. Why?" His brows knitted together, trying to figure out what was missing.

Tears sprang to my eyes unwillingly and I turned away from him. It was gone. With it, we could have bought food, new clothes, a place to sleep...

"She left it. Now we're going to starve." It was Caine's voice, dripping despair.

Nothing from Glen yet. He probably hated me so much he wouldn't speak to me. But suddenly I felt strong arms circle me. Burying my face in his chest, I gave in. He hugged me tighter, whispering encouragement. We stayed like that for several seconds, and then he nudged me, saying, "Look."

I pulled away a bit and followed his finger. Raine marched over to Caine and gave him a forceful shove.

"Why'd you go and make Lyn cry? She's doing her best for us and all you can do is tell her how awful she is!"

For once, Caine had nothing to say. He just stared at Raine. She sobered up a little and stated, "You're her friend... Friends help and- and love each other, too."

Her cheeks flared red, likely embarrassed by her sudden outburst. I grinned, wiping tears with a grimy sleeve.

"Shall we get going, then?"

I gazed up at Glen. "You're not mad? You don't hate me?"

He snickered and planted a little kiss on my flushed cheek.

"Lyn, I could never hate you. As for the money..." he shrugged, "Forget it, we'll find something else. If you feel up to it, we can plan another raid later, too."

"Thanks, Glen. It means a lot, but for now lets just see what happens."

We all set out, then, deeper into the vast canopy of trees. Glen and I were in the lead with Raine between us and Caine lagging behind, mumbling to himself. Raine told us she was hungry more than once and I think everyone was feeling slim. My stomach growled and Glen glanced over and cackled. Soon after, though, everybody's began to rumble and we all giggled in spite of ourselves.

We found a tree with clusters of moss growing around the roots and decided to bed down here. It was extremely difficult to get comfortable on the damp ground, but we finally managed to settle in after much twisting and turning. I was apprehensive about sleeping in the woods, but listening to the others' steady breathing made a sense of calm settle over me. It wasn't like we had the means to sleep somewhere half-decent.

I was nearly asleep when I heard Glen's voice.

"Lyn." He whispered, "Are you still awake?"

I grinned in the darkness.

"I am now."

"Do you remember when we first met?"

As a matter of fact, I *did* remember, quite clearly. My smile broadened.

"How could I forget"?

Ch.2 Glen

It had been a chilly, wet day and I had told my mother that I would go and watch our slaves that evening. I mounted my chocolate colored Andalusian riding with a straight back toward the field. It was a ways away since we lived on a plantation. About half way there, storm clouds rolled in and the rain came pouring down. My horse was spooky and we slipped and skidded many times, making the ride terribly uncomfortable. The downpour had taken a turn for the worst; giant puddles formed, some knee-deep in places where the dirt had caved in.

We had been riding through a very rough spot and my horse crumpled, then came back up, bucking. Much as I tried to keep my balance, in the end, I got thrown off. I remembered the sudden pain and how terrifying it had been, thinking for sure I had broken bones and recalled myself wailing and crying for help. Remembered how no one ever came.

I had just lain there, motionless while the rain kept beating on me. This hurried stranger had seen my unmoving body and stopped to stoop low over me. Out of the hazy memory, his handsome face and striking blue eyes were the things that had stood out most. He had asked me where I lived and I pointed at the long dirt road I had come by. Somehow, the boy carried me all the way to my colonial mansion without getting lost.

My weeping mother had answered the door followed by my armed father, brother, and many servants. After that, things get really muddled. I slept for a day and remembered waking to the same stranger's face. Seeing him clearly in the morning light, I realized I had spoken with the boy the day before my incident. He had been plowing fields when I came riding by and, bored as I was, stopped to chew the fat.

He must have stayed with us, no doubt courtesy of my mother, her way of saying thanks. The boy had had the loveliest smile when he saw I was awake. We exchanged names after some chattering and his took me by surprise. Glen, one of the only names that rhymed with Lyn. I had enjoyed his company so much, I invited him to come and participate in the harvesting with me early that dawn. He agreed without hesitation and we slipped down the winding stairway and out the front door. I found my horse was still missing so we walked instead.

We'd had the most wonderful time, dancing over puddles and stepping on each other's footprints in the mud. Even gathering the vegetables was pleasurable with cheerful company. On the way back, I'd asked him where he had come from. Glen told me he had been adopted, never having known his actual parents, and that his foster parents lived far away. Or rather, he'd moved away, seeking a life of his own when he was old enough. Glen had asked me the same question and I said that I had moved around a lot due to business prospects of my father. We would have continued conversing, but the sights of smoke in the direction of my home made us quiet down and hurry on.

It was a horrifying sight. The beautiful two-story colonial was ablaze, most of it already burnt to the ground. I had panicked and attempted to rush into the blaze, but Glen had held me back and towed me away. I fought the whole time, but it was a useless effort. Before we turned to flee into the wood, I glimpsed a shadowy figure riding off into the smoky haze. I tried to alert Glen, but he would have nothing of it.

That evening, when it had just been the two of us, we bed down in the hills and clung tight to each other. I had been in a fever, but from then on Glen and I had stayed together, a light in the dark for the other. All that was over two years ago, but the memory remains like it was only yesterday.

Ch. 3 Missing

I awoke to the scent of lush earth; as I opened my eyes, the soft light of the morning greeted me. I sat up to survey my surroundings and saw the empty dent to my left that told me Glen was up. I glanced to my right to see Caine snoring peacefully. He looked young and helpless while he was asleep. I examined the moss beside him and noticed Raine was missing, too. She must be out walking with Glen. They often went out early, strolling with each other.

I was about to stand when Caine muttered something. Dropping to my knee I leaned over and watched his eyes flutter open. I grinned. "Sorry, what was that?"

He sat up, wiping the sleep from his droopy eyes. "I said that was the best night's sleep I've had in days."

I cocked my head to the side, not understanding why. I was sore and stiff from dozing on the ground all night.

"C'mon, you telling me you're not rested? I didn't hear a single peep from you last night." That struck me as strange. Then it hit me.

"Wait, you mean I didn't keep everyone up yelling?"

"If you did, I didn't hear it." he and I helped each other to our feet, "Anyway, I think we should get moving, I'm starving here."

Using even a small amount of energy left me weak and my stomach seem emptier. Before long, we stumbled across a narrow, beaten-down path that had to have been the way Glen and Raine went. We followed it single file with Caine close behind and me in front. After wrestling with low-hanging branches and thorn bushes, we ended up on the rocky outskirts of a cliff that overlooked a good-sized town.

"Wonder how much we could scrounge up from that place."

I eyed Caine and could tell exactly what he was thinking; he cut his russet gaze sideways to see my reaction.

"We have to find Glen and Raine, first. It's not like them to be gone for so long."

I was beginning to worry about where they were.

Caine waltzed over and inspected the cliff side. He grimaced and said, "I think they had the same idea."

I stifled a gasp and hurried over. Sure enough there was a trail of dirt and what looked to be a rockslide down the ledge.

"We have to go after them!" I blurted. Caine tipped his head in the direction of the track saying, "Ladies first."

I moaned and commenced the descent of the rocky face. I slid down without meaning to, skinning my knees and palms in the process. Halfway down, I began to think about Caine, knowing he wasn't too fond of heights. I opened my mouth to call for him right as a small stone struck my head.

"Ow, Caine, watch where you step!"

I looked up just in time to see him plummeting from above me. I let out a diminutive shriek and scrambled for a firm foothold. I found one, but it was too late. Caine slammed into me and I completely lost my grip. Thankfully, we had scaled most of the cliff so the plunge wasn't dire, but he landed on top of me and it knocked the breath out of both of us. I ~~lied~~ lay there a few seconds to regain it; Caine seemed to have the same idea, but with him stretched out on me instead of rolling off.

I sucked in enough air to say, "Get off." And pushed, not doing a thing. Caine managed to muster the strength to haul himself off me.

"Let's *never* do that again."

I shook my head, but remembered he couldn't see me and so said, " I'm fine with that."

I turned onto my stomach and heaved, struggling to my feet. I felt my knees buckle and would have collapsed if Caine hadn't caught me.

"Alright, we need some food. Even if Glen and Raine aren't in this town, we're going in anyway."

I nodded grimly and we set off in the direction of the settlement.

It was a nice place, not too upscale nor too poor. It had cobblestone streets and the houses seemed fair and elegant. Even some people were sociable; a few returned a smile to us as we walked past.

Great. I am going to love robbing them. Not like I even had a good conscience any more. Caine nudged me slightly, whispering, "Look." He pointed to a richly clad couple that appeared to be in deep conversation with each other.

"How 'bout giving them the old hit-and-run?" he asked with a quirky glint in his eye.

I raised an eyebrow. "You think I could pull it off?"

He snickered.

"What happened to that blueblood confidence?" I shot him a look, but it only made Caine smile more, "Go with what you feel like. I'll come in if things get too hot."

With that he stalked away, melting into the crowd like a practiced thief. I took a deep breath to still my shaking nerves. Let's see if I was as good as Raine when it came to distractions.

I began to stroll lithely toward them then made like I had a tremor and went down howling in mock pain.

"Help me, please! It hurts!" This got their attention along with everyone else's on the street.

I did my best not to smile when I caught a glimpse of Caine passing like a shadow through their midst, picking purses like flowers. One of the women reached out to me and I seized the opportunity to extend the show. I snatched her bony arm, jerked the woman down and wailed, "Don't touch me!"

In the back of my mind, I prayed Caine wasn't having too much fun. To my relief, I heard the "tap-tap" of approaching footsteps. Now came the risky part.

I quieted my yelps of hurt to whimpers as I heard the planned commotion to my right.

"...Your what?" the wealthy woman's voice.

"My sister. She has these real bad seizures sometimes and mother said to keep her away from crowds." Caine was doing an amazing job of keeping his voice steady and worried, "So if you'll excuse me..."

There was shuffling and then skinny arms scooping me up. He lost his footing and I shifted to try and help, but Caine stamped his foot, the signal for me to be still. He got me away from the awestruck crowd and finally set me down in a deserted alleyway with a rusty cellar door at the end. I reached out, tugging on the latch until the door creaked open making me jump and hastily shut it.

"What are you doing?"

I turned to find Caine staring at me. "I-I was-"

"There's nothing down there so don't bother." I saw him finger his shirt. "By the way, amazing performance out there. I nearly cracked up seeing everyone's face."

I blushed and looked away. "What'd you get?"

"I'll show you once we leave this place."

This left me mildly annoyed, but I said, "We still have to search for Glen and Raine, first."

I looked Caine in the eyes, daring him to object. He only shrugged, saying, "Let's go then."

My eyes hurt, my feet ached, and even thinking was painful. I was sure Caine felt the same. We had been hunting for the good part of a day, avoiding as many people as possible in case we were recognized. I was beginning to think Glen and Raine had just up and left. No. If they had, then surely someone would have placed a sign telling us, wouldn't they?

At least we had eaten. Caine purchased some fresh fruit with our stolen wealth. I would have preferred something more substantial like meat, but the price was high and we didn't risk it.

"Well… back where we started from. What now?"

Releasing a breath of frustration, I realized we were in the town square again. "Where have we *not* gone?"

Caine assumed a defensive cast. "You're not going to want to hear it."

"Just tell me."

"The cells." I froze for a moment. Caine noticed my distress and added, "I'm not saying they're there, but it's the only place we haven't tried."

Prisons were never a place thieves wanted to go. If they were there, how would we ever get them out? We were only two kids after all.

"You think we won't find them." It wasn't a question. I turned on him.

"No. It's just-"

"Hey!"

I recoiled at the voice and Caine swiftly moved to where I was behind him and he was facing an advancing man. I placed my hand on Caine's arm to stay him. The man paused before us, breathless. "You two haven't seen some kids come this way have you?"

My instinct told me to play it safe, but I asked, "What did they look like?"

"An older boy with blonde hair and blue eyes and a little girl with curly brown hair. They were arrested earlier today, but killed a guard and escaped."

I felt sick. Caine answered for me. "Nope. Can't say we've seen 'em. Sorry."

He pushed me away and as soon as we were out of sight, I crumpled to the stones. "What is wrong with you? He could have spotted us and we'd be dead or close to it."

I just shook my head.

"He was talking about Glen and Raine."

"No he wasn't."

"Actually, yeah he was."

I gasped with alarm at the voice right behind me and spun to be met with a smirking face, framed with dirty golden locks.

"Glen." I wanted to reach out and hug him, but seeing Raine by his side, her face a mask of apprehension, I knew something wasn't right.

There was a charge of footsteps at the top of the alley; we circled around and saw a triple of armed guards hurrying our way.

"Go, go!"

We were off in a second, the cobblestone path blurring beneath our feet. I thought we were going to make it, but another curve and we were trapped by a dead end. I heard Caine curse, saw him search frantically for a way around. The men had us cornered, panting with their weapons drawn.

"All of you are under arrest." The leader said, aiming his pistol, "Put your hands up and no one gets hurt. Resist and... well." He clicked the gun.

We all exchanged glances. With only the tiniest movement, Caine nodded to Raine. She dove, screaming, on to the street; at the same time, Caine dashed forward with his knife and tackled one man, gun going off as he hit. I made for the other a moment too late. The leader was going to shoot Caine.

"No!" The deafening shot sounded as I crashed into the second guard.

I smashed his head against the ground with the impact and listened to the soft thud as another body landed next to mine. I couldn't look.

"Lyn, are you hurt?"

I nearly fainted with surprise at Caine's touch. Glancing to my left, I spotted the bloody stiff of the third guard, a bullet through his chest.

"Let's move." I looked up to see Glen putting away a silver pistol, "The noise is sure to draw attention."

Caine snatched my arm, tugging me away from the sight of dead men. That had been one of the tightest spots yet, and we had made it out. Alive.

Ch. 4 Signs

"You killed to get out?" Glen nodded, explaining the gist of he and Raine's escape as we strolled along the forest floor just now finally slowing our pace from the town.

"They were tracking Raine and I knew I had to do something." He lifted his lips into a self-pitying smirk, "I... made an impression and we both got thrown in jail."

"Least you got something out of it." Caine gestured to the hidden pistol.

"That reminds me." I began, "What about the gold?"

Caine jumped into the tale of how he stole it. I rolled my eyes, not paying attention. Instead, I watched how beams of multicolored light broke through the branches. Bending my neck, I could just make out the canvas of sky. Shades of red, purple, blue and gold combined to form beauteous patterns littered throughout the atmosphere. The scent of dead leaves, mist, and soil wafted through the air; I was merely enjoying being alive.

Caine suddenly pulled up beside me and I caught the tail end of his sentence, "- and that's how I stole the gold."

I turned on him sputtering, "What?"

He cut his gaze and I saw Glen and Raine trying to hide their grins. I became a little cross. "Listen, before you go off about how I wasn't paying attention, just wanted to let you know that I was the one who helped you steal the stuff. So let me see it."

He pursed his lips, pretending to consider. I narrowed my eyes, voice threateningly low. "Caine."

Glen then intervened. "Come on you two, don't start a fight. Caine, stop being difficult and show her the money."

"Fine."

He lifted up his shirt, exposing his belt loop. I counted the bags dangling from it. One. Two. Three...

"Six!" I exclaimed, "Caine, you were only supposed to take from the people that were speaking with one another."

He held up his hands, palms out. "Before you get torn up about it, let me tell you I stripped five bags out of six off that woman. They're filled to the brim with *gold,* too."

I opened my mouth, but said nothing. Why would a single person be carrying all that money?

"Wait, that doesn't make any sense. Have you stopped to think why one person would be toting that kind of cash around a busy town"?

This appeared to make everyone pause to contemplate. Caine spoke first with his arrogant response. "It doesn't matter. The important thing is that it's ours, now."

"No, she has a point." I looked at Glen expectantly. Maybe he had figured it out; he smiled out of self-pity. "We're either already in a whole lot of trouble, or the trouble's just beginning."

"D-Does that mean we're gonna have to run more?"

I peered down at Raine and could see the terror in her doe eyes. I couldn't answer that question because I didn't want to lie. I simply slid my arms around her, an attempt of comfort.

"What do you mean by that?" Caine, evidently still not understanding what Glen had in mind, was interrogating him left and right.

"I'm saying those people could be very influential and dangerous. They could possible be the ones who sent the guards in the first place."

Raine shivered in my arms as she said, "Lyn, I want to go to bed. Let's not run any more."

Caine and Glen were still bickering with one another and I had to raise my voice to be heard. "Guys, listen! I know we're all tired and scared, but maybe a good-night's sleep will help."

They glanced at me, but didn't argue. We walked in silence for a while until Glen found a fairly satisfying patch of grass to bed down on. Another night of sleeping on the run. I sighed, listening as my breath mingled with the sound of crickets and frogs. I followed a tiny lighting bug and held back a laugh when it alighted on Caine's nose; I had to turn away as it lit up.

I let myself drift off, wondering if my dreams would be pleasurable as well.

What was that noise? I paused to listen, but the only sound I heard was my rapid breathing and thudding heart. I tentatively racked the brush aside... There it was. My heart skipped a beat as the *thing* rotated in my direction; it looked gigantic.

I thought it was a bear, but it had horns protruding from its head. Our eyes met and its were red with madness. The fiend started toward me on four tree trunk- sized legs with dagger like claws at its feet. A demonic growl erupted from its throat when it picked up the pace.

My brain was screaming out commands to my body, but I was so torpid with fear I couldn't move. The monstrosity was barley two feet away as it rose up, still making that awful noise. I contorted myself as adrenaline rushed through my veins, twisting and grabbing a handful of moss. Then the bear came down.

Piercing agony raced up my calves and I let out a sequel of surprise as the ground moved beneath me, a trail of blood wetting the grass. I gasped as it unhooked its claws from my legs and shifted to where we were face to face. It opened its razor-edged mouth, howling in rage. Salvia coated my face and the last thing I saw was the beast's blazing white teeth and black insides...

"Ahhh!"

I sat bolt upright yelling at the top of my lungs, blinking, trying to clear the sweat from my eyes, hyperventilating.

"Lyn? Lyn, calm down. I- Glen!"

I felt Raine's tender fingers attempting to quell my tremors. Her hands were moved away gently and replaced by Glen's powerful grip.

"Lyn, look at me."

No matter how hard I tried I couldn't focus on him. Images kept flashing in my mind. The bear, the blood, the pain... I started shaking more violently; it was all Glen could do to keep me from falling over.

"Caine, bring me some water and food!"

I sensed something cool touch my lips.

"Lyn, you have to drink." I took a weak sip and Glen encouraged me to take more, "Right, now swallow."

I hurriedly drained the flask of water until there was nothing but drops left.

"Better? Can you eat?"

I nodded, answering both questions as Glen pushed a small fruit into my trembling hands, closing my fingers around it.

I lifted it to my dry, cracked lips and took a bite. Flavors blossomed in my mouth; it was sweet with a hint of tartness in the skin. Glen sat there by me, ready if anything went wrong. Caine and Raine stood back a bit, watching. When I had eaten down to the core, my tremors ended.

"Dream?"

"Yeah, but this time it was different."
Glen lifted an eyebrow in inquiry. "Could you tell us about it?"

"Well... I can't remember much, except that there was this huge creature." I exaggerated the word by spreading my arms apart, "At first, I could have sworn it was a grizzly bear, but it had bull-like horns coming out of its head."

Raine drew in a little breath, her eyes widening. Caine scowled, like usual, asking, "So you kept us all up last night because you were afraid of some unicorn bear?"

I shot him a look of exasperation and continued with my story. "If you would have been there, I'm sure you'd have been scared half to death, too. Anyway-"

"That's the point. I *wasn't* there so it's not *real*. I know you're a bit shocked, heck I am too. This has been your worst tantrum yet. I can't *wait* to see what you'll do next."

He ended on a note of sarcasm and stood. "Now that you're not screaming your head off, we'd best get going."

Raine rose and came over to hug me. "Don't worry about Caine. I'm glad you're okay"

She then took off to catch up with him. Glen helped me to my feet, giving my hand a quick squeeze before he let go.

"You tell me the rest while we're on the road. I think I need to hear it."

I gave him a half-hearted smile and went to follow Caine and Raine.

Ch. 5 Memories

We had been traveling for quite a while, but most of the woods looked alike so no one knew exactly where we were. Every now and then, we would find a fallen log or stump with fungi growing all over it to mark our path.

I had described the rest of my dream to Glen. He seemed more interested in this particular one than others we had discussed together. We hung back from Raine and Caine a few paces to have some privacy.

"And this bear... you didn't see any more with or around it?"

I shook my head.

"No. It was just the one."

Glen thought on this for a moment. I had become so caught up in the conversation, that I bumped into Caine and nearly knocked us both down.

"Good grief, Lyn. Are you sure you don't need to get your eyes checked?"

I was noticeably flustered at my mistake and apologized. I heard Raine laugh.

"Don't fret, Caine, Glen almost ran me over, too."

Glen was smiling sheepishly, abashed from having crashed into Raine.

"You two are both clueless."

"Look whose talking."

Caine gave me one of his mischievous smirks and I chuckled. It was nice to relieve some of the tension built up after such hard time on the road.

I glanced over Caine's knobby shoulder and my smile swiftly faded. It was a rough looking dirt trail. Never a good sign when you didn't want to be spotted or found like us. I took an uncertain step forward, but Glen stopped me. "Hold on."

I spun to face him. "What is it?"

"Do you see that part of the forest on the other side of the road?"

"Uh-hu. What about it?"

"There's a legend about those woods."

This pricked my interest. It was something in the way he said it that made me unsettled.

"Is this going to take long?"

My breath hissed out at Caine's impatient nature. He asks the stupidest things sometimes, I thought.

"Be quiet and sit down. We can all use a little break now and again." I looked at Glen, smiling, "And what better way to have one than hear about a legend."

Caine groaned in protest, but seated himself on the ground. Raine had an animated glint in her eye as she asked, "Is the story happy with a good ending?"

Glen laughed under his breath. "Far from it."

Raine frowned and I motioned for her to come over to me. We both sat down, with her resting on my lap. "Alright, Glen, we're all ears."

He smiled at me and began.

As Glen recited the words of the tale, my mind wandered. I glanced over everyone's faces, remembering how an unlikely group of friends had come to be. It was hard to believe it had been over a year since we'd met.

Funny, I thought smiling. Our backgrounds were so different yet here we are. There was me, the rich girl who had lost all she owned. Caine, the thief who'd been thrown out on the streets. Glen, the common working man who had never had a real loving family. Raine, who had lived with a wonderful family, but had been forced away.

I recalled the day my life had changed forever. Glen and I had been traveling together for nearly thirteen months, searching for the man on horseback I had seen the day my house was destroyed. We were much thinner and dirty, too. We had no money so we often stooped as low as thieves, stealing what we needed and praying we didn't get caught. I still feel the pang of a guilty conscience whenever I think about it.

I never understood why Glen didn't leave. He'd had plenty of opportunities for work that he was well suited to, but turned them down, even after I had told him to go in the first place. Truth be told, I was grateful in the long run. I would, by no means, have made it through the sensation of having nothing. All my life, I had had anything I wanted; servants catered to me all hours of the day and I never had to work to acquire money.

Glen had shown me how the real world worked. After having confessed to me about his childhood and uncaring foster parents, I felt a sort of empathy for him and stuck with Glen. He told me he had gone out on his own, laboring for small amounts of money to keep him going. He had said it didn't bother him, though, enjoyed it, in fact and supposed it gave him more than just money.

It just so happened, on that day, we were going to need a few skills of his. We were introduced to Caine, first.

I glanced over at Caine's angled face, remembering the time we bumped into each other. I recalled Glen and I walking down a village street after having swiped a small purse off of one unfortunate person.

A stranger, close to our age, waltzed over and brushed my shoulder with his. I swung my head around, startled, and expecting an apology. He kept on walking, a little faster than before. I stood there, dumbfounded, then Glen took me by the hand and swiftly trailed the stranger. The boy noticed us following him and broke into a gallop; we did likewise.

I had not the slightest idea why Glen was pursuing this stranger, but did not resist when I was drug into twisting alleyways. We flew around corners, sometimes painfully dragging elbows and knees on them, and sprinted down a straightaway until we finally had the boy at a dead end.

Panting, he looked from left to right. I had immediately thought of a trapped animal when I first laid eyes on him. It wasn't just in his demeanor, but the boy's physical appearance reminded me of some half-crazed wolf. His hair was dark auburn and wild, sticking out in all directions and his skin was tan, perfectly commenting the boy's russet eyes.

When he figured out there was no other ways of escape, he dropped to his knees and begged us not to hurt him. I had been upset from the way he'd treated us. Like thugs, I remembered.

Glen advanced, demanding he return my purse. A wave of confusion hit me and I groped for my money that wasn't there. I stared at the boy and gaped; he had nabbed my cash without ~~me~~ my ever noticing. Would've gotten away with it too if Glen had not have been there.

I watched as he reached into his tattered jacket and produced the bag of coins. The boy acted as if he was going to hand it over to us, but jerked away and hurled it at the ground. The cloth burst open as it connected with the stone and coins spilt everywhere. The boy had broken off to the side to try and make a run for it, but hit me in his hurry and his speed was broken, leaving an opening for Glen to snatch him.

The boy screamed as he was brought to a rough stop, arms twisted painfully around.

"Let go of me!"

He writhed in Glen's grip, spun and slugged him square in the jaw. I gasped as Glen dropped his arm, but jumped the boy before he could get away. We fought in frenzy; he tried to pry me off but I held on, eventually spotting the hilt of a blade at his waist. I dove for it.

I had just gotten my fingers around it when he seized my wrist, pinning my hand in place. I remembered glancing up at his face and seeing that charming grin on it.

"Nice try."

"Oh yeah?" In the second we paused, I had worked the knife free and flipped it to where the blade pressed into his skin. Where was Glen? There was no way I could hold my own against this boy so I thought of something quick.

"What's your name?"

He'd been struggling, and would have very well yanked free, but the question took him off guard.

"What?"

"Caine!"

We both spun to where Glen had hold of a little girl, no older than ten, and she was yelling a name. The boy's to be exact.

I heard him curse and shove me to the ground, skillfully avoiding the knife. Caine pressed on Glen until he had drawn his own dagger and leveled it with the girl's neck. That stopped the boy dead.

"Glen, don't!" I struggled to my feet, still clutching the knife. Glen flicked his eyes to me and adjusted his hold on the girl. Her gaze was steady, yet terrified at the same time, large, brown eyes locked on the boy named Caine.

"If you hurt her, I'll kill you."

Caine's voice was remorseless, "No." He snatched me around the waist, wriggled the blade free of my hand, and held me at knifepoint, "Better yet, I'll kill her."

I saw Glen hesitate, the resolve in his eyes softening.

"Glen." I warned him. He had never been reckless, but seeing me in danger might just set him off. The little girl spoke, then.

"Please, Caine, don't hurt her." She shifted in Glen's strong arms and glared at him levelly, "Put me down."

He stared down Caine, looking as if he wanted to say something, but the boy cut him off.

"You first."

I listened to Glen silently curse and he had dropped the girl like a live snake. As soon as she hit, the girl dashed over to Caine and hugged him, pressing the knife away from my neck.

I glanced down at the back of Raine's head, knowing she had very likely saved my life by doing that; I could still remember the cool feel of death right under my throat and swallowed.

The boy had looked at me as I clambered over to Glen, the girl protectively under his arm. "What do you want?"

I had scrutinized him strangely, and then the craziest idea shoved its way into my head.

"Come with us." I said on impulse.

Everyone had reacted separately. Glen had been completely taken aback, struggling to compose himself. Caine had let a slow smile spread across his face. The girl had stared sheepishly back at me, as if embarrassed to be asked to travel with us. From there, we called each other a few names, learned some background, and actually began traveling together.

Come to find out, Caine had been raised in the city, living on the streets with his parents who were, as he called them, "master thieves". I'd figured out how Caine had learned things the hard way, acquiring his stealthy skills at an early age. Once he had gotten older, his parents had allowed him to come on a few of their burglaries.

"They never got caught." He'd said. That is until they became overly confident and careless, going in a place and coming out in chains. Caine had told me they left him in safety before they went, so he ended up not getting caught. When his parents never returned, Caine had gone out and seen a prison boat leaving.

"I always had a hunch. It was the paper that confirmed it."

The next day, he had fished a dirty newspaper out of the garbage and read the first headline. *Jail Boat Sunk by Violent Storm. All presumed dead.*

He had spoken about how he wasted away for a few days until the hunger finally got to him. Caine said he had gone to the chapel, remembering their offerings to be very generous. At the time, I thought robbing a church was the worst possible thing you could do. By now, we had stolen from a dozen or so, each one making me feel a little blacker at heart.

I remembered that Caine had eyed Raine when he described going up to the church steps. He told us, after having gotten up to go to the building that this girl had been lazing around and then saw him. She had asked Caine what he was doing and then actually second guessing herself, led him right to the offering. He said it was a gesture that stopped him dead in his tracks.

"A caught thief must become a clever thief, as my folks had said. She skipped off leaving me with two choices: I either dropped it all and bailed right there, or follow her, take the money, and live with a guilty conscious for the rest of my life."

Thankfully, Caine decided on the in-between, or Raine would still be an orphan living at the church. Or maybe it hadn't been such a smart move, in Raine's case at least. I had always thought the story of how they had met was sweet.

Caine had followed the girl to the spot and tried to sneak the money out, but he said she had turned around, seeing the whole act. "Go ahead, I won't stop you. You need it more than the church, anyway."

Those were the words that had made Caine place the coins back in the velvet-lined plate. Raine had come with him out of empathy. *Her* story was one that no child should ever have had to go through.

If I remember correctly, Raine had been born into a loving, middle-class family and grown up in the suburbs of the city. She had led an average life until her father had gone out to seek his fortune; people were calling it the California Gold Rush. Raine had been left with her mother who suddenly fell ill after her father had gone. She had died shortly and there had been no way to notify Raine's father and so she had been sent off to the church and raised there. That is, until Caine came along.

Ever since then we've traveling as a foursome, helping each other stay alive and survive day by difficult day.

Ch. 6 The Waterfall

"Lyn? Hello, did you even listen?"

Caine's egotistic voice interrupted my daydream and I made my eyes focus on his thin face.

"Lyn?"

Caine looked back over his shoulder and answered Glen. "She's okay, Glen. I think I snapped her out of it."

My face flushed red at the attention they were paying me and I held up my hands to stop the onslaught of words already pouring from their mouths.

"Guys, guys! I'm fine. I feel great, really."

Judging by the look on Glen's face, he didn't believe me. Caine, on the other hand, quit the thought and helped Raine up out of my lap. She stretched and yawned, accenting her child-like features.

"Glen," she said rubbing an eye. "You're a wonderful storyteller."

He lifted one side of his mouth, acknowledging her complement. I shifted my gaze to Glen, loosening up myself. "Sorry. You'll have to catch me up on the story later."

His smile broadened and he told me not to worry.

"What we need to be figuring out is whether we cross the road or follow it from the woods."

I pursed my lips, feeling my temple wrinkle up as I considered both options. Truth be told, I would be keen on leaving the woods, but we would have to find some other form of surety to rely on.

"After hearing your story, Glen, I'd rather take the road."

Raine nodded her approval of Caine's suggestion. He eyed me to see what I purpose we do. Obviously, the legend Glen had told was not pleasant.

"Well, it sounds like the road would be our best bet if we want to avoid trouble. As for unwanted attention..." I trailed off and my party grimaced.

"I think we should follow the road, too." Glen must have come to a conclusion. "Whenever we spot someone, veer off and into the woods." He cast about our faces to see if there would be any arguing. We all decided that his was the best plan of action. After a look and a few steps forward, we continued on, expecting at any moment to be called out or shot at.

We trudged on at a quickened pace, somewhere between a fast walk and a jog. It was demanding, both physically and mentally, to be so high-strung and on the run, but if you weren't then our life would force you to it. It certainly had me.

A few hours had gone by and we hadn't encountered a single soul, save for the occasional bird gliding overhead. No one had spoken in a while and an eerie feeling fell over me, darkening my mood. I could bear it no longer.

"Does anybody have any idea where we're going?"

My voice seemed alarmingly loud, but I was past the point of caring.

"Does it look like we know"?

I felt the surge of anger rush through me and I snapped back at Caine. "No, Caine, it doesn't. I don't know why I even asked because all you do is answer questions with stupider questions!"

He assumed a vicious cast and shouted over me. "What do you want me to do about it? All I ever hear from you is-"

Glen sprung between us, pushed us away from each other with Raine in tow and hollered, "Run!"

I swung my head around and spied a whole caravan of merchants coming our way. Fast, too, like they were being chased. For a horrible moment, I felt a longing deep in my mind. I ached to run toward them and let the people take me away from this difficult life and back to my old one.

"Lyn, move!" Caine took hold of my hand, tugging so I would go with him. I saw the urgency in his eyes and let him pull me away from the path and the memory. We raced through the undergrowth side by side, breathing hard, until we came to a thicket of bushes.

"Quick, you first," he urged, scraping at the dense brush.

I clawed at the bramble, but more and more took their place.

"Would you hurry up"? Caine shoved my cut hands out of the way and put his body into it. The sound of snapping branches made me want to bolt, but I threw my weight against the wall as well. Break! As if an answer to my thoughts, the final bit of limbs gave way and we burst through, landing facedown in the weeds. I pushed myself to my feet, spitting out the grime with renewed vigor. Caine was by me in an instant.

"Are we safe?" I asked, probably echoing his own thoughts. In the heartbeat we paused, there came a sound of yelling and bushes being trampled. I heard Caine swear and flicked my gaze around where we had crashed.

"There. Come on, let's go!"

Without a second thought, he snatched up my arm and took off through the high weeds, heading for the sound of water. That would only make more noise to lure them to us.

"What are you doing? Stop!"

I tried to dig my heels in the ground, but the grass nearly made me trip and we were at the stream. The thrashings were closer, now, and he splashed into the water. I didn't follow. Caine spun to stare at me. "Lyn, come on! Please, you've got to trust me."

"But Caine-" He cut me off by leaning in close and looking me straight in the eye.

"Trust me. If it doesn't work out, well, at least we die an exciting death right?"

He was *enjoying* this. I could see it in his face. I narrowed my eyes.

"Caine, you little-"

"Now that's the Lyn I'm used to."

He caught me off guard with that smile and used the advantage to yank me off the bank and lead me upstream. We stumbled into a dim tunnel, concealed by willow branches. As they fell back over the entrance, we were thrown into almost complete darkness; the only light was that streaming through the thick canopy overhead.

He drew me to the wall of the tunnel and we pressed our backs against it, not breathing as shadows moved outside our cover.

"I could have sworn I saw people rush this way." The voices sounded foreign, strangely accented.

"Well they're goners now." They seemed nervous. " Let's go before that witch shows 'er ugly face."

"Alright- Wait, is that water?"

Footsteps plodded our way. I squeezed Caine's hand tighter, holding my breath, the water cool on my exposed ankles.

"Nice, I'm parched!"

There was shuffling and then a hard shove and the gruffer sounding voice. "What're you doing? You drink that stuff, the witch'll possess you! Let's get outta here."

I didn't breathe until the noise of the men had gone. Just when I calmed down, the thought of Glen and Raine entered my head. I spun away from the stone, clutching Caine's hands like I would blow away if I let go.

"Raine and Glen."

He stepped down, too saying, "Lyn, don't worry. Didn't you see Glen had everything under control?"

"Yeah, but-"

"We keep going," he finished for me, moving on, skidding a bit on the slick rocks. I followed; worry eating away at my calm. And what about the "witch" those people had mentioned earlier? I shook my head, sighing. Wasn't like I could do anything about it, so might as well go with the flow. Ironic, since we were following a stream.

The water was unusual; too clear to be out here in the wild like it was. The liquid reflected the rays from above beautifully on the stonewalls surrounding the rivulet. It was cold and crisp and had a soothing noise to its current.

"It's real pretty, isn't it?"

Caine glanced over his shoulder at me, a half smile portrayed on his face.

"The water?"

I nodded. "Yeah. See how it reflects the light off the walls."

He followed my finger, shrugging. "It's all right. Nothing special."

I huffed at his dismissive manner, then missed my step and slipped on the rocks. I barked out a yelp of distress, and felt a hand snatch mine before I soaked myself in the stream. Caine righted me, laughing.

"You know what's really beautiful?" His grin widened as I strung the water out of my dripping hair.

"Shut up."

He assumed a more sober expression. "What, you don't want to know?"

I glared a hole straight through him, cheeks burning with embarrassment. Still, he continued. "Well, I was going to say-"

I knew what was coming and saw my chance to quite him for good. I tackled Caine right off the ledge and we hit the vast pond at the bottom of our descent. The water was a *lot* colder than I realized.

I attempted to breathe, but only managed to take in more icy water instead. The chill seeped down into my bones and I was having a time trying to swim to the surface. Maybe this hadn't been such a great idea. The shock of the liquid took my breath away and black dots flickered before my vision in my panicked strokes for air. There was a sudden pressure at my waist, then the bite of oxygen rushing into my lungs as I broke the surface. Before I knew it, I was up on land, feet still in the water, and gulping down air.

The shakes were fierce and I couldn't tell if they were from cold or fear. I stretched out my hand and felt another encircle it.

"Lyn, I'm going to get you back for this one. And it's not going to be pretty."

I tried to make light of the situation we were in. "What? I only thought the water would cool your hothead down."

A shriek interrupted Caine before he could get a word out and I felt his grip tighten on my hand as we both sit up. A figure came into my line of sight and pounced on Caine, nearly knocking him over; next thing I knew, Raine had her arms snaked around his middle, whispering little bursts of happiness.

I was so relieved to see her that I didn't hear Glen come up beside me.

"You two are both soaked through."

"Really? I didn't notice." I shot Caine a look, but felt to blame since this whole thing was my fault. I decided to change the subject before Caine got to tell how I had tackled him and we'd fallen into the water.

"How long have you been here?"

Glen's blue-eyed stare searched my face as he answered. "Not long. Raine said she heard a splash and took off to find it. That's when we happened to see you and Caine disappear under the water."

He brushed a damp strand of hair back and tucked it behind my ear, smiling at my brashness. I had no doubt he'd seen the whole incident.

"So, here we are, stuck in the woods again. What do you purpose we do now?"

I looked up into Caine's agitated face. Now that some of his color returned, he was back to his old, annoying self. I shivered as a cool breeze blew over us.

"Where's Raine?"

"Over there." Caine pointed to the tiny girl intently watching a flowering bush growing near the pond.

When I turned my attention on Raine, I noticed a large waterfall pouring into the pond. It looked the perfect size for a cave to be behind, I thought childishly.

"Now that you've had a chance to enjoy the scenery, Lyn, why don't you get back to my question"?

"Oh, right. Well we could- uh..."

Caine threw his arms up and acted cheery. "Wonderful, Lyn, I love your suggestion. Glen do you have a better one?"

Glen gave Caine one of those stop-acting-like-an-idiot looks, but Caine went on like he didn't see it.

"No? Well then we'll just hear what Raine has to say."

He opened his mouth to call for her, but Raine yelled first.

"Come here! Quick!"

Oh boy. Was this day ever going to end? Glen and I took off first, leaving Caine to hurry behind.

"What's wrong?" I asked, already fearing the worst.

Raine was head and shoulders deep in the bush as she called out, "Help me grab it!"

I snatched a look at what it was and jumped back, slamming up against Caine.

"Raine, get out of there," I yelped, regaining my balance and grabbing a fistful of her shirt to yank her back.

"Lyn, what's-?"

I screamed as the giant lizard dashed out in a blur. I never took my eyes off it until it vanished into a broad opening in the rock behind the waterfall. A cave, I realized after staring at the stone. There was sudden laughter in the rear. I spun to glare at Caine.

"Something funny?"

He only laughed louder.

"Great, Caine's lost it. It must be that witch water those men were talking about."

Glen exchanged glances with Raine and I said I would explain later. Caine still hadn't shut up, but a voice that rose over the laughter made him quiet down.

"Who is making all that noise?"

We all watched the entrance to the cave as a shadow danced on the walls. It was hunched but moving quickly.

"Glen?" Raine's warning tone made it evident that she wanted to make a break for it, but it was too late to run now.

I took in a frightened gasp when I saw the woman; her appalling appearance really scared me. The woman's hair was a tangled black mop, dangling past her waist and her clothes were little more than rags sewn together to create a makeshift robe that skimmed the ground as she hobbled toward us. There was something peculiar about her clothing around her shoulders and as she neared us, I noticed it was the same lizard I had yanked Raine away from.

The foul woman paused in front of us, searching our faces with unnatural eyes. Her right iris was colored light blue, but the left was a deep brown, a startling contrast to each of them. She carried an unpleasant stench around her, worse than I knew we smelt. I couldn't take those eyes on me any longer.

"What do you want?"

She flicked her gaze to me and I held it. I saw a faint smile appear on her cracked lips and it chilled me as much as her stare.

"Come in, dear, and I will show you."

The woman's voice was surprisingly calm and full. She vanished back into the cave, faster than I could blink.

I stepped forward, planning to follow the woman.

"Lyn, stop!"

I turned to face Glen and asked, "Why?"

This question must have stunned him. For a moment, he looked like the sixteen-year-old boy he should have been, and not so much like the man he was forced to become.

"Why? Why! Because that woman was crazy or insane or whatever you want to call her! Did you see her? She wasn't *right*. Trust me, I've seen crazy before and it looked a lot like her." Caine seemed nervous but was taking it like anger; "We are *not* following that weirdo into a cave."

Caine sounded about as freaked out as I felt even know I wasn't showing it. Raine decided for all of us.

"Well, she invited us in didn't she? I think we should go."

That sounded like the church orphan talking.

"Now you're the one who's being crazy, Raine."

"She's right. Let's go."

Caine spun and gaped at Glen. He raised his eyebrows in that way that just made you want to disagree, but shut you up just in time. All but Caine went for the entrance. Glen went first, followed by Raine, but I hung back and asked Caine, "You sure you want to stay out here? Seems like a pretty stupid idea to me, but whatever floats your boat is fine with me."

I caught a glimpse of his scowl and knew he'd follow. I grinned at Glen when he shook his head at me. "Remind me never to argue with you, Lyn."

I giggled.

"What, you afraid of loosing?"

"No. I just know you'd find some way to turn the truth to fit in your favor."

I'd never thought about it much, but he did make sense. I shrugged the idea off, thinking it must be my wealthy background that gave me my social skills as we walked into the cavern.

It was beautiful. After being cramped in the tiny entrance, we finally came out on to a vast open space directly behind the waterfall. Mesmerized by the sparkling waters, I went to touch the falls. The clear liquid was icy on my fingertips and gave off a refreshing mist.

"Hello again, child." I jumped and whipped around to find the haggard old woman beside me, reaching out to the water just as I was, her bony fingers hooked like a bird's.

"I see you like my waterfall."

I glanced around for my party, but everyone was gone. I shifted my gaze back to the woman, eyes narrowed and ready to get some answers.

"Who are you and what do you want from us?"

She held out a clawed hand to stop my onslaught of words. "Questions, questions. Dear, Lyn, you must learn to be patient or you will hear no answers from me."

I stepped back from the woman, determined to put a little distance from a stranger who just happened to know my name. Had to have been a lucky guess, I thought. I watched the woman smile, as if she could hear my comments.

"Luck," she began, "That is what we all need more of, isn't it, dear. Luck and a bit of gold can get you far in life, wouldn't you say?"

She turned and walked off, leaving me with even more unanswered questions than before. I raced to catch up, but it seemed like she would get two paces farther for every step I took.

Blinding light stopped me and I ended up in a small chamber decorated with hanging herbs and animal skins. There were bottles of some type of liquid that were stacked on a table. The thought of poison came to mind, but they could have been medicine. What really caught my eye were the walls. They glittered, not because of moisture, but with gold and jewels. Where could a witch like that woman had accumulated all these riches?

Before I knew it, I was at the mounds of wealth, hands outstretched and ready to stuff as much as would fit into my pockets. I ran my fingertips over the perfect gold coins, longing to take and hide them away just for myself. But... Something was not right.

I swept the room with my gaze, feeling like I was being watched. I looked down at the money I had been stroking and froze.

"A test," I breathed.

Sudden, hot anger filled me and I yelled out into the open, knowing the hag could hear me.

"What are you playing at, witch?" I grabbed a fistful of coins, "Did you think I was dumb enough to steal this? Sorry to disappoint, but I don't need your fake wealth!"

I flung the money and they connected with the bottles, knocking them over and making the liquid splash everywhere. A bit splattered on my skin and the burning sensation made me recoil.

"So it *is* poison."

To think I'd almost *trusted* her! Unexpected laughter made me start and spin around.

"'Almost?' Dear, don't kid yourself; you do trust me or you never would have followed me in here."

The witch had been reading my thoughts and now she was blocking my exit. I'd had enough.

"Look, lady, I just want to find my friends and leave this place as soon as possible." I brought myself to look the woman straight in her double-colored eyes, "And right now, you're making that very hard for me to do."

I knew I was being difficult, but the witch's calm manner had driven me to it. A disapproving expression formed on her ancient face.

"My my, Lyn. You are terribly impatient. If you wish to see your friends, then, please, don't let me stop you."

She stepped aside, holding an arm out to indicate me going. I glanced at the woman, then the exit. I took a few steps toward it, then broke out into a sprint, heart soaring as I sped past her. I glimpsed over my shoulder, never slowing, and a smile of contempt formed on my lips.

"Bam!"

I collided with something solid. It must have been a person because they moved away when I hit with a grunt. Luck just wasn't with me today.

I lay there in a crumpled heap, wishing my head would stop pulsating.

"Man, Lyn, you're just on a roll today," Caine began, patting me on the back instead of helping me to my feet, "Feel sorry for Glen, though. I've never seen someone go down that hard."

"Caine, be quiet!"

Raine's voice was not the joking type, and we all saw the witch hobbling forward, the lizard back on her shoulders and with a dwarf-like man beside her. How did she move so fast?

"Oh, should've guessed."

Caine hauled Raine behind him and I staggered up with Glen. If I'd had time to notice, I would have seen the roaring waterfall behind us and the mouth of the cave to my right.

"I'm glad to see you found your friends, Lyn."

Glen and I exchanged glances and the woman smiled like she found us humorous.

"Ah, I'm afraid I have been quite rude to all of you. I am sure you want to know why you're here." She glanced at the little man, "Dos will be happy to show you."

The man called Dos began striding toward us. He came about to my waist and had massive feet. Dos paused in front of us and held out a hand as if we owed the man something. Caine bit his bottom lip, holding back a laugh, when Dos glared at him.

"What do you want, midget?" He nudged me with an elbow, "Would you just look at those feet! Man, I bet you sure can swim good with those stompers."

I started to snicker along with Glen and Raine. The small man glared at Caine and moved closer.

"What are you looking at, dwarf? Why don't you go paddle with the ducks. I'm sure they wouldn't be able to tell you apart!"

Dos began to turn toward the waterfall like he really was going to dive in. Caine noticed.

"What's wrong, little man? Can't take a joke?"

The woman had been listening in on the conversation and spoke up. "Oh yes, Dos can take a joke. Can you?"

It was clockwork. Almost as soon as the words left her mouth, Dos vaulted at least five feet into the air, spun, and kicked Caine square in the chest. He went sprawling across the moist stone with a surprised gasp. Dos landed effortlessly, prize in hand. He held the five bags of gold that had been dangling from Caine's belt loop. The man smiled up at me after noticing I was staring and went to present the witch with our money. Or rather the money we stole.

A bit aroused by his deceitful smile, I went to check on Caine. Raine was there already, giggling at his wheezing. I let a chuckle escape my lips when I saw him lying there.

"Well, Caine, that 'little man' sure got the best of you didn't he."

"Sh-shup."

I beamed at his failed attempt to speak. Glen and I helped him to stand.

"Thank you, Dos. I've been searching for this."

I saw the woman pocketing the gold, feeling a bit cross she just took it and said nothing to us. I wondered why Dos did not go for the sixth one, as well. *I stole five bags out of six off that person.* His words ringing in my head, I figured out how the woman must make her money. The room I had been in housed her strange bottled product that she sold and made the cash off of. Why then, would she live in a cave?

"You really are smarter than you appear to be, Lyn." The witch grinned at me, "To answer your other question, let's just say I like my privacy, shall we."

She was inside my head!

"So you're a witch?" I blurted the query out before realizing how rude it sounded. The woman dismissed this with a wave of her clawed hand.

"On the contrary. I am not a witch, as you so boldly put it, but a fortune-teller."

Another question sprung to mind, but she cut me off saying, "And before you ask, my name is Eggy."

I narrowed my eyes and she gestured to the waterfall. "Come now, I've kept you all far too long not to show you a bit of the real thing. Meet me by the water child, and you shall have your answers."

I thought about debating, but decided against it and went to get Raine.

"Raine, do you want to have your fortune told?"

A spark kindled in her hazel eyes and she answered, "Yeah, I want to hear it."

"Okay, then go stand by the waterfall and we'll meet you there."

She skipped over to the falls in such a carefree manner it made me slightly jealous.

"I'm not even gonna ask." Caine barely managed a whisper and hobbled much more slowly over to Eggy, eying Dos warily.

I glanced up at Glen hoping he wouldn't ask too many questions. He only raised an eyebrow and smirked, stressing his handsome features strikingly. Glen didn't say anything, but I could tell he thought I was crazy.

"Go ahead. I'll just follow your orders."

I flashed him a smile and began walking in the direction of everyone all ready at the falling waters. Eggy spread her thin arms, the mist ruffling her rags, and addressed us.

"Children, stand a few feet apart and only look at the water when I tell you."

I, along with Glen, Caine, and Raine bowed my head, feeling jittery for some reason. My troublesome thoughts stilled when Eggy's ancient voice echoed throughout the cavern.

"Listen well all of you, for I will only say this once."

In the pause that Eggy created, the noise of the waterfall seemed to dim, and her voice drifted up over the falls.

"I foretell... Oh, my. Great danger and hardships thrust upon you. Some may leave you mortified, changing your very being and thoughts toward each other. One of you holds a magnificent power. There are others... that may prove to be formidable and deadly adversaries. Beware the one with the devil's head."

She seemed to quiet and think for a moment, but then her voice came back. A warning.

"The choices will be hard, very hard, but each of you will be forced to choose. So choose wisely. You may lift your heads."

The trance was broken and I raised my head slowly, fearful of what I might see in the falling waters. At first, there was nothing, but as soon as I was about to avert my gaze, a light shifted and I became transfixed. An image started to form before my eyes. It looked like a girl; she was standing with somebody.

That's when I realized the girl was I and the tall, well-built man next to me was my deceased father. The scene was so calm and tranquil it brought tears to my eyes, blurring the image. Suddenly, it changed and my face in the picture was contorted from a sweet, peaceful expression, to one of pure terror.

The vision expanded, giving way to a large, opulent room. I was standing in front of a colossal man. His face was hidden in shadows, so I couldn't tell if I knew the man or not, but even in the effigy, his presence seemed menacing and wicked.

The scene shifted again, this time to a vast expanse of blue. Waves, all shades of azure, sapphire, and cobalt crested and broke upon the shoreline. I had never seen the ocean, but somehow I knew this was it. I longed to reach out and touch the venue, but I did not dare for fear of disturbing the illusion.

I watched as the waters became more violent and fierce, rising up, twisting, as a cloud of darkness enveloped the once beautiful setting. In the image, I saw myself look up and scream as the cloud descended. The last thing the vision showed was the devilish figure of a man with burning yellow eyes...

I came away gasping for air. It was remarkably similar to waking from one of my dreams. Clutching knotted bunches of hair, I sank to my knees, dizzied. Thankfully, it wasn't as corrosive as some of my nightmares had been and I recovered quickly. Peering out the corner of my eyes, I looked to see if anyone else had experienced what I had. Based on their expressions, I could believe they did.

Glen was frozen, looking more scared than I had ever seen him. Raine almost appeared to be in a pleasant daze, a smile portrayed on her lips. Caine was swinging his head from side to side, eyes darting madly from one object to the next.

I abruptly felt a pounding in my head and my hand instinctively went there.

"What is it, Lyn? What did you see?"

Glen was there, still with a trace of fear in his sky blue eyes, but ready to help me if I needed it.

"Th-there was a man... I-I-"

The words were there, I just could not put them together right. I shook my head, trying to rid myself of the ache there.

"Man, I *knew* we shouldn't have come in here. I knew it! And I told you and what happened? Oh that's right, we went and did it anyway!"

Caine had gotten into one of his frenzies again and I attempted to calm him, even ~~know~~ though I felt the same way.

"Caine, don't- ugh."

Glen caught me before I went down and helped me to stand. "Don't talk. We need to get out of here."

He urged me forward, motioning for Raine to come, too. I heard Eggy's voice behind us.

"You can't run from the future, children. Something big is coming and mark my words, what you just saw is but a glimpse of what is going to happen!"

My mind was now clear enough to walk on my own. I softly brushed Glen's hands off my shoulders and stopped dead at the exit. The undersized man, Dos, was blocking our path. His presence made me hesitate, but I turned only to see Caine marching this way with Raine in tow. He twisted around and shouted at Eggy.

"You're crazy, woman! You and your little man are both insane!"

He stormed past me and halted in front of Dos.

"This is for kicking me earlier, midget!"

Caine slammed his foot down on Dos's toes. The small man winced, but did not cry, only wait patiently for Caine to move.

"Gah, no wonder you don't wear shoes. Your duckers couldn't fit into any!"

The smart comment set Dos off. As soon as Caine withdrew his foot, the man landed a powerful punch in Caine's stomach. He doubled over as the breath left his body.

"Why you little-"

Caine didn't get the rest of his sentence out, because Dos reared back on his hands and thrust both feet out at Caine's exposed face. They connected and Caine fell backward with a dull "thud". He was out cold this time.

Raine gave a little shout when he hit the floor and started toward Dos, chin set in a way that meant she was about to get even.

"Raine!"

I tried to get her attention, but she never slowed her pace. I about made a mad dash, but Glen was faster.

"Get Caine," he shouted over the roar of the waterfall.

"R-i-i-ght."

Did he expect me to lift Caine? Oh well, I thought, here goes. I slid my slender arms under his head and knees. After a bit of straining, I scooped him up, staggering under Caine's weight since I was so weak from having not eaten. Salvia dripped on to my arm, making me scowl and wipe it on his head. I figured it was what Caine deserved.

"Maybe I should carry him?"

I glanced at Glen, giving him an embarrassed grin. "I think that's a good idea."

I passed Caine's body off to Glen who smoothly adjusted to his weight. I felt a dainty hand slide into mine and looked down at Raine's wide-eyed stare.

"Where'd they go, Lyn?"

I knitted my eyebrows together, not understanding what she was saying. That's when I realized Eggy and Dos were gone, vanished into thin air.

"I-I don't know."

I touched Glen on his shoulder, saying, "We need to go. This place is starting to freak me out."

He nodded in understanding. "It's freaked me out ever since we came in."

Raine agreed, tugging us both out. No one turned to look back.

Ch. 7 Pirates

It felt good to be back on the road. I savored the wind on my face and the grit between my tired toes. I peered over at Caine, still being carried by Glen. It had been at least an hour since we had gotten out of that cave.

"How's he doing?" I asked, a little worried.

"Fine, although I'd have thought he'd be awake by now."

I could have imagined it, but it looked like Caine's mouth curved up ever so slightly.

"Oh, I think he's awake."

"Really?" Glen stared hard at Caine's face. A thin smile passed over his lips and he stopped walking.

"Alright, Caine, ride's over." He dumped Caine on the ground and brushed the grime off his hands. Caine sat up rubbing the back of his head.

"Come on, don't you feel sorry for me? It's not every day someone gets knocked out by Bigfoot."

Glen and I huffed and Raine started chanting, "Poor little baby Caine."

"Raine's right, you deserved it." We all laughed at his scowling face.

"What's wrong? Can't take a joke?" I mimicked Dos's footwork by swinging my leg towards Caine. I chuckled when he flinched.

"Thanks, guys. You're all jerks."

He was able to stand, but not stay up without assistance. I scrambled over to steady him.

"Take it easy, Caine. You might get hurt even worse than you already are."

Now that I was closer to him, I could make out dark shadows forming around his nose and eyes. It was hard to believe Dos hadn't broken anything. He noticed my scrutiny and turned his face away from me.

"Don't start feeling sorry now."

He shook my hands off and I let them hang at my sides. He was still unsteady on his feet; I thought about offering my support, but didn't think it would help in the mood he was in.

"Maybe we should find a place to sit down," I suggested, inspecting Caine. He spun his head sharply to glare at me with pain-filled amber eyes. Raine ran up to him and grasped his fisted hand. She gave a tug and he looked down at her, gaze softening slightly.

"Please Caine, just listen to Lyn. She always knows what to do."

I blushed at her exaggerated compliment. Glen walked up and draped an arm around me, drawing me close and saying, "That's right. Lyn *always* knows what to do. Even if it is on the insane side of crazy."

I giggled at his sarcasm and pushed him away, thinking he could be just as mad for following through with my plans. He cackled and indicated with his head that we should follow.

"I think I've found us a place to settle down for a while."

I let out a relieved sigh and strolled alongside Glen. Sweet little Raine was trying to get Caine to skip with her, but wasn't having much luck; he merely stumbled behind, clutching her hand as she bounced up and down coaxing him to do the same.

Moments like the scene before me made me forget the constant dangers and threats that hounded us at every turn. I felt, for once, joyful and relaxed. I glimpsed at Glen and was surprised to find him staring at me with the same intense cast I had. We locked eyes, each of us with faint smiles as if holding back a laugh.

"Ouch!"

I had slammed into the thick trunk of a hickory tree and pulled away, face throbbing and clutching my nose. I heard Glen curse and opened my eyes to see him in the same position I was in.

"Aw thanks guys. I appreciate you your trying to look like me and all, but you didn't have to run into a tree to do it."

I saw Caine's smirking face and narrowed my eyes. Glen went up behind him and playfully cuffed him on the shoulder.

"Shut it, Caine." There was a bit of edge to his voice, but Caine's smile only broadened.

While my party settled themselves, I decided to go foraging for food. Strolling over to the brush, I started pushing them aside, searching for some sort of berry. An unknown sound stopped me. At first, I thought it was a creek, but after examination, found that it was, in fact, a river. I was about to step through the dense brush, but froze when I picked up on a nearby sound. Shuffling back to my spot, I bent to slyly peer through the branches. I was shocked when a burly man staggered into view carrying firewood. The man threw it into a charred pit and brushed his hands on his trousers, eyes sweeping the surrounding area.

I ducked, hoping the man didn't have a chance to see me before I went down. Who was he and what was he doing here? I wondered if there were others like the man around and if so, we could be in serious trouble *if* we were caught. Too many if's, I thought. I paused as a wild idea popped into my head. It was one of those that made people think I was crazy.

We needed to get on that river and this man (or men) had boats. And we were thieves... I ambled over to everyone, a smug expression on my face. Caine was the first to notice. "Uh-oh. Lyn's scheming something again, I can see it in her eyes."

Glen turned my way, a pained but joking look in his expression. "We're in trouble."

I rolled my eyes at both of them, although it seemed like a rather girlish thing to do in this situation. Bold Raine, of course, defended me by stating, "We are not. Remember?" She pointed to her head. "Lyn knows best."

The boys snickered at Raine's defiant remark. Caine rubbed his hands together greedily, a broad grin on his face. "Alright, then, let's hear it."

I held up my hands.

"First, you have to come see this."

Caine and Glen stood while Raine scooted over to my side. Caine rubbed his shrunken stomach, a look of yearning on his face. "Did you find food? I'm starving." He poked one of his prominent ribs and pityingly smiled. "Literally."

My own abdomen growled in protest making me wish I had actually found food. "I wish, but no. I can't explain or none of you would come and see this. So follow me."

I had few stares of apprehension, but curiosity must have got the best of everyone because they said nothing and filed in behind me. I nearly jumped out of my skin when I heard the racket everyone was making stepping on dead leaves and fallen twigs.

"Shhh!" I intensified the word by putting a finger to my lips. "Listen, we all need to be *very* quiet."

Glen eyed me suspiciously. "What is it?" I only smiled and beckoned for them to keep coming.

I parted one of the limbs and peered through the opening. I was taken aback when I spied more husky, criminal-looking men setting up camp. There was a sudden pressure on my frail shoulder, pushing down. It was impossible to resist and I had no choice but to go down with it. I opened my mouth, tongue forming the first words of "let me go", when a dark blonde head ducked beside me. Glen gave me a desperate look that meant don't move. My eyes widened, horrified that one of the thugs had spotted us. He pulled at my arm with urgency in his movements. I couldn't help myself so I asked, "What's happened?"

He stared at me like I had gone stark mad. "Did you not see those men? I could have sworn they were river pirates."

I let all of the cowardice leave my body, almost laughing out loud at Glen's overprotective concern. "No, you've got it all wrong. That *is* what I wanted you to see."

Glen raised his already arched eyebrows.

"Look," I said, indicating the sandy banks of the river where the boats were docked. "See that? I know this might sound extreme, but I think we should try *borrowing* one of those boats."

Glen's blue eyes shifted from my face to the men now constructing make-shift tents out of cloth and sticks, to the three various sized boats gently bobbing as the wind made large ripples in the river.

"*I* think it's a completely insane idea. There's no ~~now~~ way we can go steal a raft from those guys. They don't really look like the hospitable type." Caine had apparently overheard my plan and felt inclined to voice his opinion. I spared a brief glance for him then turned my attention back on Glen. "What do you think?"

"I think we should step back so we won't have to whisper so much and think this thing out."

I sighed and trudged, defeated, over to a soft patch of green grass and let myself drop into the lush feel of it. The feeling made me want to fall asleep.

"Lyn, if you're serious about taking one of those rafts, then I think I have an idea."

I looked up, hope kindled and waited expectantly for Glen to continue.

"I think we'll need to lay low until nightfall. That's when we'll strike."

He swept his sky-blue gaze over us, taking in our reaction in his intense fashion. I let it sink in while Raine wholly agreed with him. "Yeah, why not. We can pull it off, right Caine?"

Caine buried his face in his hands and moaned. "Why did I have to get stuck with the lunatics?"

I opened my mouth to say something about his snide comments but he continued.

"Of course we can do it. I mean, what else have we got to do that will get us killed quicker?"

I glared at him and shook my head. Caine only shot me a look and I said yes to Glen's idea.

"Anyway, now that that's settled, why don't we find something to eat"?

Raine perked up at the mention of food. "Uh, I already found some." She blushed as we stared at the berry stains on her fingers.

"Where at, Raine?" Caine asked, "Can you show me?"

She looked up at him, a joyful twinkle in her eyes as she started toward the thicket we had just exited. "Sure, follow me."

I yelled as loud as I dared after them. "Bring us back some, too!"

Caine held up a hand, acknowledging my request. I then situated myself in the lush grass, determined to find sleep.

"Lyn?"

Glen's voice was suddenly close. I lazily lifted an eyelid to notify him that I heard what he said.

"Just wanted to tell you I'll keep watch." After what seemed like an afterthought he added, "And to say goodnight."

I grinned, halfway opening my other eye. He returned it with a warm smile of his own, softening his hard features. After he walked off, I rested my eyes telling myself I would only take a short nap. I dozed fitfully for the first minuet and then fell into a sleep far deeper than I had intended.

"Thump-thump, thump-thump!" Went the beating of my own frantic footsteps. I soon heard the sound of another pair too close behind to make me comfortable. I felt warm, moist breath down the back of my neck and swiveled to stare into the eyes of the mammoth beast hot on my heels.

I swung around, barely avoiding a gigantic tree. The horned bear rammed its head into the trunk, and there were cracking sounds followed by ear-piercing bellows. I had tripped and fallen on a large, dead log. I waited, heart hammering in my chest, to be snapped in two by the beast's foot-long teeth.

When I didn't feel the razor incisors tear into my flesh, I hesitantly lifted my head after rolling over on my back. The abhorrent sight of the coal black bear thrashing and horns ripping the bark greeted me. It was coming apart. Not just the tree, but the world was crumbling before my eyes. I watched, torpid with panic and dread as the creature was destroyed along with everything else.

Blood coated my body and threw crimson blotches before my eyes. My screams mingled with the sound of rending bone, flesh, and wood. I surged to my feet, scrambling blindly forward and still shrieking with terror. I swung my leg out in mid-stride and connected with nothing. In an attempt to catch myself before I went down, I threw my other leg out into the void.

I could sense air gusting by my flailing limbs and tried to scream, but the breath was knocked out of me and so I fell, down and down into complete and utter darkness...

I went from a dead sleep to a standing position in seconds. I took in a lungful of oxygen, relishing the cold air as it burned my throat going down. It was pitch black in the clearing I had drifted off into earlier, but I could make out vague human forms in the haze. Squinting, I managed to pick out their faces. Caine was missing.

Mt heart skipped a much-needed beat when I did not spot his fine-boned face peacefully resting with Glen and Raine. That's when the afterthought clicked. Why was Glen here? Wasn't he supposed to be keeping watch? I bet someone had sneaked up and snatched Caine while he had been asleep. But it made me wonder why the person did not go for a girl like Raine or me.

While I was thinking about all the "what if's", a hand appeared out of the darkness and painfully clamped over my mouth, tight so where I wouldn't have a chance to bite. A fleeting notion of Caine being captured like this crossed my mind, but was wiped away as the person drew me in close to their spare body.

"Please, Lyn, don't scream."

I relaxed so much at the familiar voice that Caine had to use all his strength to keep me up after my knees buckled beneath me. "Hey, hey, are you alright?"

He removed his hand from my mouth and helped me steady myself.

"Yeah, I'm fine."

I glanced down at his arm, still tight around my waist and peered over my shoulder at him. "You can let go now."

"What?" He looked confused for a moment then traced my eyes to his hold. "Oh, sure. Sorry."

He removed his arm from around my middle, blushing a little. "Didn't mean to scare you like that. I know how wild you are after you wake up from one of your dreams and couldn't think of a better way to approach you so I just... grabbed you."

I giggled at his embarrassed manner and shook my head. "It's okay, I know what you mean. Anyway, why are you even up right now?"

I thought about mentioning my idea of him being kidnapped but figured it would only make me sound silly.

"Glen fell asleep on the job by the time he had finished eating." He shrugged, a huff of laughter escaping his lips. "I figured someone needed to make sure those pleasant fellows by the river wouldn't try to nab us in our sleep."

I nodded and he seemed to remember another thing. "By the way, we left some berries for you for when you woke up."

"I'm not hungry."

Caine let his features form a very skeptic look, but didn't pressure me when I said no. I really was lying. Not just to Caine, but to myself, too, thinking the stabbing ache in my stomach was simply exaltation.

"You two night-owls all set and ready?"

The voice made me jump and stare in its direction. I was able to make out Glen's handsome profile in the moonlight and Raine beside him, stifling a yawn even know her eyes shown with excitement.

""Yeah, we're ready. Not like we have anything to pack." I smirked at Caine's impudent but true remark.

It was time to put our skills to the test.

Ch.8 The Getaway

Stealing purses, wallets, food, and jewels, *that* was easy. How were we going to get away with a boat these pirates were napping around? The thought pounded in my head as we neared the encampment. Now that I was close to the men I could tell they took on the appearance of brigands with their rough faces and piercings, ragged attire, and blades all around. I bent to get a better look at their faces, illuminated by the firelight. I wrinkled my nose at the stench of sweat and ale rolling off their bodies.

The men's ages seemed to range from ours to mid-forties. Don't know if that will help in scouting the area, though. That was Raine's and my responsibility since we were the smallest. I held my breath and crouched down, eye-level with one of the men. Inspecting his face at close-range, I could tell he wasn't much older than Glen. There was slight trace of muddy brown stubble forming around his chin to match his unkempt hair.

My eyes were on his ear, something gleaming at his lobe. I shifted and perceived a distinctive silver earring hanging there. I reached for the earring, having a strange desire for it. Just as I was about to take hold of it, the man's eyes shot open. I snapped my arm back and cowered there staring at his emerald-green eyes. There was no way I could move in the kind of shock I was in, or risk shouting for Raine and waking the men. Not like he wouldn't do the same thing when the thug got his bearings.

That sick feeling formed in the pit of my abdomen when I saw his eyelids waver as if he was attempting to blink. I just gazed at his face waiting to be killed, but the boy's tired eyelids fluttered one last time before he let them close and he fell back into a deep sleep.

The only thing I could do was simply squat there, trembling and think about how luck had come through for me again.

"So, I'm guessing they're out cold for the night. According to Raine, of course. Not like you could tear your eyes from that guy long enough to give your friends a warning."

I jumped a little when Caine appeared beside me and shook my head, managing to stand. Glen and Raine were stalking past, motioning for us to follow and be quiet. It was like crossing a minefield. You had to be careful of where you stepped and whom you stepped over. My body felt like a bowstring, taut and ready to be let loose. I flinched every time I heard a booming snore or witnessed a man turn in his sleep. I seemed like eons had past before we got to the boats, still docked and tied down.

"Caine, can you undo this knot?"

He answered Glen after trying the rope. "No way. It's too tight and I can't see well."

"Now what?" I glanced at Raine and knew it was too late to give up now.

I swept my gaze over the mass of bodies. There had to be at least fifteen or more, so I figured one of them must be carrying something sharp enough to cut rope.

"Well I'll tell you what you *can* do," I said, spotting a large dagger protruding from one of the thug's shirts.

"What?" Caine nimbly strolled up to my side, stealthily as a practiced thief.

"See that big guy by the fire pit? I pointed to a bulky, giant of a man, twitching in his sleep. Caine positioned his face close to mine so he was level with what I was indicating.

"You gotta be kidding me, Lyn."

"You don't even know what I'm going to ask you, yet!" My outburst got a couple of hushes from Glen and Raine. They only intensified my mood.

"You know what?" I dropped my voice low. "I'll go get it myself. You're not the only one who can steal things."

I didn't wait for him to answer. Spinning on my heel, I stormed off in the direction of the pirate with the dagger. I'll show him, I thought, I'll show them all that I am perfectly capable of managing myself when it came to heists, And when it came to swiping knives off men in the middle of their sleep.

When I neared the hulking felon, my confidence slipped a bit, replaced by a strong sense of embarrassment. Had I just told them all to back off and let *me* do the dirty work? No, I reasoned, they had all done something for me; I was merely returning the favor.

Flexing my stiff fingers and swallowing the lump in my throat, I inched closer to the man, shifting my eyes form his ugly face to the blade to make sure I wasn't caught in the act. I could scarcely breathe as I reached out to grab the deadly looking knife. If I happened to slip, even once, I would either be wounded or chance waking all the other pirates. My spindly fingers encircled the cloth-wrapped hilt...

"Arrahh!"

I jolted my body so suddenly and vigorously that I practically ripped the dagger from its sheath when the man yelled. I lost my balance and swung my arms wildly, trying to find a purchase for my foot. I took a step back and stomped on something that flattened instantly, spewing out juice from the other side that coated the underside of my foot. I jerked up and firmly planted myself in the sand, expecting at any moment to be run through with a sword. No fine point ever came. Or yelp of surprise for that matter.

I was okay. I was *alive!* I let my breath out, clutching the edge like it was my last lifeline, and checked to see what I had stepped on. The revolting stench hit me as I inhaled the smell of rotten fruit mixing with body odor and brandy to create disgusting fumes that filled the air. The sticky juice that had drained from the fruit was splattered all over one of the river pirate's back and shoulders, not to mention all the gummy globs stuck in his hair.

Time to go, I thought. I skipped nimbly around the bodies littered on the riverbank still keeping tight hold on the dagger. I saw Caine, Raine, Glen come into view and I triumphantly waved the blade above my head, pleased with myself as I listened to it slice through the air. Glen looked alarmed to see me swinging the stiletto so rashly about while Raine bounced and clasped her hands together, a big grin spread on her face. Caine seemed annoyed and put-off, standing there with a scowl etched onto his face and arms tucked into one another.

I cut to the chase when I handed off the knife. "Alright, we got the blade, now start cutting." I felt the tacky pulp of fruit in the bottom of my foot and added, "Fast."

Glen took the dagger, testing the edge with his thumb.

"Hold up." Caine held up a hand to stop us. "Let's get in the boat before Glen nicks the rope. We don't want it running downstream and ruining all Lyn's hard work."

Raine moved up to Caine, prepared to take the lead. "I'll go first."

He smiled, wincing as his bruised skin stretched.

"Actually, I'm thinking Lyn should go first, just to be safe."

I saw her face drop, making her look adorable for a moment, but then she hardened and nodded, renewed fire in her eyes. Glen was shifting from foot to foot, eager to be gone. "Come on, the night's wearing thin and we don't have much time."

"Right," I agreed, stepping up to Caine. He placed his hands on my waist, adjusting his position.

"Here goes. Hope I don't *accidently* drop you." He flashed me a mischievous smile and I narrowed my eyes. With a slight grunt and hop from me, he hoisted me up to the hull of the small boat.

"Whoa!" I flung my arms out and Caine steadied me with firm hands.

We both released a sigh of relief as I regained my balance. Raine stepped up, grinning at my loud mouth.

"Ready?" Caine asked.

"Ready."

"Alright, try not to make as much noise as Lyn did." He slid me a look before he lifted Raine up to me; she seemed giddy as she was passed into my arms.

"Got her?"

"Yeah."

The sudden weight was unexpected. Thank goodness Caine had gotten there so quickly or Raine and I would have both been soaked and sandy.

"Thanks," I breathed, but Caine had his attention elsewhere.

"You can thank me later, right now we need to move!"

Almost as soon as the words left his mouth, I heard shouting coming from the bank. I added my own voice to it. "Glen, cut the rope!"

I saw him hesitate and could picture his being captured by the mad men. He must have come to a quick and witty conclusion because he dashed over to the other two boats and sawed at their tethers. By now, the pirates were waking with a vengeance, their shouts echoing in the clearing. I couldn't hear exactly what they were yelling, but it was likely orders to kill us.

"Lyn, get down!"

Caine snapped me out of my trance and I looked up to see a knife flying toward me. The next thing I saw was the boards of the deck rushing up to meet me.

"Ouf!" The impact left me gasping for air. Caine certainly wasn't helping by pinning me to the hard, wooden floorboards.

"Get off!"

I struggled under his weight, but managed to get my arms loose and shift to where I could push up.

"Lyn... Stop. Fighting me!" With a rapid lurch, Caine seized my flailing arms and pressed them behind my back, wrist on wrist. I jarred my body wildly, even tried kicking, but he never budged.

"Glen needs help. And what about Raine? She can't handle those men!" My voice was thick with panic; Caine pulled my arms tighter as I struggled more.

"Raine's hiding. Safe. And Glen can manage those guys, you know that."

I bit back tears of frustration, thinking what would I ever do without my friends to set me straight. I stilled and craned my neck to see Caine watching me.

"Look, I'm okay, now. Thanks for saving my life... again."

His thin lips curved up into that annoying smile of his. "I don't think so. Not after that performance. And you're welcome."

I heaved a sigh, letting my head drop against the panels. I focused on the water moving beneath me and wondered why it was flowing past so rapidly.

"Caine, let her up."

I immediately turned my attention to the voice above my head and felt Caine shift.

"Well, you made it. Not like I didn't think you couldn't, though. Still, you should be grateful. I just saved Lyn, you know. She'd be a match for even *you* to handle."

I felt the weight of Caine's body leave mine and my hands be released.

"Finally!"

I pushed myself off the cool floorboards and to my feet. Glen had made it. Dripping river water and nicked up, but living.

"Glen's back!"

Raine, who had apparently hidden herself in a barrel when Caine and I hit the floor, now came tearing out toward Glen. She wrapped her thin arms around his waist and he patted her back, sincere expression softening.

"Look at those idiots. We sure showed them, didn't we"?

I twisted to glance at the pirates. They were lined up on the bank, howling in rage, shaking fists and shouting things I was better off not hearing. I let a faint smile form on my lips and closed my eyes for a moment. The crisp breeze caressed my skin and ruffled my hair, smelling of promise.

I opened them gradually and laughed at the sight that greeted me. Caine threw up his arm, waving cheekily at the furious men. Raine copied him, using both arms instead of one. Their other boats had drifted so far downstream they could scarcely be seen. And it was all thanks to Glen's clever scheming.

Found it.

"I think I see some food!"

Ever since we had left the banks of the river, we had been trying to settle in, and food was a must. The thought of nourishment had not crossed my mind while the raid was in progress, but now that it was over I was ravenous.

"Where at, Lyn?"

Raine appeared with Caine to help me carry provisions.

"Right here," I said between bites of stale bread and some kind of cured beef jerky. The food really didn't taste that good, but I was so hungry it was difficult to quit stuffing myself and move away.

I followed behind Caine and Raine, hauling a small crate full of mostly ruined meat. We met up with Glen who, after having gone through miles of beer and whisky bottles, managed to find drinkable water. As soon as I set the box down, I tore into it, devouring the smelly cuts of beef and pork. I licked the salt from my fingers, noticing the others' eyes on me. My face heated up and I felt ashamed of my rude manners toward everyone. I cleared my throat and wiped my mouth with the back of my grimy sleeve.

"Sorry. I know you have to be just as starved as me. Probably even more."

I had a hard time believing that myself, but I offered the meat around. Raine smiled at me in that sweet way she had and accepted the beef. Caine came over and snatched some himself, wrinkling his nose at the scent; it made his dark bruises spread more. Glen took a few strips and set them aside, passing out water instead.

After lunching on dry bread, mushy fruit, and bitter meat, we made sure the boat was still on course and settled down on the wood boards, close to the mast. We sat in something of a circle formation, with Caine across from me and Raine and Glen to my left and right.

"I'm glad those pirates aren't chasing us any more," said Raine, attempting some conversation. I took the opportunity.

"Yeah, me too. I almost passed out cold when that one yelled in his sleep!"

"The one that slept with his eyes open freaked me
~~my~~ out. More than Lyn, even."

"Hey!"

Caine grinned and I couldn't resist either. Soon we were all giggling at each other's stories and jokes about them.

"Lyn, that reminds me." I turned my eyes on Glen as he started rummaging through his pockets for something. He saw me watching and turned my face so where I had to look him in the eyes. Smiling, he said, "Hold out your hand and close your eyes and I'll give you a big surprise."

The rhyme made me laugh, but I did what he said. Something cool and smooth touched the palm of my hand.

"Now you can be a *real* pirate."

I let one eye open first and the other followed suit. I stared, gaping, at the silver earring lying in my hand. It was the exact one the green-eyed pirate had had dangling from his ear.

"How did you-? When did-?" I was at a loss of words as I inspected the engraved piece of silver. It was really quite stunning, the way the ridges formed a design in the metal.

"You aren't the only one who can steal things." His grin warmed my insides, blue eyes with a joyful twinkle in them.

"What is it?" Raine tiptoed over to gaze at the earring in my hand and her face lit up at once. "It's pretty. Are you going to wear it?"

For a moment, I didn't understand what she meant. "Oh you mean as jewelry, right?"

She nodded. "Yeah. Didn't you say you used to have all kinds of these things you wore when you lived in your house?"

It was true. My mother had been very fond of adornments and often let me wear them. I had instantly taken a liking to the sparkling baubles and gems. I fingered my right ear, feeling the small hole I had gotten so long ago. I wondered if I could even put it in.

"Come on, Lyn. I would love to see you get that thing through your ear."

I eyed Caine, picking out his challenge. Apparently, he did not know my ears were already pierced. I positioned the small end of the earring at the indention in my ear. It slid through effortlessly.

I let a smirk develop on my face when Caine's expression went from complacent to distressed.

"How's it look?" I asked, tilting my head so my hair fell back to reveal the earring. "Glen? Raine?" I inquired, looking from one to the other. "Caine?"

"Like a pirate," Raine exclaimed.

"It looks good," Glen said, sweeping my face with his intense gaze.

"It looks the same," Caine stated, some of his old arrogance returning.

I grinned in spite of myself. Devious, I thought, take a man's earring and parade it around on *my* ear while he never knew what happened. And for the man to be a pirate at that!

Ch. 9 Fire

The blaze was everywhere, consuming everything in its path. I was sprinting through narrow breaks in the flame, getting scorched every time my arm or leg brushed the roaring embers.

I stopped to catch my breath in a glowing clearing. The trees would light up at any second as soon as the ground began to quake and I screamed, groping for something to keep me on my feet. I snatched a swaying limb above my head as flames licked up grass and bit my skin. The earth ceased its shaking and left me trembling with panic as the blaze surrounded me once again, engulfing the forest in a wild hunger that was never fulfilled.

I turned to run, but something materialized out of the orange and red flames. I shook my head in disbelief as a towering black figure appeared as if summoned from the inferno. It was the hulking bear creature with horns protruding from its head, but there was something different about it this time. It was standing upright on its hind legs like a human.

I squinted, trying to make out more of the form. I did not know why I wasn't running; the fire was going to kill me if I didn't move. I was transfixed, my watery eyes straining to see the colossal thing. I blinked, seared skin stretching as the heat from the blaze flowed over me. In the second my eyes closed and reopened, the beast had moved directly in front of me, body only inches away from my own. I looked up expecting more colored flames, but instead saw the obscure space where the beast's face should have been. Incandescent yellow eyes glared at me from the haze with such intensity that I buckled and went down.

The flames rushed over, devouring me along with everything else.

I awoke gasping down air, trying to swallow my screams. I batted my eyes fervently, clearing the sweat that dripped from my pores. The mid-day sun streamed down on my body and heated my skin even more.

"A-n-d she's awake."

Apparently Caine had been set to watch me twist and turn in anguish as dreams ravaged my mind. I felt his cool hands on my arms, but they were drawn hastily back.

"Shoot, Lyn, you're burning up." He took hold of my elbows instead.

Why was it always like this? Every time I woke it would feel as if I was on the verge of death. I began to shake madly, not because of the nightmare, but in frustration of myself.

"What's the matter?"

I choked back a sob as tears of fury and hopelessness sprung to my eyes. I leaned into Caine, resting my head on his shoulder as teardrops rolled down my heated face.

"Hey now, everything's going to be alright, I-I promise." He patted my back awkwardly as if to reassure me. I let out a shaky breath, striving for control.

"Are you okay?" He whispered in my ear. I nodded weakly in answer.

Caine pulled back, gently, moving his hands back to my elbows. I blinked my remaining tears away and he took the edge of his torn sleeve and blotted at my face with it, a faint smile on his face.

"No more crying, alright?" I gave him a half-hearted smirk in return.

"Alright," I agreed. Caine took my hand and pulled me to my feet after he stood. The world looked alive with possibilities.

"I'm going to go get Glen and Raine," I barely heard Caine say. I shook my head absently in answer, gazing instead at the ever-changing scenery that sailed by.

Since we were always traveling on foot, I never really had a chance to notice the beautiful landscapes that surrounded me. Now, looking upon it from afar, I could appreciate the raw majesty of it. I watched as we passed giant fields of wheat not yet harvested. The wind that blew across the vast plain made them dance in waves as perfect as the ocean in motion.

I closed my eyes, remembering the countryside that used to be mine. I smiled at the memory of myself running alongside the carpet of crops imagining how good they would taste later in the year. I recalled the sitting down at dinner, waiting and peering greedily at the food our chefs carried in steaming plates full of food, fresh from the fields. The bread always came first. My mouth watered as I remembered the aroma and taste of the wheat, seasoned ideally and baked until a light crisp crust formed around the edges. There never was any hunger back then.

Voices brought me back from my memories of a life long gone. I opened my eyes reluctantly and turned to see Caine speaking with Glen as they both walked toward me. Raine struggled to keep up with their extended strides and listen in on their conversation. Everyone quieted as they neared me.

"Lyn, how are you? Caine was telling me you had a rough time sleeping."

I gazed at Glen, not fully aware of what he was asking until I saw his worried expression.

"It... I had a nightmare again." I shuddered as I recalled the blazing fire and red-eyed beast. A sudden thought popped into my head.

"What did you see in the waterfall?"

Glen's temple crinkled as he asked, "You mean back with that witch Eggy, right?"

I nodded, centered on his reply. His usually calm, collected features changed as the thought crossed his mind.

"I never understood what the crazy hag was talking about." I regarded Caine with interest, saw him scowl. "I didn't see nothing."

I sat there pondering why Caine did not experience the vision I had.

"Well I did," Raine said, a little defensively.

"You did?" I repeated stupidly.

"I saw my dad. I knew it was him because I remembered his face from pictures my mother had." She paused, glancing down at her feet. "He looked… happy. At first, I was so glad to see him smiling and safe. But then I guessed he'd forgotten all about me and my mom and that's why he'd been grinning like that."

She was hurt, but trying not to show it. I figured consulting with Raine more would be wrong so I turned back to Glen. He still hadn't spoken.

"Glen?"

He grimaced as if in pain when I said his name.   "I… saw my own death."

This surprised me. He narrowed his eyes; dark lashes casting small shadows over his planed cheeks as he elaborated. "You can't imagine what seeing that was like. The scene showed myself fighting or protecting something. Then all I saw was blood and anguish; everything was over and my body lay there, still and lifeless."

After a thought, he asked, "Why are you even asking that question?"

I looked away, feeling guilty for bringing up the whole scene with Eggy. "I don't know. It's just... ever since then my dreams have gotten more violent and regular, too."

Glen studied my face, searching for something that wasn't there. "What have they been about?"

I glanced at him, debating on whether or not to tell him what kept waking me up at night.

"I keep seeing some kind of bear creature-"

"Wait, is this the same unicorn bear that you were scared of days ago?" I examined Caine's face to see if he was being smart, but was met with a serious cast from him. I shook my head deliberately, eyes still trained on his face. I noticed his angry bruises had faded to light pastels that shadowed his face.

"It's not some fluffy teddy bear with bumps on its head if that's what you think," I stated hotly, irritated at how he had taken my explanation.

Still receiving no reply, I continued, words rolling off my tongue in a frenzied manner as if they had been dammed up forever.

"At first I thought it was only some minor beast rampaging through my dreams, but lately every time

I lie down to rest it's there! With its demonic eyes and insane size. I can't find peace sleeping, much less when I'm awake!"

I felt myself becoming flustered and started to feel hot liquid forming at the corners of my eyes.

"I-I keep thinking it means something, but I can't figure it out. Either that or I'm too much of a fool to try." The tears dripped off my cheeks, seeping into the cracked, wood deck. "I was hoping one of you could make some sense of them, but... Nothing's working!"

Raine crept up to me, wary of the tantrum I was throwing and touched my arm, a soothing gesture. "Don't worry, Lyn. With all of us," she swept everyone's face and smiled, "Well, we can figure out something."

I gazed through my tears into her gold-flecked stare. It was cleansed of all doubt; so assuring, in fact, just seeing her good-natured look made me feel better.

"Hey, do you see that?"

I twisted in the direction Caine was watching. Squinting against the sun's reflection on the rapids, I could pick out a form on the rim of the river.

"Is that... another boat?"

The vague outline of the figure sure did appear to be one, but I couldn't be exact from this distance.

"I think we're going to find out soon," Caine stated, a hint of panic worming into his voice. The structure was defiantly drawing closer.

"Let's not wait around to see what it is."

We were up and moving. Tensions were rising at an alarming rate.

"Everyone, find something to paddle with; we need to move!" I barked orders while trying to locate an object myself. Upon finding one, I heard Raine holler, "Fire!" And I spun around, breath coming in labored gasps.

The mast of the vessel was aflame, tongues of fire licking their way down the wooden pole and consuming the cloth sail. I made out a single arrow embedded deep within the burning wood. That must have been what started the blaze. The whole boat seemed to be at a standstill, like we were stuck.

A loud roar behind made me jump and circle around, afraid of what I might see. There were people, nearly twenty, lined up and coming closer with each passing second. They looked so familiar, yet strange at the same time. It couldn't be the pirates we stole from, could it? I could not think of any one else that would be pursuing us. Another shout rose above the alarm accompanied by a lone gunshot burst. The tortured scream that followed made me tear my eyes away from the fire and advancing men I had so carefully been trying to place. I knew the voice the instant it touched my ears. Glen.

A tormented expression dominated his face and his hand was tight against his chest; blood spewed from between his fingers, streaking his tattered shirt with red. I saw Caine and Raine rush to his side as he staggered, doubling over. Caine caught my eyes. In my fright, I could only make out the shape of his lips as they yelled an order I was too overwhelmed to heed. He waved for me to come on and my body lurched into motion as if on que. I dashed across the deck, floorboards blurring beneath me as one thought echoed in my head: get off the boat.

I hardy felt the heat scorch my skin as I charged through it, heading for the edge of the raft, certain that solid ground was going to be there to meet me. A volley of gunshots erupted as I neared the rail. They whizzed past my head, striking sudden fear for Glen's life if one had already hit him. I spotted Caine and Raine practically dragging Glen off the boat so I figured we must have crashed land.

I vaulted over the guardrail, confident in my sprinting abilities. That self-assurance was smothered when my feet connected with mush; it wasn't land, but a swamp! The weight of my impact had wedged me down into it, knee-deep. I could hear the lunatics storming the burning vessel above me as I urged the others to move. I caught a glimpse of Glen, bloody and pale, swaying worse with each step. If we could just make it to the shelter of the thicket of the bog then we may have a chance. But I felt like I was getting nowhere wading through the thick, black waters of the swamp.

"Ah!" I yelped as I went down. My foot had gotten caught on an unseen root beneath the muck and I stumbled forward, splashing clouded water and algae everywhere before my face united with the slimy liquid. I jolted up out of the marsh, spitting out globs of gooey mud. Twisting, I witnessed the sight of the half-crazed men holding guns, other weapons, and shouting profusely. Frozen by shock, I lay there awaiting the sharp pain of a bullet piercing my skin, but no such hurt ever came.

They did not attempt to pursue us or fire pistols and rifles into the bog, but merely stand, howling and shaking their fists at the heavens. That's when I saw it, proof that these men were not the pirates from before. Even with Caine tugging at my shoulder I couldn't forget the image and move on. Mounted crudely on a tall, spear-like pole, was the green-eyed pirate's head, expression forever minted to look like his last moments had been merciless and unforgiving.

As Caine yanked me away from the savages, the thought that kept returning was the earring that I still wore. Had my greedy desire cost that boy his life? Surely not. I touched the metal and not even the seriousness of Glen's wound could keep the images at bay. I saw the boy's bloody, open mouth, his death-pale skin and matted hair that stuck to his sick, ravaged forehead. And then his eyes, lifeless and green, they stared at me with the accusation only a guilty conscience could give away. Over and over again, the vision rolled through my mind and it wasn't until Glen collapsed did I manage to somehow force the scene away.

I knelt down, soaking my clothes in the foul water to get a better view of him. The wound looked terrible, skin surrounding it swollen and an irritated color of red with white fluid oozing out of it. Blood was still flowing pretty freely and the front of Glen's shirt was completely drenched with it. I brushed his flushed cheek and saw his eyes, drowning in anguish.

"Guys, this looks bad. We need to treat it."

Caine glowered at me. "Lyn, how nice of you to finally notice! Oh, and great idea, too. I would have never thought of it."

He discarded his fake smile and asked none too kindly, "*What,* exactly do you think we should do?"

I hadn't paid any attention to how long I had kept to myself. It had been a down right stupid thing to do at a time as dire as this.

"I-I don't know. But I do know if he continues like this... he's not going to make it much longer." I glanced down at him. Glen was barely breathing as it was, so there was no way his body could take more physical exertion than it already had.

"Why don't we get out of the water, first"?

Now noticing Raine, I asked, "Where do you see a dry spot?"

She pointed to a small island just a few yards away and up enough out of the water that we wouldn't get wet.

"It's perfect." A bright smile lit up her face. It was the first time I had felt happy since the boat incident. She did so enjoy being praised for her efforts.

I leaned down and lightly rested my hands on Glen's shoulders. "Can you make it to that dry piece of land?"

Hw slowly raised his head and parted his clenched eyes. "Yeah... I'll be able to get there." His voice was filled with so much pain and loathing that I doubted his words.

"Let's get a move on. Raine's been covering for you, but she's wearing out so you helping this time, Lyn?"

I nodded to Caine, determined to express my concern through my actions rather than my words. I braced Glen on his left while Caine helped steady him on his right. "Okay, Glen," I began, "Try to help us out here if you can."

He started to stand and Caine and I shifted so we supported most of his weight. Glen groaned and took a sharp breath, shuddering afterword as if merely breathing robbed him of his strength. Raine made sure we would be able to handle Glen and went trudging ahead, warning us of deep spots and twisted roots.

After what seemed like hours we finally came to the elevated piece of land. I climbed up first, leaving Caine to stabilize Glen, and helped Raine up out of the muck. She and I took nearly all of Glen's weight as Caine walked him on to the dry island. Had he fainted? The load was too much for my scrawny body to bear, especially without Glen being conscious.

"Glen," I strained his name out, noticing Raine was struggling as much as I.

"Lyn- Ah!" He coughed violently once and then collapsed, slipping right through my hands. I gaped, staring at the open space where he had been, and then dropped to my knees to make sure he was still breathing. I pressed my ear to his chest, right above his heart, smearing my face with warm blood. Raine was right beside me, holding her breath and stroking

Glen's ashen cheek. His heartbeat was faint, very faint, but still there.

"Is he...?"

I shook my head. "No... No, he's not gone."

A sniffle, and I looked at Raine to see her smile, wiping her tears with a dirty sleeve.

"I didn't think he'd be able to hold out much longer. Looks like I was right."

Raine, flustered by Caine's remark, asked me, "Glen's gonna be okay, right Lyn?"

I looked her in the eyes, debating whether or not to tell her a comforting lie or what I *really* thought. I decided on the in-between. "I think he has a fair chance if we find a way to help heal his wounds."

"Alright, but... what do we do?" That was a good question.

I knew we had to do something or Glen most likely was not going to make it through the night. I swept my gaze over the dimly lit swamp, noticing the absence of light and realizing it would be dark soon. My eyes fell on a large clump of moss growing on the trunk of a tree that had risen up from the bog. I turned to see Glen's pale, perspiring face to confirm my plan. "I think I've got it."

Caine and Raine gazed at me expectantly, skeptic cast more prominent on his face than hers.

"We're going to need some fire."

Raine's eyes widened while Caine's narrowed. "Why? Haven't you had enough fire for one day?"

"Listen, if we're going to have any chance at this, then you're going to have to trust me."

After some rationalizing, Caine spoke again, words not as loud as before. "Fine. You said we needed fire. How, exactly, do we get some surrounded by water with no flint or matches?"

Happy he had made no further attempts to argue, I explained. "This is going to be hard, but it's all I can think of."

"We'll both do whatever you tell us, Lyn," Raine stated, ever diligent to her friends.

Caine raised an eyebrow. "If it's not something along the lines of 'go jump off a bridge', then I think I can manage."

To them, that's what this idea was going to be. "You two are going to go back to the boat, see if it's still smoldering, and bring back a hot board. I'll cover the rest."

"That's about like going to jump."

Raine silenced Caine, grabbing his arm. "But we can do it! If those guys are there, then Caine can sneak and steal a board. He's good enough to do that." She gave her sweetest grin; there was no way Caine could say no. She and I exchanged glances, smug. She certainly knew Caine's weak points.

"That it?"

I gazed at Caine, noting the absence of his bruises. He looked different without them. "Yeah. If you find supplies be sure to bring them back."

"And you're sure you can handle yourself?"

I shot him a look and waved them off. "I'll be fine."

I sat down and wrapped my arms around my knees, looking at them disappear into the haze. Watching the slight rise and fall of Glen's red chest made me want to speed up time and help him faster. A sudden snapping sound made me jerk up and stare, wide-eyed, at the source. A ragged squirrel had broken a limb bounding from one tree to the other.

I shook my head, thinking myself foolish for being startled by such a thing. Taking another look around, I scooted closer to Glen, my heart beating quicker when I found that I could no longer see between the trees. When the first beam of moonlight reflected off the still swamp water, I began to think maybe I hadn't come up with such a great plan after all.

Where were they? I knew that Caine and Raine couldn't have been gone more than a couple of hours, but as the night progressed, I began to worry. A scrawny, defenseless girl left to guard an injured boy on the verge of death was *not* a good idea. As I listened to the everlasting chorus of toads and crickets, I became aware of another sound. At first, I thought it was simply the wind rustling a few tree branches, but when I heard the same noise over and over, a knot tied itself in my stomach. I was only able to catch the tail end of it because the animals started to quiet.

There it was again. The drone seemed like moaning laughter, if there was such a thing to compare it to. My eyes darted around, and I gripped Glen's cool, motionless hand, trying to gain repose. I could have sworn the consonance was closer this time. Whatever was making the sound must know we were here; either that or it smelt fresh blood, I thought, sparing yet another glance at Glen. Nothing I could think of lived in a swamp and made that noise.

Forms moved in between the trees. I hoped it was an animal, prayed it was something that wouldn't kill us, but it shifted into two separate shapes, upright and carrying glowing wood. For an awful moment, I thought the murders~~murders~~ from the boat had found us, but when two faces were illuminated by the faint gleam of fire coming from the board, I heaved a massive sigh of relief.

"*Where* have you been?"

Caine shrugged his shoulders. "It's kind of difficult to find your way back to an island when the whole swamp's black," he replied, indifferent to the distress in my voice.

"He got lost," Raine said, pointing out his mistake. I examined the wood they had brought back and that's when I remembered what I had neglected to do while they were gone. Breath rushed out in frustration.

"Stay here. I'll be right back!" I left Caine and Raine staring after me, confusion dominating their expressions, as I vaulted off the mound. Sullied droplets of water splattered everywhere, soaking my pants up to my thighs, but I didn't care.

I stopped, mid-stride, and called, "Raine, Caine, I left a stack of twigs and grasses with some dead leaves on top of it. Light it!"

With my order voiced, I trudged off toward the oversized tree with moss thriving all over its trunk. I snatched handfuls of the damp plant and stuffed it into my pockets, then tramped back over to the mound. A pleasant, if not recklessly thrown together fire burned among the wood and grass.

"Nice job. Did you find supplies?" I followed the compliment with a demand.

"Left them over there," Caine said, indicating a cloth sack carelessly tossed to the side. Good. That was tomorrow's breakfast taken care of; now it was time to get things done.

"What about knives? Find any?" I asked the question even know I already knew the answer for the hilt of a small dagger protruded out from under his shirt.

"Yeah... Why?"

"Let me see it."

He huffed as he reached for the blade. "So much for gratitude."

"Thank you," I countered, flashing a smile. I took the knife and handed the moss to Raine.

"Lay this beside Glen." She had an inquisitive glint in her eyes, but went to do it.

I walked closer to the fire, tightening my grip on the dagger. This was going to work; it had to. I held the bottom of the blade and threw it forcefully into the flames where it became embedded deep within the burning ashes.

"Hey, what are you doing?" Caine scrambled over to where I was standing, watching the embers heat the steel. He was going for the knife.

"Don't! Leave it be." He hesitated, deciding whether to heed my words or follow through.

"Alright. But you owe me a knife."

"Done." I remained standing, staring as the metal began to glow. I nearly stuck my hand in, but common sense stopped me. I ripped enough material off my shirt to offer a bit of protection from the heat. The fact that it was wet only made for a better guard. I wrapped my hand in cloth and braced to plunge it into the coals. I thrust my hand in and snatched the dagger, gave a quick yank and it came out, hot. I bit my tongue to hold back a yelp; the fire hadn't burnt me at first, but now I was starting to feel it.

"Raine, help Glen sit up! Caine, I'll need you to hold him for me."

Raine darted to Glen's side, traces of fear in her movements, and managed to make him sit erect. Caine's features twisted once he figured out what I was going to do.

"You're sure this is the only way?" I nodded gravely, sorry too that it had come to this.

"This is going to hurt you a lot more than it hurts me, Glen." Hearing his name mentioned, Glen seemed to acknowledge Caine by attempting a smile, but it came out as more of a grimace. I came to a halt in front of him, and looked at the blade in my quivering hand.

"Just do it, Lyn!" I tore my eyes away from the lustrous steel and, propelled by Raine's voice pitched high from fright, readied myself to burn the pain right out of Glen's body.

Ch. 10 Burn

When I pressed the blade of the dagger on Glen's wound, he let loose an utterly agonizing cry of tortured madness. It took every bit of control I possessed not to let go of the knife. He writhed in anguish then went limp and the screaming subdued, leaving a faint echo to follow. Caine somehow kept him upright, Glen's smoking skin pressed tight on the flat of the blade. Raine covered her face, weeping tears in her hand.

I felt the bile rise in my throat from the smell of seared flesh, but only swallowed it and put more pressure on the dagger. The sound it made was similar to sticking a hot piece of metal in cool water.

"Okay! Raine, get the moss and make sure it's wet. Hurry!" She made haste to do what I asked despite the tears that blurred her vision. Raine gathered up the plant and began handing portions to me. Thank goodness the damp plant had held the moisture in. I pulled the knife back, wincing as Glen's blackened skin stuck, then snapped back in place. I groped for the moss.

Feeling the fuzzy tips touch my fingers, I snatched it up and plastered it over the vile, dark spot where I had burned Glen. The thought that it had been *me* made me a little sicker to my stomach, but the aches would have to wait because I wasn't done yet.

"Caine, turn him over!" While Caine and Raine busied themselves with that, I was up and running, knife in hand. I let it fly, splintering several sticks in the process of delving back into the blaze. Hotter, I thought, melt for all I care, just catch! When I heard the urgent cries of Raine beckoning me to help, I could wait no longer. Seizing hold of the blade, not worrying if the heat singed my flimsy guard from it, I wrenched it out and hastily made my way to Glen.

Since the bullet had gone straight through, it saved us the task of having to dig it out, but it also meant if we were going to be able to stop the bleeding, then we had to scorch both the entrance of the shot and exit, as well. I could feel the high temperature of the metal hilt eating away at the fabric of the shirt twisted around my hand. I couldn't imagine what it would be like to have an injury touched by it.

"He's still out cold. I won't be expecting screaming that could wake the dead this time"

"Hold him anyway!" A bewildered expression crossed Caine's face, but he complied and the harsh process of burning bloody flesh resumed.

The gash was larger in the back so I had to wrench the knife down into the puncture more. Black smoke was coming off Glen's body so vehemently I barely located the place of the blade. The smell was enough to make ~~you~~ one vomit and I was getting the worst of it, but it wasn't like I had anything to chuck up. The trek through the marsh had robbed me of my meal on the raft. I yanked back the dagger, verbally expressing how disgusting the sound was.

"Moss!" Raine appeared as if summoned from thin air with the rest of the plant. I piled it over and around Glen's wound in effort to keep out infection and heal it as best I could.

"Okay, I think I'm done." Caine and Raine gathered around me to gaze at my work.

"He looks…"

"Rough." Caine finished for Raine. I had to agree. Glen was sprawled on the bloodstained ground, smoldered from the burns. The only color to his skin was that around the plant. Otherwise, he had turned a deathly shade of white, disturbed only by the scalded skin and green pigment of the moss.

I had done all I could. Now came the difficult part: waiting. If Glen could make it through the rest of the night, and keep breathing until morning, he might have a chance.

I noticed how badly I was shaking, how exhausted I was from the day's events. I dropped the knife; it stuck in the dirt, hilt up. I stood and sauntered to a place near the campfire that was now little more than a faint gleam in the darkness of night. I passed Raine, asleep, nestled close to Glen as if she believed her presence was enough to ward off any bad things that were going to come.

Once I had settled for a patch of hard dirt, meekly illuminated by the dissipating embers, I spied Caine not too far off and sitting close to the bank, gazing out at the murky waters of the swamp. He was slouched, so I assumed he was resting, but I had no way to be sure and I didn't feel like getting up to check.

The last thought to cross my mind before I nodded off, was the eerie noise I had heard while Raine and Caine had been gone. Remembering the moaning laughter made me shudder and hope that whatever it was left us alone.

Ch. 11 Food and Sand

I awoke feeling worse for wear. My mouth tasted like I'd slept with my foot stuffed in it all night. The mud from the bog had dried and was caked in clots all over my legs and feet, even splattered up to my elbows. At least I had slept soundly. No dreams had crossed my mind, probably because I had been so drained from the day before.

I sit up to stretch, but doubled over in pain from my stomach. Moaning, I clutched my middle, grinding my teeth. The hunger felt like it was killing me from the inside, eating away at my muscles and organs because I couldn't find adequate food for it.

Wild laughing resounded in my ears, making my breath hitch. It was the sound from last night: except it was closer, much closer.

"Lyn?" The voice was hoarse and weak, but there was no mistaking it. I looked up and *sitting*, not standing, was Glen, covered in scorch marks and moss, but alive. I met his eyes with the same joy that was carried in his. The blue in them was dimmed, but they were brightened when he saw me smile. Seeing him made me forget the noise for a moment.

Noting Raine was still fast asleep; I spoke quietly, mirth and relief painting my voice. "You're awake! How are you feeling?"

He shrugged, tensing up with the movement, and then relaxing. "Better, I think." Glen seemed to be trying to push it.

I leaned in, brushing the damp hair from his forehead. He looked so weak... It was silly, but his fragileness scared me. What was I thinking; of course he'd be feeble! Glen had been razed by fire, near death, but he'd pulled through it. So far.

"Lyn, is something wrong?" I shook the thought away, forcing a smile on my face.

"Oh, no. I was just- it's nothing," I stumbled for something to say. "D-Did you hear that moaning sound from before, or was it just me?" He nodded, slightly.

"It almost sounds familiar, but I can't place it."

Familiar? Then it came to me. "Oh, you must have heard it when you and I were waiting for Caine and Raine to come back. You were barely conscious, so maybe that's why you can't remember so clearly."

His forehead creased, deep in thought, or straining to think, I couldn't tell.

"It's near." He glanced at me, sensing fear in my voice.

"I'm sure it's only some lost animal crying out. We're in a swamp, after all." When Glen saw the skeptic cast I exhibited, he said, "If someone hears it again, then we worry."

I bit my bottom lip, going with what he thought for now. As reassured by his own words, Glen asked, "Is there any food around? I think it might help ease the pain."

That brought me back to the hunger from before. "Yeah, hold on."

I spotted the brown sack still in a heap on the ground and ambled over to it. I was hopeful at first, but that optimism quickly became disappointment when I went to open it. The vile scent told me that we were not having breakfast this morning. I stuck my hand down in the bag and my hopes vanished, crushed like the rotten fruit and spoiled meat inside the sack.

"Did you find any food in there, Lyn?" I turned to receive Raine.

"I don't think we'll be having breakfast any time soon." Her pouty lips formed a frown.

"Oh... But I'm starving!"

"Aren't we all, Raine?" Caine, having climbed up on the island, was now strolling casually toward us. If I hadn't known better, I would have thought he was just some ordinary boy waltzing through the swamp without a care in the world. But we were far from ordinary.

"Of course we're all hungry. If you... What is that?" I focused on something long and limp dangling from his hand.

"Our breakfast."

I gaped at his frank reply. As he neared us, I saw what it *really* was; a dead snake, reeking of swamp stink and pink and bloody where he had skinned it, hung in his grasp.

"You're kidding, right?"

"Look, you don't have to eat it. I was feeling a little generous today, so I went out and killed this thing, almost got bit, and figured I'd cook the meal, but no. We all have to be difficult, don't we Lyn?"

He was dogging me and I knew it. I could feel my temper bubbling. "It's not that I don't appreciate what you've done, but that... *thing* is-"

"No no, I get what you're saying. I'll just go throw it in the water. Croc's gotta eat to." He began walking to the edge of the rise.

"Caine, wait!" I dashed over to him. "Stop."

I grabbed his arm, cocked back and ready to toss the snake into the mud. The touch of the cold reptile made me shudder. "I'll eat it."

I glimpsed Caine's smirking face and shot him a vengeful look in return. What a wonderful way to start the morning.

"Can you get the fire going, or should I do everything myself?"

"Yes," I replied through clenched teeth. I marched over to the pile of leftover twigs and grasses, listened to the hushed chuckles of Glen and Raine while I worked to get it stoked. After the flames caught, the smoldering coals burned brightly.

Caine stuck the snake on a sharp limb he had carved into a point and situated himself by the fire after having visited Glen who was still sitting on the ground. I watched in revulsion as he rotated the stick, like a housewife would roast a chicken over an open fire. Even know the smell it gave off made my mouth water, I did not want to put the meat in my mouth. Who knew where that thing had been! The only way I could force myself to eat would be to think about the ache in my gut that told me I desperately needed food.

After several minuets of roasting, Caine pulled the snake off and tore it into four good-sized chunks for us to feast on.

"Here," he said, handing a section off to me. I stared at the brown lump of snake in my palm.

"Hey, who knows, it might taste better than chicken." I looked at Caine out of the side of my eye, doubting his prediction.

"Wow. Caine, it's delicious!" Raine was enjoying her first bite a lot more than I was. What did I have to lose? Putting one end up to my mouth, I parted my lips and took a mouthful. A strange rush of flavors entered; it was hard to describe. The tang was similar to stringy pork mixed with chewy chicken.

Honestly, it wasn't half-bad. In fact, it was one of the best things I had eaten in a long time, but I was not about to let Caine know. Still, he seemed inclined to find out. "Well?"

"It's... Edible."

A grin stole its way on to his face. "She likes it!"

"No I-"

I decided bickering over food would be stupid so I just shook my head and kept eating.

"It's good," Glen began. "Lyn's just too proud to admit it."

"Glad you like it. How are you feeling after... last night?"

"Better, at least, not dying anymore." He still looked drained and waxy, but his voice didn't seem as hoarse and his eyes shown a little brighter.

I glanced around at the marsh. The sun reflected on the surface of the foggy water, sending off its beams in a million different directions. Glancing up, I was blinded by the mid-day light breaking through the trees. I realized we needed to get going. "Hey Caine, stop bragging about your great cooking skills and help Glen up. We've wasted half and day here and I think it's time we got a move on."

"What are you in such a hurry about?"

My mind immediately went to the laughing from before. "Let's just say there are some things here more dangerous than a snake."

He raised an eyebrow at me. "Who knows if Glen can even stand? I mean, he just got shot and saved from an early grave. Now you're going to make him walk?" I could tell he was playing with my guilt.

"Maybe if we helped he could." Raine was trying to come to an agreement. Sweet of her.

"It's okay, I'm feeling pretty good. Lyn's right, we're burning daylight."

Ironic he should use the word 'burning' to describe it. That did it, though. We all exchanged glances and unspoken concerns then went about leaving. I put out the fire, thinking if the men were still searching for us, it would be best not to have the smoke to lead them here.

Glen was leaning heavily on the trunk of a tree, clutching the moss feebly protecting his wounds and breathing hard. I went to take his hand.

"Lyn you don't-"

"*Yes,* I do. Now hold on." He gave up protesting and gratefully let me guide him off the dry land. His limping was bad, worse than I wanted, but at least he could move.

"Are you sure you can keep going?" I questioned. "Is that blood beneath the moss?"

I gently prodded an area around his chest. He gasped from the touch and flinched away. "Please, don't... leave it be. It's healing."

I persisted. "Tell me what it feels like."

Glen cut his blue gaze at me. "Awful. Like getting stabbed with hot knives again and again; it feels like my skin is tearing apart."

I thought now would be a good time for encouragement. "Well, you're doing a whole lot better than I ever would. Why, I would still be sitting on the ground moaning because it hurt." He smiled, pained, but it showed promise.

Eventually, Glen was able to walk without assistance, but slowly. Caine pulled up beside me. "Lyn, I'm thinking maybe we should split up."

The proposal sounded absurd.

"What-"

"I know, I know. We would only be, let's say fifty yards apart from each other. So if one of us got into trouble, the other would know right away."

I considered it. Caine and I should be fine. I was anxious about leaving Glen's side and not being able to see Raine. Still, I knew if we were ever going to find a way out of this godforsaken place then we would have to cover some ground. "Okay. Fifty yards, right?"

Caine nodded. "Right."

"Glen?"

He answered me without breaking stride. "I heard you. Don't worry about me." With that, he turned abruptly to the right.

"I'll go tell Raine." Caine veered to the left, leaving me to simply walk straight ahead. I hated being left alone, I really did. All my pressing thoughts swarmed in my head, the most disturbing one being the strange noise following us. I knew something small could never make a sound like that.

Come to think of it, I had not been hearing the normal birds chirping or occasional frog croak. I began to wonder if the thing with the laugh was accountable for it. The possibility became even more plausible when I came across piles of bones, some rotting and darkened with age, others white and fresh: all stripped clean.

I had no idea what to think. I fluctuated between the two extremes of being scared half to death or staying wholly naïve and ignoring it all.

"Ahhh! Someone help!" The plea shouted out made me start violently.

In an instant, I was rampaging through the knee-deep muck, muttering, "Bad idea, bad idea!"

My calves burned with physical strain. Run really was not the way to describe it. I was doing something of a drunken gallop, kicking mud and flying water everywhere. I had but one objective: find Raine.

The water, sprinkled with yellow specks, was up to my ankles and becoming thicker each step. I soon realized the specks were sand, quicksand. And Raine was drowning in it.

I saw Caine burst forth from the western side of the swamp, balancing on one foot so not to step in the sinking earth. Where was Glen?

"Caine, Lyn! Help!" Her voice came in little shouts and gasps because her frantic struggling was dragging her deeper and deeper into the bottomless pit of sand.

"Raine," I yelped. "Try not to move, you'll only sink faster!"

Her flailing stilled for a moment, but she was already up to her chest in the stuff sinking quickly. I had to do something and fast. I yelled at Caine across the basin. "Grab a vine!"

"What?"

I second-guessed myself. "No wait. Grab me and don't let go!"

Not waiting for an answer, I plunged into the slush. The impact robbed me of my breath and sent a wave of silt throughout the pit. I felt my extended arms lock with what had to be Raine and came face to face with her when the sand had cleared. I attempted to whisper reassurances to her before the inevitable happened. "You're going to be fine so don't worry. I've got you. But you might just want to hold your breath."

She gave me one final nod, puffed out her cheeks with air, and went under.

"Caine!" I could feel hard tugs on my ankles.

"I can't pull you, it's too much weight!"

I turned my head to catch a last gulp of air before I was sucked down with Raine. I could barely make out the muted shouts of Caine as my ears filled with quicksand. I held Raine in my grasp, but she made no effort to hang on herself. Bad sign.

Of all the ways to die, it had to end like this? My lungs were burning already; I wanted to cough, spit out the globs of ooze and breathe again. There was no way this could be the end. After all the things I had been through I wasn't going down like this.

I used the last of my strength to squirm and wriggle in the stink of the mud. Had I just moved? I could still feel Caine's hands around my ankles, but I thought he was stuck too so he couldn't be pulling us out. Maybe I was hallucinating, or the sand was in my brain. I moved again. Out.

The grime was dripping off my legs and my waist was soon out of the pit. I started contorting my body to get my head up before I passed out and broke the surface. I shook back and forth trying to clear the sand plastered on my eyes, and gulped down a great lungful of air, swallowing the slush as the wind forced it down my throat. "Lyn hold on. Don't let go of Raine!"

I became conscious of Raine slipping through my grasp. I snatched her wrist and tugged; her head came out! She was covered in mud, but was moving and spitting sand everywhere, just as breathless as I was.

As soon as I paused to admire the moment of peace, I was unceremoniously dropped on solid ground. Caine leaned over me and seized Raine by the arms, hauling her all the way out. After he sat her down, he offered his hand and I took it letting him pull me to my feet. "You know I'm so happy we're alive I could hug you, but..." His face crumpled as he ran his gaze over my mud-covered body.

I lifted an eyebrow, daring him to spit out the rest of his sentence. "Well, you know. I don't really want to smell that bad." He gave me a very cute, boyish smile and I advanced on Caine, throwing a fake punch. He stepped back and that's when I noticed something thick and green snaked around his waist.

I followed the body of the vine and saw where it was fastened to the trunk of a tree. And there beside it was Glen, shocked that he himself had just saved us all.

"Lyn." I looked down into Raine's bright stare, wet with tears.

"Thank you," she whispered wrapping her trembling arms around me. "I don't think I've ever been so scared in my life."

I smiled faintly. "I know what you mean."

I glanced over her head and spotted Caine conversing with Glen. "Thanks, Glen. I thought we were all goners for sure. If you hadn't been here..."

"You saved me. I was only returning the favor."

"Still." Caine shrugged.

I gently detached Raine from around my middle and went to see them. She trailed behind. I spread my arms, palms up, the look of ridiculousness. "I'm speechless."

"And dirty," Caine added. I fired him a glare then returned to Glen.

"How did you do it? Get us out, I mean."

He grinned, washing all the pain from before away. "I overheard your slapdash plan with the vine so I snatched one up on the way here," He touched one of his bandages. "I'm a bit slow today or I would have had you out sooner. Actually, I wouldn't have had you out at all if Caine hadn't ~~of~~ have been here."

"You shouldn't have pushed yourself," I remarked. "Look, you're bleeding again." I indicated the area around the moss. Red was trickling from underneath the plant, making what was left of his shirt wet again.

"Did you want me to do nothing while you drowned in the sand?"

"I... No, why would you-?"

"Then don't worry about it."

"You two come look at this!" I turned toward Caine. He and Raine were staring at something on a tree. Adrenaline sparked in my abdomen and Glen and I went over to them.

"Look," Raine said, pointing to large claw marks that had gouged the trunk.

"What do you think made it?" Caine questioned. I had an idea; my mind went to the sound from before. Running my hands over the split bark, I tried to imagine what kind of animal could have made slashes that deep in such a giant tree.

A wail, beginning softly, grew until it was booming with mad laughter. The nearness of it was enough to set the most tranquil of persons on edge. I froze in place, petrified even after the moaning had stopped. Raine, having cleared her eyes of quicksand, exchanged glances with Caine. "*What* was that?" They both echoed in unison.

"That," I began. "Was the exact sound I've been hearing since we've been in the swamp."

"Well, we know what made those claw-marks, now," Glen stated, running his blue eyes over the trunk. "Now," he turned to me, "We worry."

"You mean we run."

He took both my hands in his. "No. If it's after us, we'd be dead before the night's over. We'll have to find a piece of dry land to bed down on."

I glanced at our joined hands, my eyes lingering on the rough calluses covering his.

"That's just a plain stupid idea!" Caine thundered, fear making his words high. "We find someplace to settle down, go to sleep, and then let it eat us? I hate to say it, but I like Lyn's plan better."

"We keep watch." The tone of Glen's voice invited no argument. "Each one of us, we'll take turns so everybody can rest and rest assured."

He fixed Caine with his icy blue stare, daring him to dispute. Caine seemed to realize a confrontation would do no good. "What are we waiting for?" He grabbed Raine by the hand. "Let's move."

Ch. 12 Night

Our pace was fast, our movement rapid. We were on the run from something: a sound. No matter how swiftly we traveled, the night was catching up and it would not be long before we would be forced to set up camp. The only way I was able to keep going was by thinking about Glen. He hung on my arm to limit his falls and let me guide him over fallen logs, through high cattails, and murky pools of waist deep water. Every time I would lose my footing, he would be there to catch me; all the times he would slow, clutching his chest in pain, I was there to urge him on and keep him moving away from whatever it was we were running from.

I felt attached to Glen on our trek to safety and was unexpectedly saddened when I finally let go. Darkness had fallen like a black sheet over the marsh. We needed fire.

"So here we are," Caine proclaimed, showing the small island on which we stood with a sweep of his hand. "Now what?"

"Fire," I answered. "We find some wood or dry grass and somehow start a fire."

"Isn't that obvious?"

"You're the one that asked!" I retorted, dread making me edgier than usual.

"The question is *how*. How are we going to get a fire started? We don't have any sources and nothing that would make a spark."

"What we need is some flint," I stated, turning toward Glen, hoping I answered his question.

"Flint, "Raine repeated. "That's a rock isn't it?"

I nodded. "Yes, but it's a stone that can create a fire. Not just a normal rock."

"Well then what does it look like?" She asked, suddenly interested in a hopeless cause. No way we could find flint stone in a swamp. I answered anyway.

"I think it's got a grayish tint and feels coarse and grainy. Like you would be careful with it when you picked it up because of its sharp edges."

Raine had been taking this in mindfully, eyes glowing brighter with each word. "Is this it?" She produced a dark gray stone out of her pocket and it was almost an exact likeness to the description I had given.

"I- I don't know." I took it and sure enough, felt that rough, sinewy texture. I looked at her, dumbfounded. "Where-?"

"Found it on the boat."

"~~Wait-a-go~~ *Way-to-go* Raine," I said with a smile.

"Alright, let's get some light around here." Caine dropped an armful of sticks over the pile of dry grass Glen had gathered.

"Okay." I glanced around the dim edged of the land. "Could someone find me a rock?"

"Already covered," Caine replied, displaying a fair chunk in his palm.

"Thank you."

I took both rocks over to our makeshift pit. Please work, I thought. I struck he two stones together and there was a click then small shower of sparks to follow. Hope flared and was put out like the spark I had created. I ground my teeth in frustration, dodging the urge to throw the rocks down and give up. I tried again with the same result: nothing.

"Gah!" All this and I couldn't even light a stupid fire? I sensed a presence near and turned to see Caine.

"What?" I snapped.

"You're not doing it right." He reached out and threw a dry birds nest on the other things. "Like this."

He placed both of his hands over mine, guiding them. Caine smacked the rocks together, sending sparks flying and jarring my arms in the process.

"Now blow." He leaned over my shoulder and puffed out air at the glowing embers. I added my breath to his and, believe it or not, an actual fire burned, glorious orange and yellow mouths of flame devouring the wood and grass.

"*That's* how you start a fire." Caine removed his hands and patted me on the shoulders, grinning at his success. "Glen you've got guard duty first!" Caine yawned. "I'm catching some shut-eye."

He plopped down beside me, one arm resting on an arched knee while ~~Caine~~ he stared into the blaze. I noticed how the firelight illuminated the sharp planes of his face and reflected off of his stunning russet eyes. He cut them sideways to look at me. "Do you think Glen's gonna fall asleep on watch?"

I let a vague smile develop on my lips at his joking manner. "If you're worried about it then why don't you go stand guard instead?"

Caine diverted his gaze back to the flickering coals. "Nah, I'm good."

He seemed lost in thought for a moment. "Say, Lyn?" He twisted so his entire face was to me.

"Yeah?"

"You know I..." his voice trailed off.

"What?" I turned my full attention on him. Our eyes met briefly until he looked away, focusing on the ground.

"Never mind. It was nothing important."

I kept my eyes trained on Caine, pondering what it was he had been going to say. Raine waltzing toward me, her silhouette a dim outline in the haze interrupted my thoughts. Tearing my eyes from Caine, I asked, "Does Glen need help?"

She shook her head. "No, but he said we should sleep together in case something happened overnight."

Right. That would provide more protection and it wouldn't be so much of a hassle waking everyone.

"Sounds good to me. Why don't you sleep in between Caine and me?"

I patted the ground to the left of myself welcoming her. Raine settled down after giving me a grateful nod. Caine scooted over and glanced in our direction. "Good night, Lyn. I'll wake you when I decide I'm tired."

"You mean after you're too scared to stand in the dark any longer?"

Caine tilted his head, a lopsided smile portrayed on his face, while Raine giggled at my remark. I gave him a wide grin in return and stretched out on my back. I used my hands as sort of a prop behind my head and gazed up at the stars: they were brilliant. The black cover had holes in it; millions of white, heavenly bodies were spread and shined through the dark like rays of hope driving away evil thoughts.

I closed my eyes, still seeing tiny dots of light dancing in the night. Soon, though, it all went blank. I had let the little specks take me so I could rest.

Pressure, movement; I was being shaken awake. My eyes shot open, no doubt edged with white, and a startled gasp escaped my lips. I sit up ready to spring to my feet, but not able to stand.

"Shhhh!" Caine had hold of my hand and if he hadn't clamped his palm over my mouth, I would have let loose at the sight of him so near.

"Now who's scared of the dark?"

The coals from the fire allowed me to catch a faint smile from him, but the dancing shadows playing over his face made any other detail impossible to discern. Caine took his hand off my mouth; it tasted of grime and sweat.

"My turn?"

"Yep. I mean, if you can handle it."

"I'll be fine."

"You always say that," he retorted, helping ~~my~~ me to my feet.

"I mean it this time." He snorted, but didn't push the subject further. I spared a backward glance for Glen and Raine and found them both sleeping fitfully, likely uneasy.

I began walking to the bank, but Caine seized my wrist and I turned to face him.

"Listen," he said, looking at Glen and Raine. "Wake me when you get tired."

Concern wrinkled my brow. "But didn't you just-"

"Let them sleep and don't exhaust yourself." With that voiced, he let go of my arm, stalked to a spot beside Raine, plopped down, and shut his eyes.

He's the one that needs some sleep, I thought, continuing to the land's edge. I paused, staring out at the ebony water. Clouds covered the stars so they no longer reflected off the swamp.

161

Surely nothing would happen with my standing watch if nothing had gone wrong so far. I cursed myself for not asking Caine if he had heard anything suspicious. It would have helped if I knew the moaning laughter was not nearby.

My ears picked up on a swish of water to my right. I jerked my head in its direction, heart accelerating as I squinted in attempt to see through the blackness. I calmed myself thinking it had to have been a tree limb or toad splashing into the water. Still, I was picking up on this indistinct rippling liquid.

"Swish!" This time it was behind me.

I twirled around and faced the smoldering fire, still seeing nothing out of the ordinary. Light, that's what I needed. Hurrying over to the burning coals, I grabbed an armload of sticks and grass and threw them on the embers. It caught instantly, flaring and illuminating the island several feet out. I turned a full circle and, despite the firelight, was not able to spot anything unusual.

Giving up my panic, I crept cautiously back to my post, eyeing the bank warily. I couldn't hear any more flowing because of the overwhelming crackle and pop of the blaze. I paused a few feet away from the rim, squinting, thinking a shadow had shifted. I inched closer and a sudden hiss pierced the darkness, making me jump backward with a startled cry.

A massive alligator burst forth into view, mouth agape, razor teeth flashing, and spitting aggressively. I back peddled faster than I thought I could screaming, "Run!" That is until my heel caught on someone's body and I plummeted to the ground.

The breath was knocked out of me and when my screams were hushed, the hissing alligator took over. There was a grunt and a splutter as Caine got kicked and I broke my fall with Glen and Raine. I sucked in as much air as my lungs could muster and yelled "Wake up!"

I tried to scramble to my feet, but only succeeded in tangling myself up more with everyone. I glimpsed Caine rise to his feet.

"What in the world?" The sight of the huge reptile stunned him into silence.

"Run!" I hollered, but my desperate words had no effect. I clamored to my feet still trying in vain to move everyone as another hiss broke the night.

A burning chunk of wood went sailing through the air and struck the giant hard on its skull. It snapped its mouth shut and tossed its head ardently from side to side. Then it ruptured with a great, booming roar and stormed us, moving at an unimaginable speed. I shrieked in terror, frozen, awaiting my death.

"Kapow!" The sound of a gun being fired mixed with my screams.

Blood splattered along the ground; for a second, I believed it was I who had been shot, but when I looked up the gore poured from the scaly beast's head and not mine. Even ~~know~~ Though the bullet punctured it, the brute charged on like the gunshot had never phased it.

"Lyn move!" I heard Caine's tragic shout, but the enormous reptile was already upon me, mouth opened and positioned to kill.

A pair of gunshots was discharged in rapid succession, each one striking home: the alligator's skull. I was yanked out of the way of its snapping jaws by two couple of hands and landed roughly on my backside in between Caine and Raine.

I watched in horror as the beast twitched and struggled, still hissing. Glen raised his silver pistol and placed his finger on the trigger.

"Pow!" And that was it.

The only thing left was a vibrating echo and a single dead alligator.

Ch. 13 The Chase

"Can you not hear or you just that determined to get yourself killed?"

Caine seemed furious that he just saved my life and was now yelling at me. Since I was still partly in ~~shook~~ shock, I did not argue, but tried to calm him. "Hey, I'm alive aren't I? Thanks for jerking me out of the way."

Caine opened his mouth to dispute, but Raine cut him off. "She's right, Caine. There's no need to shout because Lyn couldn't move fast enough."

He turned on Raine. "Don't you start! I... thought we were too late."

While they continued to bicker, I stood and hobbled over to Glen who was inspecting his pistol. "You know you're the quickest thinker I've ever met."

"He looked at me, a peculiar expression painting his face.

"Not really," he held out his gun. "Those were my last bullets."

My eyes widened. I refused to believe what he'd just told me. "What do you mean 'those were your last bullets.'?"

"Exactly what I said. They're gone.

Dread returned. "What are we going to do?"

Glen shrugged, letting my question flow over him like water. "We'll think of something else," he replied, stowing the gun away.

He smiled, *actually smiled,* and told me, "We can always throw Caine in front of it next time."

Despite my mood, I laughed at his light-hearted humor.

"What?" Caine challenged.

"You heard me."

Raine and I chuckled at their play jokes.

"Say Caine," I began. "Since you're the only one with a knife why don't you go skin that alligator." I indicated with a tilt of my head. He narrowed his eyes, gaping a bit.

"Yeah, Caine," added Raine, patting her stomach. "I'm starving"

"Alright already!" He threw up his hands. "I'll go cut up the stupid thing."

I stood there, hands resting on my hips for a moment and studied the sky. Light was returning, awake and ready to drive the darkness away. I then shifted my gaze to the fire. We wouldn't need its glow, but the heat would be required to cook the alligator. I decided to go and get it going again.

"Hey, come take a look at this!"

I skidded to a halt and swung to Caine. He was crouched and staring at some reeds. Forgetting the fire, I hurried over to the spot.

"What, something wrong?"

"If you call this wrong," Caine held up a smooth, white sphere, "Then, yes."

I picked one up myself. It looked like an...

"Are those eggs?" Raine asked my question.

"Alligator eggs," Glen breathed. I glanced behind at him, understanding now why the beast had attacked so aggressively.

"The alligator must have been a mother protecting her young." I felt foolish sympathy well up in my chest.

Caine noticed. "Don't start getting sentimental on me. Look on the bright side," he said showing one of the spheres. "Now we have eggs to go with our bacon."

My stomach flipped when he mentioned that.

"How are we going to cook them?" Asked Raine, sounding about as interested as I felt.

"We're not," Caine replied, handing the damp, round thing to me.

"What?" I nearly dropped the egg in surprise.

"You're hungry aren't you?" Caine rose and went to go slice more of the gator.

"How bad can they be?" Glen gently edged past me, brushing off wet moss so we had a clear view of them.

Fourteen. Piled on top of each other, looking like the most unappetizing thing I will have ever eaten. I swallowed the lump of revulsion wedged in my throat and tapped the egg on a nearby rock. The smooth shell fractured and I lifted it to my mouth. Pressing my thumb against the crack, I tipped my head and let the slimy yoke slip past my tongue.

I shut my eyes wanting badly to swallow the nasty, raw lump. A smidgen went and I managed to force the rest of it down my throat, but the bile had already been building from the taste and all of it came back up. The acid burnt my mouth and the tang was almost unbearable. I could still feel the sticky fluid plastered on my mouth.

"Keep going." Glen had moved close and pressed another egg into my palm. "It's always easier the next time."

I have no idea what made me do it, but I took it and ate the thing. He was right, though. The taste had not improved, but I kept this one down. Craving suddenly tore into me and before I knew it, I was groping for more. By the third egg, they were just sliding down and I became oblivious to the taste. All that mattered was food.

When I reached for the fifth, Glen caught my wrist. "Lyn, stop, you're going to make yourself sick."

"I already am sick," I stated groggily, and meekly struggled in his grasp. He only pulled me tighter.

"Lyn." That tone told me to drop it, but I was drugged. I yanked harder and felt another hand touch my shoulder. Next thing I knew, hot meat was being wedged into my fingers.

"And I was the one who thought you didn't like raw eggs." Caine's manner was meant to be humorous, but I detected a hint of worry mingled within his voice.

While I feasted on the meat, (it was much better than the eggs had been) I watched Raine scurry to gather the remaining embryos. The others divided them amongst themselves; the act made me rather gruff. It wasn't like I was going to beat them up and wolf down the things.

After our bellies were full and we sit watching the last bit of fire simmer down, I tried getting every one to talk. "I can't remember the last time I've been this full."

The others looked at me. Raine spoke first. "It feels weird. You know, like we're not in trouble anymore."

Caine huffed a laugh. "Yeah, I'd be full, too if I ate twenty alligator eggs, Lyn."

Raine and Glen exchanged glances and giggled. I shot Caine a glare and proclaimed, "I did *not* eat twenty eggs!"

"Okay, sorry. Thirty."

They snickered and even I had to hide a smile. I noticed them shift and spoke again for there was no reason to let this rare moment of serenity to go to waste.

"What do you miss?" This quelled their movements. "From before we met, I mean."

"I want to see my dad again," said Raine after some thought. "We always used to have so much fun together."

She frowned. "Until Mom got sick... What about you, Lyn?"

I didn't have to ponder long. "Me? I wish I were back on the plantation. Life was easy."

Now that I thought back about it, my life then was pretty leisurely. When all you have to do is jump on your horse and check up on slaves doing work, it's hard to think of anything better. I sighed letting the thought out with my breath and looked to my right at Glen. "Glen, anything to add?"

He smiled like he was embarrassed. "I have to agree with you. Some of my best memories were when I was on the farm with you, Lyn."

I lifted the corners of my mouth, feeling the blush creeping up my neck.

"Well you know what I think?" Caine broke in, ruining the instant. "I think you guys are crazy. We don't set in the middle of a swamp and talk about what makes us happy in life."

He stood. "I don't' know about you all, but I'm going to find a way out of this place."

The three of us exchanged mocking glances and rose to join Caine.

Everyone was so focused on trying to keep stable footing and staying semi-dry, that we had no time to converse. We had been walking since morning and it was now midday. The odor of the swamp was suspended over our heads, collected in a sticky cloud. Pulpy mud and ooze clung to our clothes and slowed us down.

The bog's massive trees were covered in moss; it was draped over their limbs and hung like bed sheets on a clothesline. These dense, green tapestries made it difficult to see, not to mention the blocked sunlight. Only a few rays broke through the tops of trees, but they never made it to the ground, just shone with sparkles. Everything was still deathly quiet. The only noise was that we made sloshing through the muck. No one had heard the crazed laugh from before and I took that as a good sign.

Glen was doing exceedingly well, compared to his not being able to stand the other day. Most of the moss had fallen off, leaving an intense scar across his chest. Whenever Glen would stumble and I'd catch him, we grinned instead of grimaced. It made me feel better all over.

I was just beginning to test the ground in front of me when I picked up on a sharp, snapping noise. I looked back over my shoulder thinking somebody had tripped. Everyone had stopped, heads swiveling, searching each other's faces and the swamp.

"Did someone fall?" I questioned.

"I thought Caine did," Raine said, glancing at him.

Caine shook his head. "Glen, you trip?"

"No."

"Well," I began, jumping to a conclusion, "It must have been the wind."

Caine turned toward me, a scowl on his face. "There is no wind."

"Then what do you think it was?" I snapped back.

"Crack!"

I gasped and spun in the direction of the splintering bark. "Was it just me, or was that closer."

I looked at Glen and knew he could spot the fear in my eyes.

"That was closer no doubt about it. We need to move." Caine was scanning the trees in every possible way, but the moss obscured our view of the marsh.

There was a sudden splash behind us, followed by the unmistakable wailing laughter. That sound sent shivers throughout my body and sent my heart racing. "Go!"

We bolted into the bog, not stopping to catch our breath. I tore through the stinking mud and reeds like the Devil himself was after me, tossing up murky water and ooze everywhere. I did not dare glance behind me. It felt as though something was breathing down my neck, and if I turned around my heart would explode so I just kept running.

The noise of wood breaking and bending along with the fervent rip-roar of water drowned out all other sounds. I jarred my legs in my wild sprint, hurtling deep pools of mud and landing in muck up to my knees. I glimpsed ahead; Caine was in the lead. When Raine fell behind he would snatch her by the hand and pull her forward. Glen kept steady pace, probably wondering if he should push it. So that meant I was dead last.

I spied, though the moss drapes, some very tall grass farther along. The blades appeared unusually thick with thin edges. Only a few more paces and we would hit it.

I went down on one knee and heard a deafening crack and splash behind me. A fierce wave of adrenaline and terror overcame me and I was flying into the grass, cut grass, to be precise. As soon as I entered its sharp foliage, I was smacked and clipped by the grass blades. I tried to cover my face with my arms, but they only whipped me more, slicing my wrists all the way down to my elbows. It felt like millions of tiny paper cuts except several times worse. One nicked me across my eye and I soon felt warm blood welling and trickling down my face. I balled up and dropped, finally free of the biting grass.

Ch. 14 Sightseeing

"Lyn, get up!" Glen was tugging on my arm, smearing fresh blood everywhere. My last bit of strength was used to haul myself up and stagger a few feet more before collapsing.

"We... we gotta keep going," Glen panted.

I willed myself to move, but couldn't muster the strength or breath to run farther. My wounds stung from sweat and the blood felt grainy and tacky on my skin. I could feel it running in rivulets down my arm. Holding my air back, I noted that other than our breathing there was no other sound. All the crashing had ceased.

I chanced a look at the swamp, but the only thing that was there was the tunnel we had come by, no hulking, howling beast, simply grass.

"Did we just imagine that?"

I hadn't realized I had spoken out loud until I heard Caine answer.

"There's no way. It was right behind us, I'm sure of it." He didn't sound so sure.

"I- I thought we were dead," Raine's words hovered in the air around us. "Thought that whatever it was was going to kill us."

"Maybe," Glen began. "But we're not dead yet."

"Just bloody," I added, swiping at the crimson fluid dripping out of my temple cut. And scared half to death, I thought to myself.

"Ah well," said Caine. "It'll dry."

I stood with an emotionless laugh, wincing as my pulled muscles contracted and stretched. I instinctively glanced at the grass one more time to make sure nothing suddenly popped out.

"Where are we?" Raine asked.

I turned around, my back to the marsh, and was stunned. We were standing at the edge of a vast field that looked as if it had not been tended to in quite a while. The crops were overgrown and rotten, the grass was up to your waist, and wild vines had overrun fences that were broken and lying in the weeds. Several yards away a shallow rise began, leading up to a mound. It gave us a lead.

"Why don't we make for the hill," I said, pointing and starting off in the direction of it.

I saw Raine glance at it and assume a miserable cast. I knew if we were tired, she had to be exhausted. Glen noticed her change in mood and sauntered over to her.

"Raine." She looked up at him. Glen turned so his back was facing her and squatted down. "Get on."

Raine took up an adorable surprised look and then placed her thin arms around Glen's neck. He stood with a slight grimace, lifting her off the ground and supporting her weight with his hands. Raine rested her face on Glen's back, smiled, and closed her eyes, looking the picture of innocence.

"I guess you want me to carry you on my back now?"

I tilted my head and glared at Caine through my lashes inquiring with my expression, 'Did you really just ask that?' He grinned slyly.

"Yeah, you're right. You weigh *way* too much for me to hold you up."

"Shut it Caine." I added a bit of edge to my voice to make sure he got the hint.

"I love you too, Lyn."

I rolled my eyes, breath sizzling out, and marched ahead, not understanding how he could joke around under these circumstances. We had almost been eaten and Caine was laughing about it! Oh well, I thought, if he didn't then who would?

By the time we had gotten to the foot of the hill, large, gray storm clouds had rolled in, looking foreboding and blacking out the sun. I along with everyone else was feeling the burden of the dried muck from the bog clinging to our clothes and slowing us down. If I attempted to pry it off, more stuck to my fingers than garments so I eventually gave it up.

The rise was a steady incline: not too steep, nor completely flat. Being accustomed to lengthy distances, it was still enough to make me wish there would be food waiting at the top. I gazed up at the darkened sky and a drop of rain splattered on my nose. I shook my head to clear it, but was soon being pelted with more cool droplets. Before long the rain came poring, bursting the cloud open like a pin would a balloon.

Raine, who had been sleeping on Glen's back, now woke up to the nippy downpour. She ran her fingers through her curls trying to dislodge some of the mud and buried her face into his back. Glen readjusted his grip and pressed on, heavy drops bombarding him in the face and thoroughly soaking his clothes.

"Ugh! As if it could get any worse." Caine had apparently lost his humor from earlier.

He slipped once and nearly lost toppled to the ground. It made me think about the positive things the rain brought. No more mud or swamp stink for starters. Sure it wasn't a first-class washing with soap and fragrance, but at least it got the grim off.

I noticed daylight was fading and we needed to find shelter before nightfall. I caught a glimpse of what appeared to be a large, thick willow loaded with billowy branches, except they weren't very billowy at the moment. Laden with rainwater, the limbs sagged and dripped with the liquid, making muddy puddles form and collect around the base of the tree. I figured it might be dry underneath it.

"Guys come on. I think I see some dry ground." I beckoned them with a wave of my arm, wet sleeve flapping and saturated with water.

We climbed the rest of the hill and pried apart dank limbs, soaking ourselves even more with flying droplets. I ducked under, leaves streaking my hair with wet. I could not stand up and be comfortable so I stayed in a crouch and waddled to walk. It wasn't much, just enough coverage to keep the worst of the storm off. In some places water was pouring off the branches and forming sloshing puddles along the ground.

I hobbled over to the trunk of the willow and plopped solidly on the ground, leaning back against it. Everyone else did likewise. Raine came to sit on my right while Glen lowered himself on my left. Caine finished wringing his sodden hair and rested beside Raine.

"That was fun," he said, tilting his neck so the back of his head was up against the bark.

"Glad you enjoyed it," I commented sarcastically.

Caine shot me a look, a faint smirk on his thin lips. "So now what?"

"I want to stay here," Raine made a show of wrapping her arms around herself. "It's not so cold."

I wished I could agree, but when I thought about things like the sound in the swamp or the men who killed the pirates, I didn't believe sitting idle was such a good idea.

"It probably would be best if we did stay here. Just for the night. Not like I want to go back out into that mess."

Raine's eyes were on me, urging me to go with Glen's words. I knew I couldn't say no to that look.

"Alright. We'll stay."

She leaned against me, grinning from ear to ear. "Thank you, Lyn."

"Great. I *love* sleeping when I'm soaked to the bone."

I turned my gaze on Caine. "Stop whining."

He lifted his hands and acted desperate. "Fine, fine. I'm done." He threw himself on the dirt floor and said, "Good night."

Raine snuggled down beside him, her back pressed against his and shut her eyes.

"Night." A slight tremor passed through me and I scooted nearer to Glen, resting my head on his broad shoulder.

"Thanks for what you did earlier," I said.

He slid an arm around me and leaned his head against mine. "And what was that?"

"You know," I answered, watching as the storm shook the branches. "Carrying Raine. It was sweet."

He laughed softly and pulled me closer. "I'll have to carry you next time."

I smiled and closed my eyes; grateful I shared Glen's body heat. "Does your chest still bother you? From where you got shot?"

He enclosed my hand with his when I brushed the area lightly and held it in his lap. "Not as bad, but it still hurts sometimes."

"Like a knife stabbing you?"

"More like a person kicking me, now." His warm breath tickled my forehead. "Funny how you worry so much about it even know you shouldn't and I've told you not to."

I only smiled. What else could I do? Whatever message I sent must have been enough because we quieted. Glen whispered something, but I was already asleep, safe within the circle of his arm.

Another and another; they just came out of nowhere. I tried running but they would be there, blocking my path of escape. I would turn and dash the other way and nearly collide with five others. Men were everywhere, surrounding me. They were armed and some even had horses.

I staggered back to the center of the circle they had formed. I swung my head from side to side, ocarching for a way oul. lliere was none. I was trapped and the cage was getting smaller. My breathing was erratic, fierce and uncontrolled, and accompanied by a pounding heart thudding wildly in my chest.

Feeling a tremendous presence behind me, I spun, whites showing fully in my eyes, and witnessed the terrifying sight of the horned black bear. My breath hitched and I couldn't take in more air, just watch as the mammoth creature rose up to its full height, electric yellow eyes locked on my own. It opened its mouth studded with razor-edged teeth and let loose an ear-splitting roar that set the men off.

They all surged forward, pouncing and pinning me to the ground. I screamed and hollered for help, but it did no good; I was being crushed by the mass of them. The last thing I was able to see was the shadow of a huge man standing with his arms crossed, watching me struggle and writhe in agony. He had horns just like the beast's protruding from his skull...

"Stop!" I had forced Glen up against the tree trunk, gripping him by the collar and yelling in his face.

I unclenched my eyes to catch a glimpse of his startled features, blue eyes shining wearily with indecision. I drew in a quick breath and launched myself backward, breaking a few damp branches with my back. I stood there rooted to the spot and panting heavily, looking at my dumbfounded friends watching ~~watch~~ me.

An overwhelming wave of embarrassment hit me and I ducked under the willow's limbs, welcoming the crisp, morning air that cooled my skin. There was shuffling behind me and a quiet voice followed ~~follow~~. "Lyn, are you okay?"

Raine came up and stood beside me, features of concern on her face. She looked older than she ever should like that. I swallowed hard once. "I don't know, Raine. I'm a little scared to be honest."

She hugged my leg, resting her cheek on my hip.

"What are you scared of?" I knew if I answered Caine it would turn into an argument by his tone so I remained silent, putting an arm around Raine's dainty body.

"What are you scared of?" he repeated, louder this time and closer too.

I still gave no reply.

"Lyn, look at me."

"Why? So you can stare and call me crazy?" I felt my fear transform to fury. Caine was only making it worse.

"No, I-"

I twisted to face him, dislodging Raine from around my waist. "So you can laugh and say I'm hallucinating? So you can rant about how it wasn't real and won't *be* real?"

I had marched forward, pushing him back down the slope. Caine's rage was building, too. I could see it in his expression.

"Lyn quit it! It was only a dream."

"See," I fired. "See how you don't listen to a word I say!"

Raine raced up and grabbed the back of my shirt. "Lyn, don't! Please stop."

"Raine. Let go." My voice came out precariously low.

"Lyn, *you* let it go." I sensed a hint of provocation in Glen's words and, for once, I was able to drop it.

I inhaled deeply then let out a shuddering breath. Caine hesitantly took a step toward me. "Are you good now? You're not going to go cra-, I mean a little... touched in the head?"

"I'm fine," came my reply, cool and steady as the dawn's breeze. I twisted so I could see Raine, still clutching my shirt.

"Raine," I tapped her hands. "You can let go."

A tiny flicker of doubt crossed her eyes, but she masked it quick and dropped the cloth. "I'm sorry Lyn. I didn't-"

"Don't be," I interjected. "I'm the one who should be apologizing."

I stepped past her and was going to by-pass Glen, but he snatched my upper arm and looked me in the face. "Are you sure you're alright?"

I held his gaze. "Yes."

His eyes narrowed, mistrust in them. Glen could always tell when something was troubling me.

"Really," I said, laying a hand on his strong arm to reassure him.

He let me go, but the disbelief was still there. I wandered over to the top of the hill and glanced to the way we had come. We'd made good progress considering the holdup the rain had created. I then looked the way we were heading. Flat land mostly and not a thing in sight, but when I squinted, I could just make out a silhouette...

"A town," I exclaimed.

"What?" Caine along with Glen and Raine hurried up to my position overlooking the outline of buildings.

"Well whatddya know. It is a town." Glen spoke as if to confirm it.

Caine patted me on the back. "See Lyn, you're not crazy just a little... off."

I let this one slide.

"What are we waiting for?" All heads turned to Raine. "Let's go get some food."

I chuckled at her demeanor and heard Glen say, "Oh no. Caine you're rubbing off on her."

Caine raised an eyebrow. "And that's a bad thing?"

"In most cases, yes."

Raine repealed Glen's statement. "Not all the time. If I'm like Caine then I'll always know what to do."

She said it so matter-of-factly that I couldn't help but laugh. Caine snorted. "Well Lyn obviously doesn't think so."

I placed a hand over my mouth, appearing taken-aback. "Why never, Caine. I think you set the best examples to follow. Especially for an eleven-year-old girl."

I knew he could ~~her~~ hear the sarcasm in my voice.

"I can see you're feeling better."

"Come on you two," Glen cut between us and headed in the direction of the village. "Let's go."

I stopped teasing Caine and jogged to catch up with Raine, but not before flashing him a playful smile.

Ch. 15 Deserted

The day had past quickly; it was already evening. The sun shone on the mountains so they cast huge, long shadows over the land and the sky was streaked with a rainbow of colors ranging from the brightest gold to deepest violet splashed upon fading blue canvas.

We could make out bits of the town, but nothing more than a few rickety-looking buildings. I wondered if we'd scrounge up enough from the place. I sure hoped so because I was beginning to feel the sharp pang of hunger gnawing away at my gut. By the time we arrive, night will have fallen, providing perfect cover for our unexpected heists.

"Hey Lyn, Raine! Hold up." I came to a sudden halt at the warning of Caine's voice. Raine and I exchanged worried glances and waited for the boys to catch up.

"Is something wrong?" I asked, searching their faces for clues.

"Be quiet," Glen said in a hushed whisper.

From habit I started hunting for cover or somewhere to hide, but we were in the middle of nowhere. A few lousy bushes sprinkled the landscape, other than that we were stranded.

The beat of horse hoofs touched my ear; the sound was distant, but drawing closer, and fast. Then I saw it. A lone rider galloping toward us like he did not know we were there, suddenly yanked back on his mount's reins, making it throw its head and stop. A gentle breeze ruffled the steed's bronze mane and tail and its rider's peculiar clothing. He was dressed better than a regular commoner; the man's garments seemed to have no rips or tears in them, unlike our patched garb, but it was coated in dust as if he had been on the road for a while. He sat there on his eager-to-be-gone horse, staring at us with an unreadable expression masking his face. We had nowhere to run so we stared back, incoherence plainly etched into our features.

The man's eyes abruptly grew larger and he jerked his mount's head around, bounding away swifter than before and like he was afraid of us rather than us of him. The whole thing made no sense. Who in their right mind would be scared of a bunch of ragged teens with a pitiful little girl tagging along?

"Is it just me or was that stranger than normal?"

Not real sure *what* normal was for us, but they got the point.

"No, that was defiantly weird," Glen replied, his eyes still watching the man ride away.

"Well he's gone now. Let's keep moving before the guy changes his mind and comes back."

I flicked my gaze to Caine and debated with myself. What if that man belonged to the town and was searching for suspicious travelers? Surely we weren't that obvious. Besides, I reasoned staring at the disappearing figure, he wasn't even heading in the right direction.

"Hey Lyn, you coming or not?"

My head swiveled back around to find Caine walking towards town with Glen and Raine a little way behind, Glen's arm protectively around her as they glanced at me. I ran to catch up, letting my thought to be blown away with the wind.

"Well... I was expecting more."

Caine's statement was under exaggerated.

"*I* was expecting a lot more." I gave my opinion, still stupefied at the state the village entrance was in.

What appeared to be a wooden arch was now broken and decaying, scattered in the dirt. It may have been more colorful at one time, but the paint was chipped and peeling in such a way, the image was completely destroyed.

"I hope the people are nicer than this town looks."

"Me too, Raine," Glen added.

"We won't know until we get there," I said, lithely strolling past the rubble.

I couldn't see much because of the dimness of the night, but there was an unusual, musty smell coming from the whole place. I listened to hurried footsteps as the others caught up to me.

"No lights," pronounced Caine. "That either means people are poor, or they don't come out after dark."

"Or maybe they don't want us to be here."

I looked at Glen, previous thoughts returning. That man had been traveling in the wrong direction, but it could have been a mere distraction to throw us off.

"I don't see any light in the houses either," Raine remarked.

She was right, too. Not a soul to be seen anywhere. It was just plain eerie. The only noise was the wind blowing, but it almost sounded hollow, as if it were wafting *through* the buildings.

"This could mean trouble."

"Glen?" I called, uncertain if I even wanted to find him from the tone of his voice.

"You guys might want to come see this."

I followed his voice with Caine and Raine. Glen was standing by one of the precarious buildings, his eyes on the structure of it. When I neared him, I saw what he was staring at. I drew in a quick breath, covering my mouth with a hand. The place was wrecked and looked as if it had been burnt.

There were large holes in the stone foundation where they had caved in. the wooden upper-half was mostly remains of what may have been a fairly nice shop, but had now fallen into disrepair.

"Someone or something burnt this place," said Glen, fingering the charred edges of the wood boards that were left.

"Think they didn't like the guy who lived here?" I asked nonchalantly. "Why don't we invite ourselves in"?

True, it was risky to claim a place so close to where we were going to raid, but if it had been empty and forgotten it would offer perfect concealment for us.

"Lyn have you lost your mind?"

Of course Caine had something to say about it.

"No, she makes a good point," Glen broke in, eyeing me approvingly. "If we stay here, the townspeople wouldn't think anything about it. Especially if we're careful."

"If there are any people here."

Raine's doubt was catching. It was unlike her to be so cynical.

"Well alright, then," said Caine, testing the ground on the other side of the crumbling substructure. "Hope the floor doesn't cave in."

I lifted my leg to step over, but the sharp rock snagged my pants and I began to fall forward not being able to catch myself.

"Ah!"

Glen caught my swinging arm and allowed me to right myself. "Need any help?"

I turned my head and smiled sheepishly at him. "Thanks."

"So graceful, Lyn."

I twisted to see Caine offering his hands to me, that arrogant smile in full view.

"I just tripped is all," I explained, grasping his hand and leaning on him for balance when Glen let go of my arm.

After he steadied me, Caine patted me on the head saying, "That happens sometimes when you get a little top-heavy."

"Hey!"

I smacked his hand away and hit him half-heartedly. Caine backed up, shielding his face with his arms. Something cracked loudly and I was suddenly watching as I fell down *through* the floor. Caine and I both shrieked in unison as we plummeted to the ground. I landed roughly on top of Caine, knocking the breath out of him and me.

"Caine, Lyn!" I heard Glen call from overhead. "Are you okay?"

I attempted a reply, but all that came was a wheeze. Caine shifted beneath me and I felt hands pushing up on my stomach. It sent fresh pricks of pain racing throughout my abdomen.

"Caine!"

The pressure ended and he exhaled agitatedly. I pushed the upper-half of my body up so I could see his face. In the dimness, it looked like he was blushing profusely. It made me grin and color creep on to my cheeks and I told him, "Thanks for breaking my fall."

Caine lifted one side of his mouth and said, "Just tell me next time the floor's going to break. Maybe we can land on our feet instead of stacked on top of each other."

"Deal."

I rolled off him and sit up, listening to the hurried shuffling of Glen and Raine above, trying to find a way down. It was pitch-black and cold where we had fallen. The sound of Caine getting to his feet made me swivel to where I thought he was in the blackness.

"Still can't see a thing," he muttered. "Lyn where are you?"

"Right here." I imagined him sticking a hand out so I reached out too and felt fingers touch mine. Caine jerked back a bit like my touch startled him, then our fingers intertwined and he helped me to my feet.

"We need some light," Caine stated.

"Think we can find some candles?"

"What gives you that idea?"

"I think it's a root-cellar," I answered, tugging at his arm to get Caine to stay with me as I felt for some kind of wall.

He walked behind and I felt his grip tighten from a sudden tense. "Lyn, you sure know how to land and hit those tender spots."

I huffed. "I'm just glad you hit the floor first. Softer to land on a person than dirt even if you are all skin and bones."

My outstretched hand connected with something solid that had indentions and my palm soon hit a shelf. I inched my hand forward until it came into contact with what felt like a glass jar. I picked it up and gave a shake.

"Find any candles?" he asked.

"No. It's a jar, but I can't see what's in it."

"Probably food. Can I-"

A sturdy "thump" resounded in the cellar and we both jumped. Caine let go of my hand and positioned himself in front of me. I placed a hand on his shoulder. "It might be Glen and Raine."

"Whoomp!"

Cracking, then soft moonlight spilled forth from the shaft and illuminated rows of shelves, the dirt floor, and the surprised faces of Glen and Raine as they came flying through the trapdoor.

I darted out from behind Caine after having set the jar down and caught Glen before he stumbled to the ground. Not expecting his weight, I nearly went down with him, but he snaked a strong arm around my waist and banged into the shelves to keep from falling.

"Need a little help?" I mocked when we were steady. Glen flashed a grin and held me at arms length, surveying my person.

"Are you alright? Caine didn't do anything stupid did he?"

I giggled. "The usual. We fall down a hole, get rescued, you know."

Raine walked over to us holding a candle, glowing as the flame ate away at the wick. She smiled. " If you're hungry Caine found some food."

You mean I found food, I thought. "Where at?"

She motioned for Glen and I me to follow. We came upon Caine, sitting with jars of food arrayed around him. We formed a circle around the consumables.

"I think I got all the tops off," Caine said. "Sure did dull my knife, though."

I picked up a container near me and examined its contents. I couldn't see much because of the candlelight, but made out what I believed to be preserves. After unscrewing the lid, I stuck in a finger and tasted the jam. Its sweetness surprised me, but it had a slightly odd aftertaste, like it had been here past time to be eaten. Still, it sated the ever-present hunger in my stomach so I didn't mind.

We feasted on canned vegetables, fruit preserves, and washed the meal down with water, all the while thinking about where we would sleep. Since it was too cold to stay comfortable in the cellar, we moved up to a stable piece of the floor, reclined, and gazed at the stars, conversing until we were too run-down to speak anymore.

"I wonder what happened here," I stated.

"Don't know," came Caine's answer.

He was resting to the right of me, Raine cradled on his left arm asleep, while he propped his head up with the other. I picked up on a huff of laughter from him.

"Whoever sabotaged this place must've been pretty angry, though."

I nodded absently in agreement. "Who do you guess did it?"

"Think it was those people we saw the day the boat caught on fire?" Glen had his arm stretched out so I could rest my head on it and I felt him shift as he mentioned the raft incident, no doubt remembering getting shot.

"I could see them doing that the way they attacked us," I said, mussing over the silver I still wore in my ear. I had thought about doing away with it, but decided against it for fear I would start seeing Greeneyes appear in my dreams.

"Yeah me-" Caine sit up suddenly, throwing dozing Raine off his arm. "Hey, do you see that?"

"See what? I asked, rising with Glen.

A vivid whirl of hues grabbed my attention. Fire was streaming down the far-off mountainside, prominent in the night, and moving fast in a straight line. The flames penetrated the darkness to where you could clearly see the outline of the wavering glow. The whole thing looked as if a volcano had erupted, but only one steam of its fiery inferno slithered down the mountain.

"What *is* that?" Raine breathed.

"A forest fire maybe?"

I shook my head at Glen's response. "It can't be. The ground's still wet from the rain."

"Think it was heat lighting or something?" Caine, like all the rest of us was trying to make some sense of it all.

"Heat lighting doesn't light mountains on fire."

Everyone was silent, at a loss of what to make of the alien sight before us. Raine finally broke the quiet.

"Caine," she said, reaching for him. "I'm scared."

He circled her in his arms and told Raine, "There's no need to be. It's just nature freaking out."

She smiled at his pun, but didn't let go.

"Come on," he said, lying down with Raine. "I bet if we sleep it'll be gone tomorrow."

She nodded and closed her eyes, ready for sleep.

"Why don't we rest, too"?

I settled back down with Glen, my head situated on his shoulder and arm slung across his chest. He rubbed my back in small circles like he could sense my unease. "Are you thinking about dreaming?"

I smirked out of self-pity. "More like nightmaring."

Glen was quiet for a minuet. "Don't worry. It's not like they're dooming you to some inescapable future."

"You're starting to sound a lot like Caine," I mumbled harshly.

"I'm just saying..."

"But what if they *do* mean something? What then?"

"Then we'll deal with whatever they throw at us."

"We won't have a choice."

"We'll make one," he stated defiantly.

He brushed his lips across my forehead and they sent shivers along my skin when he spoke. "I-We will all still be here when you wake up."

I shut my eyes comforted greatly by Glen's words, but how long that comfort would last, I had no idea.

Ch. 16 Complications

Home. I was back and standing at the top of a hill overlooking my quarterly estate. There were fields filled with too many crops to count and there, there stood my family, smiling and waving, beckoning me. I offered no resistance. Running, I gave a little shout of joy and spread my arms wide, ready to welcome my mother's warm smile, brother's heartfelt laugh, and father's solid embrace.

While I was loping toward them, I noticed my family begin to fade. Their faces blurred and went completely out of focus; they stopped waving.

"No!" I shrieked.

I tried to run harder, but the distance kept increasing. My mother and brother disintegrated, leaving only my father to be whisked away as well. I sank to my knees, surrendering him to the black, heartless void. Tears pooled, rendering me blind until I blinked them away.

A monstrous, swarthy cloud with two radiating points positioned like eyes that pierced the ink like haze consumed the scene, the entire plantation. They were glaring at me, somehow making me feel accountable for everything that had happened in the past three years.

"It's not my fault," I whispered, voice breaking like glass being hit with a bullet on every word.

The darkness whispered something back, but it had already taken me. Back to the place I now called home...

The ground quaked underneath me, making me crash into consciousness.

"Come on Lyn, move!" Glen was tugging me to my feet, coaxing me to go with him.

I was brazenly yanked toward the trapdoor leading down to the root cellar. I caught a fleeting glimpse of the sunlit view and something charging us. I placed my foot on a step, still groggy from my dream.

"Lyn jump, we don't have time!"

Was Glen crazy? If I vaulted from this height I could break my leg. I hesitated.

"Go!" He shoved my down into the hole and I lost my footing.

I screamed, swinging my arms, trying to find a purchase.

"Gotcha!" I landed none too gently in Caine's arms, but it was better than the ground so you didn't see me complaining.

He sat me down asking, "Did you see Raine anywhere?"

I heard much anxiety in his voice. "Wha- No. She's not with you?"

He shook his head, distress increasing with the news. "We don't know where she is. When I woke up Raine was just... gone."

Great. One more thing to worry about.

"I'm sure she's fine. Raine's a smart girl, she'll know what to do." I said it more to calm myself rather than Caine.

The light source coming from the door was diminished as Glen dropped to the floor, dust flying where his feet hit the ground.

"Did you find her?" Caine questioned. His last ray of hope vanished when Glen answered.

Caine shook his head; something was *defiantly* wrong.

"What's happening?" I asked.

The ground gave out another violent tremor, worse than the first. Glen snatched me by the wrist to stabilize my flailing.

"Raiders," he whispered.

My heart sank to my knees and the small amount of breath I had left me. I staggered to a shelf and placed my hands on it to regain my composure. What did they want? Had they found Raine? In the back of my mind even a consideration of my dreams crossed my thoughts. My weak legs gave out and I sank to the floor, willing my vitals to return to normal.

Caine and Glen came to sit beside me, fear that was surely plain on my face showed in theirs. Glen took my hand; I could feel his shaking slightly. I grabbed Caine's and he looked at me, a worried smile forming on his lips. The tremors had stopped for the most part, but the silence was filled with other noises. Footsteps, shouting, weapons being drawn, and people overhead made us quiet our breathing and still quivering limbs. I looked up at the floorboards and saw light seeping through various cracks and holes in them. Shadows danced and moved in time with the footsteps, sometimes pausing for a few agonizing moments then playing along the other wall.

It was too cool in the cellar to sweat, but I still felt the prick and flow of my pores attempting an outlet then freezing in the process. I didn't want to squirm too much because I was afraid of the tiniest movement alerting them. Voices broke out above us that sent my heart skipping.

I strained my ears to catch some of the words, but it sounded like gibberish to me. Either that or my brain was so paralyzed with fear I couldn't focus. The unnerving noises died away slowly, leaving nothing from before. I finally mustered the courage to whisper, "What do we do?"

Glen's grip tightened on my hand. Caine answered, "At least we have food."

Glen shot him a look across me.

"Shut up," he breathed and then paused. "We're going to wait these guys out. They've got to leave after they realize what they're searching for isn't here."

I nodded slightly, agreeing with his idea. We wait, that is, *if* we didn't get caught first.

Several hours passed. The morning brightened to noon light that shone brilliantly through the upper level. None of us had made any attempt to move, only stretch out our legs while we shifted our backs against the shelves. No sounds from before were present and we heard no thumps or sudden outbursts of voices.

I felt Caine move to get up, and turned to see him stiffly rise to a squat. Glen reached for him, fingers spread as if he could stop Caine from his position on the ground. "Wait."

Caine glanced at him, confusion wrinkling his brow with that same panicked cast in his dark eyes.

"We've held out this long," Glen began. "Let's stay until we are absolutely positive they've left."

Caine reluctantly settled back down, eyeing the steps to the door longingly. I let out a heavy sigh, not sure whether to be relieved or worried that we weren't moving yet. Glen squeezed my hand, giving me an understanding look. I held his gaze, tracing the silvery blue pigments in his eyes. Caine's paranoid muttering made me break away.

"-finding Raine..." He trailed off when I grasped his hand.

I made a mute hushing shape with my mouth, signaling him to quit talking. Caine gave me a look that spoke volumes. I knew he was concerned ~~fro~~ for Raine, heck we all were, but we just could not risk going out yet. So we waited.

I knew it couldn't have been more than a couple of hours, but it felt like days. Physically I was sore and cramping from being in one spot for too long. Mentally I was a wreck. My mind darted from unanswered questions, the situation we were stuck in, and all the 'what if's' in between.

"We've waited long enough," said Glen quietly, moving to his feet. "That and I can't sit here any more."

I rose to follow him, heartbeat soaring to a crescendo. When we came to the foot of the stairs leading up to the trapdoor, Glen stuck out an arm to halt Caine and ~~I~~ me from going ~~further~~ farther. "Let me go first."

I bit my bottom lip to keep from telling him otherwise while Caine nodded and agreed. Glen crept up the steps with cat-like grace you wouldn't expect him to have. I did not possess the nerves to let him go alone so, a heartbeat later, trailed Glen, muscles tight and trying to walk as silently as possible.

I didn't let him know I was there until we were at the top. Caine appeared, thieving stealth letting him move like air, on the other side of Glen who shot me an irritated look. I pleaded with him through my expression; he gave it up and placed his hand on the latch.

Ch. 17 Captured

I remained, still as stone, at the top step while Glen cautiously poked his head out. I did not breathe or blink, I'm not sure my heart kept beating in those torturing moments Glen took to scan the area outside the door. He checked everywhere, twice, save for behind since the door obscured the view.

"Clear."

I let out a breath that shook as badly as the rest of my body. Glen crawled out and Caine followed. It took a few more seconds for all the tremors to stop, but I finally managed to drag myself out of the hole. I gulped down fresh air, glad to be free to the stuffy underground. In the daylight I could tell that the building had been burnt. The blackened pieces of wood lay scattered everywhere and most of the infrastructure had been smashed, rocks in piles around it.

A strange feeling overcame me. There was no noise; none of the boys had said a word and even my breathing seemed loud. Did someone stumble across Raine? I turned, and the shakes came at the heart-stopping sight. There were at least a hundred or more of them. Men standing and on horseback were in a perfectly straight line waiting, just like we had, for us to appear. Caine spun around. "Run."

Glen whispered back, "We can't."

The men began advancing on us, strolling at a quickened pace like they knew they were in complete control of the situation. The only problem about that was they were. As we got forced backward toward the town's center, more men emerged from behind buildings and other parts of the ruins. I realized, terrified, that they were cutting off any chance of escape.

I thought about busting out and making a run for it, but figured they'd only be able to kill me faster. My back touched one of the people and I yelped, jumping forward and turning so I was facing them; my mouth went dry at the sheer number of them. Some were on horses, most on foot, I noticed as I tried to pick out similarities in their clothing to see if they were part of some kind of gang. It was impossible. Some were dressed finely, their suit tails draped fashionable over their mount's hindquarters while others were bare-chested, wearing feathers in their hair and paint on their faces. *That's* who had been speaking earlier, Native Americans. I didn't have time to see much else for they started tightening the circle, closing in until one shoved me to the ground. Glen and Caine landed shortly after.

I panicked. When you're surrounded by a bunch of demented men, the ground is the absolute worst place to be. I struggled to get back on my feet, but my motions were rapid and quaking. I wasn't going to make it. A few men surged forward out of the crowd, stomping on us and kicking. I got hit hard in the stomach, doubled over in pain, and a foot rammed into my face, making blood run.

The other men laughed and hollered at our pain like it was some sick game they played. The beatings continued and I knew I would be covered in cuts and bruises in the morning. That is, if I even *survive* until then. Through the haze that encompassed my mind, I heard a howl burst forth from the voices. Did they have dogs to come chew on us now?

The savages that were left in the center hurriedly scrambled away. One strode on my leg and I let out a ragged scream, feeling bones pop sharply. The rest of the feet either hammered me in the side or back of my head, leaving throbbing aches everywhere. I opened my clinched eyes to narrow slits and witnessed the men move to form a pathway, lining both sides with their bodies. The shouting ceased and the sound of one pair of footsteps was the only thing to break the silence.

It looked like a bear, a horned bear, walking on its hind legs. It was huge. As the massive figure neared me, I noticed it was a man wearing the skin of a black bear that had horns sticking out of its head. It reminded me of my unpleasant dreams. The giant man stopped, towering over me. I craned my pulsing neck to see him better.

He was a white man, but his entire face was covered with coal black paint. The head of the bearskin was pulled over the man's like a hood, casting his face in shadows so I couldn't make out much. What really captured my attention were his eyes. They were a brilliant shade of yellow, gleaming like a cat's when the light shown on them. Those eyes stared at me and I was captivated by the shocking color they emitted. This man had a powerful, dangerous presence about him and just being around him made your skin crawl.

The man knelt down; my heart flopped wildly in my chest when I saw an alarming smile form on his face. When a man like this grinned, it meant trouble. He spoke in a deep, bone-chilling voice, lowered so that only I could hear. "You've grown."

About a million questions sprung to mind when he uttered those two words, but before I could speak, the man snapped his fingers, stood, and walked back the way he had entered. The pack of what had to be his followers encircled us again.

I tensed, readying myself for the thrashing; it was their hands this time. I moaned as they patted me down, feeling for hidden weapons or money. It seemed like everywhere a hand touched it would make an injury flare up and burn. Someone clamped his calloused, filthy hand over my mouth to muffle the wails and as soon as I felt skin I bit it as hard as I could, tasting grit and blood mix with my spit. Their hand drew back with a yelp of surprise then came back and smacked me across the face.

I was yanked to my feet and the sudden strenuous pain pressed a gasp, nearly making me topple over. My hands were forced together and a rope tied around them, tight enough so that my slender wrists couldn't slip through. I glanced at the strange knot; it looked tricky to tie and rougher to untie. There was no telling how many victims had been knotted up this way since the men sure did seem to know what they were doing. The rest of the cord was fastened around my waist, painfully squeezing my shrunken stomach.

A person shouted an order in foreign tongue and another length of twine was connected to mine, belonging to Caine's binds. He was trying to fight them, jerking this way and that, head-butting a few men then getting pinned by a dozen more.

"Get off me you freaks!" They ignored all of his insults; one even had the nerve to slug him in the face. That shut Caine up.

Glen was brought, constricted like the rest of us, in front of me. The man who fastened Glen's ropes looked bruised and had a bloody nose. It gave me some kind of ridiculous satisfaction to see Glen had clearly landed a few punches of his own. That content was wiped away when I saw the shape *his* face was in. Glen's left eye was swollen shut and he had a nasty gash above it extending to the new bump in the bridge of his nose. He had blood smeared across his lips and dripping from his forehead wound.

One of the ruffians on horseback was given an end of the cord; he laced it around the saddlebags hanging from his mount. When the man saw me staring he smirked, a teasing twist of the lips, and tipped his Stetson at me in mock chivalry. I glared back with hatred in my eyes, but he only grinned wider, showing off yellow teeth, turned, picked up the horse's reins, and signaled for a fast walk.

It bolted forward, throwing Glen off his feet, wrenching my hands and body with him, and sending Caine sprawled out behind me. The horse didn't stop and my skin ripped apart on the ground.

"Stop!" I screamed, but if anything, the animal sped up.

I attempted to haul myself to my feet, but was connected to Glen and the pressure drove him into the dirt. If he didn't stand up, none of us would. I felt the tears coming, not just from the pain of being drug and fettered, but from fear we wouldn't be getting up.

The group paid us no mind even know Glen and Caine were yelling too. The savages walked, trotted, or ran to keep pace with what I thought was the center. A sharp rock cut across my side and I shrieked in hurt and fury. "Glen pull up! Caine stand with me!"

I was lugged forward as Glen drew himself up, struggling trying to get a foothold. I jerked my legs to the front, skinning my shins and ankles badly but rising as well. I was not yanked back down so thankfully Caine had stood as I had.

"Lyn, keep moving!"

Caine shoved me into a jog too quickly and I tripped. Yelling as I went down, the feeling of hopelessness overwhelmed me as I hung suspended between Caine and Glen. It wasn't like they could help me with the stupid horse moving like it was.

"Hold on, I got you." Caine was trying everything he could to help, but it was no use. The earth dug into my chest and face, but I was powerless to do anything about it.

A rider came thundering by and I soon felt the rending cease. Glen and Caine helped my to my feet. They were asking things like 'are you alright?' and saying 'we're okay now', but I wasn't paying attention. My eyes were on the stranger who made the horse quit rampaging. Vision blurred from the dust, I could only make out the back of the man and hear some of their conversation.

"-easy on the girl."

Our rider spoke back to the one in a fancy suit. "I can't help it. It's 'em that's falling down."

There was silence, then the cool voice from before. "Just look back every once in a while to see if they're still breathing. Keep the Boss happier."

With that the man rode off, coat tail flapping in the breeze. Our man glanced behind at us and said, "Might wanna start walking, rats."

He clicked his tongue and the horse gathered itself into a trot. We were forced to run to keep up. There was no way any of us could maintain this pace for long.

I swept the crowd with my gaze as if daring them to knock us around again. Not real sure what I'd do it they did, though. A few snickered in amusement, the rest kept walking. A throbbing pain in my side drew my focus to it. My shirt had splotches of red around the placed I had slit open on the rock. It stung something fierce, but there wasn't anything I could do about it. Running certainly was not helping.

"Woah!"

I skidded to a halt, slamming into Glen as the horse put on the brakes. I glimpsed over his shoulder to see a crowd we couldn't get through easily. The man leading us grumbled and muttered, "Well ain't you kiddies lucky. We're walking for a while."

I looked toward the heavens, saying a silent prayer. The whole scene made me think of Raine. Where was she? They could not have captured her or she'd be tied up with us. Maybe they had killed her. I could not bring myself to even imagine that. There was a possibility that she had escaped or stayed hidden. What would she do when she figured out we were gone?

Just focus on putting one foot in front of the other I told myself. I did.

Ch. 18 Long Road

There was no stopping, no food, and no water.

It was as close to death as I'd ever felt. Pain, terror, and weariness: that was all there was in my life right now. After the first hour had past, I was ready to give it up then two, three, four; the minuets lapsed into hours and day quickly faded to evening.

The ground and I kept getting better acquainted with one another as time passed. I hardly cared about all the pinpricks of pebbles, raking my skin off, and what not being covered with dirt felt like any more. Wasn't like these men were going to do anything about it. They were the cats and we, the mice caught between their paws.

The continuous pain from being dragged came to a sudden stop. My arms were wrenched upward as Glen rose. By himself or by force, I did not know, but I used the ropes that dug into my wrists as leverage and balance when I got to my feet. Three men were lined up opposite us. The amount of sunlight allowed me to see some details that showed the diverseness of this ruthless group we had gotten tangled up with.

Two were white, the other dark skinned; they all looked rough and dangerous. One of the white men scowled at me when I glanced at him, making his round face even more unfriendly with his short nose and beady, sunken eyes. The other smiled, not a real smile, but a mocking twist of the lips. A slight wind blew his long, shockingly orange hair covering his gray eyes. The boy wasn't bad looking compared to the rest of them, but I caught a strange air of menace about him that I couldn't quite put my finger on. The black man was sturdy and lined with muscle, his cold eyes perfectly matching his stony expression.

Someone walked behind them issuing orders as he past, duster neatly clipping over grass as he went. I heard blades singing through the air to my left and right and I yelped in astonishment as the roped connecting Glen and Caine was severed. The two people behind us shoved them: Glen to the stocky white man, Caine the rigid black one, and walked forward with coils of braiding dangling from their hands. The heavily clad white man pulled a double-barrel shotgun and smacked resisting Glen across the head with it. He landed with a solid "thump." The Native American with the ropes began looping them around Glen's arms and legs then cut the bonds with one of the numerous knives hanging from his belt.

Blackie had Caine in a stranglehold while another midnight dark man hogtied Caine with practiced skill. My brain was screaming run, get away from here. I took a step back and the redhead frowned.

"I wouldn't if I were you, girlie."

I froze in my tracks, paralyzed with dismay that he was speaking directly to me.

"Why not?" I choked out.

"Because," he said, promenading toward me, "I hate seeing pretty little babes like you get cut up."

"You sure didn't seem to mind when I was being towed behind that horse."

I knew I should not have said anything, but couldn't help myself from being snappy. The young man laughed at my comment. "You're a feisty one ain't ya"?

"Leave'er lone, Dev. Everyone's waitn' on you."

Alright alright," Dev replied, grabbing my wrists. "Hold your horse, Morin."

The man called Morin snorted and kneed his bronco on. He was missing an arm I noticed as Dev led me to his mount. He placed his hands on my waist.

"Right, sweetie, don't try anything stupid once you're up there. I'd hate slicing your throat."

Dev hoisted me up after his threat was voiced and I did my best to hang on despite my constricted hands. He mounted after me, picking up the animal's reins and giving a soft click with his tongue. The horse took an experimental step forward then, adjusted to our combined weight, kept going. The motion made me sway dangerously to one side.

"Woah, hold on!" Dev snaked his left arm around my mid-section and pulled me back against him. "Whew, thought I'd list ya for a minuet."

He peered down over my shoulder, eyebrows raised in what I believed was amusement. "Dang, girlie, you're skinny as a pole. 'Spose ya-"

"Dev, would you shut yer trap? Boss's orders, no talking ta da prisoners."

A lanky, coal-black man on foot trotted up to us, his torn army uniform flapping with the wind.

"C'mon, Jeven, I was only getting better acquainted with-"

"*Boss's* orders," Jeven repeated, flashing both of us a look that meant, to me, obey or die. He dashed ahead, colt like legs carrying Jeven swiftly forward.

By 'Boss', he must mean the man with the golden eyes. I shuddered just thinking about seeing him again. On the other hand, Jeven's little speech had given me a delicious idea. Dev didn't seem the type to keep quiet for long so maybe I could get him chattering. If I were lucky, the Boss might personally take care of him, which would leave me with a chance to find Glen and Caine.

Of course, it could go completely wrong and I utterly fail. *I* could be the one ending up getting punished by the Boss. I swallowed, telling myself that every choice had its consequences; you just had to find a way around them. First I needed to find out where Glen and Caine were.

"Say, Dev," I began, glancing over my shoulder and up at him. "Where did my friends get taken?"

He stared down at me, a sly grin plastered on his face. "Your boys is right over there, girlie."

The hand around my waist pointed and I traced it. For a moment, I could not breathe. Cages. They were trapped in nasty, rotten enclosures. It looked like the pens had originally been for some kind of animal, but they had perished, leaving behind rust colored blood, bones, and a reeking scent of death.

Glen was still unconscious and the hair on the back of his dark blonde head had darkened and was matted where the blow from the butt of the gun had drawn blood. Caine was sitting on his knees hunched and banging his body on the iron bars when the cage he was stuffed in was jostled. I shook my head in disbelief. Forget attempting an escape with them, I wasn't even going to make it a foot away without their help.

I bit my bottom lip, assessing all my options. My mind was so muddled and unclear I couldn't think straight, and the absence of food and water was not making it any easier. I started seeing lights and, for a moment, I thought they were hallucinations, but when a footman close by struck a flame and lit a torch I realized the burning dots were quite real.

I groaned noting that we were going to be traveling through the night with no cessation whatsoever.

"You getting hungry, too?" Dev asked. "Hang tight."

I almost corrected him, but a sudden urge from him made the horse nudge up beside another rider. A thick, portly man sat atop his ebony stallion chewing

228

on... well, food I guess. It looked like some pig thigh that had been poorly cooked then stepped on.

"Hey there, Ossy. What's that you're eatin'?"

Ossy grunted and took another huge bite of meat, slapping his flabby jaws disgustingly and acting like he didn't hear Dev. The man probably couldn't the way he carried on chewing.

"Mind if I..." Dev dropped the reins and reached out to Ossy.

What on earth was he thinking? I was about to find out. As soon as the vulgar Ossy opened his mouth to take another bite, Dev snatched the meat out of his grubby hand, stuffed it into *his* mouth, took up the reins, and we both high-tailed it out of there. Ossy yelled, "Dev, ya scoundrel, get back here!"

I doubted the pot-bellied man would give a chase, but Dev did not slow until we had put several yards and people between Ossy and us. He dropped the lead again and took the food out of his mouth, laughing.

"That fool Ossy had it coming," he stated, gnawing on a mouthful. "Not like he can't stand missin' a few meals."

He held the foul piece of meat in front of my face. I wrinkled my face in revulsion at the half-eaten thing. When I didn't make a move to eat he said, "C'mon, girlie. It ain't gonna bite."

When I still held back, Dev spoke again. "'Sides, thought you was hungry."

He moved it away and I stopped him. "Wait!"

The hand quit moving. "Change your mind?"

"What else is there to eat around here?"

He chuckled at my dry humor. I bit it; the flavor was not at all pleasant. It tasted of meat that had spoiled a *long* time ago with hot spices on it. They made it taste worse.

The tang of two men's saliva and some kind of after jolt went rampaging down my throat and I hoped I didn't get indigestion. "What *is* that?"

"You know, I'm not real sure," Dev replied over another mouthful.

I felt him shudder when he swallowed. "Sure does have a kick though don't it?"

He held it back in front of me. "More?"

"Don't you have anything to drink?"

"Thought you might ask that, he said, producing a cloth-wrapped flask from his belt.

After undoing the stopper, Dev took a swig then offered it to me. When he made a move to put it to my lips, I interrupted him. "I can feed myself just fine, thank you."

"Suit yourself, sweetie."

I managed to get bound fingers around the flask and drink. I tried not to think where the nozzle had been. Several drops splattered on my neck and shirt; I blushed when Dev laughed at my clumsiness.

"Thank you," I growled through clenched teeth.

He took the canteen and stowed it away.

"You know, girlie, if you're gonna be traveln' with me we may have to fix that attitude problem you've got. I can think of a few ways..."

I could think of several, none of them pleasant.

"You wouldn't," I whispered, heart increasing speed.

"Sure I would," Dev said, fingering my hair. "I could start by chopping some of your lovely locks off. Although, I gotta tell ya, I'm kinda reckless with a blade. It might slip and stab you in the head."

As he said this, the fingers tightened, jerking my hair so hard tears sprung to my eyes. It made me remember that even though Dev may have a wry sense of humor about him, the man was still as merciless as the rest of them.

A booming shout resounded in front of us. I inhaled sharply and stared at a large mob gathering around something.

"Speaking of knives..." Dev trailed off and spurred his horse into the midst of the crowd.

They parted and the ones that didn't or were too late got trampled. A man cursed Dev rather nastily and he spat back, "Move next time!"

He reined the animal in when we were almost at the outer edge of the circle the onlookers had formed. Torchbearers had made a ring, their flames lighting the center like a great bonfire. Two men were there, brawling.

One was a grand, hulking beast of a man. The hair on his tanned head was cropped short, but that wasn't the story for his shaggy chest and back. The other was thin and frail-looking, black hair sticking to his head with sweat. The massive one was throwing punches, each striking the feeble man mainly in the face and upper body. He was getting hit, but barely. Every time the beast would swing, the other shifted slightly so the fists just grazed his cheek or shoulder. The little man would jab at the husky guy then return to his strange method of defense. His expression was masked save for a faint twist of those thin lips, like he was having fun getting beat.

A startling voice propelled itself over the uproar from the gathering. Everyone got quiet as a man on horseback rode forth, resplendent in his attire. A shock of gold fell to his shoulders from under a top hat and a jet-black cape covered the man's back, fastened at the front with a silver clasp.

There was something vaguely familiar about him, as if I knew the stranger. Probably ripped him off somewhere down the line, I thought. Seemed to catch up with me a lot lately.

The two that were exchanging blows untangled themselves and backed away a few paces, glaring at each other with their skin shining with sweat.

"What's happening here?" The man's voice was cool and detached, the tone of someone that held authority.

The skinny man flicked his chin at the one he had been fighting seconds earlier. "He stole something of mine, and I want it back."

The bulky one opened his mouth in protest or accusation, I couldn't tell, but the fancy man cut him off.

"Very well, but let's go about this in a more civilized manner, shall we?" He glanced at both men, cold slate eyes giving them an indication.

The big one gave a grin that stretched from ear to ear, yellowed and missing teeth showing fully as he drew an enormous dagger, blade as broad as his arm. While the slim man's expression remained the same, there was something in his stare like a wolf that had spotted easy prey. He drew two considerable smaller knives, looking more like stilettos and less like broadswords, holding the one in his right hand down, left with it up.

Both men's eyes glinted dangerously. The man on horseback's words set them off.

"Go to."

Ch. 19 Blades

The giant man gave out a bloodlust roar, hoisting his dagger above his head and charging at the thin one. The silence before was gone, replaced by hollers and bellows from the crowd.

The feeble guy merely stood there watching as the other man's legs propelled him forward, torchlight reflecting off his upraised edge. Is he just going to let him kill him? Take his life and not even a fight to protect his honor?

When the beast was only two strides away, the lanky man adjusted his stance slightly, expression still unreadable. The bounds were taken, giant's blade positioned to kill, but the knife came down on air. The skinny man was in motion, twisting directly out of the broadsword's way. As he vaulted through the air, he drug his dagger along the beast's left shoulder; the blade was colored red when he landed gracefully behind the big man who's hand had flown to his wound, howling as blood poured from it, racing down his now useless arm in a drenching downpour.

The mob went mad and the uproar of voices increased at the sight of blood. The large man staggered and spun back around, raw animosity showing in his eyes. He swung his blade at the other man who, unconcerned, stepped smoothly back and about a hair's length away from the gleaming razor edge of the knife. A wild light manifested in his cruel, black eyes and he smiled viciously.

Lunging forward, he began hacking away at the large man's exposed chest. He screamed in agony and sliced through the air where the other one's head would have been.

I looked over my shoulder at Dev, wondering why he wasn't hooting and hollering like the rest of the savages. He was rummaging through his saddlebags for something. Dev cut his eyes to catch me staring and I quickly thought of something to say.

"Why aren't you watching the fight?"

He turned his head all the way facing me, a lopsided smirk making him look dashing and dangerous.

"The big guy made a huge mistake, taken' something from Razor, but the new ones is always the dumbest." He went back to his bags and kept talking. "He must've thought we call 'em Razor because he's skinny."

Dev huffed a laugh of what I guessed was pity. "Big guys bluff and muscle their way through life."

He turned back to me. "I'm pretty good with a blade, but if I went up against Razor I'd use a gun."

His eyes flicked to the men and I followed. The man Dev had called Razor was dicing the giant into little pieces like a jigsaw puzzle. The crowd roared their approval, delighting in the sight of gore and hurt. Dev's voice came from behind me.

"I seen him cut people up like that before. Cut 'em up so bad they can't move then stand there and laugh."

I tore my eyes away from the bout and looked Dev in the face to see if he was serious.

"Razor's a strange guy; I try ta stay away from him." He stared through his orange mane of hair at me. "You will too if ya know what's good for you, girlie."

My eyes widened a bit and I twisted back around, half-way expecting Razor to be there waiting for me, but he was still engaged in the skirmish.

Razor evaded, knife breezing past his head then kept slashing. Needle thin red lines decorated the other's upper body. He started throwing punches and swinging his blade to get the other man to stop. One of his fists must have connected because Razor suddenly dropped to the dirt and the noise died down. The giant, sill standing, appeared surprised he'd landed a hit.

He took a step forward and the motionless Razor sprung back to life, lurching at the large man's right leg. He brought his blade up just in time to parry the blow, but Razor ripped his other knife from the man's ankle and stabbed him in the wrist, stunning him for a moment. Razor tore the blade out then, shining with crimson, buried it in the other's right shoulder, rendering both arms and right leg ineffectual.

Since no weight could be supported on his leg, the man crumpled to the ground, struggling to stay upright with only his left leg for balance. He screamed as he went down. The shrieking turned my blood to ice.

"String him up! Fun and games are over."

The well-dressed man was suddenly beside us calling out an order that was immediately obeyed.

"If you're wondern', that there's Lieutenant," Dev said as I took in the familiar stranger's full appearance.

He had a very narrow face with sunken cheeks and aristocratic bone structure. The man would have almost been handsome if not for his slate gray eyes that turned you away.

"'Lieutenant' what? What's the rest of his name?" I asked, taking in Dev's analysis.

"No one knows his real name. We just call 'em Lieutenant because he used to be in the service. Guy's a darn shark at cards, though. You could probably tell 'cause of his clothes."

They made this cool, indifferent man stand out even more. He wore a black top hat with a cream feather elegantly attached to the band around it. A shirt's white collar protruded from under a polished, silver vest and he had on a midnight suit and a velvet cape that came to his elbows.

"He's been away searching someplace for the Boss. Just got back, too."

Then it struck me. That man on horseback with his fine clothes and bronze mount *was* Lieutenant. He had been looking for us, but the thing I didn't understand was the reason.

A cry of anguish tugged me from my thoughts, back to Razor and his victim. Razor was standing, smiling, with both knives raised, the other man's blood making their reflection dim. At least twelve people had surged forward to tie the gory man up, and each one robbed him of something. They stripped him down to his pants, taking all his weapons and belongings.

The man simply lay there. He kicked out with his left leg weakly a few times and wailed every time someone moved him. They looped a rope around his neck and picked him up. After hauling him to the nearest tree, the man that had robbed him of his knife caught the end of the twine as it came down from being thrown over a limb. He pulled; the other's feet left the ground and his moaning ceased. The body hung there, lifeless. The man fastened the rope to a root and walked off to join the rest of the band.

I watched in horror as Razor approached the dangling body, thinking he would chop the man up worse than he already had, but he didn't. He only slipped his hand into the corpse's pocket and withdrew it a second later with something shining brilliantly in his palm then the man stowed it away.

"You done watching the show, girlie?"

I was too scared to do anything but nod. I heard Dev chuckle faintly and knee his mount on. Lieutenant was not there so I assumed he'd melted back into the crowd.

We rode past a small gathering of footmen fighting over the dead man's horse. I supposed one was next in line for the animal because he shoved the others out of the way, hopped on the steed, and urged it to a brisk trot.

The ruthlessness of these people far exceeded my first guess. They were brutal, remorseless barbarians who made the rules as they went, killing whoever seemed to be in their way and not caring if who they murdered was wrong. They stole whatever they desired heedless of the trail of blood the savages left behind.

I could only hope Raine's blood was not part of that trail. I certainly missed her, though. Her bright smile and lively eyes pushed away the darkness when no one else saw through it, and I missed Raine so badly that I almost wished she'd gotten captured with us.

Almost.

Ch. 20 Trouble

And like a Christmas ornament nobody wanted, we left him hanging. All of us rode on into the night. I constantly shifted my position, trying to get comfortable, but it was near impossible. My sores and bruises flared every time I moved and when I finally settled in a dull throb would pester me until I moved again. Dev offered me to lie back against him, but I declined, several times. The man still kept one arm around my waist and I doubted it was to keep me from falling anymore.

I had no idea how these men were able to keep going through the night. I would have imagined the footmen having the hardest time, but they were moving at a steady trot, keeping pace with the horses even. I never saw them eat, drink, or slow for that matter. Had Glen and Caine been fed and given water? I could not bear to be withheld from them any longer.

"Dev, I need you to take me by my friends."

I prayed he didn't object or get smart with me, but it was bound to happen.

"I might've considered it if you'd asked me nicely."

I suppressed a heavy sigh and devised a different approach. I eased myself backwards until I was nestled up against Dev's chest. After swallowing the lump of tension in my throat, I put on what I hoped was my most compelling look and caught his eyes. "Could you please? I would *really* appreciate it if you'd let me just see them."

He met my gaze evenly, tugging me a bit closer and smiling. "So now you're gettn' sweet on me?"

I ground my teeth together, biting back a reply, and just grinned a little more. Thankfully, Dev clicked his tongue to make the horse pick up the pace.

We slowed when the animal neared the cages. I saw them; Glen was stuffed into the enclosure closest to the front, slouched with his arms draped over his knees and staring into space. Caine had curled up into a ball and appeared to be sleeping.

Glen looked up sharply when he heard the mare approaching. He tensed, positioning himself as far away from us a possible. I stared hard at him, willing him to recognize me. Glen's eyes narrowed at the sight of two riders on one horse. I desperately longed to throw my arms up and wave so he would know it was me.

His eyes finally met mine, blue pools overflowing with pain. Glen's lips formed my name, indecision as plain as day on his face. I shook my head fiercely, feeling hot tears brim in the corners of my eyes at the sight of him so... defeated. The blood that coated his body with red specks and filthy coat of grim over that didn't help. When I answered him it was like the hurt in his eyes multiplied, but he seemed to actually settle back down seeing that I was alive.

I began to open my mouth to 'silently converse', but Dev took an abrupt turn to the side leaving my only family behind.

"Can't have you two plotting an escape can we, girlie?"

As much as I wanted to snap back at him I couldn't. Seeing Glen had drained me emotionally. It was like a wave had washed up on the shore then drew back, soaking all my energy with it.

Dev wasn't going to let me go so I leaned back against him. Sleep took me as soon as my eyes closed.

There it was again. I let my ears guide me through the dim, twisting corridors. I could hear a voice; it was unclear, but still there. I rounded another corner and froze in my tracks heart skipping a much-needed beat as I gazed at the scene.

A colossal man stood before a mirror, matched so perfectly with his height that I could not perceive the reflection. Was he speaking to himself? No. There were two voices, each conversing in unison to where it sounded like one solid voice.

I have no idea what impelled me to do it, but I stepped forward and the man quit talking as he turned. Those incandescent yellow eyes locked with mine and he smiled. So did the *other* man beside him. They advanced toward me and I spun around to run.

One of them snagged me by the arm and my legs flew out from under me as I was yanked roughly backward. I screamed in panic, swinging my free arm at my captor, but a strong hand stopped it. The other had tight hold of me now.

They began to pull. Wailing in misery, I knew I had no chance of breaking away. The men shouted, enraged with one another and the hurt in my arms became unbearable. I was hauled back and forth, this way and that, like a sick game of Tug-of-War; I was the rope and they the competitors. I writhed in torment, shrieking in pain as my shoulders popped radically.

Then it was all brought to an end. I landed, face first, on the floor with white light dancing around my vision. Faint whispers touched my ears and grew to bellows. I wanted to cover them, but the aches rendered my arms dysfunctional. I soon realized, though, my voice worked just fine.

"Stop it!"

I screamed and screamed and screamed some more. So much that my head became weighted with suffering and I blacked out...

Along with a bitter intake of breath, my eyes flew open and I jerked ramrod straight up in the saddle, smacking the back of my head into Dev's face. I knew I'd hit him because the hand around my waist dislodged itself and went straight to it.

"Ugh! Dang, sweetie, ya rammed me right in the nose," He sniffed once. "Hope you don't mind blood in your hair."

He ruffled my tangled mess then shook his arm.

"'Bout time you woke up, girlie. I think ya put my arm to sleep. If we're going to be traveln' buddies then you'll have ta learn to keep your balance when ya doze in the saddle."

"I-I'm sorry, Dev."

I swung my head in an attempt to clear my muddled thoughts. The dream made no sense at all (not like any of my others did either), but this one was totally different from any I'd had so far. It was probably the result of sleeping on a horse in a stranger's arms, I reasoned, stowing the notion away for later. How long had I been resting?

I blinked, clearing my eyes and looked around. Daybreak. The tender morning light kissed the horizon, spreading soft sheets of blue over the black. The sun was behind us so we were still heading in a westward direction, still moving at an unrelenting pace.

I noticed we had entered a forest. The sunlight shining on the trees created dark shadows that layered the forest floor and the early-morning dew was thick on the grass blades and leaves. I could pick out hoof and footprints from the group in the places where moisture had been knocked off the green. The scenery might have been peaceful to me if the situation hadn't been so grim.

"Hey!" A shout of distress roused me from my daze.

The cages were to the right of us and the voice belonged to Caine. Men walking close-by were prodding him and Glen with barrels of guns and tips of knives.

"Wake up ya rats! We're here."

I very nearly yelled at them myself, but the words were choked in my mouth when the cool press of steel was on my neck.

"Calm yourself, sweetie, or I'll do it for you."

I grabbed Dev's arm with my bound hands, wrists screaming as the rope dug deeper into my blistered skin.

"Don't-"

"Let the men have some fun. You just might wanna worry 'bout yourself right now, though."

As he said this, the blade bit into my neck and blood mixed with sweat. He's going to kill me. All that song and dance meant nothing.

Dev did something completely unexpected; he pulled my arms away from his and, in an almost stylish motion, flipped the knife, bringing it down on my bonds and slicing the rope in a clean cut. I was so dumbfounded that I simply sit there staring at my smarting skin.

"W-Why did you-?"

A young man, likely my age, came riding up on a worn buckskin mare cutting my bewildered words short. Dev took both my hands in his, concealing the absence of my constrictions and gave a somewhat forced smile to the boy. I saw him glance at Dev's fingers over mine and raise an inquisitive eyebrow. Dev had to have winked because the boy crudely smirked, returning the gesture. Men, I thought, resisting the urge to roll my eyes.

"Bring 'er up front. That is, if you two can stand being separated for a bit." The young man laughed, speeding off again with his traveling cape flapping in the wind.

"Thought those ropes might be bothern' you," Dev said, running his fingers over my irritated wrists and squeezing the horse with his knees for a quickened pace.

We began to move past groups of footmen and others on horseback to the front of the herd. It still amazed me how diverse this crowd was. There were men ranging in age from mine to well into their forties. The ensemble they wore varied from deerskin wrapped around their waist, decked out gunmen equipped with holsters and bandoliers, heavily garbed people that were covered in high collared dusters, pocketed trousers and leather boots, to men like Lieutenant with richly decorated uniforms, vests, suits, and capes.

The idea of being at the head of this pack sent shivers down my spine.

"Why are we going to the front?" I asked Dev.

"Shut up," came his reply, cool and crisp.

I was rather taken aback, not expecting Dev to answer me in such a rude tone. The man didn't seem his chatty, laid-back self. It was like he was nervous or tense.

We had progressed to the front; the forest had cleared, making way for a rise about half a mile out in a vast clearing. There was a hulking silhouette almost castle-like. That was the direction we were heading. If things were bad before, they just got a whole lot worse.

Ch. 21 The Fort

A fortress, I thought, gaping at the massive stonework barricade. The heavy wood doors swung inward and we were greeted with more brutish savages. They appeared muddy and soot-blackened, like they'd been involved with fire recently.

Our boat. They had been the ones who set it aflame. I hurriedly composed my features making it look like I couldn't care less about men with guns and knives and the one pinning me in a saddle. The brutes probably ravaged that village they'd pulled us out of, too. What on earth could be the reason for the pillages?

Before they ushered us inside, I caught a glimpse of our escort scattering. Many didn't even enter the fort, but disperse off into the woods, brandishing blades and guns as they stalked off. Others produced a mat and plopped down on the ground, seeming asleep as soon as they hit, and some sauntered over to boiling pots of what I believed was stew, eating heartily.

I returned a few sneers and scowls from the 'boat burners', but Dev clutched me tighter, bending to whisper, "Don't bait 'em, girlie. 'Less ya think you can handle them later."

I didn't look anyone [handwritten: anyone, crossing out "anymore"] in the eyes after that.

It was like a small community inside. Houses made of log and mud brick dotted most of the fort's edges and in the very center was a gorgeously refined stone building. Of course that was the place we were heading.

I swallowed, feeling tension tie my gut in knots so I quickly diverted my gaze to something else. They had women here, but not of the American race. There was an abundance of Chinese females doing various chores such as cooking, washing, hanging pelts to stiffen, and ladling soup for the men to eat. I wondered if they did this willingly or if the women were forced to work as slaves. Based on what I'd seen so far, I went with the latter [handwritten: latter, crossing out "other"] notion.

We had arrived at the porch of the grand stone house and stopped. I waited, still as the rocks that supported the dwelling, for something to happen.

"This is where you get off," Dev said, nudging me. He must have meant by myself.

I swung my left leg over and slid down, crumpling to the ground when I landed. The pain was horrific and my legs burnt like fire was razing the muscles from within.

"Just stay there a minuet," Dev commented on my position. "You'll be able to walk. I think."

He rode off out of my sight and I managed to straighten, regaining my composure, but not without a few gasps of searing hurt. I finally stepped forward testing my weight on the first step of the porch and, being able to support myself, went to the top.

I glanced at the beautiful mahogany wood door and wondered if I should enter. I turned to check if anyone was watching and spied a few familiar faces. Razor was conversing with the big, burly man that had taken his victim's broadsword knife. The one-armed man, Morin, was arm wrestling the messenger boy at a nearby table. Lieutenant was still nowhere to be found, but I saw Caine and Glen.

I stared, transfixed, as their cages were unloaded, knocking them around roughly. Men with horrible grins began pushing the pens into some kind of horse stable. Caine and Glen both looked awful with heavy bags under their eyes, hollowed cheeks and torn and bloody clothes. They probably haven't eaten or drunk a thing since I had last seen them.

My eyes darted around the inside for food or water sources. The well I spotted would be perfect for liquid and there had to be rations in the horse troughs. All I had to do now was go get it. While I descended the steps I thought, what's the worst that could happen? They hadn't killed me yet so hopefully that was out of the question and I could talk my way out of torture. Maybe if I messed up bad they would lock me up with Glen and Caine. My foot touched the bottom stair, chest swelled with confidence as I brought my other foot down on solid earth.

"I'd go in there if I's you, girlie." Dev's voice made me freeze to the spot with one foot on soil and the other still positioned on the step.

I jerked my head around to see him on his horse and peering out from the corner of the house. He smiled in a disarming fashion when our eyes met then disappeared back around the edge, out of sight. I stood there a moment longer, not able to tear my gaze from the bend. I bit my lip, flicking my eyes to the stable, but finally decided to heed Dev's warning.

I trudged back up the stairs, going against everything my heart said yes to. I've got to be smart about this, I argued with myself, standing once again in front of the studious door. Placing my hand on the smooth, golden knob, I took a deep breath, preparing myself for whatever was coming next. I twisted the handle and pushed, letting the door swing in on its own, soundlessly.

I stepped through, senses on high alert. I considered leaving the door slightly ajar for a quick getaway, but figured if I closed it no one could sneak up on me.

I surveyed the interior of the home in awe. As soon as I entered, a magnificent chandelier caught my immediate eye. Candles were arranged in gorgeous shimmering rows, throwing their light across the room and making the crystal insets sparkle with surreal beauty. The candlelight from that and many ornate oil lamps allowed me to behold the regal splendor within the residence.

Soft, plump sofas and chairs lined the dark walnut paneled walls and brought the stone to life. Bear, wolf, and cougar skins had been made into lush rugs; heavy, polished tables displayed handcrafted works of fine art and glistening treasures. Then I saw it.

I stumbled to the alluring garment hanging on the wall. It was a dress, notably presented in all its splendor and glory. I reached out to feel the silk bodice, taking in every detail of the frock.

Its collar was wide, stretching from shoulder to shoulder and lined in white lace studded with pearls. It had no sleeves; cream-colored silk looked as though it had been poured on the dress, making it catch the light ever so softly. The waist was encircled with a rich royal blue sash that accented the ivory color and the skirt puffed out, ending in gentle ruffles with more lace lining the bottom, pearls shimmering sweetly.

It reminded me of my plantation days when I would throw on a dress like this and go parading about town, showing off my style and grace.

"Why don't you try it on?" The deep, steely voice turned my blood to ice and nerves to water.

I spun to witness the last person I ever wanted to see. Those inhuman, yellow eyes bore into me when I tilted my head to look this towering man in the face. He was smiling faintly, though it looked like a smirk. That awful bear head had been pulled back to reveal raven black hair styled in a soldier's cut. The man's black face paint had been removed, showing a very noticeable, jagged scar running down the right side of his face and ending below the chin; it was a startling discoloration to his tanned, leathery skin.

I got over the shock of the man's presence and attempted to speak.

"Who are you and what do you want? Why did you bring me and my friends here and what use are we to you?"

He stopped my flood of questions with a great hand. I thought he was about to slap me so I flinched away. He only smiled more.

"So many questions and none of which you need to know the answer to," he gestured to the dress behind me. "I… *acquired* that pretty little thing just for you. As a matter of fact, put it on and join me for dinner."

That particular idea didn't sound too appetizing to me.

"No." Good grief why did I go and say that?

His eyes darkened menacingly, but the smile never faded. "Alright, we can either do this the easy way or the hard way."

I had a death wish; that was it.

"You get dressed and come or your *friends* will pay the price for your foolishness."

He paused here to let me consider. How could Glen and Caine survive worse than what they already had to endure? I couldn't live with myself if they were killed because of me.

"Okay. I'll come." The words were barely audible, but his grin turned to one of bottomless contempt.

"I thought you might change your mind," he indicated a door forward and to my left. "Go get dressed."

The muscular giant left and entered another door a ways down the wall. I unhooked the beautiful garment and began to move to the room he had pointed out. My fists tightened on the fabric to keep them from shaking as my thoughts whirled in my head. I don't need to do this; I don't have a choice.

When I entered, I was surprised to find three Chinese women standing next to a steaming bath and a glass of white liquid, most likely milk. The one at the front spoke.

"We help?" She gestured to the dress I was holding. I shook my head, dumbfounded for a moment.

"Uh... No thank you."

She bowed low as did the others and before deserting told me, "Take bath, milk. Come dinner."

I merely nodded, agreeing to her odd speech. This was certainly going to be awkward.

I swept the room with my eyes, checking for any place someone could see through before I stripped off my clothes and submerged myself in the piping hot water. I gritted my teeth from the shock of heat, but relaxed after warming up to it. The feeling was a step away from heaven.

I scrubbed down with the hand-made soap, turning the water brown. There was dirt and grim in places I don't care to mention and by the time I had gotten out, the clear liquid from before had transformed to midnight black.

While wringing my hair out, I was suddenly conscious of how badly it needed to be cut and realizing what I must have smelt like after all these long months on the road. I dried the rest of my body with a wool towel draped over an exquisitely decorated bedpost.

I loosened a few of the ties that would hold the dress on me and slipped it over my still damp head, feeling the smoothness of the silk as it soothed my many cuts and bruises. After tightening the knots back up, I noticed a gold plated mirror and went to appraise the gown. It fit perfectly, showing my slender, somewhat shapely figure quite nicely. My shrunken waist was a bit of an offset to this, but the vibrant blue sash made up for it. If only my hair looked a little nicer.

I sighed and ran my fingers through it a few times, but the tangles only worsened so it appeared like long and shaggy would be my style for the meal. That's when I remembered the milk, still setting on a small table beside the tub.

I went to pick it up and sniffed. Nothing seemed wrong save for a faint, sour smell. I took a sip; my features twisted into a look of displeasure from the bitter taste and thick cream texture. Goat's milk: fresh too by the lumps of cream that slid down my throat with the strong liquid. I shuddered and put the empty glass back. What a perfect way to start the evening meal off.

I spied a pair of formal slippers left by the luxurious bed and tried them on. Too small. Wonderful, I thought, padding barefoot to the door and exiting the room.

The large foyer was just like it was before I changed: stunning. I sauntered to the door the man had passed through. Closing my eyes, I let the air out of my lungs, wishing my edginess would go with it. Turning the gold knob, I slipped through and shut the door behind me.

There he was, sitting at the end of a long oval table with a beautiful glass finish lining the top. The man grinned smugly and I regarded him with cool indifference, ambling to an intricately carved chair. I lowered myself into it gracefully. (Well as graceful as one can be with shaking legs)

Almost immediately after I was seated, three Asian women burst through another door, bearing smoking platters and glasses containing blood-red wine and water. They hustled around the table placing the delicious-looking plates in front of us with savory fumes rolling off fire-grilled rabbit, vivid vegetables, and sweet fruit. The scent alone made my mouth salivate profusely. Water was set beside this along with dazzling silver culinary pieces.

I didn't touch it. There was no way I was going to cave into my hunger and give this man the pleasure of seeing me submit. In the back of my fool mind the thought that he could be doing all this to help me actually surfaced, but my heart knew it wasn't true.

I listened to the clinks of silverware as he sampled the delicacies, sensing the man's yellow eyes on me. I looked through my lashes to confirm that feeling. Suddenly, he ceased eating, picked up his plate and glass, and began strolling toward me. I tightened, body going rigid as he put the plate down to the right of me, settling himself in the chair closest to mine. The man then took up his fork and started chewing once more, eyes still trained on me.

I felt the tremors come. What in the world was it about this guy that made me so... terrified? I finally snapped, launching to my feet and hearing the scrape of the chair as it scooted along the polished floor, hoping it scarred. The man didn't even move when I threw open the door and raced out, listening for the slam of it.

Flinging the entry panel wide, I scampered out on the porch, but stopped dead when I felt cool steel pressing on my neck. I slid my gaze sideways to see Dev, holding me at knifepoint, crack a smile.

"I'd go back in if I's you, girlie."

I inhaled slowly and stepped away from the blade, glancing at him. He arched an eyebrow under his orange mane, daring me to make a run for it. I backed all the way inside and he shut the door.

I stood, fuming at Dev and myself for being so scared. Sensing tears of hopelessness, I shook my head; I was *not* giving up that easily. Alright, I thought walking back to the dinning room, I'll play their game for now.

Ch. 22 Realization

When I entered the man was still calmly enjoying his meal. Sparing me a glance, he spoke. "I thought you'd change your mind."

Once I did not make to seat myself he ordered, "Sit."

I walking stiffly to the chair and sat, eyeing the food longingly. Just leaving it to spoil would be like cutting off your nose to spite your face, right? Besides, I thought, picking up a silver fork, if I were going to play along, then I might as well act the part. My mouth gushed with the juices from the rabbit after the first bite of succulent paradise. I became ravenous, making a serious effort to restrain myself from appearing wolf-like as I feasted on the savory meat, earthy vegetables, and juicy fruits. It had been so long since I'd had a decent meal, yet alone something as gourmet and substantial as this.

The man, finished, now began to speak. "It's been a while since I've seen you, but a father has his reasons for not keeping in touch."

I nearly vomited when I heard his words. Did he just say "*father*"?

"Those people you thought were your parents and sibling fulfilled their purpose well enough, though I must admit, it took me a while to track you down." A faint smile creased his lips. "We ransacked your house and killed those people you were living with before we set it ablaze so they didn't burn to death at least."

I was going to be sick; I dropped my silverware and had lost my appetite, feeling more revolted every time he uttered a word.

"We searched, but you weren't there. Pity, really. You would be much more comfortable here if I had found you then, but the whole tracking business was time well spent."

I could feel my heart about to give out with shock. Has my whole life been a lie? The man kept speaking and I hated him more with each sentence.

"I needed time to get this organization together. Since it's grown in the past years, I fear someone may come up with the senseless idea of challenging my authority so I figured it'd be a fine time to bring in family. Someone I can trust; my daughter."

Daughter. How could he even say that word?

I swallowed the bile and mustered the courage to ask, "If you're my... father, then what happened to my mother? Where is-"

He cut me off with a hand, sneering as he

answered, "Last I heard, she traveled to the west-coast. Place called, California," he huffed. "That's where my brother lives."

He paused in thought. "Should've killed them when I had the chance, but their time's coming soon."

I tried not to think about what he meant by 'soon'. The man's lucid, yellow eyes were sizing me up, that wretched scar creating a yet more ominous air about him.

"Your time is now."

After those sinister words were voiced he rose, garmets billowing around him and told me, "I've got to go take care of some business. We'll talk more when I return. Think on it."

He started toward the door, but I stopped him. "Wait!"

He paused, looking over his massive shoulder at me. I was stunned into silence by his gaze, but mustered the guts to ask, "What happens to me?"

He made a dismissive gesture. "You've got free run of the place. Dev'll keep an eye on you."

With that he left, leaving me ill and with a piece of rabbit I'd forgotten was there.

I decided to go back outside. It was dark, but torches burned bright in a few places, dimly lighting the fort.

I started down the porch steps and spied Dev coming toward me. I slowed to a total stop at the bottom. Don't know why I did since I presumably had the entire place to myself.

"I have-"

"Free run of the place. I know, girlie, the Boss told me."

"Good."

I moved to pass him, but he stuck out an arm. I stared at Dev, vexed.

"Free run only goes so far."

"But-"

"Look, sweetie, why don't you go to bed and explore tomorrow?"

Seemed like he was giving me no choice.

"Where will I sleep?" I asked, though it was probably a stupid question.

"I hear there's a nice soft bed in the house. Remember stealing it from some rich woman's place," he grinned shrewdly. "I can escort ya there if you'd like, girlie."

I felt my face redden. "N-No thanks, Dev, I know where it's at."

I turned to walk back up.

When I entered the bedroom I noticed that a fresh pile of clean clothes had been laid out on the plush linen sheets with pajamas beside them. I was too worn out to think much about it so I stripped off the fine, good-looking dress and slipped into weightless, pjs. Even the nightwear was presented with a certain degree of unexpected elegance with lace lining the sleeves and trouser bottoms of the fresh silk attire.

I climbed into the sumptuous bed, letting the velvety sheets glide over me, but despite these comforts, I could not find peace. My mind kept wandering to thoughts of Glen, Caine, and Raine. Sure, my belly was full, but what if Caine and Glen were starving? And Raine? She might not even be alive. Then there was me: apparently the daughter of some madman with a bunch of barbarians following him. No wonder my mother left.

I shook my head, sighed, and sunk back into the goose down pillow. My thoughts threatened to keep me from sleeping, but the bed was clean and the sheets were soft...

Ch. 23 Trapped Inside

I awoke without any trace of pain, cushioned by what felt like clouds. Wonderful smells wafted through the air making my mouth water. When I opened my eyes, I was startled to find three Asian women watching me, two holding delicious plates with cured ham strips and boiled eggs stacked on, the other with more goat milk in a glass. They bowed to me then approached and set the delectable meal down on a shined mahogany table beside the bed. They stooped low again and backed away.

I stared at my morning meal, used to raw eggs or wild game half-cooked with dirty water to wash it down with, not this. It was like I had become Princess of the Outlaws overnight. Was this what it would be like? Protection from the wilderness, meals to eat when hungry, people catering to me, an actual bed to sleep in...

Thoughts of the boys and Raine returned. What am I thinking?! I couldn't live with myself if I left them to suffer while I lived not having to worry about if I'd still be alive the next day. Not after all they'd done for me, after all we'd been through.

I swung my legs to where they dangled off the bedside and began stuffing myself with succulent ham and fresh eggs, thinking all the while about how to get Glen and Caine out.

After I got dressed in new cotton and silk clothes, I went outside, squinting at the early noon light. It made my heart jump when I closed the door and saw Dev leaning casually against the stone, hands in pockets, red hair carelessly swept to the side of his face.

"Good morning," I said.

He glanced at me and raised an eyebrow in mockery. "Thought mornin' was six hours ago. Have enough time to catch up on your beauty sleep, girlie?"

I sighed and walked to the edge of the porch, gazing at the stables. Alright, I thought to myself, eyeing Dev, let's just see what kind of clout I've got.

Turning to him, jaw set in what I hoped was a determined way that would provoke no argument, I spoke. "Dev, I want you to let my friends out of those cages."

To my dismay, he started laughing.

"What, you think 'cause the Boss likes ya that you're gonna make me do whatever you say? You got some real nerve, sweetie."

I countered his smart talk with something I willed would work. "My father wouldn't want me to be unhappy while I'm here and he's gone."

That shut him up.

"Wait... Your *father?* The Boss's your old man? Ha, you really had me going there for a minuet!"

Dev tried to blow me off, but I spotted doubt in his eyes and attacked it.

"Going where? To the stables?"

Devs cockiness subsided and he was quiet for so long I thought I'd gone too far.

"Yeah," he finally said. "I'll catch up to ya."

As he stalked over to the stables, I let out a relieved breath, leaning on railing to support myself. Just what had my father done to get this group, these savages, to obey him? Was it fear?

I could believe that. Simply being within a few feet of the guy made you want to cower at his raw might and powerful presence. Then again it could be something completely different. Better not think too much on that, I told myself.

Glancing toward the stables, I saw Dev speaking with a tall, stout man and gesturing my way. I decided now might not be the best time to drop in and speak to Glen and Caine, but my whole body burned with desire to see them, talk to them. Caine with his arrogant, sarcastic way and joking smile; Glen with his calm composure, handsome face and sapphire eyes.

I will get to see them, I reasoned, looking on at the husky man shake his bald head and produce keys, just not now. But surely I could help them by finding a way out of this place.

While Dev was engaged with the man, I slipped off the steps and around the back of the house. There were more dwellings but in much poorer shape. The brick was made of mud and the roof of hay. Around the houses, Chinese women shuffled about, clad only in rags. This must be where they stay. By the look of things, the horse stables would have been nicer than their quarters.

A few cast a glance my way, but all in all they seemed wholly unconcerned I was there inspecting every square inch of the place for faults.

"Whatcha doing, girlie?"

I jumped when I heard Dev's voice behind me and spun to face him. "Nothing. Just walking around, stretching my legs."

He arched an eyebrow and smirked. Sure didn't do a good job of answering.

I decided to change the subject. "What about my-"

"Your boys is in the cells."

Did that mean more pens?

"But you-?"

"Got 'em outta the cages. It'd be plain stupid if we let them roam," he eyed me. "Since you're already lookin' for a way out."

I figured denying it would only make me more suspicious so I said nothing and turned to keep searching. Bad move.

Dev shifted, quick as lighting, snatching a fistful of my hair. I gave a shout when my head was yanked back and he moved in close, drawing his knife.

"Mistake, girlie," he breathed into my ear. "Never turn your back on someone. 'Specially me."

Just keep calm, I told myself, he is not going to hurt me; it's only fun and games. I was finding that *extremely* hard to believe feeling the sharp metal blade beneath my chin.

Some of the women stopped what they were doing, but hurriedly got back to it when they caught Dev's eye.

"You scared, sweetie?"

I answered, careful of the knife when I spoke. "Let me go, Dev."

He chuckled. "Someone else would hurt you, girlie."

"You won't."

About that time the young messenger came flying. "C'mon, Dev, quit scaring your girlfriend. The cockfights is startin'!"

He finally released me, but clamped a hand on my shoulder, pinning me in place. "'Bout time," Dev began walking, pushing me along with him. "You'll like this, girlie."

Now what? I was grateful the boy had made Dev stow the blade away, but it felt like jumping out of the frying pan and into the fire.

Dev led me to a large gathering, not unlike the one that had amassed when the knife fight took place, and muscled his way to the front still dragging me behind. I wrinkled my nose at the stench coming from the nasty men and shivered whenever I brushed past a hairy arm or leg. We arrived after much pushing, shoving, and yelling. I looked down at a circular enclosure constructed out of knee-high logs. In the center were two men holding roosters, attaching knives a couple of inches long to their spurs. One man held a tall, iridescent black chicken sporting a great, white plumed tail. The other had a burnt orange cock with chestnut outlining its feathers.

I swept the circle of people with my gaze; they were nudging each other and pulling out pieces of gold, silver and jewelry. Where the men making bets? Much of the mummer from the crowd died down when a short, dark Mexican stepped into the ring of logs. He flashed a smile and threw up his hands. "You ready for chicken fight?!"

All the men roared their approval, raising fists to the sky. The Mexican gestured to the other Latino holding the burnt orange rooster and said, "Let go, brother! We in for easy win."

He dropped the cock and the other white man did also. Both hurried out of the enclosure while the one that had spoken melted back until he could view the arena from every angle.

The roosters just stood there, stamping their scaly feet, apparently not used to knives being attached, when all of a sudden they stopped, staring each other down. The black one gave a loud crow and the other answered, stretching its neck and shifting to its toes. The long-legged, ebony chicken charged, cutting-edge making niches in the dirt. The other did a bit of a hop-skip, flapping wildly and squawking, striking out with its dangerous feet.

"Bam!" They connected in mid-air, red liquid flying, dotting the dirt and streaking their feathers.

I gasped as the black chicken bit and flogged the other in a savage, frenzied manner. The chestnut–lined one cried and flailed with its feet, slicing a few wild feathers off the other and making cuts in the ground, but otherwise not doing it any serious harm. The dark cock wouldn't let go of the other chicken's comb; it had it right where it wanted, able to draw waterfalls of blood with each successful kick.

Some men were cheering, others moaning while the orange rooster was being mauled. I myself stood there holding my breath, not able to tear my eyes away from the brutal sight in front of me.

"Juan and Julio," Dev said from behind me.

"What?" I answered, not diverting my gaze.

The orange chicken had finally managed to break away, but was staggering quite severely.

"The Mexican brothers that run the show. That rooster must be the one Juan's been braggin' about," He huffed. "Looks like it's gettin' the fire knocked outta it."

"Is Juan the one that spoke or the one that was holding the chicken?" I asked, flicking my eyes to and fro the Mexican brothers.

"Juan's one that spoke."

He was a smaller man, shorter than *me* by a head at least, and looked to be in his late twenties. His hair was closely shaven (you could see scars where the knife had caught) and he whore a leather, moccasin jacket with too-large pants and boots. Julio had long shaggy hair and a thin goatee. He was a little taller than his brother and slimmer, too. The man was dressed in similar attire and shared the same short nose, round cheeks, and dark skin as his sibling.

"Oh man, Juan's cock itn't looking so good."

Hearing Dev's words, I turned my gaze back to the arena. Both roosters were staggering with crimson blood pooling beneath their split feet. The bloodstained burnt orange one looked to be having trouble breathing with the gore coating its beak; it began to kneel over.

Juan rushed forward, shoving the crowd away. "Stop, my chicken not done!"

He shimmied over the logs and snatched the rooster, letting its feet rest on his hands, knives narrowly missing them. Juan encircled its neck and placed his mouth over its beak, slick with red.

I watched, mouth agape and utterly disgusted, as Juan sucked the blood up in his mouth, held it, turned his head to the side, and spit out a gory blob on to the dirt.

"Getting' the blood out of its lungs. Not a bad idea," Dev glanced at me. "Whadda you think, girlie?"

I merely shook my head, too sickened to answer properly. He laughed.

"Yeah, I'd've already killed it. Juan must *really* be wantin' for a win."

Finally, Juan set the cock down, smiling with chicken blood splattered on his teeth and lips. It stumbled a bit, but steadied after a second. The black rooster had been waiting, breathing hard and bleeding, for its opponent to return.

It gave a cry and launched into a drunken gallop of cutting blades and bloody feathers. The other simply stood there, already seeming much livelier than before. When the black cock was little more than three feet away and gaining quickly, the orange chicken propelled itself up into the air in a flurry of wing beats and cackles, lashed out with renewed vigor and lust, and struck it down, blades puncturing deep.

It landed a fatal blow; the other chicken's neck was split open and it collapsed in mid-stride, blood draining much too swiftly. The remaining rooster crowed, long and loud, and was joined by whoops and cheers from the men. Juan and Julio grasped each other by the hand and cried out bellows of enjoyment in Spanish as many a grumbling gambler handed over precious stones, gold, and other treasures to them.

I felt a sick place in the pit of my stomach when one Chinese woman pushed through and picked the dead chicken up by its neck. She spun it a few times then snapped the bird like a whip. I watched, bile rising in my throat, until I saw her slam it on a plank of wood and begin yanking its bloodied, iridescent feathers out.

Feeling someone nudge me, I reopened my eyes to stare at Dev.

"What you bettin'?"

I was caught off guard for a moment. "Wha... Nothing. I don't bet."

He arched an all too familiar eyebrow and barked out a laugh. "'I don't bet.' Ha, that's rich, girlie! So, whacha bettin'?"

I ground my teeth; he grinned and flicked his eyes to my ear.

"How 'bout that earring?"

My eyes widened in surprise and my hand flew to the hoop of silver still dangling in my ear. With all the bad luck that thing had brought me I didn't care it he *took* it.

"Fine. What do I get if I win?"

His smile broadened and Dev stepped close, reaching down into the neck of his shirt.

"This," he answered, producing a lovely, twinkling diamond that he had looped a string about and tied around his neck.

I would have rather had that than my silly earring any day. With everyone else throwing and flashing his wealth in plain view, I wondered why he was so discrete with showing it to me. I pushed the thought away.

"Deal."

"Alright," Dev said, slipping the beautiful jewel back inside his shirt. "Pick a rooster."

I turned around, startled to find two more cocks about to assault each other. One was a gorgeous fire-red color with a large comb and tail. The other was speckled gray and white with abnormally long spurs and flowing tail feathers. Those spurs looked dangerous, but seemed to put the dappled chicken off balance a bit.

Let's go skill over power, I figured. "The red one."

Dev snickered. "Looks like all show and no kick to me, but it's your loss, babe. My money's on the spotted one."

We'll just see about that.

Ch. 24 Guilt

*I*t was over in a matter of minuets. My flame-colored chicken easily evaded the other's fatal attacks, almost dancing to an unknown beat. Then it got careless. Taking a stab to the breast, it struck out one last time with the attached blades. The dappled cock had been sliced pretty badly and made no attempt to dodge; the knives entered and departed from its abdomen and it was dead before it touched the ground. The red rooster clucked and sank to the dirt, not breathing anymore.

"Did I lose?" The words left my mouth and only then did I realize how despicable I sounded. Just like everyone else.

The two Mexican brothers stepped forward again and Juan spoke. "Never seen tie before, but Ash went first so Pot 'O Blood win."

The cheers came along with the women. I had seen them prepare the other roosters and drop them into the stew pot: dinner was going to be hard to swallow. I heard Dev curse behind me.

"Well, girlie, ain't you the lucky one," he said, yanking the diamond loose and handing it to me.

Dev smiled, a lie to go with his words. "Better keep it outta sight or you're not gonna be lucky for long."

I took it, feeling a foreboding knot settle in my stomach that told me something was wrong. Then again it could have had to do with the fact that I had just witnessed *and* gambled with another living thing's death.

I have got to get away from here. The sun had sunk much over the course of the day, a lot faster than usual, but I had slept pretty late, too. Why not go check on Glen and Caine? Yeah, that's what I'll do. Maybe it would ease my troubled mind. I was off with a hop and bounce, almost giving a little shout at the thought of seeing them again.

That gleeful feeling dwindled as I neared the old, beaten down building that was their prison. My fingers dug into the apples I had snatched from the troughs, anticipating at any second to be spotted by the repulsive guard Dev had spoken with. Thankfully, he was nowhere to be seen.

Before entering the heavy iron door, I checked the barracks and risked a glance at the cockfights: nothing. I slipped in wincing a bit as the rusty hinges squeaked. I paused to let my eyes adjust. Afternoon light trickled in through a few barred windows, but besides that and flickering torches it was dark and musty smelling. There were two shallow steps leading down into a small room. That's where the cells were.

I swallowed audibly and descended with slow, timid steps, thankful for the little light the windows provided. But oh man, was I nervous about seeing them again. How long had it been? Four, five days? It felt like forever. I wondered if they would even recognize me in my fresh, pressed silk clothes with no grim or filth to coat my skin. What if they hated me for not coming sooner, for getting food, water, and a bed handed to me?

I had stopped at the bottom, throat closed up and questioning my being here. Then I heard a rustle, muted footsteps just barely perceivable in the silence and a voice, not rising above slightest whisper.

"Lyn?"

My name. Not girlie, not daughter, not you. Lyn. I tripped over to the rows of bars and cleared my eyes of tears to see.

"G-Glen? Caine?" Why was it so hard to speak?

"Lyn." Glen came close to the iron bars; I couldn't breath.

There was urgency in his eyes that unnerved me. That and the shape he was in. Glen looked frailer and thinner than before, his chiseled features more severe with clothes ripped, filthy, and in terrible condition. Blood was caked in his blonde hair, incredibly tangled and dirty. Caine was no better. He, like Glen, had lost a lot of weight to where he almost looked ill. Caine's face had always been gaunt, but now his jaws had hollowed and sunk and his auburn hair was (if possible) wilder than before, sticking out in a hundred different directions and unclean.

"What the heck are you doing in here?" The voice nearly made me jump out of my skin.

I gasped and spun around, dropping apples in the process. The guard. He smiled, a nasty, rotten smile and said, "Gimme those apples and get out."

"But- but," I stammered. My head was completely disheveled.

The guard moved and snatched my collar, lifting me almost clear off my feet. I heard a hurried movement and yelp behind me and the man drew his pistol, nearly dumping me in the sloppy way he pulled it.

"You, shut up. Less ya want bullet through yer head," he glanced at me. "You, get outta here. If ya wanna talk to the rats, go outside." I was released.

I scampered out, shaking off tears and slamming the door behind. Sucking in a deep breath, I considered the ugly man's words. Outside? He must mean the window. There had to be one in their cell, I just needed to get to it.

After loping around the shabby prison, I came to another window (this was my third try) and, spying a crate I could use for height, went to pick it up. I placed it under the opening and climbed up, stretching to my tiptoes and calling their names in a desperate whisper. "Glen, Caine! Where are you?"

Caine's thin face appeared behind the bars and Glen came shortly after.

"Hey," Caine said.

"Hey..." I was stunned into silence once again by the weakened state they were both in. I recalled shoving two more apples into my trouser pockets and fished them out. I eased them onto the ledge between the bars.

"Here, I brought these for you. Thought you might be hungry."

A large, calloused hand and slender, knobby one reached out and took them.

"Thanks, Lyn." I heard a crunch, and then spoke in attempt to relieve some tension.

"We're sure in a bad mess this time."

I listened to them chuckle at my humble manner.

"Don't worry, Lyn," Glen's voice. It's pretty hopeless in here."

"Same out here."

I heard Caine snort and remark, "You don't look hopeless to me," he pointed to my shirt. "What is that? Silk? Man, I can't remember the last time I wore silk... Who'd you steal it from?"

I felt my face redden and exhaled, reminded just how Caine could be. "I didn't rob anybody. I-"

This time Glen cut me off asking, "What's happening, Lyn? Why are you out walking around instead of caged like us?"

I quieted and stared at his pale, azure eyes, wondering if I should tell the news. No, not a good time, especially since I had no idea how they would react.

"I really don't know." I decided to deny the truth for now.

Glen looked hard at me. "They're not... you know, *touching* you, are they?"

I felt the blush tinting my cheeks when his question registered. Glen meant something along the lines of fondling. I hoped.

Caine must have taken my silence as misunderstanding because he elaborated. "That redhead that's been following you around... He feeling you up?"

"Wha- No!" I flushed profusely when his blatant inquire gave me *that* image of Dev. The boys must have noticed I wasn't going to clarify since Caine changed the subject to another problem.

"What about Raine? Have you seen her?"

I bit my lip, trying to pull my thoughts together, and then answered, "Not since you have. I miss her bad, though."

A rare, pained expression crossed his face and I tried to change the subject; stretching even more, I leaned up close to the bars and spoke quietly. "Just hang in there, guys. I think I've found- Ah!"

Next thing I know, I'm plummeting to the hard, dusty ground. I landed with a solid "thud", lights flashing when the back of my head connected. My vision cleared and I was staring up at Dev's grinning face. I never heard him come. The man had kicked the box right out from under my feet.

"Visiting hour's over, girlie."

I attempted a reply, but could not muster the air needed for it. I saw another shadow appear behind Dev. He must have noticed it too because he nearly trampled me in the act of pulling his gun and barking, "Hey!"

I managed to claim a little breath and struggle to my aching knees for a better view of this person. My heart ricocheted off my ribs so hard it hurt. Razor, stood in my line of sight with his midnight gaze piercing me to the bone.

This was the first time I had seen the man up close. He wore a tight shirt, showing his prominent lean muscle underneath a leather jacket that hung loosely on his slim frame. His hair, I noticed, was jet black and greasy-looking, not dangling in his face like I'd last seen in the fight but slackly pulled back and tied in a band. The man had a long, deadly face that showed no emotion: a cold-blooded killer. With his wild eyes locked with mine, I realized I could not speak. They had a demented, inhuman look that made this man dangerous.

Out of the corner of my eye, I spied Dev lower the gun a fraction. Razor's gaze flicked to him and the weapon froze. He stood like that for several seconds longer then turned away to keep on walking.

Dev and I both released out held air. He stowed the gun and shuddered. "That guy gives me the creeps."

I stood stiffly, dusting off my soiled garments, wincing a bit as I rose. I finally found my voice. "I don't know why. He really seems to like you."

Dev twisted, still nervous from the encounter, and opened his mouth to counter my sarcastic comment, but a torrent of voices and clanging of bells silenced him. Chinese women were ringing and shouting; men were converging in on them.

"Dinner," Dev glanced at me. "You hungry, girlie?"

I nodded, realizing I hadn't eaten since breakfast.

"Come on, then." He started walking.

Razor must have really freaked him out because I would usually be getting drug there regardless of what I said. Looking at the prison window, a sudden sad pain swept through me and I took a step toward it. "Guys?"

"Girlie, let's go!" So he *hadn't* been that stirred up .

Before I turned away, two hands stuck out of the bars and waved. Tears brimmed and I waved back, but another hand clamped on my shoulder, squeezing hard and making me stagger away from the touch, gasping. It didn't let go.

"I *said* come on."

I tried to pull away from Dev, but the pressure only increased, turning my sympathetic tears into tears of hurt. I did not resist anymore, but my shoulder throbbed under his touch. He released me when we were a few paces from the dinner crowd.

Dev seemed to walk faster than normal so I guessed Razor must still be on his mind.

I lolled behind, massaging my shoulder where his hand had been. I watched him enter a line and saw three others get behind Dev. The line seemed to be moving at a steady pace so I decided to take a spot. The men in front of me noticed the instant I stopped.

One I recognized as the one-armed man, Morin, turned and sneered unbecomingly. I held his gaze for a second then looked away. Listening to him speak to the two around him, I soon noticed them circling me. That's when I got panicky.

I met their gazes as evenly as I could and moved to go out of the circle.

"Excuse me."

A sturdy hand halted me and shoved back roughly. "Just where do you think you're going?"

Before I could answer, another man jostled me and asked, "Why's a fragile thing like you even in this line?"

I crashed none too gently into a bulky chest and felt hands close around my slender arms. Looking up, I witnessed the man's pockmarked face twist into a very unpleasant expression. "Are you hungry, baby?"

I jerked, kicked, squirmed, and shouted, but the few that took heed weren't going to do anything.

"Hey, hey! Leave her alone you idiots!"

Dev pushed through the men and snatched me, wrenching my arms from the other man's grasp. I heard Morin give a teasing yelp. "What's wrong, Dev? 'Fraid we'll hurt your girl?"

His friend gave a nudge and added, "He always been possessive, Morin. Never learned to share."

If he caught it, Dev either didn't care or choose not to acknowledge the shrewd comments.

When we were several feet away from the crowd, Dev spun my body to face him and shook me hard. "*What* are you doing? Trying to get yourself killed?"

I had never seen him this angry before. Dev's normal, laid-back self had been smeared by Razor's appearance and he was apparently dishing his fear out on me. "I was just getting dinner."

He looked at me from under a heavy brow, derision unconcealed on his face. "*Your* dinner's inside."

"Oh..."

You could not imagine how stupid I felt after he said that. I broke away, trying not to let Dev see my abashed blush.

I thanked and dismissed the same oriental woman ~~that~~ who had catered to me earlier. I changed then slipped into smooth, velvety covers, content with my full stomach. Dinner had been splendid, as always, but it had taken a bit of will to eat the same birds I had seen alive earlier that day. Still, when the warm, tasty broth touched my lips, I could do nothing but wolf it all down. The fresh chicken soup seemed to be seasoned just right and none of the bloody residue remained from the bout.

Good! So there I lay, staring at the well-made roof and thinking (the one thing I shouldn't be doing). I thought of Glen and Caine, how they had been and acted: Raine, likely dead by now because we'd left her: Dev and the other men, the whole group in general: my father's offer... and lastly of the cool, beauteous diamond around my neck. I left it on even ~~know~~ though it was uncomfortable to sleep with. Dev was the only one who knew I had it, and I wanted it to stay that way.

I suddenly felt hot pricks of water poking at the corners of my eyes. Before I knew it, tears were streaming down my cheeks and wetting my hair. How was I ever going to get out of this? I'd brought Glen and Caine into the mess and probably killed Raine; it was all because of me.

Me, I thought, a sob escaping my mouth. *It's always me...*

Ch. 25 The Plan

A rooster crowed. I opened my swollen eyes, felt the salt from my tears stretch my skin. I lay there, but becoming aware of little inklings trickling through my head, got up. No clothes, no breakfast. Strange. What time is it, I wondered. I saw a pretty blouse draped over the golden mirror and some pants under that. There was nothing else to wear so I put them on. The pull-over felt good on my skin and the lace collar was low, exposing my neck. The pants were comfortable if not a little baggy. I paused to look at my reflection.

My eyes were a bit puffy and red from crying through the night. My hair was windswept and tangled, like always, but not horrible. I couldn't tell if I had put on any weight; my clothes billowed about my lean frame, but I did not feel undernourished.

All in all, I was the same: long, streaked blonde hair, dark cobalt blue eyes, slender limbs, and a waist narrower than my pinky finger. A pretty face, some would say. I sighed and walked on, exiting the room as quietly as I could.

When I stepped out on the porch, I was greeted with cool, fresh air ruffling my hair and caressing my skin. The morning rays peaked through distant mountains, spilling light over the fort, casting it in an ashen radiance. Once again I was stunned into a peaceful silence upon witnessing such a sight from within these walls.

Dev wasn't up yet so that gave me some content to see I had beaten him. I waltzed over to the stone bench and seated myself, thinking breakfast would be quite tasty right about now. The spot gave me a very nice view of the fort. There were a few men out, none of which I recognized from this distance.

I scanned the walls; no way to escape and the large double-doors at the entrance appeared impenetrable. I lamented inwardly, glancing toward the old prison. A brief thought of going to see Glen and Caine crossed my mind, but after the incident yesterday I shouldn't try to risk it. I traced the distance from the cells to the stables, stables to the door…

"Well, looks like she got up a little earlier today."

I turned toward Dev walking up the porch steps, lifting the corners of my mouth. "Have enough time to catch up on your beauty sleep, Dev? Didn't think a guy as good-looking as you needed any."

He smirked dryly. "Don't get cocky just 'cause you heard the rooster crow first, girlie. I bet you haven't even had breakfast made for ya."

He was right, but I directed the comment on a different route.

"You're right, but I told them to hold off because I wanted to ask you a little favor..." I trailed off to perk his interests.

Dev raised a quizzical eyebrow. "And what could that favor possibly be for you to skip your mornin' meal?"

Here, I tried to look bashful and embarrassed.

"Well," I began, eyes straying up through my lashes to lock with his. "I was hoping you would share breakfast with me."

Laughter bubbled up from his chest. "Wow, girlie, I'd love to. But no."

Irritation sprung to my mind and was followed by sudden anger.

"Why not?" I snapped back, letting my fury get the best of me.

Dev's sardonic grin widened. "For one, I can tell you're plotting something."

I cut him short before the man could continue. "I just wanted some company."

I was having serious trouble keeping my temper in check, but I had to make him believe I really craved this.

"It gets real awkward simply sitting there with those Asian women watching me. I mean it's not like I can carry on a conversation with them," I paused dramatically, choosing my next words with care. "I figured inviting you might help relieve some of the... tension."

Dev appeared to actually be considering my offer.

"Some of the *tension*? Well, sweetie, when ya put it like that I guess I can't say no."

He strolled over to me and extended his hand in a courteous manner. I held back then decided to take it. The man yanked me to my feet, clutching my hand so forcefully, I gasped.

Dev jerked me close and bent to where his face was barely inches from my own, smiling savagely. "Just remember, girlie, I got the knife."

The morning meal was even more high-strung than usual. Asian women were waiting as soon as we entered, bearing steaming platters full of deer and eggs over easy. I decided to have breakfast in the dinning room with the large table. It gave me a strange sense of déjà vu, but if my scheme was going to work I had to go through with it.

"Whew! I don't remember the last time I's this full," Dev remarked when we were finished and exiting the house. "Ya sure weren't very talkative at the table, girlie. Somethin' I should know?"

I locked on to the stables, never diverting my gaze when I answered. "I was just thinking how nice it would be to ride around, get some fresh air..."

Dev snorted. I finally glanced at him.

"Why don't you and I go for a ride?"

"Please," I added for good measure.

"You must think I'm crazy, girlie. I ain't gonna risk it."

Not giving into my rage, I decided on my next choice of words.

"What harm could it do?" I inquired, staring him full in the face. Well, what I could see of his face; the wind was intense today and it whisked his orange hair everywhere.

"You'd be surprised."

"Really?"

I danced closer, placing a hand on his arm. "It couldn't be wrong. I mean you, a big, strong guy taking a helpless little girl like me on a ride around the fort," I flashed a smile. "It'd be fun."

"Plus," I leaned up to whisper in his ear. "I'd make sure we didn't get caught."

"Alright," Dev growled, finally giving in. "It's gonna be short so let's go."

I let him walk ahead, grinning madly behind his back.

"Just open the dang door, Ossy."

Well, we'd gotten a horse, mounted, passed the morning crowds, and stopped at the gate. I felt like someone had hit me hard in the stomach when I saw the nasty, round man, Ossy, at the exit. The feeling only worsened when I heard his words.

"I ain't lettin' ya filthy food-nabbers out."

I could tell Dev's patience was being tried from the great outlet of breath frizzing my hair. He could just give up now. Dev did *not* have to do this; I'm not even sure how I got him to in the first place.

"Oh c'mon, Ossy! It was justa piece of meat."

The fat man puffed out his cheeks in a look of annoyance, facial expression making his share a strong resemblance to a pig. "Piece of meat that was darn good too."

I felt Dev shift behind me and turned to look at what it was he was doing.

"Oh yeah?" Dev inquired, reaching down into his pocket and producing a piece of deer leftover from breakfast. "Better than this?"

He wagged it back and forth and Ossy's eyes followed it, looking like a half-starved mutt.

"G-Give it here!" He commanded.

"Open the gate," Dev replied.

It set Ossy to grumbling, but he complied, waddling to the heavy wooden door and undoing the lock. He pushed it open and Dev clicked softly with his tongue, signaling the horse to move.

It was an unexpected jolt and threw me off balance. Dev's free hand tightened around my waist when he felt me slide and he tossed the sliver of deer to Ossy who immediately snatched and stuffed in into his mouth. Dev squirmed a bit in the saddle with me, but eventually we both settled in.

When we stepped outside of the entrance, I was greeted with a burst of the engrossing sensation of freedom. I saw the distant mountains beckoning me, deep forest enticing me… And then I was pinned back in the situation I was stuck in.

Dev was mumbling to himself so I looked around us. There were dirt pathways leading off into the woods or around the fort; everything else seemed to be dense wilderness. A good place for crooks to hide, I thought, no one within a few miles of the structure.

"Wonder when the Boss's gonna be back."

I picked up on Dev's more audible mummer now. I decided conversation might lighten things up.

"Do you know where he went?" I asked.

"Nah. No one does 'cept the men he takes with him."

I considered his words while Dev paused.

"This one must've been pretty important," he huffed a laugh. "I'm surprised he didn't take that freak Razor."

Dev nudged me and said, "You're lucky the boss took Lieutenant and not me."

"Why?"

"Lieutenant's second in command around there so he's usually left in charge when the Boss is out. I'm sure if *he* saw the way you act, you'd never got out of your room. The guy's wild when he's mad."

I remembered Lieutenant well enough. The man had been easily recognizable by his stately attire that far exceeded the other men's garb. His aristocratic features made Lieutenant naturally handsome, but he had the mien of someone that could be pushed to kill if angered enough. He was likely the type that seemed all cool and collected until he snapped.

During our talk, I noticed we had covered some ground, maybe more than Dev intended. Perfect. I was feeling a little personally needy anyway.

"Uh, Dev, can we stop?" The embarrassing part would be saying it.

He gave me one of those 'are you serious' looks and asked the inevitable question, "Why?"

I flushed pink.

"Well..."

"'Well' what?"

I exhaled and spit it out. "Look, I have to use the bathroom, okay?"

He grinned. "Don't worry, we're turning around right now."

I jerked up a little in urgency. "But I have to go *now*. There's no way I can hold it."

Dev cocked an eyebrow and appeared to be calculating the distance from here to the fort.

"There's some bushes over there," he said, tipping his head toward some shrubbery.

I let my mouth fall open slightly as we pulled up beside the bushes.

"Well go on," he prompted, giving me a little shove. "I'll wait for ya."

I slipped down in silent fury and trudged over behind the bramble. I became angered even further at all the waist-high grass I had to wade through.

Once I found a decent enough spot, I relieved myself, wondering if this really was an okay place. I was going to give Dev a piece of my mind if I caught him peaking. I heard the man's voice.

"Hurry up, girlie! We gotta go. Storm's coming fast."

I turned my gaze skyward, now noticing the hefty breeze had picked up too. There was a dark slate, almost black color to the sky, creating an ominous air. I could not believe how sudden it all came on.

"Do I need to come help you?"

My shaky control shattered when his words touched my ear.

"Go help yourself!" I snapped back.

"What?" There was a warning edge in Dev's voice that meant I had nearly crossed the line. Or maybe I already had. I didn't care either way.

"Go ahead, pull your knife on me. I bet you're too scared to use it anyway, *girlie!*"

I slammed my mouth closed, bracing for him to come tearing through the bushes, dagger in hand, ready to end my life.

I listened to a "thud" besides my pounding heart and, still fired up from my rashness, inquired, "Did you fall over?"

No answer.

The wind whipped my clothes and hair, rustling the bushes. I chanced a look at Dev. The sight I saw made me stop dead and I think I forgot to breath.

Raine.

Ch. 26 Escape

She stood there, trembling slightly, staring at Dev's unconscious body, and the large rock lying beside his head, red hair splayed out in a circle on the grass. I could not speak for a moment because of her sudden appearance.

She looked every bit as bad as Glen and Caine did; her brown locks were tightly curled and wispy, her clothes were torn, dirt-stained, and spotted with blood. Her body was pencil thin, but her eyes were bright and glowing with a fierce determination far past her age.

"Raine!" I cried, stumbling forward out of the brush, arms open wide.

She gave a little start and her doe-eyed gaze pierced me to the bone.

"Lyn!" She bounced over to me, giving me a good squeeze.

I hugged back, never wanting to let go again. Finally, I pulled away, crying, but still holding her elbows. There were small specks of water in the corners of Raine's chocolate eyes too.

"We all thought you were dead. How did you find this place?"

She smiled through her tears and explained.

"Well, before everyone woke up the day those people came to the town, I couldn't sleep so I decided to explore the house and see what I could find." Raine turned her stare from mine, embarrassed by her childishness.

I was too elated to tell her she should have told one of us where she was going. She continued.

"About the time the sun started coming up, I was heading back, but heard this rumble and saw the men charging toward us. I should have told you all but... I was scared. Instead I climbed up the old chimney and stayed there."

I didn't want to, but I had to ask. "So you saw us..."

"Get beaten? Yeah," Raine swiped at her eyes. "I-I was frozen and I could hear you screaming, but I *wouldn't move.* I saw them take off and followed, telling myself I would get you out."

I was amazed.

"How did you eat?" I asked, knowing the boys and I always caught the food.

"There were lots of jars and stuff in that cellar so I took some with me."

I gaped inwardly. Raine's smarter than the three of us put together. She gestured toward the fort.

"I've been hanging around this place ever since you went in. A couple of days ago, I saw a bunch of guys leave with this giant man that had horns on his head. When I found out none of you were with him..."

So she had thought *we* were the ones dead. But Raine had stayed, had hope. Maybe that's why we needed her so badly; she had hope and the strength to keep going.

Something cold and wet hit me on the arm. I looked down and saw a drop of water, glanced back up and perceived other drops falling. The sky was coal black, its wind blowing harder than ever. It was perfect cover.

"Raine, we have got to go back in."

She stared at me like I was out of my mind, but the thought, *it's Lyn,* must have gone though her head and Raine nodded. "I'll follow you, Lyn."

I spied Dev's mount grazing over at a nearby tree and an idea popped into my head. "Raine, go get that horse."

"Right!"

She sped off and I glanced down at Dev, still

out cold. I knew this was going to work; it *had* to work or we were plum out of luck.

Squatting, I flipped Dev over and began undoing the buttons of his duster. I slid it off, starting to work on his shirt. Raine was going to need something to wear besides rags if we wanted a fighting chance. After threading his arms out, I searched the man's belt, packed full of what I wanted. I snatched the knife he'd pulled on me a hundred times, his old pistol, and some extra bullets from his pockets. Smiling, I tucked everything into *my* new belt, a courteous gift from Dev, and thought about my hair.

I shrugged the overcoat on thinking about how blonde my hair was in contrast to his bright red, almost orange mane, one of the man's most noticeable features.

"Lyn, I got it."

I looked up to see Raine with the animal, still munching on grass. His saddlebags!

"Good, Raine. Now get on her," I said, reaching into one and finding a hat.

"What?"

She was obviously intimidated by the steed, but we had no time to waste; the draft was really picking up, rocking the tree limbs violently and showering us with rain.

"Come on, Raine, I'll help you."

She gulped and I hoisted her onto the horse with her tiny hands gripping the horn tightly. I handed Raine Dev's shirt and told her, "Trust me, just put this on, stay up there, and don't say anything." She nodded, panic lighting her eyes.

I took up the reins and led the horse ~~with me~~ after having stuffed most of my hair under the hat. The animal was jittery from the wind and rain, making it difficult to lead. I left Dev in the grass, striped to his pants, hoping he wouldn't miss his clothes and belongings too terribly.

By the time we had gotten to the gate, rain had turned to hail and the gusts were enough to rip you from the ground. Men were hurrying this way and that, shouts drowned out by the raging storm. I picked up the pace too, thinking someone was bound to notice me, but I may just have Lady Luck with me today. The others might only see a shorter, hoarse-sounding Dev towing a smaller, dark-haired me back inside.

We were finally at the entrance, ice mauling us and gales whipping our garments. I let loose a breath of relief seeing a thickly set black man instead of Ossy at the gate. I halted before him and made a show of trying to settle the horse. I kept my face down to hide as many features as I could and strained my voice to make it sound deeper with a bad accent. "'Scuse us, but girlie and I's need to get through."

Would I pass as Dev? Please let us go, I prayed.

The man scrutinized us like he could care less and waved us in. I quickly guided the steed to the fine stone house, tied it there, and helped Raine down. I could not believe this was working!

The wind was even worse inside the fort; walls trapped it in and the gusts spun madly, tearing roofs off houses and stirring up all kinds of dirt and debris. No one took heed of Raine and me dashing to the old prison and slipping through the rickety door.

We both paused to catch our much-needed breath. The sound mixed with that of the air wafting through the bars. The gusts had nearly taken my hat with them, but I managed to keep it on despite the blonde strands that had fallen out.

As ~~was~~ we started down the two small steps, I heard shuffling.

"Who's there?"

My heart wedged itself in my throat. The guard! I groped for the gun and pulled it, leveling it with the fat man's bloated face.

"Woah, Dev, easy with that thing! It could..." He trailed off, taking in my facial features, hair, and size, realizing I was not Dev.

The guy's eyebrows shot up in a look of shock and he reached for his gun. I ~~clicked~~ cocked the pistol ~~once,~~ giving a warning. He jerked up slightly, perspiration forming around his pudgy face.

"Y-You're the girl Dev's always with! W-What'd ya do to 'em?"

He was nervous. Good.

"Open the cell," I commanded, a sudden rush of power zipping through me.

The man hesitated and I put my finger on the trigger.

"Do it or I'll shoot!" Thankfully, the threat was enough to set him in the right direction.

I watched him fumble for the keys and Raine sneak up behind him. She had defiantly learned a trick or two from Caine; I never saw her move, and the guard apparently hadn't either.

He turned the keys and pulled a latch, the barred iron door swung open. Just before the boys hurried out, Raine wacked the portly man across the back of his head with a rusty crowbar and he went thundering to the ground, knocked senseless.

"Haha, nice one Raine! You have no idea how long I've wanted to do that," Caine commented as he embraced her.

"Caine!" She cried, voice breaking.

I smiled, tears of joy blurring my vision. Glen walked over to me, arms spread wide, and I stepped into his solid embrace, melting like butter in a hot pan. Sobs racked his body and he pulled me tight against his chest. I didn't care if he smelt worse than some of the savages, I was just glad to be back in his arms.

"Hey, Glen, give me a chance too, would you?" I heard Caine say.

We pulled away, smirking, and Glen said, "It's good to see you, finally."

He went to hug Raine, as amazed as all of us seeing she was still alive.

I saw Caine's trademark grin welcome me and we hugged, squeezing each other tighter than I could ever remember.

"Man, Lyn, I missed you," he whispered into my hair. "More than Glen, even."

I giggled faintly. "*You* missed *me*?"

He moved back to where we could see the other's face. "Hard to believe, isn't it? That I can actually *want* to see your scowling face and hear your complaining voice."

I merely smiled more, thinking the exact same thing.

"Come on you two, we've got to get out of here," Glen said.

Caine and I released, but I stopped everyone. "Hold on," I pointed to the guard drooling on the floor. "We need to do something with him first."

Glen nodded, speaking to Raine. "Go find us some rope. Caine, help me drag this guy in the cell."

"What? Are you serious?"

"I'll help," I volunteered.

Caine gave all of us skeptic looks and rolled his eyes. "Don't say I didn't warn you when this thing gets dropped."

"Hush up and push, Caine," Raine told him, shoving hard, rope in hand.

We pushed; the three-hundred-pound man moved about two inches.

"Harder!" We all dug our feet into the dirt and after much panting, straining, and a final burst from Glen did we get the man into the cell.

While Glen and Caine busied themselves with tying him up, I stretched my weak muscles. Someone's shadow darkened the steps and since I was the only one standing, I saw whom it belonged to. I opened my mouth to scream, but my throat had closed up on me. He was right there, no more than six feet from us, razor edged blades glinting softly in the dim torchlight. Raine did the shrieking for me and it made Glen and Caine speed out of the cage, slamming the door behind them and stopping dead with me.

I had a gun, but Razor had his knives. Glen had the same idea and I glanced over at him in horror as he reached for the guard's pistol he had taken. I shot my hand out to stay his arm.

"Don't!" I barked.

He froze and Razor flipped one of his deadly weapons, speaking for the first time since the fight. "You really think you can pull that gun before I take your head off?"

The man's voice was unexpectedly deep and rich, solid to where when he spoke, you would wait until he finished to give your opinion. I felt myself shaking, recalling what he could do with those knives. But there was something in his eyes...

How I got up the nerve to move, I'll never know, but slowly, I eased my hand down into the neck of my blouse, feeling the large diamond resting against my skin. Razor's coal back gaze followed my every move; I kept my eyes on his blades. Those hands could move faster than lighting. One twitch and I was finished.

"W-Wait," I stuttered, working the jewel out.

There was a light in his ebony stare that had not been there before. The man extended one of his daggers, never breaking focus with my face. I removed the diamond from around my neck and carefully hung it on the tip of the knife, aware, if Razor moved, he could take my hand with the jewel.

The man tilted the blade to the light, making it catch the gemstone and dazzle.

Somewhat satisfied, he raised it more and the necklace slid down on his arm. Razor spoke directly to me even know̶ his words were aimed at us all. "I knew Dev had it all along. He was scared so he gave it to you, but that idiot may have saved your life."

I thought about speaking, but decided to remain quiet. Razor snarled a little, looking devilish. "Since you held on to this for me, I'll let you go, but if I ever see any one of you again I'll kill you."

My knees were trembling so badly, I almost crumpled then and there, but stood only by sheer force of will. I couldn't believe my ears; he let us go free. Well, he *said* we could go. For all I knew, the man could stab us in the back for trusting his word. I wondered if having confidence in Razor could come with consequences.

The man leaned back against the metal bars, stowing one knife away and flipping and twirling the other in a blur while he inspected to great jewel.

"Go, guys, I'll follow," I urged them to move.

"Lyn..."

Caine sounded uncertain but Glen broke in. "Caine, Raine, you two go first. Lyn and I will trail."

They nodded, edging past Razor, never turning their backs to him. I made Glen go before me even *Though* know he wasn't happy about it, and tagged behind, locked on the man. His black eyes linked with mine and the breath left me when his knife quit moving. I do believe the only thing that saved me was a groan from the fat guard in the cell. Razor broke contact, flipped a dagger, and threw it between the bars. I gasped as the blade buried itself in the guard's neck flesh, killing him instantly.

Glen finally snatched my hand, gave a firm jerk, and we sped out of the building, never looking back.

The storm hit me like a pail of cold water on a hot day. Wind threw me to the ground, rain and hail smacked me in the face, beat my body. The clouds had turned the sky black as Razor's gaze and it was difficult to see through the madness. I made out the stables and knew that was our destination.

Struggling to my feet, I pushed forward shouting, "The horses. Get to the horses!"

When we had gotten close, I spied a spooked horse, tied and saddled where its rider had left it.

"Glen, grab that one and meet me at the big stone house!"

He appeared slightly baffled, but compiled while I hastened to the beauteous structure. Caine followed.

"What the heck are you doing, Lyn?!"

"Trust me!" I called back.

Gripping the porch railing for support, I hauled myself up to the untarnished door. It opened without warning and I jumped back into Caine who stumbled a bit, but steadied us both.

The Asian woman stepped out carrying a small sack. I gaped at her when she handed it to me and said, "Good luck."

She then closed the door and I, having regained my composure, dashed to Dev's mount still tied on the pole.

"Who was that?" Caine asked, stunned while I tucked the satchel in the saddlebag.

"A friend," I replied, fastening a strip of cloth over the animal's head to keep it from spooking.

"Come on!"

I had untied the horse and was leading it to the exit, unrelenting gale attacking me ferociously. We were almost there; I could taste freedom, but I wouldn't be safe until I swallowed it.

Raine and Glen met us at the gate. All we had to do was get through…

"Oh no," I breathed, legs giving up.

No one else heard me, but they all paused as well. I felt Caine's hand on my shoulder.

"Lyn, we should g-oh." He saw it too.

Dev had gotten up after regaining consciousness and tracked us all back to the fort and now he stood about ten feet from us, looking haggard. The man's bare torso was slick with water and his skin had thin lines of red on it from where a few wild brambles had snagged him. Dev's orange hair had turned brown and his face had a strange expression on it.

I didn't know what to do. Here we were, a step away from freedom and we're stopped dead by the same fool who'd been keeping tabs on me for days. I watched, petrified, as Dev started to walk. Something was wrong, though. He was shuffling slower than I would think possible under these circumstances, throwing a foot out then stumbling. Dev actually tripped and did not catch himself, plunging face-first into the mud. That gave me hope; he was still out of it from being slammed with that rock.

"Which way do we go?" I yelled over the roaring winds.

"Not the way we came from!" Caine shouted back.

"This way! I think I see something." Glen started a hard dash for the woods, tugging the frightened horse with him.

I ran after he, Caine, and Raine, full of joy and more than a little anxiety...

We crashed into a good-sized hill upon exiting the forests. The storm had not let up. If anything, it had gotten worse. The great bellows of wind hounded the trees, making them bend and scream with pain and hail beat us to death along with the branches that scarred our faces. Thank goodness we found something solid to keep the worst of the tempest off.

Too worn to go over the large mound, we hurried around it, still lugging the animals.

"Look," Raine said, pointing.

I glanced up and couldn't believe our luck. There was a rock overhang cut into the side of the hill that was perfect for cover. We began the difficult task of scaling the slope them collapsed after reaching safe haven under the rock.

"W....We made it!"

I shook my head, surveying everybody. We all breathed hard and shook, from physical exertion, no food, and the suddenness of our escape. I'm sure the rain and hail had something to do with it, too.

Raine looked frail and drenched, her curls were twisted horribly and tangled on top of that. Caine was the definition of exhaustion, slumped back against the stonewall, wet hair plastered to his head and hollowed cheeks. Glen looked worried, but tiredness ruled his emotions, seeming to stretch his skin tight, making him appear older with more defined features, a rough kind of handsome, if you took it that way. That would mean we were *all* a rough kind of handsome, I thought with a smirk.

Despite all this, it was so good to have them back.

"Lyn, are you alright? You're shaking pretty bad." Glen's concern was touching.

I smiled more. "I'm okay. Just..." What was the word?

"Excited."

"Excited?" Caine repeated, deeply sarcastic.

I turned my eyes on him. "Yeah. Aren't you?"

"If by 'excited' you mean scared half to death, then yeah, I guess I am."

I listened to Raine's twinkling giggle and her say, "Well then I'm the *most* excited!"

We all chuckled; Caine even ruffled her hair. We needed Raine's ability to change little things like that into something light-hearted and humorous.

"I think the horses might have you beat there, Raine."

Glen was probably right. The animals couldn't stand still and you could easily see the whites of their eyes as they tugged relentlessly on their reins.

I thought about the men from the fort while I watched the violent squall, wondering if they had realized we were gone and if they had found Dev's sorry body outside yet. We needed to move, fast. From what I knew, their trackers could tail us for miles and if we got caught again... I didn't go there. The storm may be enough to hinder them or at least buy us some time. Razor did not seem like the type to squeal, either.

"Whoa. Look at that." We all followed Caine's gaze and froze.

A tornado. Its rotating vortex looked like a funnel of draining water, large at the top and narrow at the foot where it touched the ground. The cyclone's winds were strong, but we were safe under the overhang, rock wall taking much of the brute force off us. It looked like the twister was rumbling toward the fort. That was good.

It meant we had a head start. All we needed to do was keep it.

The spinning tempest hit the fortress without mercy. I watched from our spot as it sent roofs flying and massacred the shabby slave buildings. What am I doing? Tearing myself away, I stood, tugged on the horse I was leading and began marching in the opposite direction.

"What, we leaving already?" I listened to the hastened scrambling as everyone followed me.

Glen walked up beside me and said, "After the weather calms down we can get on the horses and maybe cover some ground."

I nodded in agreement, wishing we could ride now. I glanced over at Dev's horse and noticed it was the same color red as his hair. Had the man come to his senses, yet? When he did, I had no doubt he would be furious. I wondered if he would think someone else had taken his things, but knew I was only daydreaming. My luck was never *that* good. Dev would likely round up a bunch of men and hunt us down. Find us all, too. That would be my luck.

If my father came back and found out I was missing... Why, just seeing the way every savage responded to 'The Boss' gave me the impression they could all be dead, murdered by his hand. Dev certainly would be since it had been his responsibility to watch me.

My father. The big secret I didn't want anyone to know. How would they treat me if they knew? If they found out my father is some madman committing horrid crimes and playing leader of a bunch of bloodthirsty hooligans?

Exactly why I'm not telling them, I concluded.

Ch. 27 The Ride

*A*fter a few miserable hours, the sky cleared, leaving bright afternoon sun and lazy clouds. I couldn't take anymore walking.

"I think it's time we got on the horses," I stated, slowing pace.

"It's *been* time," Caine added, relieving Glen of the dappled bronco he was leading.

"Why don't you and I ride together, Glen?" I asked, smiling at him.

He grinned back and my heart did a little flip. I had forgotten how lovely that smile of his was.

"Alright, Raine and I'll double on this one," Caine said, giving Raine a boost up to the saddle.

I paused before I mounted, trying to remember if Caine had ever ridden before. Glen stopped too, hands on my waist to watch.

Caine swung his leg up above his head and hopped like a monkey before he got his balance. He snatched the saddle horn and his foot came out of the stirrup and he hung there, dangling, before dropping to the ground.

"Caine do you-?"

"No!" He interrupted me. "I'm just a little rusty, that's all."

He braced himself and was about to jump, but Raine held out a hand.

"Caine let me steer it." After receiving a ridiculous look from Caine, she added, "Please. It'd be easier."

"Raine, I-"

"I know you can't ride."

That was the end of it. Red-faced, Caine scampered up behind Raine and wrapped his arms around her. I laughed, having watched the whole scene, and got a dirty look from Caine and a giggle or two from Raine.

"Well that solves our problem," I said, letting Glen lift me effortlessly to the saddle.

He mounted after and grabbed the bridal line with practiced skill. Glen and I were excellent horseback riders; we had been riding since we learned to walk: him for travel and work, and me for enjoyment and quick ways to get around town. Caine had been trapped within the slums of the city where only the wealthy could afford to keep horses, and Raine...

"Raine, where did you learn to ride?" I asked, curious.

She looked at me, grinning. "Back when my mom and dad were around. Almost every weekend, we would go up to this farm that had horses and the landlady that owned the place liked me so she let me ride them. So I guess that's how I got pretty good."

It made sense enough so I didn't press for more facts. The last time I had ridden was with Dev. Hopefully the last I'd ever see of him, too.

Being in the saddle with Glen really took me back. It made me think of the time we first saw each other.

I had been going out to parade about town on my brand new Andalusian horse, wearing my latest silk dress. While trotting down the fence line, I noticed a worker pause and watch me (which wasn't unusual, they often did), but this one kept staring. Most of the time, I only needed to glance at the laborer and they would get back to work; not this one.

I slowed my mount until we came to a complete stop and I was locked on to the stranger. We stared at each other for a moment and I was captivated by how blue his eyes were: bluer than the clearest day's sky and as shiny as crystal. The boy broke into a grin that dazzled me. He was very handsome, what, with his dirty blonde hair, chiseled features, and lopsided smile that could make you smitten over him.

As much as I tried, I could not keep my refined mannerism up so I gave in, dismounted, and began chattering away to this stranger. The boy had been incredibly easy to talk to, open without concealed schemes or false smirks, so unlike the men in politics I'd had to deal with when my ' father' took me to some of his meetings. I reminded myself that he was a field hand, possessing little to no money, but the thought did not stop me from befriending him. And thank goodness it didn't.

If it had then I wouldn't be here now, but with that group my father leads. We weren't in the best situation, but it was a heck of a lot better than what it could be. Be an optimist, as Raine had taught me.

"Are you tired, Lyn?" Glen whispered in my ear so only I heard him.   "Exhausted, but I can't sleep now."

I heard him chuckle softly. "Why not?"

"I would fall off the horse."

I could imagine him smiling.

"Oh yeah? I'll keep you on so lean back and you don't have to sleep, but rest your eyes a bit." I lifted the corners of my mouth, thinking it was unnecessary, but didn't resist.

I tipped back, supporting my head with his shoulder, cradled under the angle of his jaw line. I closed my eyes, calm and at peace for the first time in weeks...

I listened to the labored sound of my breath and the "slap, slap" of my bare feet on the stone. Where was I even going? I stopped in mid-stride and broke left only to pause again in sheer terror.

Two identical men were standing on a long piece of metal, their stances provoking and voices raised. The room seemed to shrink and I soon realized the only safe place was the beam of metal. I was forced toward the bickering men, heart trying hard to break out of my chest when I noticed whom they looked like.

Yellow eyes, high cheekbones, bearskin garments, and towering bodies rippling with muscle. One of them began trudging toward me and the other faded back to where he could barely be seen. I receded away from my father's double, soon to the end of the steel bar.

I glanced down: nothing but white; I glanced at the man: nothing but death. Drawing in a deep breath, I leaped off, falling. I spun in the air and let loose a cry of shock when I saw many more people waiting at the bottom to catch me, but I fell straight through them, feeling knives bite into my skin and watched the white before my vision turn black...

My eyes flew open and I suddenly lurched forward. Glen looped his arm around me, hardly able to keep hold of the horse. He was the only thing between me and the ground, but I didn't know that.

"Stop!" I shrieked, struggling in his arms, not knowing it was Glen. "Let go of me!"

We both wrestled for control in the saddle while the horse danced in place, throwing its head and snorting in fear.

"Glen, I got the bridal! Grab her," Caine shouted.

I was scarcely a match for one of Glen's arms, and did not stand a chance when he pinned me with two.

"It's us, Lyn," said Raine. "You're gonna be fine."

"I-I know," I gasped, wriggling my sweaty hands out and placing them on Glen's powerful arms.

"Then stop acting like a lunatic!" Caine snapped, still holding our horse's reins.

"I'm glad you think it's so easy to come out of a nightmare all fine and dandy, Caine!"

Feeling bold, I added to his anger. "Why don't you ride side-saddle some more?"

His face turned bright red, with rage or embarrassment, I did not know, but I was pretty sure it was fury.

"Shut up you-"

"Caine, stop it!" Raine's cry of distress made all our attention gather around her.

I could see trickles of water running down her cheeks as she kneed the horse forward, wrenching our animal from Caine's grasp. He swung his arms out for balance then snaked them around Raine for support.

"What's wrong with you, Raine?!"

I couldn't tell if the night air was getting to him or what, but Caine never yelled at Raine that harshly.

I heard her tiny voice through sobs. "I-I can't believe you want to fight more... Not when we just found each other."

"Raine, I-" Caine ended with a great sigh and began mumbling to Raine.

I felt a terrible sense of pity and noted I could not bring my hand up to wipe my eyes dry.

"Glen," I whispered. His arms had squeezed me tighter ever since Caine opened his mouth.

He loosened quite a bit when I said his name. "Sorry, Lyn. Lack of food's making me slow, I guess."

I realized that everyone must be starving if I was hungry since I had eaten this morning and they hadn't in who knew how long. The blue sky was now black, stars glimmering like little holes in the darkness.

"It's making everybody slow," Caine said as Raine pulled their mount back up beside ours. "Let's see what that Chink packed for us."

To my sudden alarm, we stopped, dismounted, and started digging through the saddlebags for the package. Stop? We can't stop!

"Why are we stopping?" I asked, attempting to make my voice sound casual.

"We gotta eat, Lyn," Caine replied, peering down into the bag.

"We can eat on the road," I declared, snatching the sack from his hands.

"Hey!"

Glen put a hand on my shoulder. "Lyn, we need the rest and so do the horses."

"But we can't," I yelped, moving the food out of Caine's reach, knowing my control was shattering.

"Why not?" Raine questioned.

I thought up the best way to avoid the truth. I've got to stretch the facts, I thought.

"Because we've got to put as many miles as we can between us and that fort." My party looked baffled and mildly irritated.

"Is there some reason they would still be searching for us?" Glen inquired, thankfully before Caine.

Ignore it, I told myself, get them to go with you.

"I'm not... Yes, yes, I think they're still out there looking." I fumbled, passing out little chunks of food then stowing the bag away.

"Lyn, you're acting weird. What's-?"

"Please, Caine," I interjected. "We *need* to keep moving."

They all just stared at me, and for a horrible moment, I believed I was going to have to come clean. But I felt firm hands on my sides and my feet leave the ground as Glen lifted me to the saddle. Caine and Raine mounted while Glen got into position behind me.

I nibbled on the piece of meat I had grabbed for myself, guilt making my appetite weak. My heart said tell them here and now, but my head told me no, put it off. How are they going to react? They would probably hate me; I would be rejected, likely dropped off the horse and left for the group to come pick me up. It wasn't like they needed my friends. Just me.

I looked up. Raine seemed so grown-up with her head held high, night breeze gently blowing her curls. I couldn't tell anything different with Caine; the boy had this shell he could hide all his emotions in when things got rough and you'd never know what he could be thinking. I glanced over my shoulder at

Glen, seeing a man worn and beaten down by the tremendous burden of responsibility before he caught me starting and gave a light smile, softening his hard features a bit. I curled my lips faintly in return then gazed ahead.

The night was misleading; it was calm, peaceful, tranquil, and the stars seemed to twinkle with good-humor, dark background letting them shine even brighter. It was like the storm had cleared everything. The breeze tasted of purity, cool and flowing, a nice contradiction to the warm air surrounding us.

The darkness put the lie, 'everything's going to be alright' in your head. I'd all but given up on the fact that I would never feel the sense of safety again. Why did everything have to be so confusing, so hard?

I just wanted to wash it all away.

The night faded to dawn; you could barely see the sun trying its best to rise above the clouds. I'd had better days.

There was no getting comfortable riding double and Glen and I often passed the reins back and forth to give the other a break. The horses were slowing dramatically and we were all exhausted, as well. Not to mention food-deprived. I didn't want to, *really* didn't want to, but having to stop was inevitable.

"Is that water?" Raine asked. We all followed her gaze to a moderately sized creek, shaded weakly by a few trees.

"Thank God! I don't care what you say, Lyn, I'm going for a swim." I kept quiet, wishing not to bicker with Caine as we rode over and dismounted.

"Ouf!" That uncomfortable riding-for-too-long sensation swept through me when my legs hit the ground, and I stretched a bit to get some blood flowing.

"See, Lyn, don't it feel good to rest?"

No, I thought, no it didn't.

"Feels like we should've stopped hours ago," Glen remarked, leading our mounts to the water that they drank greedily.

"It does," Raine added. "I'm hungry."

"And *I'm* thirsty."

"Good!" I snapped. "Go wash off in the creek. You stink."

"What and you don't?" I ignored Caine and got food out for Raine.

She looked me straight in the eye when she took it. "Lyn, are you okay?"

"Yeah, Raine," I lied. "I'm only tired."

"Mh."

Something in her manner made me believe she did not trust my answer, but I could simply be worrying too much. Stress did that to you. So does lying to your friends, I was painfully reminded. Surely all I needed was a place to cool off. No. All I needed was to tell them the truth.

I stood back, hand resting on the horse's hindquarters, and watched them. I could not remember the last time they all looked so happy. Just like children playing, I thought.

Everyone had found an area about waist-deep and started splashing. Caine got Raine in the face a few times but she only shrieked with glee, slapping the water. Glen pounced on Caine, shoving his whole head under and laughing. Caine came back up sputtering and whipping his eyes until Raine charged him, looping her arms around his neck and forcing him under again. Glen laughed some more then glanced my way.

He threw up a hand and motioned for me to join. I took a step towards them, but stopped myself. We did not have time.

I still had some food in my hands so I called, "Guys, let's eat!"

They all hauled themselves out of the water and came over to me, dripping.

"What's wrong, Lyn?" Caine teased, taking some fruit from me. "Afraid of the water?"

I rolled my eyes and finished passing out our meal. It's now or never.

I took a deep breath and let it all out.

"Look everyone, we can't stop." I trained my eyes on them. "There's someone you've never met. You may have seen him; the leader of that group we escaped from. He's this huge man with glowing yellow eyes and he wears a bearskin with horns stuck in it."

"You mean that wall of muscle that spoke to you when we were surrounded?" Caine questioned.

I nodded. "Yeah. That guy told me I'm his daughter."

There was a shocked change of facial expressions all around, food halfway to their gaping mouths. I hurried on before anyone could cut in.

"Listen, I don't believe it, but he said he knew those people *who* ~~that~~ raised me on the plantation. Said he paid them to keep me until he was ready to take me back." I slid a glance at Glen. He had a quizzical cast to his face that told me he didn't believe it either.

"I don't trust the man, but he's convinced himself I'm his daughter and I think that's the reason he's kept us alive until now." I swept them with my gaze; frozen. "All of those guys at the fort are his followers. Don't ask me how he got them, I just know every one of them are scared to death of the man and will do anything he says."

Not able to hold their gazes any longer, I focused on the ground, forcing the rest out.

"He didn't seem like the kind of person to put off getting what he wants and I don't have a doubt he'll send those savages after us so that's why... That's why we *can't* stop." I met all three pairs of eyes evenly.

The only break was the sound of a horn in the distance and a rumble to follow. My party jumped and Raine asked, "What was that?"

"Dunno," Caine answered, "but Lyn's been keeping some serious secrets from us."

"What are you talking about you 'don't know'? It's a train!" The whistle sounded again, closer and Glen sprung to life, grabbing my hand and tugging me to the horse.

"If Lyn's right about this whole 'hunt us down' story then we've got to catch that train."

To my surprise, Caine barked a laugh, snatched Raine, and dashed to their mount. "Glen, you're even crazier than Lyn!"

Glen lifted me up to the saddle, dampening my clothes when they brushed his and commented back to Caine after swinging up behind me. "We're not crazy, Caine, we're desperate."

Caine and Raine were climbing on to their horse; Glen snaked a strong arm around me and breathed, "Hold on."

He kneed the mount into a gallop, my back pressed against his wet chest, gone ridged with tension. I perceived Raine and Caine's horse keeping pace behind us as my nerves flew to the moon when we hurdled the creek, thundering toward the noise. We broke out on level land, romped a few paces, then skidded to a jerky halt, Glen holding me in the saddle as the steed danced, trying to rear.

The blare let loose once more. "Which way's it coming?"

Everyone searched from side to side; I saw it.

"There!" I yelped, pointing. All heads swiveled to the left.

The locomotive was just cresting a hill, black smoke billowing from its stack as it rumbled down the tracks. We were going to have to jump it.

"Glen." It wasn't a question.

"Lyn, do you-?"

"Yeah. Back up."

He pulled on the reins and the horse turned in place, hastening back to the shelter of the sparse trees. Raine fought with her mount as I watched, petrified by anxiety, Caine holding her tight with one arm while the other grabbed the bridal line. He yanked the frightened animal around and into our concealment.

"What's going on?" Raine asked, trembling a little in Caine's arm.

"Let me guess," Caine began.

"We jump the train," we said in unison. He looked at me, smirking, a quirky glint in his eye I couldn't place.

Raine seemed to panic more. "But Lyn I don't think I can make it."

She made me pause to consider.

In reality, none of us could. We were three scrawny, undernourished teenagers and an eleven-year-old girl. It sent my mind racing. We *had* to make it on the train or else chance getting captured again. "It's coming too fast. We won't be able to hang on, yet alone make it." Caine stated my thoughts.

My breath rushed out in frustration and worry.

"Wait, what about that hill?" I turned to where Glen was indicating, hopes kindled fiercely once more.

"That's it!" I exclaimed, "We keep going up until it hits the hill and slows. Then we jump on."

It made sense. When the locomotive started up the hill, it would loose momentum. We'd ditch the horses and grab ourselves a train. I smiled to myself. If only it was that easy.

"Glen, you think you can make the top of that hill before the train hits?"

I felt him shift and answer, "If you can hold on."

I grinned, bracing myself as we broke through the trees into a hard gallop for the rise, noise from the rails in hot pursuit behind. Come on, I thought feeling Dev's horse laboring for breath underneath me, just a little more. We crashed the slope, Glen squeezing the animal for all it was worth.

The motion was extremely uncomfortable. The horse would shoot forward in a lunge, slamming Glen up against me, then struggled to keep its back legs moving with it as I was thrown into him, all the while feeling the quaking of the tracks. It felt like riding thunder with the beats, booms, and racing pulses. Then, in less than a split second, we went down.

I let loose a cry of surprise when the animal buckled, crumpling to the ground and pitching Glen and I over its head. The dirt gave us a brutal welcome, knocking the air out of our lungs and the pep out of our step; we skidded to a burning stop. Oh no, I yelled to myself, we've lost it, we've lost our chance!

I tried to push up, but a sharp pain kept me in place. I couldn't breath. The rumbling was still there, but did not come as quickly, like it had just started up the rise.

"Lyn, Glen!" Raine dropped her reins and tumbled off the horse. Caine pounced off, rolling as he hit the ground, but coming up in a sprint for Glen.

"Lyn, what happened? Can you walk?" Raine's tiny hand slipped into mine and helped me to sit up. I sucked in little tidbits of hurtful air, shuddering from shock.

I glanced up and there was the train. We could make it. I just had to move.

"I can walk," I said, barely able to stand. "We've got to get to the train."

"Lyn, don't- okay." Raine second-guessed herself and helped me hurry to the boys who where almost at the train.

Caine glanced at us and yelled over the thunder of the rails. "Where are we getting on? We're almost outta cars!"

I looked up just in time to see a half-open boxcar pass in front of me.

"That one!" I shouted, forcing my throbbing legs to a fast hobble.

I could see it: a handle protruding from the door and a small step jutting out from under. I covered the last bit of ground with painful lunges, feeling the burden of running uphill, and jumped for it. My hands circled the latch, but my feet never found a purchase. I screamed in terror as I hung there, unable to pull myself up. "Help!"

I saw three forms enter the car out of the corner of my eye, heard the rolling thuds of each body when they hit. I just kept swinging, arms getting weaker by the second as the train picked up speed.

"The messes you get into, Lyn," Caine's voice. "I'd swear you *want* to meet death!"

I turned my head in his direction and he extended his hand. I stared at him like the boy was crazy, but when he shook his arm in frustration, I knew exactly what Caine wanted me to do. I braced myself both mentally and physically then reached for his hand. I shrieked as my body sunk lower to the tracks and he yelled, "Jump!"

This was insane! Caine yanked and I let go of the handle, swinging toward him. We collided and hit both Glen and Raine to keep from crashing to the floor, well, from *almost* crashing to the floor. They mainly took some heat off our impact when I landed in Caine's lap and he against some crates.

I stayed there for a moment, head resting on his heaving chest, one hand still locked with his, and with Caine's other arm draped over my back. He gave me a pat.

"Lyn, you crazy psycho..." He wheezed a laugh in at the end.

"Need some help?" Glen asked.

"She does, honestly," Caine replied, playfully tugging at my hair.

"You're the one who needs help, Caine," I said as Glen and I stood. "No sane person would know how to professionally jump trains."

He smirked and, assisted by Raine, got to his feet wincing.

"You pick up a few things here and there being a thief and all."

That was true, I thought. I certainly had learned things that never would have occurred to me when I had everything.

"So, Lyn," Caine began after having seated himself on some boxes. "What other secrets are you hiding from us?"

I didn't answer, only got that sick feeling in the pit of my stomach again. We weren't safe I knew that. Not even the sense of tracks rumbling underneath my feet and sound of the whistle could assure me.

"Lyn, don't worry," Raine said, taking my hand. I felt several rough calluses on her palm that should never be on any little girl's hand.

"It could help if you talked about it," Glen added.

I twisted my lips faintly.

"Well…" Everyone had his or her eyes trained on me. "I've just about told you everything important. Any thing you *want* to know?"

"Oh I can name a whole list," Caine commented. "So were you out walking around while we were penned? Going anywhere you wanted, doing anything?" His dark eyes narrowed shrewdly. "And what about all those *guys* hanging around you?"

"So you know, I *still* have my innocence in tact, and no, I wasn't able to roam around everywhere I wanted," I had to cut him off before the questioning got out of hand. "I did get to wander inside the fort, but never without someone watching my every move."

Caine looked as if he was going to ask something else, but Glen got there first. "Speaking of other people, who are some of the ones we should be worried about?"

I sat on Glen's question for a moment. "There's a lot. Some main ones are this red-head named Dev, Razor-"

"Whoa, you know their *names,* too?"

I glared at Caine. "Of course I know some names! I was around the savages for three days. Anyway, Dev's the one you saw at the gate, and Razor was the man with the knives that nearly killed us in prison. The other one is a man called Lieutenant. I don't know him as well, but I've heard he's like second-in-command, some prideful guy with gold hair and expensive clothes. You'd know the man when you saw him."

No one had spoken. They all just sat there with these strange looks on their faces. What on earth could they be thinking about me?

"And you learned all this while Glen and me were locked up and Raine was lost in the wilderness?"

I shifted my gaze to the floor, guilty. "Yeah."

"You attract trouble like light attracts moths, Lyn," Caine finished. It certainly did seem that way.

I nodded absently, feeling the full effect of exhaustion. It was suddenly difficult to move. The day was cloudy and dreary, making me even drowsier. Nobody made any noise so I guessed they were all half-asleep, too. Glen came over and wrapped an arm around my shoulders saying, "We can worry about all that later since we're beat down. Let's rest."

"Let's," I agreed, slipping down to the wooden floor and reclining back against crates.

I saw Caine slumped on top of boxes with his arms and legs dangling off. Raine strode over to us and curled up with her head situated on my lap, asleep as soon as she closed her eyes. Looking at Glen, I found he was dozing, as well. I stared; it was the first time I had actually noticed us getting older.

Light blonde stubble sprinkled Glen's chin and I suddenly realized he might not *be* sevnteen any more. Maybe he hadn't been in the first place. We didn't have time for birthdays and no need to know our age. I'd thought I was sixteen, but I honestly did not know any more. Whatever my age was, I shouldn't have been through what I had *already* been through in a lifetime.

Days are days, I thought. The world doesn't quit spinning because one person has it rough. No. It keeps going, oblivious to the awful things it throws us into.

Ch. 28 Destinations

Something bright was in front of me. I opened my eyes to narrow slits and lazily put a hand up to shield my vision from the radiant sun. There was noise to my left and movement. I turned my head, feeling my neck crack, to look at Glen.

"Good morning," I said, then put my hand up to my mouth. "Oh, sorry, it's not morning anymore is it?"

I saw him grin; Glen's smile was a little higher on the right, but that only accented his handsome features more.

"The day looks beautiful, but I'd rather be in here than out there walking in it."

I agreed. "How many miles do you think we've covered?"

"More than a couple week's worth of walking, that's for sure." I glanced at Caine as he slid off the boxes and landed, stretching.

"Hey," Raine mumbled from her position on the floor.

"Hi sleepyhead," I replied, stroking her hair.

"Do we have anything to eat?"

Of course she'd ask that. We *had* had food, but we ditched that luxury with the horses so we were back to starving.

"No, Raine, I don't think we do."

"Hold on, hold on!" Caine ordered, throwing up his arms. We all stared in expectation.

"We're thieves, right? People who take what they want? Look around," he swept the car with his gestures. "Just what we need."

It was full of crates, packed with who knew what. For once *I* was skeptic.

"Hey, genius, how are we going to open them?"

He gazed at me and smiled. "Remember back at the swap when you said, 'I owe you a knife'?"

I narrowed my eyes. "Yeah?"

Caine extended a hand. "Now's when you pay up."

I didn't know what he was planning, but I reached for Dev's belt I was wearing and drew his knife. I held it out and Caine took it.

"Thanks, Lyn."

We all watched him go over and ease the tip of the blade under one of the lids. He wiggled and rotated the dagger and a nail soon popped up. Caine got to work on the other corners and then the top was off.

"What the-? Clothes?"

We exchanged confused glances and went to peer in. Everyone but Caine was ecstatic.

"We can use these," I stated, pulling out a shirt and holding it up to myself. It was way too big, but it might fit Glen.

"Nice, Caine. Now go open the other boxes."

He huffed, but complied. "Yes, your Highness."

I rolled my eyes and kept going through the garments, eager to wear something besides my ripped blouse and baggy pants. Being a thief wasn't good for your conscience, but it sure came in handy in tight spots.

By the time everyone had changed, Caine had pried the lids off the boxes he could get his hands on. It wasn't much, but thankfully they were not all full of clothes. We all sat down to eat in our clean attire, feeling refreshed. It was amazing what fresh clothes and a little food could do for you.

The meal was mainly raw vegetables, dirt on and fresh from the field. There was some pork and beef jerky mixed in and the salt really helped the greens. I noticed the new clothes on us made everybody look as nice as we had in years.

Glen found himself a white shirt, open to where you could see part of his chest, a duster to go over it, and some dark, pocketed pants. Caine threw on a black collared shirt after having cut the collar out and trousers he had to tie a rope around to hold up. Raine dressed in a puffy-sleeved blouse that had loose thread hanging from the bottom with worn pants that came just past her knees. I decided on a lightweight top, trimmed in lace and that tied around the waist. The bonds dangled past my thighs, but it was about the only thing that didn't swallow me. Can't really say that about the pants, though; I copied Caine's 'rope belt' and miraculously, they stayed on.

I sat facing the open door, mesmerized as the landscape passed by. It was the hottest part of the day and prime time for nature's beauty to shine. There were flat plains, rolling green hills, and snow-caped mountains past all this. It was breathtaking.

Wildflowers sprinkled the ground and the breeze made the flowing grasses move in waves. The sky was a brilliant blue, disturbed only by white, fluffy clouds that made the whole canvas complete.

"Railroad travel's pretty sweet," Caine stated after finishing off the last of his meal. "You don't have to watch out for people, you don't have to drive... Just sit back and enjoy the scenery."

He paused then asked, "How long we going to be living the sweet-life?"

Fear settled in behind my breastbone, knowing the men could be there waiting when the train stopped. "We can't wait until it restocks at a station or town. The men could have already tracked our next stop."

"How are we going to avoid that?"

"Simple," Glen answered for me. "Whenever it starts slowing, we stick our heads out. If we see a town, get off."

"While it's going fast?" Raine questioned, eyes a little wide.

"Don't worry," I assured. "It will be going slower, promise. Why don't we go west from there?"

Glen gave me a funny look, smirking slightly. "Lyn, we've *been* heading west for months."

"What?" I replied stupidly.

"I read the stars," Glen explained. "Little trick I taught myself when I traveled alone."

I smiled, ending the conversation before anyone thought to ask why I was so determined to go west. Turning away, I gazed back out at the ever-changing scenery. I could hear Glen and Caine conversing in the background, saying something about knowing how to tell where you're at.

"Hey Lyn." I looked at Raine as she came to sit beside me.

"You know, Raine," I began, a faint smile on my lips. "I wonder sometimes where we'll end up."

She nodded, eyes tracing a bird skirting the ground. "Yeah, me too."

Raine paused. "But as long as we're with each other I don't care because I know, in the end, everything's going to be fine."

I managed a movement of my head in reply, but felt myself drifting, endless thoughts pestering me. Closing my eyes, I could still see the picturesque setting before me. 'Everything's going to be fine.' Really, I thought, it's that simple?

I didn't think on it too long, I was very tired so I let the sweet wind put me to sleep...

Dusk. I knew before even glimpsing it. Why had I slept so long? I forced my eyes open, clawing at the sleep in them as I pushed myself to a sitting position. The scene I was greeted by was much more peaceful than I had expected.

Raine and Glen were slumped on crates, napping. Caine was standing at the open door, gazing out at the beautiful sunset over the mountains. Not knowing why I was so jittery, I rose quietly, trying to make as little noise as possible, and went to join Caine at the entrance. He cut his eyes to glance at me; they were very dark, but the fading sun reflected off them like fire.

"You're up unexpectedly silent."

I colored a bit.

"Why aren't you sleeping?" I asked. He shrugged, hair gently moved by the breeze to where I could see his severe and angled profile.

"Couldn't. Too excited to know when we're getting off. Why are you awake?"

I figured telling him I thought we were in danger would be a silly reason so I said, "Same reason you are except I can't wait until we stop."

Caine smirked, that smile of his just as charming as ever.

We both stared out; I did not see wilderness anymore, but farmland. Rows of crops were prominent and barns with silos were common. The sights made my pulse race. This was not good. It meant our 'excitement' about getting off might happen sooner than anticipated.

"Caine, grab on to me," I instructed, waltzing over to the edge of the door.

"Whoa, Lyn, hold on!" He snatched my arm and I twisted to meet him, a small grin passing my lips.

"Calm down. I'm only going to lean out so I can see in front of us instead of the side view."

Caine looked at me, uncertainty wrinkling his brow. "And you want me to sling you out over moving tracks so you can?"

"Yes," I answered, matter-of-factly.

He huffed and shook his head, but looped an arm around my waist, holding my hand with his other. It almost felt like we were about to dance instead of lean out of a train.

"What'd you see?" Cain asked after my head was past the door. Oh no. This was bad, *really* bad.

There was a good-sized town straight ahead and the train was slowing down, no doubt about to stop. So my instinct wasn't crazy, I was jumpy for a reason.

"Caine!" He pulled me back suddenly, stunned by my tone of voice.

"What's going on?"

"Wake Glen and Raine. We're out of here!"

He shook them both full awake and I herded everyone to the door.

"Jump!" I exclaimed, bunching up and releasing.

"Bam!" I hit the ground and rolled, curled up to avoid as much injury as possible. The roaring noise of the locomotive thundered by, earth trembling under its force. I did not move until the sound of wheels scraping the tracks quieted.

When I stirred, every bone in my body seemed to crack. I grimaced and sat up shuddering, waiting for the pain to subdue. Swiftly surveying the spot we landed in, I was quite relieved to find us safely by the tracks, concealed from prying eyes by tall grasses. Still, it felt like something was there... Light! I could see a glow in the distance that didn't come from the town.

Oh, was I happy at first, then another thought crossed my meddling mind. My father's men, camped and ready to ambush this town we would have pulled into. I bit my tongue, thinking I had just cost these innocents their lives. "Lyn?"

Glen's voice made me start and face him. How the boy had managed to crawl beside my body without me noticing was a mystery.

"What are you staring at?"

I tipped my head in the direction of the radiance, "That."

"So I'm not imagining it either," Caine said, inching in alongside us with Raine right by him.

"You don't think it's the men do you?"

"Wouldn't they be closer if the train's pulling in?" Glen asked. "I would already be attacking if I were them since they would have full control of the thing."

He made a good point. I eased back a little.

"Then who or what do you think it is?"

"How about instead of lying here talking about it we go see for ourselves?" Raine covered a giggle at Caine's distinctive cynicism.

I rolled my eyes. He was right, though, staying here discussing the light was going to help us no more than staying on the train would have.

We all got up and started moving, always checking behind our backs for signs of the savages in pursuit.

"Stay down!" Caine whispered as loud as he dared. We were on our stomachs, peaking through the tall, useful grass.

People had set up a small camp on the outskirts of the town; we had seen the glow from their fire. That could have been a good or bad sign. Good in thinking these people were not very smart in concealing themselves, but bad since the openness they left could mean they weren't afraid of attackers.

"I don't think its-"

"Shhh! Look." After Raine quieted, we focused.

A woman stepped into view, clothed in gorgeous fabrics and decorated with colorful beads. We watched her, holding our breath, until she disappeared inside a tent. Had women from the fort been dressed like that? No, but... there was a man! I stopped my motion of rising and froze, locked on his face. He caught me in the act of staring, but seemed more surprised than I.

Run! I blinked and spun, making a mad scramble backwards before the man called for his buddies. I barely heard the mumblings from my party as I withdrew from our protection. After my first few lunges, I collided with *another* man, hammering us both down into the dirt.

I was out of it for a second, but that wasted second was all this guy needed to grab me. (After all, I *had* been dumb enough to fall on him).The commotion behind me hinted the man who ~~that~~ spotted me first had called for help and had his friends waylay everybody who was with me.

I struggled and beat my captor on the chest, but none of it fazed him. Not going out without a fight, I jerked my head back and slammed him square in the face. It stunned the guy, but the only problem was it stunned me more. In that dizzied moment, the man had quit the easy arrest and gotten angry. He worked his fingers tightly into my hair, painfully yanking my head away, then rolled to where he was on top of me, pinning me roughly into solid earth. It gave me a sliver of satisfaction to see his nose dripping blood.

"Take it easy and you won't get hurt," he said as the man hauled me to my feet. "Try another dirty move like that and you'll be under before you can bat and eyelid."

I sprung forward, knowing it would only make his grip stiffen more. "I'd like to see you try."

"Watch me," he growled. I smiled, liking this one already.

We ended up at the large tent the elaborate woman had entered; three others detained Caine, Glen, and Raine and they shoved each of us in. My man spoke.

"Madam Castella, we brought a few visitors to see you."

I listened to a rustle of cloth and out from behind a flap of curtain stepped the ornate woman. Her glossy black hair hung straight, flowing past her hips and woven with gems. She was dressed in a vibrant scarf gown that had beads dangling off the bottom, waist, and sleeves and had some of her thick hair stuffed in a bandanna.

"Visitors? At this hour?" Her voice was coarse and rough, but she sounded more amused than surprised, as the woman looked us over, a smile playing across her red lips. "Why, they're only children," she said, gesturing at us, bangles clinking as she moved.

"We ain't kids," Caine cut back. My heart sped *sped* after he addressed Castella with that arrogant tone. It was one thing to mess with the guards, but when you started insulting a power position... Let's just say things don't go as smoothly.

"Well, what else can you be, boy?" She still seemed calm and unfazed. What was this woman playing at? Instinct warned me we could be up against someone tricky.

"Castella, was it?"

She looked at Glen sharply. "That's *Madam* Castella to you, child."

Glen's features hardened, but he cooperated. "Listen, *Madam* Castella, we're passing through like the drifters we are, and mean no harm whatsoever so why don't you let us go and we'll be on our way."

He paused, a daring glint in his eyes. "Sorry to bother you, but we've already wasted enough time here."

I bit my lip as Castella's sly grin grew wider. "Are you scared, boy?"

Glen's eyes narrowed and his fists balled up. The man who was holding him tensed; I felt my chance to intercede.

"Who *are* you people?" I asked, hoping to redirect the conversation.

The woman glared at Glen for another moment then her dark gaze lingered on me as she answered. "Gypsies."

I was speechless.

"Gypsies?" Caine clearly wasn't. "Heard gypsies are good thieves."

Castella chuckled, shaking her beaded head. "That's a misconception. Gypsies are merely travelers borrowing what we need along the way. What made you think us thieves?"

Caine's smile surfaced, pride all over his face. "Justa rumor I heard once. But, like I said, only a rumor. It's obvious you guys aren't any better than me." I gaped at his insolence. Did I really just hear that? To my astonishment, the woman started laughing, her great hoop earrings tinkling softly.

"Oh really? Since I don't believe you, you'll have to show me your skills in the next town we come across. Besides, you will owe us for taking care of you children."

She's plotting something, I thought, this woman's smarter than she is letting on. I held back a grimace when Caine agreed to her terms.

"Do we get no say in this?"

Castella faked perplexity saying, "Darling, you had a chance to speak, but I'm afraid it's passed. You work for me now."

I nearly exploded, but the man's grip on me kept me under control.

"Garcia, show our guests to one of the empty tents. I'm going to catch some sleep before we haul out."

She drew up her skirts, but paused to stop us one more time. "I'll be seeing you children later."

Ch. 29 Strangers

We were escorted to a large tent towards the outside of the camp. The guards let everyone go, but Garcia held me until they had entered. When he released me, I didn't move; the delicious concept of running took over my mind.

"Don't worry," Garcia whispered. "We'll be out here all night."

What he really meant was he would be monitoring the tent so none of us would make a break for it. I gave him a look, getting the point across that I got his underlying message before I slipped in after my party.

The inside was dimly lit by an oil lamp in the middle and somewhat cozy. Even with all this I did not feel calm.

"It's not as bad as I expected," Caine stated, striding to a spot beside the lamp and sitting. I unfroze myself and went over, too.

"Kind of nice to have a roof over our heads." I glanced at Raine. It was the first thing I had heard her say since we got off the train. She must be all shaken up from this.

"I don't feel it," Glen commented as he plopped down by me. "Castella doesn't seem like she can be trusted. I'm not going to sleep good until we leave."

"We're a lot better off than we were."

This time. Raine pitched in with Caine. "Yeah, they said they would take care of us, *feed* us."

And give us a place to stay. All too good to be true.

"It could be a way to win us over," I reasoned.

"We're already supposed to help them out for all this," Caine began. "Do a little work and get paid. Nothing to it."

"They're using us," Glen said. He was right, in my opinion.

"Well, maybe they are," Caine mumbled. "But it sure doesn't feel too bad being used like this."

With that voiced, he eased back, apparently determined to sleep some of this excitement off. *good!* Raine lay down, too, and Glen and I figured it wouldn't be so bad to catch some shut-eye. We reclined on our sides, facing each other. He lifted a corner of his mouth, but the anxiety was much too plain of his face.

"The one time I'm *supposed* to sleep sound, I can't."

I smiled sadly, wishing there were something I could do to cheer him. I rested my forehead against his and Glen opened his eyes. Looking into them, I noticed they were a shade darker tonight, glistening, still swimming in blue. The color reminded me of how they were in the swamp and I impulsively asked, "How is you scar?"

His hand instinctively touched it, but he acted as if the movement were only putting an arm around me. "I barely feel it anymore. I still can't believe I'm alive when I see the thing. It looks awful."

Glen smirked in a perplexed way. "You never will forget it either."

I could believe that. A grin surfaced after I yawned; the pleasant feel of Glen next to me and homely tent had actually led me to exhaustion. He could tell I was tired and cradled my head under his chin saying, "I'll see you in the morning."

I couldn't even manage a good night.

I awoke to the steady din of voices outside the tent. No dreams so Glen still had his arms around me and chin over my head. Light filtered in through the door flap and cracks in the bottom of the shelter.

"Glen."

After I said his name, he jumped, opening his eyes swiftly.

"What's going on?" He asked, extracting himself from me and sitting up.

"Nothing," I assured, rising. "Well, nothing life-threatening like usual."

Sudden laughter from beyond us caught my attention. I glanced at Caine and Raine's spot on the floor: empty. They hadn't woken us up.

Feeling put-off, I helped Glen to his feet and pushed open the door. Early morning light blinded me momentarily, but I soon focused on three figures. One of them was Caine, the other Raine, but the stranger was new to me. It was a woman, I noticed as Glen and I drew nearer to her. She must be the cook since she was passing out steaming bowls of food. Woman sure did have a mouth on her. She became aware of us and turned, flashing a wide grin.

"Hello," I said, smiling hesitantly.

"Why hello, dears. I've been speaking with your sweet friends here. Have you traveled together?" The woman spoke quickly with a slight accent, smile never wavering from her plump face.

"Uh, yes, for a while. Who are you?"

The woman's surprisingly tiny hands flew to her mouth. "Look at me! I'm sorry, dear; I've forgotten my manners. My name is Hona the head cook around here."

Hona handed Raine and Caine bowls of what I believed to be porridge. She reached out and patted my cheek, 'tsking.'

"Thin as a rail. Pretty little thing like you needs some more meat on those bones. Sit tight, I'll be right back!" With that, Hona rushed off, leaving me with the impression of a busy woman who could do with a break.

"'Sweet friends' huh? I can understand Raine, but I'm scared to ask what you said to her to make Hona think that about you, Caine."

He swallowed the mush and raised an eyebrow at me. "Come on, Lyn. Don't think I'm 'sweet'? You know it's the smile that gets 'em."
Of course he showed it off for me.

"Don't worry, you'll have us thrown out by the time this is over," Glen countered. "Food any good?"

"It's terrible!" He nudged Raine. "Right, Raine?"

She giggled and nodded, not doing well at keeping a straight face.

"They probably poured some dirt on it for you," I said, smirking. Caine returned my grin, about to say something, but Hona came back, shoving the smoking bowls into Glen and my hands.

"Enjoy!" And she was off again.

I stared at the porridge in the container. It didn't smell bad, bland mostly, but the stuff looked very unappetizing.

"I think they spit in yours," Caine remarked. He really shouldn't say that since they could have spit in this and you would never know by glancing at it.

"I think Lyn thought it was going to be a first-class meal like she'd been getting, not the normal stuff," Glen joked.

"Shut up," I mumbled, blushing and stuffing a spoonful in my mouth. It was surprisingly warm, salty, and had a gooey texture. I was pleased to find, after I finished, that I felt quite full and satisfied. While everyone talked amongst ~~himself or herself~~ Themselves, I sat back, surveying the group we had mixed up with.

There were scraggly men packing and lifting boxes into caravans that were covered and horse-drawn. Their garments were not as colorful as the women, but you could still tell they were gypsies by their dark skin and hair, bandannas and beads. Women were sprinkled in here and here, vivid-colored dresses flashing and arms covered in bracelets. Children even dashed about, oldest looking to be our age and ranging to an infant in its mother's arms. They certainly did seem to be in a hurry loading up, though. Like the people were afraid of something...

I pushed the thought out of my mind, realizing it was a very small group, no more than fifteen in all, and compared to my father's savages, realized he would have no trouble taking every last one of them down.

"What are those guys staring at?" Caine's accusing voice brought me back from my repose. I turned to see four children looking right at us. Two were our age; one was likely around eight, and the other six or seven.

"Hey!" Raine's sudden outburst made us jump and the kids' blink. They came over.

"Are you four new?" The oldest girl asked.

"We're not staying," I began. "Just doing what we can to help this good cause out."

She smiled, picking out my sarcasm, and tossed her thick, curly black hair back, exposing a very round face. "Well aren't you guys the odd ones. No one in their right mind helps us gypsies. Less they got a debt to pay."

"Why do you need to know why we're here so badly?" Glen pried. The girl shifted her dark gaze to him; it lingered a little longer than necessary.

"Just curious is all. Anyway, my name's Layla," she pointed to the boy beside her, still focused on Glen. "This is my brother, Lamar."

Lamar grinned shyly, running bony fingers through his short hair.

"And this is-"

"Angelo," the eight-year-old finished. He seemed short for his age and very dark, like he'd stayed out in the sun too long. Angelo elbowed the youngest boy who shot him a nasty look then kept glaring at us. This boy seemed the most unfriendly and unusual.

The boy had light skin and blonde hair that looked like it had been dyed brown once. Instead of sorrel or copper eyes, he had sea green painting his irises. He noticed my observations and glowered at me before spinning and stomping off the other way.

"Ike, wait!" Angelo yelped, chasing after him. I saw Layla sigh.

"That's Ike," she explained. "He's 'adopted' as we like to call it. We found him abandoned on the side of a road one day and Castella took him in so he's been with us ever since."

I was wondering why he seemed so spiteful, but after hearing *Castella* took him in, understood. Speak of the devil, I thought, spying the woman waltzing our way. Maybe it was just bad judgment, but I was not fond of the her.

Lamar noted my attention and twisted, startled to find Castella right behind him.

"M-Madam Castella," he stuttered, bowing his head and making some kind of sign with his hands. "It's a pleasure to see you this morning, mam."

Layla followed her brother's movements a moment later. Castella smiled, that deceptive twist of her lips, and nodded to the siblings.

"And a very good morning it is," for the first time, she took notice of us. "I see you've found our new guests."

"Uh, yes," Layla answered. "We were just about to show them around."

Castella clasp her hands together and said, "Good, but I desire a word with these two." She tilted her head in our direction.

"But do show the others around. They'll catch up."

Castella's little order, no matter how nonchalant she made it sound, put me on edge. Why did she want to speak with only Glen and me?

"Of course, Madam," Layla replied, ushering Caine and Raine away, after a lasting glance at Glen. Lamar dipped his head to me and went with his sister.

I cut my eyes at Glen; he was watching Caine and Raine leave.

"So," Castella began, walking on, apparently presuming we would follow. "I trust you had a restful night?"

Glen and I quickened our pace to catch up.

"It was... a change from sleeping in the dirt," was all I could spit out without allowing doubt enter my voice.

Castella swept me with her dark chocolate eyes, knowing she was up against someone as manipulative as she. "Surely it was preferable to where you've been sleeping."

I was about to object, but she kept going, strolling by a cluster of strong men packing valuables into covered wagons.

"Anyway, let's get to the point shall we?"

I instinctively became defensive; Glen stayed silent, striding nosily to the right of Castella.

"I see your other friends have settled in nicely, but I couldn't help but notice that you two seem... detached."

I knew this was coming. Thankfully, Glen played for us.

"Detached?" He repeated. "What makes you say that? We've only been here a night."

Castella huffed a laugh. "Please don't play dumb with me. It's obvious how both of you feel. Just look at how closed off you are now."

I liked this woman less and less.

"Listen," she stopped and spun to face us, jewelry clinking with her movements. "We're moving away from this town, heading west to toy with luck. Our place to restock is called Jerome. That's where your *talents* come in."

I was quiet, mind considering all different scenarios, good and bad.

"Think of it as shadowing, improving your skills," she reasoned.

"Madam Castella," said a gruff, middle-aged man. Castella turned, annoyance unmasked but covered fast.

"Good morning, Belvin. You desire my attention?"

While she was distracted, Glen and I conspired together.

"What do you think?" I asked, searching his blue eyes for reassurance. His face was impassive.

"We already know Caine and Raine's choice."

They were not going to leave I knew that.

"She's baiting us, you know." I nodded, smiling sadly. "It's tempting." The woman was devious in scheming. " I don't want to stay, but-"

"You don't want to leave Caine and Raine either, right?"

I shut my eyes, exhaling heavily. Glen had hit the nail on the head. He placed his hands on my shoulders and I opened, locking gazes.

"I'm not going to leave you, Lyn. It isn't like I have anywhere better to go."

"I know that."

"Good," he said, that cute curve to his lips coming out. "Just making sure you didn't forget, whatever you decide."

"Mind telling what all that whispering was about?" Castella's voice made me jump; caught in the act.

"We're going to stay," Glen made up for my silence. "For now."

The woman broke out into a wide grin. "Good. Very good," she swept up her colorful skirts. "I'm needed elsewhere so I'll leave you two to get about your business."

With that, she left, moving around camp with her commanding air. Alright Raine and Caine, I thought, leaning on Glen, we are going to try this out.

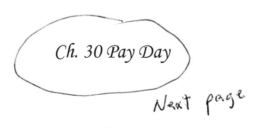

Ch. 30 Pay Day

Next page

Two weeks went by in a flash. There were days when I felt at home, like I belonged, and then I would come to my senses realizing these people were complete strangers. The whole thing was hard to believe. It was the first time in forever that we were around other humans not trying to kill us.

We became friendly with the four gypsy children. Layla was very outgoing with her mass of curly black hair and circular face; I didn't doubt she had a fondness for Glen. Lamar was quieter than his sister, but kind-hearted toward all of us, especially me. Angelo acted as our tour guide, quite knowledgeable about his camp. Ike, on the other hand, was not sociable or particularly nice. The strange boy seemed to avoid us every chance he got.

I have to say that the gypsies were one of the most unique groups we had ever been tangled up with. The people ranged from dazzling lady dancers and magicians, to men that put on shows with fire and swallowed swords. The sights and diverseness *almost* made me forget where I was. But when someone returned my smile with a glare or didn't acknowledge me, I was abruptly reminded we did not belong. All of us were outsiders, more mouths to feed, not family.

Caine and Raine seemed to be growing apart from Glen and me everyday. Caine acted like he never saw the disdainful sneers or heard the rumors about us. Raine appeared to thoroughly enjoy these people, but she was treated with what had to be forced kindness and sympathy. They were the only reason we were here.

"Glen, do you enjoy being with these people?" I had asked him one night when we were alone.

He exhaled, staring up at the moon. "I want to, Lyn, honestly. I just can't shake the feeling we're being played. Do you like being here?"

I shook my head.

"Not at all. Castella doesn't seem trustworthy and everyone else treats us with... I don't know, forced hospitality. Even Layla and the others are closed off at times. And you see how Caine and Raine are getting." An edge crept into my voice. "They don't see any of it."

"We can leave, you know. It'd be like old times before we met Caine or Raine." Glen had gazed out at the open landscape so longingly as he said this I nearly agreed to split then and there. He was right; nothing but ourselves was holding us back from simply walking away and not looking back. That was one reason why I liked Glen so much, he never committed to anything unless it would benefit one of us. That and he could always state the truth.

"We need to stay, see how the whole offer thing come out."

He had smiled, that pitying, sad smile. "I knew you'd say that."

I reconsidered. "But we can go if you want to."

Glen laughed, looping an arm around me so I could rest my head on his shoulder. "We'll stay, Lyn, don't worry."

He knew as well as I if we left Caine and Raine we would never get over the thought of what could have happened to them. So we stayed, for the next week. Then came the raid.

It was the afternoon of the robbery and the kids were briefing us while we hid out in one of the horse-drawn carts.

"Alright, newbies," Layla instructed. "This isn't like pick pocketing one easy target."

I bit my tongue, holding back a smart reply. Layla wasn't the best person to be briefed by. I exchanged glances with Caine, knowing he was doing the same.

"Yeah, you guys just do what we say and you'll be fine."

Layla rolled her eyes at Angelo and Lamar finally spoke up. "It's not as bad as they make it sound. Stay with your group and you'll make it."

"Group?" Raine repeated. "Will we be together?"

"Who knows," Ike sneered. "I'll probably get stuck with you." He said this with unrestrained distaste, but it was a step up from glaring all the time.

"Who divides us up?"

"Madam Castella."

I did my best concealing my grimace. Ever since I met the woman, I'd had a strong dislike for her, somehow knowing she was never up to any good. Though I will admit she hid it well behind fake smiles and carefully picked words. The flap to the wagon's entrance was slung open and we all jumped. A stick-thin woman gestured angrily at us.

"There you are! Come on everybody's waiting."

Ike was the first to raise, an evil grin plastered on his face. "Now's when things get interesting."

The other three left without another word. Before Caine got out after Glen and Raine, I snatched his arm.

"What?"

"Remember what we're here for," I said.

He smirked, removing my hand. "*You* don't get yourself knocked out. This is a big group so there's bound to be stragglers."

"Is that concern I hear?" I teased to see if he was still all there.

"Am I really that bad?" He asked, helping me down. Boy was I glad whenever I glimpsed that old twinkle in his eye.

Layla waved us over to a large group gathered around Castella and two male guards. This must be the entire gypsy camp, I thought. No more than fifteen people at most and they were all listening to the woman, displayed in her colorful finery, boost moral.

"As many of you are aware of, we will be having some fun tonight."

A few whoops of enjoyment came from the crowd. Castella only smiled.

"There are certain items I would advise you to keep an eye out for. Hona would appreciate cooking supplies and *I* would be tremendously pleased by jewels, coins, and whatnot." People snickered at her comment, elbowing and likely betting who could win the most favor with the boss.

Castella raised her hands for quiet. "The ones I have spoken with, you know who you are, need to gather now."

Everyone began to move and I glanced around in confusion until feeling a tug in my arm. I turned, expecting Glen, but it was Lamar that towed me to a small gathering. My friends had disappeared. I cursed Castella because I knew the woman had split us like this.

We paused with a group of five, Garcia, of course, was the leader. My scorn for Castella burned even hotter. He was dressed in a dark wrap shirt and tattered pants with a bandanna around his neck. He took notice of us.

"How nice of you two to join us," Garcia said sarcastically, gaze lingering on me, no doubt remembering the bloody nose I gave him. "Watch this one, Lamar, she's nothing but trouble."

I couldn't keep the smirk off my face; Garcia snorted and shook his head. Out of all the gypsies, I had a strange connection with him the most. I guess I liked his personality.

"Nothing to worry about, Garcia," I began. "You watch your back and I'll watch mine."

He half-smiled and walked off, giving orders to the others in line.

"What are we doing?" I asked Lamar.

"Grouping."

"Grouping?"

"Yeah," he explained. "Like military formations or something. Our group's-"

He stopped; we were moving. "Hold on."

Lamar guided me in with the pack Garcia was piloting. My heart accelerated as we merged and everyone seemed excited and tense.

"Just stick close to me. I'll tell you what to do."

I simply nodded, moving towards the town, wondering if Glen, Caine, and Raine were as nervous as I was. The sudden impulse to see them set me looking, but all I was met with were dark faces frowning at me. Please stay safe, I prayed. Things were about to get crazy.

We were approaching town. The sun had gone and we were enveloped in darkness. Only several yards to go and we would hit Jerome. I had not seen Glen, Caine, or Raine since the caravan and my anxiety had grown to bursting. Lamar was the only one keeping me with these people.

I tried making out others I recognized in the front, but it was too dark. No moon shone in the sky so that only heightened the black, but that was good; we had more cover for the raid. Everyone slowed and I watched them disperse to the right, left, back, and straight up front. Lord, we were up next. I didn't care how much Caine and Raine wanted to stay; Castella had crossed the line, throwing us into this mess. The woman was at the back, the safest position there was.

"Lyn, we're moving," Lamar yelped, dragging me out of my bitter mindset. He pulled me around the wall. Were we going in a side entrance?

We bypassed the edge completely while the rest of Garcia's group went in and were met with an ivy-covered wall. I looked over at Lamar to see if he was planning what I thought he was. The boy tugged on the vine a few times then motioned for me. "Come on, I'll give you a leg up."

I hesitated. Climbing a wall wrapped in plants was not my cup of tea.

"Come on," he repeated.

I figured I had no choice so I stepped up and he cupped his hands together.

"You ever climbed vine before?"

I shook my head.

"All you gotta do is-" he grunted, lifting me. "Grab a branch!"

I lurched forward and snagged a whole cluster of green, flattening against the wall.

"I can't... Find a foothold!" I yelled, tearing limbs and leaves off the side, dangling in frustration.

"Lyn, be quiet!" He whispered. Lamar grabbed a handful of my shirt and tugged, making me yelp in pain.

"Stop it!" The pressure released and I listened to him sigh. Faint scrambling touched my ear and I craned my neck to see him disappear over the edge. I went off.

Fuming, I stuffed my feet into the vine and slung my arms up to snatch another cluster of branches. I scaled the wall in a rage, planning to take what I wanted, grab Glen, and leave. I was sick of these people, this raid, this whole situation we never should have gotten into. Upon reaching the top, I paused, realizing how badly I was shaking. I based the observation on the fact that I was hungry and not because I was jumpy.

Glancing out, I could see silent shadows drifting in between houses and shops. For a fleeting moment, I felt like part of the gypsies: drifters living on the move, getting close to people, then turning around and stealing their treasures. And in Castella's case, using every being she could get her claws around.

I'd show them how things were *really* done. Creeping forward, I tried to recall my street skills from Glen and thieving techniques from Caine. Spying a train station in the distance, I slunk to it, but froze mid-way hearing voices from the deck. My adrenaline kicked in and I dashed for the wooden overhang, diving under it, scooting as close to the panels as I could. The voices had ceased in my sprint for cover and footsteps took their empty place. I was praying hard that no one found me eavesdropping when, over the sound of crickets, I caught someone speak.

"Did you hear that?"

My stomach contracted in such vigor; I believed I was about to vomit. The footsteps stopped right above my head; all they had to do was glance over...

"C'mon, sir, that deep listenin' in cards got ya all jittery."

I passed out for a split second after I put *that* voice with a face. The comment back confirmed it.

"Shut up, Dev! You're the one who caused this whole mess with Brogen."

"Lieutenant, listen-" There was a sharp turn and rough jerking to choke Dev's words off.

"The dead don't speak. I've heard you're miserable excuses for letting her get away. You're a lucky fool since Brogen's decided to keep you alive this long, but since you've already made all your defenses, maybe he'll shoot you instead of stringing up your sorry neck."

A yelp and barely perceivable whispering followed.

"You're a corpse, Dev. Even if you find that girl your life's already been decided." It sounded like Lieutenant shoved Dev to the floor. "I only hope I'm the one who gets to do the honors."

A rustle of clothing then receding footsteps told me Lieutenant was gone. Why was Dev still here? I was paralyzed, having trouble breathing normally, and shaking uncontrollably.

"Why, girlie, why'd you do this to me?" I felt sick, too ill with fear to check if he was actually speaking to me. "I'm gonna die because of you, sweetie."

He chuckled sadly. "But I hope I'll get to see the look on your pretty face one more time before I bite the dust."

I was not breathing or blinking, my heart throbbed so hard it hurt as I listened to Dev's boots thud away. I finally released my held air, very weak in the knees. ~~Laying~~ *Lying* there, breathing in the fumes of the dirt and watching the stars twinkle made me wish I ~~was~~ *were* here by my own will, not the force of the looters that called themselves gypsies.

They were still searching for me. I knew my father would never give up that easily but I had not expected him to keep such a tight trail on us. I mean the man had beaten us to town! I could not believe the force he moved with, the secrecy he tracked with and the atrociousness he attacked with. Somewhere deep down, I felt a pang of guilt for Dev's predicament. I had killed him, not literally, of course, but I might as well have. It seemed he was treated like the scum of the earth now that I had gotten away by using the man.

I wondered if this 'Brogen' character was someone I should be concerned about, but I figured I would find out sooner or later so I inched my way out of my hidey-hole and stood, stooped low, not wanting to be too obvious. I took a few steps and my knees quaked worse with each one. There was no way I was going to steal something tonight. But it wasn't like I could back out after coming this far.

I need higher ground, I thought, sweeping the area with my gaze. The sight of an old, abandoned clock tower became my target. Now came the issue of reaching it. Maybe if I walked it wouldn't look so suspicious.

Moving, I found, was strenuous. I felt like jelly, barely keeping my form and about to melt with any sudden surprise. It was the first time today I realized I was hungry, famished even. The encounter with old enemies had utterly drained every ounce of my strength. The shadows moved and rippled between the buildings; I shied away from more than a few. There was one outline that stayed right with me no matter which way I turned. It passed too close for comfort and I jarred myself into a mad dash to the tower.

Blood roared in my ears and my adrenaline became my last resort after I barreled through the stairwell door and started tackling the steps. I bit my tongue to keep from screaming as I went down on hands and knees, my foot having caught on one of the stairs. Still, I kept going, finally dragging myself to a spot where I had a nice view of the town in silent turmoil below. My eyes traced their shadowy movements like an owl would a mouse.

The gypsies would climb rooftops, conceal themselves in bushes, and pass sacksful of loot off to collectors who were stockpiling it. Lamar had been right, it was like cleverly executed military maneuvers. These people worked as if they were well-oiled machines.

Despite all the hype and talk about the raid I knew, deep down, this was wrong. Stealing what you needed from a few was how the poor stayed alive, but taking anything you *wanted* was a different matter. We were robbing a whole town and, somewhere in my long-lost conscience, I wondered if there could be consequences later because of this. I sighed, focusing instead on a figure I recognized below: Garcia. The man looked as if he had just made a nice fortune for Castella, toting a full bag with him through a window. A fast-moving shape caught my eye. No thief should ever move that quickly unless he was trying to outrun trouble.

It sprinted toward the gypsy and I half-stood, expecting a hectic getaway cry from him. I watched, stunned, as Garcia turned and screamed when the other man connected. The shadow drew back, staring as the gypsy crumpled to his knees, hugging his side tightly.

The silhouettes had stopped moving upon hearing the shriek: all but one brave soul. I was probably the only person ~~that~~ who saw it. Another gypsy materialized out of the black behind the man with the knife. This one had some kind of weapon too because he rammed it into the man's back, covering his mouth with his free hand to muffle the guy's last cry of pain. He dropped to the street in a heap, making no effort to catch himself so I assumed he was dead. The gypsy ~~that~~ who killed the other man helped Garcia to his feet.

I could do nothing but watch events happen. A boy I thought was Angelo burst into the street, saw

Garcia, spun back around, and darted to get the word out we were leaving. Gypsies hunkered over their goods and got out of there while the more considerate ones helped Garcia walk. I wanted to lend a hand too, but when I saw everyone's loot, decided against it. What would they think whenever they saw me bring back nothing?

This was bad. It had turned into our worse case scenario in a matter of seconds. The town was soon to wake and my father's men may still be here. I roused myself and trotted down the stairs, but paused in the exit, letting the shadow from the wall conceal me from the other's view. *Everybody* had something. Everybody, except me.

It was too late to rob houses now, I'd get left behind, but what would happen when I came back with nothing? I could offer my earring. The stupid thing had caused me so many problems, yet I knew giving it away was something I just couldn't do. The only thing that lightened my mood was the sight of Caine at the back, carrying a bag full of who-knew-what that was bigger than I was, smirking, looking like the cat that swallowed the canary.

In the end, I choose to wait until the last left then show up late, making them think I had either

398

been held up or lost my spoils. The group had moved pretty swiftly and I soon watched the last of them disappear through the front gate. Getting to my feet, I planned to follow, but a mummer of voices made me cease. Townspeople were waking and had noticed the slaughter in the street. I struggled to listen in on the commotion.

"Oh, Lord... Someone go get the chief!" There came a rising burble from the crowd until another man rose above, quelling the sound.

"My son!" He wailed. "They killed my son, stole my valuables, hurt my people!"

My blood turned icy cold. We didn't murder some poor beggar brave enough to attack a thief, but one who held power.

"Make them pay!" The gathering chanted.

"Grab your weapons, men! We shall have revenge if it's the last thing we do."

Enough was enough; I ran.

Ch. 31 Bad Choices

I bolted into the gypsy camp through the back entrance, weaving past tents and arrogant crowds toward Castella's voice. Panting heavily from my sprint, I slowed to survey the proceedings for a moment. Castella had them all lined up; one would display their findings while the woman inspected it. I could already see other lavish offerings she'd taken before I arrived adorning her clothes and body. The man that was up offered bronze and turquoise jewelry and Castella dug her greedy fingers in it, pulling out dazzling copper-colored and stone inlayed bangles. The witch slipped them on her garlanded wrists and waved him on.

It made me furious.

"Hey, newbie," Layla said, cuffing me on the shoulder. "You showed Madam Castella your goods yet?"

I rubbed the spot she'd hit and shook my head. "No and I don't intend to."

There was no way I was letting Castella make me look a fool in front of the others for not presenting anything. Layla raised an eyebrow in warning. "You got to. And don't think she's lettin' you off 'cause you're *guests.*" She grinned meanly. "Your boy didn't cover for you, Lyn."

By that she had to mean Glen.

"He never needed to," I replied. Layla was by no means my favorite person and she sure wasn't trying to get on my good side.

"You're gonna be in serious trouble. No one says no to Castella, newbie." She turned to walk away. "Good luck. You'll wish you had it."

I narrowed my eyes, but did not press the argument. It was a waste of effort. No one says no except me, I thought, stepping into line.

As it progressed, I was able to see what valuables were shown off. It was pretty evident who the suck-ups were and who wanted to leave. The woman in front of me was defiantly a suck-up. She had given up a solid gold necklace with a good-sized diamond hanging on the chain, no doubt worth a fortune. Castella snatched it without a second thought. I was next.

I waltzed up to her, Castella basking in her precious stolen things, and waited for her to focus on me. She was going to get it. I was equipped with a speech and hard wit for reprimanding the smug witch.

"Well?"

I lost it soon as I met her dark gaze.

"'Well' what?" Stupid, senseless chattering to buy me time. Castella huffed in exasperation.

"What do you think, child?" She inquired, gems, bracelets, and necklaces swinging from her hand. I swept the wealth with my eyes, biting my lip, aware that I was becoming the center of attention.

"I have something more valuable than treasure." What a way to draw it out.

One bold man decided to yell from the assembly. "That means she ain't got nothing!"

Others back him and a faint smirk passed Castella's lips as she held up a hand to quiet them.

"What, my dear, could possibly be more valuable than this?" She asked, loud enough for everyone to hear, gesturing to the vast array of riches around her. The woman knew how to play a crowd; they were all silent.

"Knowledge," I said firmly.

She laughed, they all did, and Castella repeated, "Knowledge?"

I took a deep breath, preparing myself for the spiel. "I stayed in town longer than anyone else, trying to scrounge up what little I could, then witnessed it." I could play effortlessly as she could.

"People woke up, sensed the mayhem... Saw the body."

I could almost hear the intake of breath when I finished. Castella's smile had vanished.

"What body?"

My eyes sought Garcia and found him, slumped and bleeding while the murderer applied ~~slave~~ *salve* to his wound. He watched me.

"Their victim," I answered, indicating the two. "They killed the chief's son from what I heard. Nobody's happy and they're coming for payback."

I had done my best to warn them, my last honorable act for these people.

"She's a liar!" What a waste, I thought.

I twisted and put a face with the voice. Garcia's caretaker had left, marched up to us, and put my good words to shame.

"We already took what we wanted from those scum. They don't even-"

"Pow!" A gunshot whirled through the air and plunged into the man's back. He was dead before he hit the ground right between Castella and me. I turned my gaze on her and smiled. The woman stared back with no readable expression, her eyes blacker than obsidian.

Insanity broke like a wave across the gypsy camp. I caught the briefest of glimpses of people barreling toward the camp, weapons hoisted, intent on revenge then "bam!" I was run over by a gypsy mother dragging her children along behind, trampling me. I curled up, protecting my head as best I could until they passed then scrambled to my feet, still getting knocked this way and that.

Gunshots, screams, and clangs of metal rang out over camp. I rammed into the flood of groups trying to flatten me, searching franticly for Glen, Caine, and Raine. Twisting out of a fleeing man's way, I collided with something jagged; feeling flesh rip open on my arm, I clamped my hand over the gash and hot, tacky blood oozed between my fingers. I ended up staring into the deranged eyes of Ike. He had tried to kill me, but I eluded his fatal blow when I dodged the man. His now cherry knife dripped blood as he shrieked, "This is all your fault!" The rest of his words mingled with cries of pain from the multitude, but I caught the last part.

"I'm going to end your miserable life!" The crazy boy brandished his blade and advanced. I pitched backward into a person and crashed to the dirt. Ike fell flat on his face, barely a foot from me, blood pooling about, gone.

I stared in shock at the sight of death right before my eyes. Sudden pressure got me moving again as my wounded arm was yanked upward.

"Let go!" I spun and my fist connected fully with my captor's face; grunt and he released my arm, clutching his nose.

I nearly took off, but the sight of dark blonde hair brought me to a standstill.

"Glen! I-"

"No time now!" He cried, grabbing my hand and weaving through the stampede.

We had to evade bullets and dropping bodies but it was better than encountering someone head-on so we made it to the outskirts of the battle, breathing hard.

"You saw *this* coming?"

"Not this," I panted, noticing his bloody nose for the first time.

"Uh, you've got…" I finished by pointing to my own nose.

"I know," he growled, swiping his face with a reddened sleeve. "I had no idea you could hit that hard, Lyn. Remind me never to sneak up on you and not tie your hands."

Blushing, I muttered, "I thought you were someone else."

We pranced a few more paces until I skidded to a stop. "Wait, what about Caine and Raine?"

Glen heaved a sigh. "We can't go back for them unless we want to risk getting shot."

He was several paces in front and expected me to follow, but I couldn't just leave them. I turned halfway around then got slammed with a rope tight across my throat, nearly choking me.

"Thought we didn't see you?" The man taunted, yanking my scream out and pinning my arms with his.

I saw Glen twist to see what the commotion was. My captor drew a pistol and aimed it at Glen. I was going to loose him!

"No!" I shrieked, jerking as hard as I could to throw the shot. The blast went off and the bullet missed Glen's head by mere inches.

The situation must have finally registered because Glen came dashing toward me, but to my dismay, was jumped by another. I watched helplessly as he tried breaking free. Glen swirled away from the man's grasp and nailed him across the cheek. He went for another blow, but the other caught his arm and bent it, making Glen yelp in pain and double over.

I joined his cries.

"Stop," I croaked, voice ragged from being throttled. I put up as much fight as I could, but a gun to the neck quelled my struggle.

"Don't think about escaping, you're coming with us."

I pinched my eyes shut when Glen got kneed in the face and heard him drop to the dirt. Tears streamed as my man wrestled me into a walk.

"Snatch the boy and let's get back, Pepper!" he called.

"Don't hurt him!" I hollered, heaving roughly in attempt to break his hold.

"You need to worry about hurting yourself, doll." The man yanked my arms further and a squeal escaped my lips.

"Hey, Pepper, hurry it up!" The man was turning then suddenly went ridged. I jumped out of his grip and he hit the ground. I braced for the worst.

"Raine, that never gets old."

I gaped when I saw the two men down, rocks beside both their heads and Caine and Raine there smiling.

"Glen, you okay?" Caine asked, helping him to his feet. Glen's cheekbone was purplish and his nose was bleeding more from the knock to the face.

"Y-Yeah just let me rest a minuet." He looked dizzy.

I felt Raine circling my hips and I grinned. "You sure know how to use those rocks," I joked.

She giggled and I gave her a squeeze before letting go.

"Thanks for leaving us back there."

"We thought you ran this way," I replied smoothly, embracing Caine.

"Hold on," he mumbled, pulling back and taking my arm. His russet eyes widened as he turned it over, exposing the full view of my cut.

"Lyn, this looks bad. How did it happen?"

Adrenaline had suppressed the pain until now. The wound was a lot worse than I had originally thought. A deep, bloody incision ran the length of my arm up to my elbow, gushing dark crimson.

"I, uh, backed into something sharp trying to dodge bullets at camp and slit my arm." It wasn't a complete lie, merely bending the truth to fit my needs. I had to make them believe it didn't hurt that much. Oh, but it did.

"Ow! Quit!" I yelped when Caine prodded my cut. I yanked it away and put my hand over it; my palm was quickly coated with wet.

"I think you might have hit a tender spot."

He scowled, knowing I was bluffing. "I think the whole thing's tender."

"Don't worry about me," I said, stepping back from Caine. "We've got to keep moving."

"Lyn," Raine warned, fixing me with that gaze.

"At least do this," Caine instructed, ripping the complete bottom of his shirt off.

"I'll help Glen and go. You guys hurry, too." Raine took off, understanding my want for urgency.

"Hold your arm out."

I hesitated, feeling the throb of the wound under my blood-soaked fingers, but released it and extended.

"Here," Caine said, guiding my to a squatting position. "Rest your elbow on my knee."

I did as told, watching in wonder as he wrapped my arm with the material from his shirt. Caine was rarely gentle, only giving slight pressure whenever he fastened the end. I gritted my teeth, withstanding the sting, until he finished.

"You alright?" He asked, smiling. "You were awfully quiet."

I flushed red. "I wasn't expecting you to be so... proficient."

"Proficient?" He snorted. "You mean professional!"

I grinned. "Sure I do."

Caine rolled his eyes. "Whatever. I learned a few skills from my parents other than how to steal things."

He noticed my picking at the bandage, reached over, took my hand away and pressed my arm against my chest.

"Why don't we keep it from getting worse, Lyn? Let your arm rest close to you so it has a chance to slow the bleeding."

"Alright, Mom."

He tried to look annoyed, but only grinned boyishly. I joined in too, laughing for the first time since we arrived at that camp. I was glad we were free from it and Caine, Glen, and Raine were with me. It was about time we started doing things *our* way again.

Ch. 32 Together Again

"*I* think I found something!" Raine called.

It had been a lot harder to move away from the gypsies than we thought. The possibility of pursuers made us search for a place to wait out the worst of the attack. We had made it to the edge of some sparse trees and foliage around them, but the branches were too high to climb and the brush was too thin to use for cover.

"Raine, is this a joke?"

She glanced at Caine, confused. "No, what's wrong?"

I bit back a laugh on seeing the face Caine made even knew though I was thinking the exact same thing. Raine had found a thorn bush for us to hole up in. It looked nasty, but she apparently saw something in it we did not.

"Nothing's wrong, Raine. Why don't you lead the way?" I stared at Glen to see if he was being funny, but his features were calm, if not smiling. Lead the way? To what, I wondered?

I turned to Raine and she grinned. The girl got down on her hands and knees and crawled through high weeds, disappearing *into* the barbs. The rest of us just stood there, baffled until a shot rang out and a bullet stirred up dust barely twenty feet from us.

"Move!" I dove into the grass, waiting for the bite of thorns on my skin, but none were ever felt. Caine and Glen piled in right after me, making the hollow middle more crowded, but it wasn't bad at all. It was perfect.

"Raine, you're amazing," I gushed. She turned pink, looking absolutely adorable as Glen and Caine praised her as well.

I diverted my attention outside, peering through the bramble. I wasn't able to see much, just a few fleeing and lurking bodies that made me uneasy. The distant gunshots and screams breaking the air gave me goose bumps and I kept anticipating the next bullet through the bramble. I had no idea why I was so jittery. We were safely obscured from prying eyes and protected by spikes then Caine said, "Lyn, let me see your arm again."

I half-turned toward his voice.

"Why?" I could have slapped myself. "I-I mean no!"

Glen rammed his finger up against his lips, signaling me to quiet down, but it wasn't going to happen.

"Caine, y-you're crazy. Please no..." I had diverted to begging when I saw them.

"Lyn, I've got to. You'll be fine," he replied, shifting the needle and thread to his other hand and stretching for my arm. I jerked away, yelping when I stuck myself with sharp branches.

"You're not touching my arm."

"It's only going to hurt a little," Glen tried to comfort me. "Caine's got to do whatever it takes to stop the bleeding."

"Ha! Yeah right." I shook my head and actually looked at the wounded area.

My bandage was as red as a robin's crest and wet to the touch. Why wouldn't the blood stop coming? I chewed on my lip, not able to calm my heart down, knowing everyone was right.

"Trust Glen," Caine said, gingerly taking my arm and working on the bandage. "He had his wounds roasted."

Glen's expression changed to painful when Caine brought up the time he'd gotten shot and we had had to burn the bullet injuries to quell the bleeding. Raine made a face, remembering it too, and curled up under Glen's strong arm.

"It's just that... I don't like needles." I was already feeling queasy and trembling badly.

"Yeah, well maybe you should have paid better attention to where you were going."

It was Ike's doing; his naïve attempt to kill me, but I had played it as my own clumsiness, not wanting anyone to worry. Look where that got me.

"Ow!" I gasped as Caine tugged to break the last of the binding loose. My mouth dried up when I took in the full effect of the slit. There was a gaping chasm running the length of my arm. It bubbled with hot red and white ooze; the wound pulsed with blazing pain. And Caine was about to stick a pin through it.

I swayed dangerously to one side, but powerful hands steadied me. I was fading, bright stars danced before my vision.

"Don't fret, Lyn," Raine's tightly controlled voice. "Caine'll do a good job."

He huffed and scooted closer. "Learned it from my mom, remember?"

I nodded weakly, sick. A flash of vivid, profound hurt in my arm then everything went black.

"Caine, it's a bunch of junk. Leave it here." Glen's voice was the first thing to touch my ear, followed by Caine arguing his way.

"It took some skill to steal this!"

He continued explaining while I made an attempt to move. Of course I used my right arm first, but the blaze of anguish stopped me. A moan escaped my lips as I quivered.

"Lyn's awake!" Raine was the first to notice.

"Hope you had enough time to catch up on your beauty sleep."

I was aware of a hand placed on my shoulder.

"Take it easy," I heard Glen say. I realized my head was resting on his lap with my hurt arm supported by his leg and the other arm was draped across my body.

"How bad do I look?"

Glen smiled, brushing a strand of blonde out of my face. "You look beautiful."

"Don't trust my handy work, Lyn?" Caine asked.

"I'm scared to see what you did to my arm."

He faked a pained expression. "Oh, Lyn, that stings." Caine broke out into one of those charming grins of his. "You really should be nicer to the guy who saved your life *again.*"

He emphasized 'again' like I needed rescuing everyday. I nearly cut back, but when I thought on it, it sure did seem that way.

"I think Caine did a really good job," Raine pitched in, her sweet face smiling at me. I guess I had no choice but to check the injury.

I turned my head to glance at the spot. It held my gaze; Caine had done considerably better than I'd imagined. The skin was bloodstained and pink. It had been fastened together with black thread, crisscrossing then delving back into the smarting skin. I ran my fingers over it gingerly, feeling the stitching, the pain from my touch.

"Surprised?" Caine questioned.

I nodded my head, smirking in a dumbfounded sort of way. "Actually... yeah."

He chuckled.

"I kinda surprised myself, too."

"How did you ever find needled and thread?" I had wondered about it in the first place, but the thought was in the back of my mind, being pushed aside by the notion of getting pierced. A more realistic approach came to mind.

"Wait, that's not your hair, is it?"

"Heh. No it's not. I wouldn't pull my hair out for you, Lyn," Caine joked.

"Look at all these scraps he scrounged up." Glen gestured to what appeared to be a pile of junk behind him.

"They just don't appreciate my technique," Caine muttered, shuffling to the items.

With everyone quiet, I listened for the racket from before. It sounded like things had calmed down for the most part. Nothing but the noise of nature took its place.

"Do you think it's safe to move out, yet?" I asked Glen, touching him softly on the arm.

"Safe?" He repeated, taking my hand in his. "I don't know the meaning of the word anymore."

I sighed and looked at our conjoined hands, pondering still how slender and delicate mine were compared to his powerful calloused one. It was a hand I had seen with the strength to hold men off, but the tenderness to sooth with contact. Hands I trusted.

"I think I've picked out everything we can use," Caine said, shambling back from the pile. "Since Lyn slept most of the day away, it'd probably be a good idea to get going."

"Can you move alright?" Glen questioned, running his thumbs over my hand when he noticed me staring.

my

"Yes. Will you help me up?"

He eased me to my feet. I swept the brush for sign of Raine, fresh panic flooding in when I saw she wasn't there. I was about to call, but Caine spoke first.

"Raine?"

Her innocent face popped through the exit and answered.

"It's clear."

We all waddled out of the thorns, looked around, and then started toward the woods.

"Why don't we stop here for the night?" I suggested, knowing Raine might not last much longer. I caught her eye and she lifted her lips in thanks.

We had pushed farther and farther away from the gypsy camp and were now deep in the foothills of

the
^mountains, no civilization in sight. Dark was falling and we had seen better days. Being beat up, filthy, and hungry all the time got old quick. The mountain air was frosty and crisp, making you shiver when it blew.

"So Caine," Glen began, "Got any flint or matches in your junk?"

"Believe it or not, I do," he stated defiantly, rummaging through his pockets for a fire-starter.

I was going to gather stones and dry grasses for the pit, but Raine stopped me. "Lyn, you leave the hard stuff to us. I don't want to see your arm hurt again."

She took the supplies; I stared for a moment, smiled to myself, and went to find a place to sit.

In no time, Caine had kindled a fire and it gleamed cozily in the dark, warming the nippy air around it. I was seated in between Raine and Glen with Caine on the other side of Raine, each of us leaning on the other for warmth and comfort. I decided now would be a good time for catching up.

"So did anyone steal as much as Caine in the raid?"

Raine adjusted under my arm and shook her head. "No. Castella took all of mine and Glen's stuff."

"She would have taken Caine's too if he hadn't hid half of it," Glen added.

"Yeah, I've never seen a greedier hag in my life. By the time I'd given up all my good stuff, you showed up, Lyn." Caine got up and threw more fuel on the fire then came to sit back down. I let Raine stretch out to lay her head on his lap.

"Speaking of the raid," Glen began, "I overheard a few familiar voices."

This instantly pricked my curiosity and sent my nerves to tingling.

"When I was sneaking in between houses, a scene caught my eye and I swung by, eavesdropping from some nearby bushes. A man was addressing a group of ten or so followers that looked an awful like the guys from the fort."

"Hold on," I interjected, "Could you describe the man?"

Glen didn't speak for a moment. "From what I saw, he was dressed up nicely, suit and vest, and had chin-length blonde hair. The guy seemed harsh and wealthy."

Glen had no doubt overheard Lieutenant speaking. This could mean trouble.

"Anyway, he said the 'Boss' was calling everyone in. The crowd reacted and there was a lot of whispering, excitement about something bad."

None of this was making sense. Dev and Lieutenant, when I'd heard them, were searching for us still. Why would they call it off if my father was so desperate to get me back? When they were so close?

"No way," Caine said, a bit perplexed. "So that means they're not chasing us anymore, right?"

I made a puzzled face. "Why would they quit?"

Caine shrugged and smirked. "I guess they figured we're the smarter crew."

"You mean the cowards that won't stop running away. I don't understand if they're this close why the men don't just capture us."

"Maybe your father found a replacement for you."

I narrowed my eyes at Caine's cheeky suggestion. They were blowing it off, but deep down, I could feel something stirring even ~~know~~ *though* the surface was calm.

"Don't let it get to you, Lyn," Caine said.

"Yeah," Raine put in, "You've still got us."

They chuckled and after telling Glen and me goodnight, reclined and dozed. Maybe Caine was right; I shouldn't let it get to me.

"Lyn, are you going to sleep?"

I looked at Glen. He hadn't debated much with the group, probably because he didn't know which side to choose. He extended an arm, but I smiled and declined, patting my legs.

"Why don't you lean on *me* tonight?"

He grinned, a humorous twinkle in his blue eyes, and spread out to where his head rested comfortably on my lap. I smiled warmly back and stroked his hair, fingering the light and dark blonde highlights running through it. Glen gazed up and commented, "The mountain stars sure are beautiful."

"Mh," I mumbled, never taking my eyes off his face. The firelight burned, throwing the chiseled planes of his jaw into shadow and making that blue seem less like ice. He noticed and turned his full focus on me.

"What's wrong?" He asked. "My nose ruined from where you hit me?"

I glowed red but the embers hid it well.

"No. I was only thinking."

"About what?"

"How handsome the firelight makes you look." I brushed his cheek with the back of my hand, feeling the fine shape of the bone. Glen reached up and caught it, locking eyes with me.

"Lyn, promise me something."

"What?"

He moved my hand over his chest so I could sense his heart beating.

"Promise, that no matter what happens, wherever life leads, you'll never leave me."

I leaned down and lightly kissed him on the cheek, close to the side of his mouth.

"It's a promise."

Glen's lips lifted and he told me, "Good night."

He let go of my hand, reassured by my words, and shut his eyes, those long lashes casting thin outlines underneath. I exhaled and leaned against a good-sized boulder, thinking it silly my heart was thudding faster than normal. The only thing that could spoil a night like this would be a dream.

I frowned, but was able to shove the thought away. Just focus on where we've got to get to, I told myself; California.

"Show me!" A booming voice demanded, echoing throughout the cavern and ricocheting over the waterfall.

"A-Alright!" Rasped another.

The vision came into view as I watched a man, covered in a horned bearskin, drop an old witch-like woman to the stone floor. There was a man with large feet staked to a wall and a dead lizard draped across his shoulders that sent me shivering. It looked like others were standing in the shadows; the witch was surrounded. The woman stood and limped over to the falling water then she was still, facing it.

"Now, hag!" Came the deep, guttural growl from the man. "I am sick of waiting and not amused by your games."

He drew a perilous looking pistol from underneath his pelt and aimed it at the woman. She turned sharply and yelped, "It cannot be rushed you wicked man! I must-"

He fired, the shot drowning out her screams whenever crimson gushed freely from her leg. The woman went down; I felt a strong sense of revulsion watching her struggle, but could not muster the will to break my sight.

"'Wicked' am I?" He inquired. She reached out in desperation to the man, but he brushed her aside with a vicious kick. "You, my dear, have not witnessed *any* of the wickedness I am capable of."

My stomach churned because I knew it was true. I knew this man. He glanced up at a scene in the waterfall. It showed a girl walking toward a woman and another man. My father howled in rage and charged through the water. His followers ran to catch up, trampling the old woman and leaving everything for dead.

I saw him heading away, urged on by what he saw, then the waterfall transformed into blood. The liquid stung my eyes and tasted metallic in my mouth. I was drowning and there was no hope of escape...

I woke to red, gore coating every last inch of my body. I heard shouting, howling, and my wails with it.

"Stop it!" I shrieked, flinging my arms out in poor defense. They connected with the rock behind me, making me convulse in pain as my stitches bit deeper into my skin.

"Caine, Caine! She's awake!" Raine's cries were distressed and I could do nothing to calm her in this panicked state.

"Lyn, easy." Caine must have caught my face because I quit ripping my head back and forth. Opening my eyes, I was overcome with vertigo. I swayed and gripped Caine's thin arms to steady myself. Blood drizzled on to his arm.

"Dang it, Lyn, you're bleeding again."

I saw splotches of scarlet, thinking I was going to be sick.

"It's okay, you're fine, you're fine." He drew me in, repeating 'you're fine' over and over. I pinched my eyes shut and wrapped my arms around Caine, breathing in his familiar scent, until the tinny aroma of blood touched my nose. I lurched back and vomited up clear, brown liquid. It burnt my throat like acid, but at least didn't smell.

"Lyn, *what* is going on?"

I wasn't able to speak; my voice was as scorched as my throat so I just shook my head and buried it in his shoulder. Feeling Caine shift to ease me away, I tightened, rasping, "Please, don't."

He exhaled and held me, rocking with me and smoothing the shock into place. About the time my spasms had been reduced to tremors, I sensed someone come toy with my hair. I tore my face from Caine's shoulder and saw Raine, alarm ruling her delicate features. When she met my gaze, I don't know how, but the girl smiled.

"Caine sure can be sweet when you need him, wouldn't you say? Too bad he's such a dope the rest of the time." The joke was such a sweet way to break my fear I gave a little chuckle.

"Thanks, Raine, you're so kind," he sneered back, but could do nothing else but laugh with us.

"Where is Glen?" I asked, voice ragged.

"He went out to hunt earlier," Raine explained, handing me some wild berries to eat. "I think he should be back any time."

I pecked at the fruit, but their sweet, crisp flavor made me ravenous and they were soon gone. Caine gripped my arm, inspecting the stitches.

"Your dreams are going to have to go away if you ever want this place to heal."

I spared a glance for it, steadying myself for the sight of blood. The liquid bubbled around the black thread and my skin was puffy with aches.

"I'm afraid to ask, but what happened in your head?"

I looked at Caine and recalled.

"My father-"

"That's all I need to hear," he interrupted. "That guy could scare the life out of me in a second."

"Keep going, Lyn."

I listened to Raine and told them, "He was with his gang and they were all in some cave with an old woman. He yelled at her to make a vision appear in the water behind her, but she refused and my father shot her in the leg."

"Ouch," Caine mumbled, rubbing his own leg. At least he and Raine were paying good attention.

"I think he saw a girl with other people. Whatever it was, he howled, plowed through the water, and his men followed, trampling the witch to death in the process." I trailed off, trying not to remember it.

"Eggy." Where did *that* name come from?

"That sounds just like the woman you described," Caine reasoned to Raine and my gaping faces. "Same creepy cave and everything. Dos there too?"

It took a moment, but the man staked to a wall had no doubt been him. "So Eggy's… dead?" Raine was baffled as well.

Caine shook his head. "It's just another of Lyn's crazy dreams."

"Are you kidding? Of course it means something." Glen came trotting down a slight slope, hauling two rabbits and a squirrel over his shoulder. He set the animals down on the smoldering coals from last night and came toward me.

"I thought you were going to get the fire started again," he accused Caine.

"Well if Lyn here hadn't of had a meltdown then, yeah, maybe I would have" Caine cut back. "And what are you talking about with her dream?"

"Think on it," Glen said, squatting so his silver eyes could look me over. "All Lyn's nightmares have come true in some weird way."

Once he was satisfied I was fine, Glen extended a hand to help me to my feet. "If that whole thing she described was right then we don't have time to cook these things. We need to move."

Ch. 33 Little Thieves

*I*t felt like we were getting nowhere. The mountain terrain was too treacherous to traverse in a straight path so we were forced into a crazy zigzag, slip sliding down crags or fighting for hand and foot holds on the way up.

"You know what I wish we had?" Raine asked as she stretched for a rocky crevice.

"Food?" Caine yelped, snatching my hand as quick as lighting when I slipped on loose rubble. Glen took my waist and steadied me the rest of the way down.

"Horses," Raine finished, managing to lower herself enough so Caine could support the girl to the grassy flat of the foothill.

"Horses sure would speed this walking up," I stated, thinking of Raine's wish. "Then again, food would be great, too."

"Don't wish your life away, Lyn," Caine joked. He must be as hungry as the rest of us were. The rabbits and squirrel were tasty, but all three of the animals Glen trapped and cooked were scrawny. Nothing like the lavish meals I used to have at the fort...

No need to dwell on that now, I told myself. Even if I had the chance to do it over again, I wouldn't change a thing. I could not shake the fact Glen pointed out from my dream this morning. The horrid truth we could still be being tracked. A squeal broke my repose and I jumped along with the others.

"Get down!" I whispered urgently. We all dropped; I started inching back, but Caine's voice stopped me.

"Wait!" he hissed, shimming up to peer over the rise. "I'm hearing kids not danger."

I crawled to his position and what I saw made me do a double take. There was a fairly large waterhole full of children younger than us by a few years. Watching them dive in and come back up splashing made me ache for a time long past. I yearned to have my childhood years back, the times I was able to ride across my farm without a care in the world, when I knew food would always be on the table when I came home, and when I slept with a roof over my head and cushions under my back.

"Horses!" Raine blurted. I snapped my head in her direction, alarmed by the outburst. Three mounts were tied to a fallen log, not terribly far from the pool.

"They must be the kids'." I speculated.

"Well they're about to be ours." Caine crept down the slope, no noise coming from his footfalls. His sudden movement surprised me and I had to scurry to keep up. The children were too engrossed in their games, but if someone happened to glance our way...

"Caine, I don't know if we should do this." I had caught up to him just before he reached and untied one of the animals.

"Raine wanted horses," he said, pulling away from me. He dispatched of the first knot and passed the lead to me, flashing a smile.

"So horses she gets."

I frowned, eyes sweeping my mount. It had no saddle or bridal, for that matter. Riding was going to be rough, not because of lack of tack, but the animal was skin and bones.

"Leave the last one, Caine," Glen instructed, taking the rope from my hands and indicating I should move. Caine huffed, but did not press it.

I shook my head when he acted as if he was going to mount up with Raine. Waving franticly, I got them to follow. We retreated with hurried steps and two stolen horses.

"This is as good a place as any," Glen said, gazing around at thick grass and the beaten-down trail we had discovered.

"Alright! Caine, help me up." Raine could barely contain her excitement. Truth be told, I was pretty thrilled to be off my feet for a bit, too.

"Same as last time?" Caine asked, hoisting Raine to the horse's back.

"You embarrassed too much to be chauffeured by a little girl?" I mocked, catching Caine turn a shade of red at my cut.

"Don't worry, I'll *try* not to throw you off."

"Funny, Raine," he mumbled, wrapping his arms around her tiny frame. She grinned and gave a squeeze with her legs; the steed began moving, seeming accustomed to carrying more than one rider so at least it wouldn't be spooky.

Glen lifted me up and mounted after, circling my body with his arms and clicking to make the animal walk. I took a handful of the horse's mane and the rope to keep us in place. We didn't have to steer much since it followed Caine and Raine's horse so I relaxed a little, leaning into Glen's muscular chest and allowing his heat to warm me from the chill of the mountain air.

I took in sights of the flourishing valley life. Greenery adorned the gentle slopes and lined the dense pathway quite charmingly. The surroundings smelt of musky earth and distinct hints of bitter plant life. Looking up, I noticed the sky was dappled with wisps of white and pools of blue.

"What do you keep staring at?" Glen's voice triggered a laugh from my chest.

"Can't you tell?" I asked, grinning from ear to ear at his puzzled expression.

"All I see are trees," he said matter-of-factly.

"Exactly."

He snickered, meeting my hands with his. Glen's touch brushed my wound and I recoiled, deciding it was a bad move the second after I did. I held my arm close, pretending I had simply shifted, but he of course knew better.

"Show me your arm, Lyn."

"There's nothing to see."

"Quit lying," he muttered, grabbing it anyway. "You're no good at it."

I gritted my teeth in both frustration and pain when Glen's fingers found the incision.

"Why haven't you told us?" I was in for it now. "Lyn, have you seen the cut?"

I shook my head and developed some backbone. "No and I don't want to. It's healing, that's all."

I pulled away, catching a brief glimpse of my arm and stopping to stare. It was worse than I'd thought. The skin had gone from pink to an irritated shade of red with puss swimming around the stitches. It was bulging and sensitive to touch. I falsely reassured myself by telling Glen, "Besides, what can we do about it?"

He didn't respond; Caine and Raine's horse slowing to a stop in front of us dropped the conversation. Good, I thought, they don't need me to worry about.

I looked up, wondering why we had quit moving, and saw a couple of old log cottages nestled in the folds of the valley.

"What's the matter?" I asked. "Caine feeling guilty about stealing those kids' rides?"

This got a laugh from the others and a scowl from him.

"Are you kidding? Thieves *never* feel bad about what they stole or who they stole from because they need it more than the other person." He said this like it was a rule of some kind.

"Not even if those people were little boys and girls struggling to survive out in the wilderness?" I knew I was playing him, but I had to do something to take my mind off the cut.

"That sounds a lot like us, Lyn," he replied back.

"You've got to admit, we have several years on them," Glen added, throwing his lot in with mine, making me all the happier. Raine even joked along, knowing the mood needed lightening.

"Caine, it wouldn't be right to take these horses away from their home. They're probably the nicest thing the kids own."

"Since when do we do the right thing?"

"You want your record to be even dirtier than it already is?" Glen dropped the lead and dismounted; the animal, having stared at the homes this whole time, now went trotting toward them, seeming content. "Let it go."

Caine gaped for a moment then was forced down when Raine got off and the horse took off behind the other.

"You three are crazy people," he grumbled, gazing after the steeds like they were the last he would ever see. "I'm glad you all love walking so much."

None of us were listening to his complaints, but watching as the horses reached the door and whinnied. A woman came out to comfort the animals and must have noticed the children were not with them. She called and, receiving no answer, turned toward a field I'd not noticed until now, yelling out names. I saw the modest heads pop up from the pasture, listen to the woman then, like it was the easiest thing in the world, go out to search the waterhole.

What a simple life, I thought, walking on, when the only thing you had to worry about was finding a few kids, fixing dinner, and plowing the fields. A basic life none of us would ever have, only dream about.

A few days went by without much excitement save for the occasional hunting we did. I would say that the only good thing about the valley was the abundance of life to keep our ubiquitous appetite at bay. We nabbed a few rabbits and squirrels and had those for meat with whatever else we could round up. It was usually tart berries or bitter plant leaves and I'd swear I was hungrier *after* the meal than before.

We finally stumbled upon a sign of civilization: dirt roads.

"Hold it," Caine hissed, blocking Raine with his arm. We were crouched silently in the brush next to the path, peaking out at it.

"I think we're clear." Everyone looked at me as I inched out of concealment.

I was about to motion for them to follow, but the sudden sound of an engine came rumbling our way. Like a naughty child caught in the act, I froze even ~~know~~ though the others were shouting for me. A vehicle sped my way and, either they hadn't seen me yet, or had no care if they ran me over because the *car* was not slowing.

A hand on my waist and over my mouth muffled my yelp of surprise as I was yanked off my feet, into the bushes again. I landed curtly in Glen's lap. He grunted, but stayed still as we watched the automobile go by.

"No way," Caine breathed, staring after it.

"Someone knows how to travel." Raine was transfixed as well.

I looked over my shoulder at Glen's relieved features. "Thanks."

He broke into that striking smirk of his, blue eyes twinkling with witty sarcasm I could tell he was itching to spit out. Raine and Caine helped us to our feet and my thoughts returned to the car.

My 'father' had owned one back at the plantation, but I never got to ride in it. He would always use it for 'business' or something like that so I just stuck with my horses.

"Whaddya say we follow that car?"

I turned my attention to Caine, knowing he was plotting every way to steal the thing and playing it like we would simply trail it to find a town. I held his sly gaze, letting him realize I'd figured him out. Caine smiled as Glen and Raine agreed that would be the best plan of action and started walking. I allowed Caine to come take my arm in his and wink as we strolled behind the others.

"C'mon, Lyn, loosen up," he whispered in my ear. "You'll thank me for it later."

I narrowed my eyes, doubting his arrogance. "How sure are you you can pull this off?"

He leaned over and kissed me on the cheek, grinning at my surprise.

"As sure as I know you'll let me get away with that."

I turned my face from him, but couldn't keep the twist from my lips. Let him feel good, I thought, it might just get us a car.

Ch. 34 Now That's How You Travel

We followed the dirt road in the direction the car had gone and found the town. It was a whole lot larger than ones we had previously raided, offering up tantalizing prizes as we pocketed a few worthy valuables that traded for food. Still, no prize had been as tantalizing as the one was stared at now.

All of us were hidden in the shadow of an alleyway, dragging the unconscious body of a bum that had tried to mug us behind a dumpster. The job taken care of, we crept up to the corner, right where we had view of the vehicle.

"Is that it?"

"It's gotta be."

Raine's excited voice interrupted my and Caine's mumblings. "We're *really* going to steal that?"

"Sure are, Raine," Caine replied, pride unmasked on his face.

"And you're positive you know how to drive?"

"Of course," Caine answered Glen, "I'm a city boy, remember? I used to sneak around all the richies' cars and take them for a spin." That last part was likely exaggerated; Glen and I just exchanged knowing glances, letting Raine drink it all in.

We gazed at the car parked outside a bar the people before must be in. It was prime time for the saloons: dusk, right before nightfall. Glen had conjured up a plan. We four make a break for it, Raine jump in the front and maneuver the wheel while the rest of us push the automobile clear out of town. When we had stolen our goods to be traded, everyone mapped out the best route to press through and be the least suspicious. Once the thing makes it out, we hop in and take off. Now if only it ~~was~~ were that easy.

I swept the area one more time then made a run for the vehicle, the others in step behind. After lifting Raine in, Glen came to join Caine and me, positioning himself to push. We strained and dug our feet in, but the car simply squeaked in protest, flying our nerves sky high.

"Raine, is the brake on?" Caine gasped.

"How should I know?" She was as panicked as we were. If someone came out to say, have a drink or smoke a cigar, we were finished.

Caine exhaled, darting to the front. He fiddled with a lever and a screech let loose, jerking the car forward. In a flash, Caine was back by my side, giving it all he had.

"Move, move!" We gritted our teeth throughout the haste it took to get past the alleys and out the exit.

"This is it," Glen breathed. "Keep it straight, Raine!"

As soon as we made it out, Caine quit pushing. I dropped to the ground, feeling the extra weight.

"Come on, Lyn," he said, tugging me to my feet. "I want you up front beside me."

Grateful for the relief, I swung myself in. Glen and Raine piled in the back, car swaying gently from their movement. Caine turned the hand-crank to start it, but no engine sounded.

He spun it faster in agitation. "What's wrong with it?"

"Hey, don't ruin the thing!" I steadied his arm.

"Try the other way," Raine suggested. He did and the rumble began immediately.

I glared at Caine who smiled weakly, red with embarrassment.

"And you said you knew how to drive," I cut.

"I do!" He retorted. "It's just been a while..."

"Look, whether you run off the road or not, we need to get away from here!"

Caine took Glen's advice and floored it, on purpose or accident, I don't know, but we sped out of sight, leaving the place in dust. Now I say 'sped' but we were only doing twenty miles an hour, which felt like speed to us.

The car had a panel that served as a door and four little seats squeezed inside the framework. Headlights that didn't work would pose a problem in the coming night, but at least we could cover some ground before then. I supposed we knocked the lights loose on our mad trek through town, but I was honestly still shocked we *had* made it.

This was really the way to travel. You could sit back and relax, but be moving quickly. A train did the same, but it was on a set course whereas a car was not. I had to give the automobile another plus since it was compact and not bulky, allowing for solid moves. The people who owned this must have paid a pretty penny for it; not many in this world were privileged enough to own such a fine way of transportation.

I smiled to myself. Not like we were either. It just so happened we could get away with stealing a car and escaping the wraith of owners before lady luck deserted our sorry selves.

It seemed like she was still with us for the meantime. We were having a great time, chattering, giggling, and feeling the late evening air against our faces, ground running beneath us. Caine was able to drive a lot better than he rode, but that wasn't saying much. He was jerky with the wheel and we hit our fair share of bumps. The black night drawing near made him even shakier.

"Caine, you think now's a good time to pull over and settle in for the night?" I suggested when he swerved to narrowly miss a rut in the road.

"Do you want to cover some ground or not?" The tension must be getting to him. "I thought you wanted as much distance between you and those guys as possible, Lyn."

"I do, but we'll never get there if we're killed with your driving first!" I snapped back over the noisy engine. It seemed like the rumble had grown louder all of a sudden.

"*Me* kill us? Sorry, Lyn, but that's your job. You just haven't done it yet!"

"Caine, be quiet and listen!" Raine yelled, alarm in her voice.

The car's engine defiantly sounded off; it was too rhythmic, too powerful. Hoof beats.

"Horses!" I shrieked, "Caine, move!"

By 'move' he must have heard 'run off the road' because there we went. The turn was too sharp and I knew whiplash would spread through my spine as soon as the adrenaline stopped gushing. My shriek of panic became wedged in my throat as we plummeted downward. The gully was a great deal steeper than I'd originally believed.

I listened in mute terror as the vehicle slammed into bushes and crashed over rocks. The wheels flew over bumps and got hammered into the dirt, our windshield cracked more and more every time a branch struck it, and the clatter of bending metal tortured my ears. I hung on for dear life, feeling as though death was in the driver's seat, waiting for something to go wrong, and I was helpless to do anything about it.

"Bam!"

Caine and I slammed up against the windshield with glass-shattering force when a tree abruptly stopped the car. I caught a glimpse of a stagecoach being towed by horses, hanging lanterns adorning the sides, race by.

Blotches of silver, red, and black dotted my vision when I tried to look through the pain. I could scarcely feel the wet blood drip down my forehead, fighting for consciousness instead. The sharp taste of gore coated my mouth and I spit out drops of it, any amount of energy used making me extremely light-headed.

"C-Caine?" I rasped. I thought I saw him sprawled over the wheel, not moving, likely bleeding.

Any movement I made hurt, but I had to get to him. Reaching over, I brushed some of his wild, auburn hair out of his face and picked out blood coating his nose and mouth. I pictured what I must look like and finally lost it...

I tried to move. "Ugh."

The soreness was dire and my bones cracked painfully as I awoke to the morning sun in my face. I automatically reached for my arm; it was dangerously swollen and raw to the touch, especially around the stitches.

"Lyn?" A voiced wheezed my name.

I twisted through the stinging pain to see Raine, encircled by Glen's arms, staring at me. He must have snatched her when we went rolling down the hill and taken the roughness off her impact. Just a few angry bruises and knots were all I could tell. I had to get Glen off her.

"Hold on, Raine." I moved where I was in contact with Glen and shook him, sending burning sparks throughout my arm. He moaned, cringing when his body started to stretch out, but he somehow managed to force into a sitting position.

Since Glen and Raine had been in the back, the seats had taken most of the crash off them instead of the windshield. Raine kept gazing at Caine's body still draped over the wheel and I took notice.

"Is he okay?" She asked.

I hesitated with my answer. "I- I don't know. He hit pretty hard... I'm really worried."

I glanced at his face and to my surprise, saw him *smile.*

"Aw, Lyn, that's so sweet of you."

I flushed bright pink, more annoyed than embarrassed.

"Caine, I am going to kill you," I growled, steadying him as he rose.

"Just leave me lying here. That should do the trick."

"I should!" I snapped. "By the way, you can't drive well enough to miss the broad side of a barn!"

His gaze didn't hold mine and Glen pulled me away before things got too hot. The collision must have drained Caine's usual sarcasm because we would be in a heated argument right about now if under normal circumstances.

"If the stagecoach would have hit us, maybe we'd still have a ride," Glen mumbled, casting one final look at the devastated vehicle.

"It was fun while it lasted I guess," I said, lightly feeling my enlarged temple and running my fingers across my bruised cheekbone.

"Caine is a terrible driver after all," Raine commented, walking with us, inspecting some nasty spots on her arm.

"Alright, I get it!" Caine marched up beside the rest of us, picking at dried blood under his nose.

We were all pretty beat-up. Along with my face, my wounded arm was more bothersome than before. It had subdued to a dull ache prior to the crash, but was now a sharp throb that flared up, nipping at my skin. I tried not to let it pester me, thinking Caine got the worst of the impact. The skin around his brow looked blackish and he kept massaging his chest as if it hurt.

We had followed our skid trail most of the way up and paused for breath.

"I think we should steer clear of the road anyway," Glen remarked. "Just in case those car owners are on the hunt for us."

Great, I thought, sighing. More walking.

Ch. 35 Sickness

"And tell me again, why do we have to go all the way to California?"

Caine, like the rest of us, was feeling the negative effects of the heat.

"So we can meet up with family connections and straighten some of this mayhem out."

"Okay. If it's *your* family why are *we* going?"

I shot Caine a vicious look and barked, "Because you don't have anything better to do!"

"Lyn's always helped us out." Raine, worn as she was, tried to ease the tension. "She's the one who holds our sorry group together."

Glen chuckled, sliding me a glance. "I don't know where I'd be if it wasn't for her. Don't want to think about it either."

Raine grinned. "Life's just not as fun without Lyn!"

"It sure isn't as crazy or complicated, that's for sure," Caine remarked.

I smiled weakly, not knowing how I was holding myself together, yet alone everyone else. The tiredness and hunger I was used to, but the way I had been feeling was worse than both of those. At times I was slow and groggy or cold then hot. Almost like I was sick.

The hurt from the crash had sunk in since it had been a day, but it left its mark. Purplish bruises and scratches would heal on their own; it was my arm I was worried about. The wound bulged and a pool of pink and white fluid oozed around the barely visible stitches that held the blood back. Anguish had spread to my muscles and they blazed when I tried to move.

"Lyn, did you hear what I said?"

I answered on hearing Glen's voice.

"N-No," I muttered, shielding my eyes from the sun. "I think the heat's getting to me."

But I felt cold, even though the sweat was coming in streams down my skin.

"There's a tree up ahead," Caine said, "We can rest when we get to it."

The short walk it took to arrive robbed me of the little energy I had left. I plopped on the ground, shaking, arms wrapped around my knees.

"I still have a few stale biscuits from town." Caine fished them out of his pockets. "Probably won't taste very good, but at least it's food."

He started handing them out and I declined when offered a couple. "I'm not hungry."

"Haha. Funny, Lyn, but you've got to eat." Caine pushed the bread into my hands.

"Caine, really I'm not," I insisted, shoving the food back.

"We haven't eaten in hours and you're not hungry?" Worry crept into the edges of Glen's face. "Is there something we should know?"

"Yeah, Lyn, you look really pale," Raine commented, moving near me and touching my arm just a bit too hard. I gasped as the pain multiplied, pricking at my skin. Feeling the bile rise in my throat, I quickly turned and coughed up bits of food and liquid.

"What'd I do?" Raine was panicked.

"Been hiding your pain, huh? I knew you were holding up too well."

I made an effort to glare at Caine, but my head was spinning wildly, dizzied from lack of nourishment.

"It's infected."

Glen was suddenly beside me; holding my clammy hand in his, he felt my forehead.

"She's got a bad fever, too," he concluded, tucking a sweat-dampened strand of hair behind my ear. Those icy pale blue eyes stared into mine, flooded with anxiety.

"Is it her arm?"

Glen nodded, shifting his gaze to the injury. "We never cleaned it."

"It's not like we could have!" Caine snapped. Seeing Glen's expression must have wound him up more. "What? You think she's going to fall over dead or something?"

Glen fired him a ruthless look.

"S-She's not!" Raine exclaimed, tears of dread wetting her face. "We can find a doctor and Lyn'll be fine."

"That's a great idea, Raine." Caine sounded sarcastic. "Only two *big* problems: one, we have zilch for money and two, the nearest town's about a four day's walk away."

"B-But we could-"

"Be quiet, both of you!"

Caine and Raine watched in silence as Glen scooped me up off the ground and staggered on. My head rested against his chest; his throbbing heart matched that of my head.

"Glen, you don't think-"

"No, Lyn." He cradled my body close. "You are going to be just fine, I swear. I'll carry you for a bit until you get your strength back so rest now."

He pressed his cool lips to my hot forehead and the contact reassured us. I soon drifted, asleep, shivering in his arms...

"Okay, Lyn, just make yourself comfortable and don't worry about moving, we'll pull."

I was having a hard time taking in all Glen's words so I merely nodded as he laid me out on our hand-made stretcher. Raine's idea, for it had been crudely thrown together with scrap sticks and wild vine. Glen had promised to carry me until my strength returned, but it never did. Caine persuaded him to pass my body back and forth to give the other a break. After a day of this, the boys were walking dead.

The whole situation made me mentally sick along with whatever I had now. Pain, I was used to, but it was always some kind of physical hurt not sickness. The torment was *inside* and I knew there was nothing I could do to help it. That's what made me feel... useless.

"Here, Lyn." I was vaguely aware of a biscuit being put into my hand and fingers closing over it. "If you eat you will get better faster."

I sighed softly at Raine, and raised it to my lips and took a bite. The bread crumbled and was chewy, tasting like mold and cardboard mixed together. After finishing, it seemed like I had a clearer head.

Forcing my rigid body to relax was no easy task; I could still feel the shakes even know I was sweating, but the sky's personality this evening made me think of other things besides my health.

The ball of yellow brought the memory of my father and his group to mind. I could unmistakably see those vibrant golden eyes glaring at me from under the animal skin that hid my father's scarred face, imagine his rage whenever he realized I was gone. Spying a wave of brilliant orange, I was reminded of Dev. Was the man dead yet? He sure did seem to think so back at the gypsy town, Jerome. I was almost saddened by the thought. Sure he'd been as violent and crazy as the rest of them, but Dev had been the only one to show virtually any kindness toward me.

I flinched away from a rock scraping my side and remembered Razor. Had he been the one to give it all away? The man said he knew about Dev and the diamond all along so he could have given Dev up just to see some scandalous revenge. Still, I could not believe it. Razor was too cold and withdrawn to hand over anything without a price.

I never figured out why my father called off the search, either. He struck me as the type of man that [who] always had a reason for his motives and a plan to make sure they were achieved without fail. I shivered at the thought of what some of those plans may be.

While watching the first stars appear in the colorful canvas of dusk, I overheard voices and running water.

"Why don't we stop here?" Glen sounded absolutely exhausted, like he could fall over any second.

"Yeah, it'll work," Caine told Glen.

My makeshift stretcher was lowered gently to the ground.

"Go lay [lie] down with Raine. I'll take care of Lyn."

I waited for Glen to object, but Raine cut in first. "I wanna help her, too!"

457

"You can take morning shift, Raine." She must have agreed with Caine because the next thing I heard was him kneeling next to me. The back of his hand pressed against my forehead; I opened my eyes and snatched a glimpse of Caine's features twisted into an awfully upsetting look. He caught me staring and lifted the corners of his mouth, pulling off a rather blue smile.

"I thought you were asleep."

"It's okay, you didn't wake me." It scared me a bit to see a strong sense of dread coloring his dark eyes instead of Caine's usual sly twinkle. He noticed my shaking. "Are you cold?"

I huffed a laugh. "I feel like it but I'm sweating"

"Fever does that to you."

Caine seemed to have a thought.

"Hold on," He said rising, "I'll be back in a sec."

I wondered what he was doing when I listened to the rip of fabric and splash in the water. The cool, damp piece of cloth that lay on my forehead made me jump when he returned.

"Cold creek water," he explained, plopping down next to me. "Thought it might help with your temperature."

"Thank you, Caine," I said with a weak smile. The kind gesture made me settle in more and gaze at the sky once again, thinking it odd how quickly the sun could disappear. Rays of glistening light shot thought the colorful hues and provided a perfect intro for the moon and stars.

I flicked my attention to Caine. He looked dog-tired, sitting slumped, eyes heavily lidded with his hair a tangled mess and body layered in filth from days on the road. And yet here the boy was watching out for little sickly me, sacrificing his own peace just to make sure I was safe... I felt as if I could never repay the debts and favors I owed to everyone.

I reached out and grabbed Caine's hand, but he started and jerked away. "Sorry. I'm kinda out of it."

"Then rest."

"And leave us with no watch? I don't think so."

My muddled mind searched for an idea. I snatched up his hand again.

"I'll keep watch."

He looked deeply skeptic.

"I can squeeze your hand if I hear or see anything. If that doesn't wake you up I'll just yell."

Caine blew out in exasperation and stretched out beside me, still holding on. "I'd love to hear you try to yell in the state you're in."

"I can to!" I persisted, an unwelcome rasp entering my voice.

"Always the stubborn one eh, Lyn?"

"Go to sleep."

He chuckled and lifted my hand to his lips.

"Here's to luck," he stated and kissed my fingers.

I rolled my eyes and made some sarcastic comment, but soon heard the steady, rhythmic breathing of a dreamer.

They all do so much for me, I thought, tracing patterns in the stars. Maybe I was returning the favor in some crazy way.

"Lyn?" I focused on Raine suddenly at my side. She put up a finger and said, "You can rest. You need too more than me. I know how to keep watch."

I couldn't do much else but nod. Or maybe it's just what friends do.

Ch. 36 Rails

"Lyn? Lyn, wake up."

I opened my eyes and, for a split second, felt rejuvenated. Glen peered down at me. "I'm going to set you up on this cart. Don't worry about moving too much, I've got you covered."

I blinked absently, trying to recall what happened. I remembered waking by the creek and roasted rattlesnake for breakfast. Caine had stayed by me all night, slept about as much as I had, too. To my dismay, I awoke even more sluggish than the day before. Moving had gotten harder and harder; our stretcher had broken and I hazily recollected Glen scooping my feeble body up in his arms then black greeted me.

Sensing the heat of Glen's body leave mine was what waned me. I was freezing and tried to curl up, but my whole being ached. The platform I was on rocked slightly and Raine's gentle presence was beside me.

"Lucky Lyn," she said, taking my hand, "You got Glen to carry you."

She giggled though it sounded forced. "Caine was too scrawny to haul me for long."

I knew she was trying to ease the tension. The floor swayed and, with Raine's help, I managed to sit up.

"Where are we?" I asked to no one in particular. My voice was misery made over.

"On some ancient hand-car," Caine answered. I glanced around, finding I was on a wooden platform with a steel lever jutting out the middle with a handle on each side. We were back on rails, I noted with a start.

"I'm afraid to ask, but who'd you rip this thing off of?"

Caine lifted a side of his mouth and narrowed his eyes. "We *found* this one." He went up to a grip, grasping it with both hands. "Instead of using our legs for travel, we thought it'd be easier to use our arms this time."

Glen took up the other handle and began pushing down while Caine pulled up. They strained quite a bit, but the car only squeaked in protest, rolling about an inch. We were going to need more power to get the thing moving.

"Raine, let's help them," I said, struggling a great deal to get to my feet.

"No, Lyn!" She eased me back down. You stay put and I'll do the work."

The thought of protesting crossed my mind, but I knew I would get nowhere. I cursed my frailty, feeling like the biggest burden in the world. Watching dejectedly, I saw Caine and Raine brace for pushing the lever up while Glen got into position to pull down.

On the count of three..."

Go!" Raine's outburst cut Caine's words short. After them came a great deal of creaking, sweat, and struggle, but whatever they did got the cart to move. We were off!

They continued on like that longer than a few minuets and soon had the handcar rolling about as smoothly as we'd get it to over the tracks. The boys were able to keep it going without too much effort so Raine slumped behind me, her back against mine, breathing hard. "I'm hungry again!"

I had to smile at her complaint. True, rattlesnake and water did not keep a person satisfied for long. Not that I wanted to eat anything, though. My appetite had gone down ~~considerable~~ considerably since the illness had gotten worse.

I had to look haggard with my sweat-dampened, tangled muddle of blonde hair. My cheeks were sunken and sharper than before. Instead of slender, I felt bony and frail, weighted down only by fever and muscle soreness. All that was scary enough on its own, but the real terrifying part was I wasn't getting any better.

I stared at Glen and Caine miserably as they wrestled with the old handle. Caine ran a hand through his wet hair slicking it back out of his face and asked me, "Why do you look so depressed?"

"I... I want to help, do something other than sit here." your

"You getting well will help us, Lyn," Glen huffed, pumping the car. We left it at that.

Caine and Glen did not let up and we were covering much more ground than we ever thought of walking. Still, it was laborious work; both of them were wearing thin, quick. Whenever we'd hit a small hill they would about exhaust themselves until Raine had to assist to get us over it. We would end up coasting, pending the car to stop then start all over again.

I simply sat there, concentrating on the barren landscape that passed us by instead of my building fever. The sun had been sizzling, but was now sinking, giving us some relief. It felt like we'd been rolling for days, but I'm sure it was only three of four hours. Our pace slowed throughout the time, but we kept going.

Gazing ahead, watching the tracks vanish under the handcar, I kept thinking I was hallucinating. The sky was marred by puffs of black and the air rippled as if from some heat source around it. What could be burning, shrubs?

"Hey, slow down." We didn't. I said it a little louder since no one heard me.

"Slow down!"

"Lyn, it's good to know you're still with us, but can't you do it in a less annoying manner?" Caine's back was to the strange sight so of course he wouldn't understand.

"Something's burning up ahead," I defended. It sounded about as stupid as I thought it would.

"Burning?" Caine mocked. "Have you seen what we're around? Dirt and dry bushes. Lyn, nothing's on fire."

We were not braking. The smoke looked like it was moving.

"Hold up." Glen quit pumping, perspiration coating his body. Caine was forced to stop when he let go.

"Glen, it's her fever," he whined, "Don't tell me you're seeing things, too?"

Coasting, but still not stopping.

"Caine, turn around and look." Raine finally talked some sense into him because he scowled, took an eyeful. We all stared, dread building, suspended above our heads, ready to drop whenever one of us figured it out.

"You've got to be kidding me." Glen knew. "Please don't tell me that's a train."

I shook my head in denial, refusing the truth. The squeak from the cart had quieted, letting us listen to the full effect of the rumbling tracks and high-pitch whistle break the silence.

"No! We're finished!" Caine wailed.

"Get off!" The handcar's fate had been decided and I had a plan not to be part of it. Everyone except me scrambled for the edges and slid off, thunder from the rails muting their grunts of discomfort as they struggled.

I was inching toward the rim, inflamed muscles begging for rest. It was impossible; I couldn't make it. The resounding din from the locomotive drew closer and the crashing shook my feeble platform. I only hoped the others got off in time...

"Lyn, wrap your arms around me!"

Why was he not running? Through the haze, the noise, I locked eyes with Glen, heard his desperate shout. Even if I was prepared to give up, they were not going to let me go without a fight.

That desperation told me I wasn't moving fast enough. My right arm was useless so I swung my left for all it was worth and looped it over Glen's neck as he drug me off the cart. I buried my face in the cave of his jaw when I felt him reel backward, barely supporting my weight, then turn and bust for the open. One, two steps pounded the earth then were wrenched from the ground as steel met steel with bone-crushing force in the deafening crash that sent us flying. Raines screamed as she hit the ground with Caine and Glen positioned himself to where his body took most of the impact off mine.

It wasn't so much the jolt that robbed me of my breath, as the pain. When we fell, I could do nothing to hold the shriek of anguish back; my arm was ablaze in horrible hurt, feeling as if the stitches had ripped the skin apart and blood was pouring from it.

There was a great deal more squeaking as the train rumbled by, likely assuming we were dead.

"Lyn," Glen breathed, the rest of his words choked by pain.

"I can't- my arm…" He somehow sat up, took my arm, and reassured me, "It's okay, your arm's fine. You're- *We're* alive!"

I picked out right away the way he changed our focus to the sweet fact we were still kicking, but I could not shake the throb or muster the spirit to look at it, for that matter.

"Oh no!" I saw Caine stagger toward the demolished handcar; it lay in a heap of unrecognizable metal and wood. "Glen, Glen, maybe we can do something about it! Please, no…" He had entered into one of his moments again.

"It's more trouble than it's worth, Caine," Glen sighed, gently testing the shoulder he sacrificed for me. I heard sickening cracks before he called Raine over.

"I can take care of her," Raine said, switching spots with Glen, supporting me while he stood.

"Glen's going to go find something for us to eat," Raine explained to me, trying hard not to stare at my ravaged right arm.

468

"Good, but he might need your help, too."

"Lyn, I can't leave you by yourself." Raine tried to argue, but my manipulation skills far surpassed hers, even with the state I was in.

"You don't worry about me," I told her. "None of you are where you can't hear me so go. I can sit here by myself, at least."

She bit that lip, but a hard stare from me sent her away. I wanted to be alone, prepare for what I was about to see. Swallowing the lump of apprehension in my throat, I finally examined my cut. The sight was worse than vile. My wound had swelled to bursting, white, yellow, and red fluid swimming among my broken stitches. The entire part of my arm from the shoulder down ached and pounded with each movement, increasing the amount of revolting juice around the black thread.

I tore my eyes away, afraid if I kept staring I'd make myself vomit.

"We're back to square one: walking," Caine remarked, settling down beside me, a pitiful expression masking his face.

"Can we rest until tomorrow?" Raine asked, dropping a rueful-looking pile of dry grasses and sticks on the ground.

"What else have we got to loose?" Caine pulled his flint and, after a few goes, lit the stack.

"I feel like I got ran over by the train," Glen commented, kindling the fire to set the meager fuel burning. "Is it just me or does anyone feel the same?"

"I feel like I'm still under it," Caine joked.

"I feel cold." Raine snuggled closer to the fire as a crisp wind stirred the embers, chilling the already cool night air. It set my teeth to chattering and caused my body break out into a clammy sweat.

"And tired," Caine added, letting Raine rest her head full of curls on his shoulder. "Good night."

I wanted to say it back, but couldn't stop the clicking of my teeth. A hand felt my forehead, then wiped at some of the sweat. Nothing had changed because it was withdrawn soon after and wound around my narrow waist. I gave in and reclined against Glen, wishing all our troubles would just go away.

"You feel weak," he whispered, pulling some of my sticky hair back out of my face. "Why can't we get rid of this sickness?"

"Give it time." I was just lying to both of us now. That's why I didn't say anything else.

"We keep this up, you're not going to last much longer." His rough fingers stroked my face, cold where my skin was hot. "Don't think I haven't noticed the way you move, the fact you can't walk."

Glen leaned his forehead against my hair; I sensed his warm breath on my neck, realized how irregular it was. Now I felt like *he* was the one who needed soothing.

"Glen…" Only, I didn't have the words.

"Go to sleep." His voice was choked with emotion.

What could I do? I closed my eyes, letting Glen's silent tears that dampened my hair put me to rest.

Ch. 37 Hope

𝒜 sharp prick in my side woke me with a gasp. I opened my eyes, started violently, and tried to back away. My arm made any attempt futile so I was forced to take the prodding. Glancing around, I was horrified to find myself surrounded by dark-skinned people, their weapons trained on us. Knives lay beside Glen and Caine, but a gun to the head must have made them drop.

We were in deadlock; I thought the people would shoot if we so much as took a breath. A sudden yelp had my nerves jumping again and the offenders move off. Someone tall and thin strolled up and squatted down by me, locking eyes with me, probably wondering why I was moaning so much. The man had a ragged cap of dark hair sticking out from under a feathered headpiece. He was dressed in Native American garb with an embroidered vest and hand-made breeches. His features were strange for a man's, though, softer, almost feminine.

I glared as strongly as I could into those muddy eyes until he broke, snapping something in a crisp, rather high-pitched voice. The people converged in; hands began to lift me up.

"Hey!" I heard Caine shout, "Don't touch her!"

Glen surged to his feet along with Raine, meaning to take action. The sound of guns being readied to fire filled the air. Glen nailed the man who had been holding the rifle to his face and Raine dove from behind him, knocking back the first shooter to pull the trigger.

The man ~~that~~ who had looked at me spun and rammed Glen into the dirt, barking something I couldn't understand to the others. They lowered their guns. Raine was frozen, gaze locked on Glen, but Caine lunged for his knife. My man shifted like lighting, pulling his pistol and butting the barrel into Caine's chest before he could act with the dagger.

"Drop it." So he could speak our language. Caine cast a quick glance my way then let the blade go.

"Girl and you come with us," he explained. "Run and die."

The masculine man ~~that~~ who was carrying me started to walk.

"Don't hurt her!" Raine demanded, dashing out of the circle and latching on to my carrier's thick arm. She was nearly trampled when the lead man steered his horse right beside her.

473

"Walk!" That oddly shrill, accented voice belted Raine back with Caine and Glen, not uttering another word. I had to do something.

"Le-go." My words were slurred and my resistance sloppy. The man leaned down and whispered something in my ear but I couldn't understand his dialect.

Tears burnt the corners of my eyes and stained my cheeks with wet. Was this it? The entire struggle and fight for nothing? I felt my hands being tied, as if I could move them anyway, but the act made me think about what these people were going to do. I faded in and out a couple of times until a rather violent shake snapped me out of it and I noticed we had stopped in the middle of some camp, dark-skinned natives gathering around our captors.

My body shifted and I was set down. The man obviously hadn't expected me to fall to my knees as soon as he let go because I hit the dirt hard. I dug into my lips, biting back the yelp of pain as he helped me to stand. My cheeks glowed red since I knew everyone's attention was on me, even my friends were looking on, and quiet filled the air.

He released me again and I staggered; the man grabbed my right arm in frustration and I let loose a scream to make the dead shiver. I saw Glen break out and start toward me, saw him forced back by the lead man. I wouldn't, couldn't stop screaming. The man came and slapped me flat across the face, sending me to the ground. I lay there and shook, fever at an all-time high, blurring my dizzied vision. Let me pass out, I wished, let me go and never come back.

A voice broke through my haze. I thought it spoke to the man.

"Our kill." He must have answered a question about us. Great. If we were *kill* then that meant dying. I could only hope they'd make it quick.

The ragged voice uttered more gibberish and the same man answered with his actions. He pulled me up and the only way I did not fall was his clasp on my good arm.

I was met with a short, elderly woman, skin tanned and leathery, her hair black and braided. She studied me strangely with muddy brown eyes, unusual flecks of green sprinkled throughout them. I couldn't imagine how appalling I had to look to her, but something clicked in that gaze and the elder spun to the man holding me. She spoke and it had to be contradicting to the man's ideas because he retorted, "Spare them? Why? They trespass."

The woman gave him a firm stare and explained. He glanced over me, scowling like I was foul scum that needed disposing of.

"Spare all?" Her nod confirmed it and I jumped at his tightened grip.

The woman motioned for him, and the man scooped me up, following her into a mud and clay building. I was laid on a long bed, low to the ground. After a nasty glare from my carrier, he left, leaving me with only the old woman for company. She had gotten a bowl of strong-smelling herbs and was crushing them together, still staring at me as if trying to work a difficult puzzle.

The elder set the basin down and finally tore her eyes from my face to inspect my arm. I felt hands on it and immediately attempted to break her grasp, but the coarse fingers squeezed and I wailed in pain. Black flickered before my vision when she probed the wound, such excruciating hurt was enough to make me loose it.

"Let me see her!" That sounded like Glen.

"No! Back." The leader's voice responded along with noises of fighting. I badly wanted to see him, too, and for about the hundredth time longed for this sickness to be gone.

The woman took no heed to whatever was going on outside, but finished pulverizing the mixture, wrinkles intensified as she dipped her free hand into a red paint. She placed her fingers, tipped with cherry color, on my wrist and applied pressure. It hurt, but nowhere near as much when she moved her grip up my swollen arm. I cried out in frenzy, fever burning my inside while her witchlike hold scourged my body. Glen had to be unconscious or otherwise this awful hag would be on the floor by now.

"Stop it!" I rasped, attempting to pull free except nothing moved. The hand at my shoulder released. One glance at my arm was about all I could take. The splatters of color reminded me of blood and I'm sure some of it was.

The elder muttered something and threw a handful of withered leaves into a basket suspended over my head. Millions of tiny pieces broke and spiraled down, alighting on my face and torso. Each spot touched tingled then went numb. There was a magnificent cool sensation along my right arm. The last thing I saw before inhaling the sweet-scented plant was the ground up mixture of green being spread over my battered arm...

Ch. 38

"*When* will we be able to see her?"

I smiled over my bowl of warm rattlesnake stew hearing my companions' quarrel outside.

"Soon if calm." The voice belonged to Wolf, the leader who had brought me here five days ago. I had believed her to be a man, but when I saw her without male garments on, I realized my mistake.

The young woman entered the building in a soft rustle of hand-tailored clothes with the hard grace of a tracker, her tall, spindly frame towering over me on the little bed. I guessed her to be around twenty-five, youthful, and the only one I'd heard speak any kind of English. I caught that customary frown before she gave a thin smile as remembering to be nicer to the girl she had slapped silly five days earlier. The woman had that air of the army about her that put me on edge.

"Better?"

I nodded, offering a slight smile to her. "Yes, much."

"Friends of yours are... pushy." She rubbed a bruise on one arm, raising a side of her mouth. "Fair-haired boy mostly."

She was talking about Glen, of course. Before I could ask any details about them, the old woman hobbled in. She was like my savior, turning the most horrific agony into little more than the softest of bumps. The swelling of my arm had decreased, shrinking back to normal size and the look of the wound was no longer inflamed and oozing, but precisely knitted together, producing a startlingly jagged scar.

I set my bowl of food down, still not having completely regained my appetite, and prepared for the woman's daily inspection. Why was Wolf here? She was never present unless she had to be. What could be different? The notion of killing flashed through my head, but I pushed it away. It made no sense if all the work that had been put into me only readied me to be murdered.

"Is... something wrong? Am I free to go?" I could have pinched myself for being so blunt. Here I was, spitting out full sentences in a language the woman couldn't understand.

I opened my mouth to revise my words, but Wolf held up a hand and addressed the elder in their tongue. *That's* why she was here: a translator. I watched the old woman smile, wrinkles looking more like leather, and speak back to Wolf, gesturing to me.

"She says you're free. But listen."

I did. Wolf assured the woman she could go on.

"You have same eyes as a man I met." Wolf was speaking her exact words to me. "He help me, took me into shop in place called California."
I was instantly rooted to the spot at the mention of that name.

"People hurt me, but man take me in, nurse me back." The woman and Wolf paused as if reminded of the time. Her eyes locked on me.

"You same as woman in his shop. He hurt by others for helping me. I repay debt by helping you."

"Wait," I interrupted, "Where was this place and what was it called?"

The elder listened as Wolf explained my question.

"*Merchants'*. A trading post."

A trading center would clarify how the woman got caught up in that mess.

"And the location?"

"San Francisco."

I inclined my head; that was all I needed to know.

"Thank you. For everything." I looked at the tiny, ancient woman. "You've paid off any debt you thought you owed and more."

She seemed to understand what I meant and touched her hand to her heart, bowing her head to me. I grinned, repeating her movements. The old woman spoke to Wolf, giving her instructions. Probably something about letting us go.

After the elder departed, Wolf told me, "Come."

I rose to my feet, feeling a renewed sense of ambition pushing me closer to the truth. The sensation of walking was fresh to me and I could not describe how happy I was to be moving by myself again.

When we exited the humble dwelling, sunlight greeted me, warming my skin. I inhaled, savoring the pure, wispy air. The leggings and rabbit skin vest I was dressed in felt good on my now lean frame and the delicate breeze that made strands of my fair, creamy hair dance put a wonderful smile on my face. I once again had gotten lucky to escape with my life.

"There she is! Lyn's okay!" Raine's doll like features lit up as she and the boys rounded a corner and spotted me. She raced into my open arms, encircling me. Not able to keep the grin from my face, I stroked her curls, noticing they all had new clothes and looked healthier.

Raine took my arm. "It's like nothing happened except for the scar," she observed, tracing the discolored skin.

"Lyn." Caine flashed a trademark smile, indicating my body. "You look like new money," he nudged Glen. "Doesn't she?"

Glen nodded, laughing as spots of color stained his planed cheeks. "We all know what you look like, but how do you feel?"

"Amazing," I answered without a second thought. "I haven't felt this good in a long time."

Glen appeared dazed a bit by my arrival as he shook his head sputtering, "I just can't believe you're..."

Caine broke the silence. "Oh go on and hug her! You know you want to, heck I do too."

I couldn't help myself from letting out a giggle. Glen surrounded me with his arms and I breathed in his familiar scent of grass, dirt, and sweat. It was just about the happiest get-together I'd had.

"You're alive," he said, drawing back just enough to tuck my wind-blown hair into place.

"And you thought I'd never last," I teased, looking into those sparkling azure eyes and smiling. Over Glen's shoulder, Wolf seemed to materialize, waltzing toward us with a small bag and pouch in her hand.

We drew apart; Wolf gave me the items. "Here, take."

I accepted and opened the sack. It had money inside along with knives and food that would keep for the road. It was our going away present, a way of saying 'you need to leave now.' Still, it seemed like a lot.

I opened my mouth to give a reason we shouldn't take this, but Wolf cut me off. "Take. Elder's wishes, not mine." She pointed to a hill off in the distance.

"Elder say go there and see California. Blessed travels." With that voiced, Wolf turned and left.

"So, in other words, our stay just got cut short." Caine stated my exact thoughts. "I guess we get to that hill and go from there, right?"

My party nodded. Raine broke the gloomy mood by skipping in front of us and saying, "Well that's fine with me. I never wanted to stay with these Indians anyway. They were mean."

"They fed you, Raine," Caine countered.

"And you know what? It wasn't that good." She got a good laugh from all of us, improving the tone as we started for the rise.

Glen and Raine were ahead, me lagging behind. Caine dropped back, strolling with me. "So we don't have to carry you. I'm not sure if I know what to do."

I rolled my eyes at Caine's snide comment. "It's an improvement, at least."

He grinned, stopped me in my tracks, and embraced me. It caught me napping, but I swung my arms around his thin shoulders, returning the hug.

"It's about time I got mine. I thought Glen took the last one."

I glanced at him, smirking. "Oh, please. You've got Raine."

He huffed, sliding a look their way. "She loves him just as much as you do."

"What, you saying you're lonely or something?" Before he could answer, I stepped back, grabbing his hand. "We can walk and talk. Don't want to get left."

"I'm saying I think it's sweet how you saved a little for all of us." What a way to change the subject, I thought.

We walked in silence for a while, hands still linked. I took in the scenery around us, pondered over how different it was from previous places we'd been. The plains spread out forever, ending in steep banks and high mountains. There were hardly any trees, simply shrubs and a few cacti. It was a beautiful day; the sun was bright and cheerful and the winds brought promise with their gusts.

I gazed down at Caine and my joined hands, tracing the vivid scar up my arm. Every time I saw it, it brought back memories of the image I had been keeping at bay. My father. I could easily visualize his tanned face, see the startling flaw of white running the length of it. Both marks looked identical, jagged and imperfect.

A squeeze of my hand snapped me out of the reprise and I stared at Caine's dark russet eyes. "What do you look so sad for?"

I searched for another reason than the one I had been thinking of. "Nothing. It's just... I feel like we'll never see those people again."

Caine snorted rudely. "Yeah right. Don't worry, Lyn, I'm sure we'll come visit every week or so."

I glared at his sarcastic demeanor, pulled my hand away, and threw the thought out of my mind. When I turned to keep going forward, I ran smack into Glen's back. He stumbled, but managed to catch me before we fell. Out of habit, I braced for the tremendous pain from my arm, but none came.

"You know, that woman really did some amazing work," he said, scrutinizing my scar. "Too bad she didn't fix your balance problem."

I only smiled faintly. Glen gave me an odd look, as if he could tell something was wrong. I'd know that blue-eyed gleam anywhere.

"Before you ask, I'm fine."

He drew his perfect brow together. That face took on a strained cast, dangerously accenting his natural good looks and making me feel instantly guilty of snapping. "I wasn't-"

"Hey you two!" Caine's shout cut us off. "Come get an eyeful of this!"

After exchanging glances, Glen and I scaled the rest of the mound. The view of sprawling San Francisco was glorious, twenty times as large as any town I had ever seen. The buildings there looked huge even at this distance and the vast land beyond it appeared to be sky stretching out forever. That had to be the ocean.

I swept my gaze over what it would take to get there: nothing but immense wasteland dusted with sparse foliage.

"How many days do you think?" I asked.

"On foot, I'd say around five," Glen answered. I grimaced, thinking of walking through the blistering heat and itchy sand.

"Well we're not getting any closer just standing here." Caine tested the hill heading for the city. "Let's get moving."

"San Francisco here we come," I told myself, inching after him, still staring at the magnificent metropolis.

Ch. 39 Getting Warmer

The sun was sweltering and the sand was roasting, cooking right through the soles of our shoes. When the wind picked up, grit flew into our clothes and stuck to our sweaty bodies. Water was a must. We had some from the Indian reservation, but not nearly enough to sustain for five hot days.

Glen had fished the canteen out of the bag and sipped on it. He passed it to me and I passed to Raine after a small swig.

"Go easy on the water, Raine," I heard Glen mumble when she took a good-sized swallow.

"Give me some!" Caine snatched the container out of her little shaking hands and started draining it.

"Quit!" I wrenched the thing from him and maneuvered out of the way of his groping hands.

"Don't think you're getting it all to yourself, Lyn. Let it go," he demanded, advancing on me. Caine pounced forward, but I dodged and he went flying; whimpers of pain followed.

I looked to see him plucking thorns from his shirt. That gave me an idea. I glanced at the larger cacti and figured the plants had to have a source of water in them; we just needed to draw it out.

"Lyn?" Raine touched my hand, making me look down, surprised to find a dagger in my grasp.

"I had an idea," I explained sheepishly, avoiding those worried doe eyes.

"And it involves you with a knife, how?"

I smirked at Glen, proud of my plan. "We want water and the cacti have it so if we dig in them water should be there. How else do you think they're living in this heat?"

"And I thought you'd been fixed," Caine sneered, picking a thorn from his leg. "Looks like I was wrong."

Did he not understand? Between Caine, the sun, and lack of food and water, I broke.

"Listen, Caine, if you want to dry up and die out in this misery, you can because I won't stop you. Look past your self-importance and think for once!"

His expression turned nasty as Caine growled, "If one of us doesn't do something with that attitude of yours then you'll end up killing us all. I'm the only one with enough sense to do anything about it!"

That stung. I lunged for him, catching a fistful of his shirt and jerking the boy in close. Caine gripped my arm with both hands, glaring hard at me.

"Shut up." There were senseless tears in my eyes, cutting my words short.

"Lyn, calm down and let me go." He was trying to be reasonable, but after his earlier actions I would have nothing of it.

"Did you not hear what I said?" I gave an angry shake.

"Lyn, Caine, Glen's got some water to drink! Please just... come with me." Our stupid fight probably frightened Raine.

I looked at the hand clutching Caine's shirt and became even more infuriated when I saw it trembling. With a fury, I pushed Caine away and it seemed like all my energy went with him. He stumbled, shot me one more look, and then stalked off, suddenly reminding me of the wolfish boy I'd met barely two years ago.

I knew I shouldn't have let myself go off like that, no matter how much pressure or heat I was under. Maybe the desert was getting to everyone, not just me.

"Lyn." Glen's quiet footsteps stopped behind me and his arms encircled my waist. His cheek pressed against mine, his azure gaze cut to look at me. I swiped at wet tears in my eyes.

"I know you're thirsty," he whispered, nudging my head. "Come over and have a drink. It's not very tasty or cold, but the stuff's wet, at least." I smiled at him through my tears and he gave a sweet grin in return.

The water was bitter and difficult to swallow, but it was indeed wet. I only wished there was more of it. Glen's incision in the plant had run dry much too quick. I supposed now we knew not to travel so much in the daytime and reserve our energy for night.

Everyone gathered themselves and managed to press on. Caine and I kept a fair distance and Raine and Glen tried to ease the friction by stirring up idle conversation about how dry the desert was or how empty their stomachs felt. The attempt of relief even made me add in the 'sand in your clothes' problem that brought a much-needed laugh. It wasn't long until afternoon sun flowed over the dust and the badlands became cooler.

"Why don't we take a break?" I asked, casting my gaze around a few scattered rocks that would suffice as shelter from some sand.

"Wouldn't it be better if we traveled through the night?" Caine questioned. I couldn't tell if he was being serious or trying my patience again.

"You keep walking if it makes you happy," I said, slipping over to one of the stones. "I'm going to rest a little before I collapse."

I saw him scowl, but Caine did not keep moving. He, Raine, and Glen decided my idea was our best bet for now and we settled in, unpacking bits of food from the Indians and nibbling on our scarce supply, each bite making us yearn for more. We chewed slowly, watching in silence as the beams of sunlight surged over the yellow sand, turning it a dark gold bathed in rich crimson color.

"What's that?" Raine broke the noiselessness. We followed her eyes off in the expanse of land. Something luminous sparkled and danced on the horizon, growing brighter as the sun sunk lower.

"You think it's the city lights?" Caine questioned, shielding his eyes from the rays.

"It's so pretty." Raine rose and daintily stepped toward the radiance, temporarily forgetting her empty stomach and parched throat. I watched them, too, saw how the lights fluttered and shone bright one moment then vanished the next only to be replaced by another.

I looked at the sight for such a long time, I was hardly aware of Glen's presence beside me. I blinked, glanced at Caine and Raine to find them asleep, then turned to Glen. He leaned against the same large stone I was resting on, gazing solemnly at the glowing spectacle in front of us.

"What's on your mind?" I asked, brushing his sandy hair to the side of his forehead. It accentuated his handsome profile quite nicely.

"Just thinking," he answered, never diverting his eyes from the lights.

"About what?" I pressed, figuring since Caine and Raine were asleep and that meant we were on watch, I had time to spare. Glen cut his gaze to look at me, half-smile crossing his lips.

"Family." His response surprised me.

"Family, huh? Our sorry family isn't doing that great right now, is it?"

My question got a chuckle from him, but no answer.

"I didn't mean *our* kind of family," he explained. "The type with a mother, father, kids, grandparents... What was it like, Lyn? To have family that cared about you?"

I took a moment before saying anything. Remembering my family only brought me a hollow shell where there should have been tenderness because I couldn't call them that anymore. I supposed they cared, though.

"It felt nice. Safe. Almost like you were surrounded by people that would protect you no matter what happened." It was a rather poor description, but it was the best I could come up with.

"Do you wish you were still with them? The people before all this."

This time, I was intent on his reaction when I replied. "There are times, but back then it wasn't as..." I searched for the right word. "I don't know, exciting?"

We both laughed. Having foster parents that never wasted a thought on you must have been hard on him, especially growing up. I recalled him telling me that was why he had left one day; they had no idea he ever disappeared. Still, I wondered what brought it up.

"Why the sudden talk about family?"

He shrugged. "I'm not sure. I guess you and your dad had me thinking." It had me thinking, too. Worrying myself to death was more like it.

I let the conversation drop, feeling drained of my energy. I leaned my head on Glen's shoulder and pulled my knees up in my chest with my hands. Closing my eyes, I knew he, Raine, and Caine were all the family I needed.

Right before I went to sleep on his arm, Glen asked me, "Lyn, you ever think you'll get married?"

That question woke me back up. Marriage? Truth be told, I actually *had* thought about it. The concept had come up multiple times in my head, silly, really, to me at least. I guess with him around me all the time, how could I not? It wasn't like I was going tell Glen now, though.

"You know, I've never really considered it." I assumed my answer was subtle enough.

When surviving day by day, love was just not a luxury we could afford. Aware of my close proximity to Glen, I figured I tactfully went after it whenever I could. Stupid, I know. Still, it wasn't like he gave me reason to stop. On the contrary, Glen's actions breached the distance between us more.

"I suppose I'd like to one of these days," I elaborated more on the topic. "Do you think you'll ever tie the knot?"

Glen smirked, smile higher on one side than the other, and said, "If I ever, I think I'll have a time doing it."

I raised an eyebrow thinking that impossible with his looks. "Oh really?"

He looked at me. "Really."

"Well, we've got plenty of time to think about it." I huddled back down on his shoulder. "Let's go to sleep for now."

"And worry about everything later," Glen added, draping his arm around me so I had a more comfortable position for my head.

Worry about everything later. Wouldn't that be nice...

Ch. 40 Worried about Water

"How do you guys feel about it, honestly?"

I had to finally break the silence in our long trek through a gully we had been traveling in. Questioning the others about my *family problems* seemed the best way to do this.

"I think you're in the right." Raine was the first to answer. "When you want to know something you shouldn't stop until you figure it out."

"Or end up dead," Caine added under his breath. I simply rolled my eyes.

"Raine's right," Glen said, "To an extent."

I raised my eyebrows, repeating, "*To an extent?*"

Glen gave a helpless grin that made me ease off his explanation. "You have taken it to a bit of an extreme, putting it mildly." A rush of temper came over me, but I had asked for it so I kept my mouth shut.

"I don't know many people who would travel half the country, flirting with death and spitting in the hands of fate just to see relatives they've never met before."

I diverted my gaze, knowing without a doubt he was exact in the wording.

"You don't even want to know what I think," Caine said.

"I asked all of you so go ahead and give me your worst."

"Well alright, but I'm not going to sugar-coat anything for you, Lyn."

I huffed. "Since when do you sweeten your opinion?"

"You're insane." He smirked lopsidedly when Caine saw my expression. "Told you it wasn't sweet."

"Oh stop talking and keep walking." I tried to play it off as a joke, but my red cheeks gave me away when Glen and Raine started giggling.

Everyone somehow drug themselves on. We decided to stay in the rut since the sand there wasn't so yielding, but packed and hardened. Thoughts of my now scarred arm often haunted me when I caught a glimpse of it, but the nearness of my destination kept my mind busy thinking how I was ever going to find the store in that sprawling city.

For a change in scenery, I turned my gaze skyward expecting blazing blue and skinny white wisps. The garish sight of deep gray obscured my vision instead.

"Is it... raining?" I asked to no one in particular.

"Do you see any drops falling in your face?" Caine cut back. "Please explain what made you say that, Lyn."

"Look up."

We all did, slowing in unison. The black cloud was about as natural as dogs flying as far as I was concerned, but it made me think of heavy rain in the desert. Flooding. A glance around the ravine we were in started to look an awful lot like a dry riverbed.

"If it is rain then maybe we can have a shower while we walk," Glen joked. "I'm going to climb up and check how far we are from the city."

He scrambled up the narrow side of our gully, rising and assessing our miles until San Francisco. I couldn't tear my eyes from the dark mass behind us.

"You think we shouldn't be standing here?"

Raine looked quizzically at me then at the cloud while Caine said, "You know rain in the desert's about as likely as my getting struck by lighting right now. It's probably some stupid sandstorm that kicked up a lot of dirt."

"It *does* shower here," I barked. "What if we're just waiting around in this ditch about to get washed away and we don't even try to move when the water hits?"

"What, now you think it's going to flood?" Caine's tone was ridiculous. I thought of something sensible to say, but nothing that seemed right came to mind.

"I just felt some water." We both turned on Raine who was staring at a puddle on her arm. I opened my mouth to justify my point, but a heavy drop smacked me in the lips. It tasted salty, like dust in the air. More droplets began pelting us.

Just as I started feeling content with myself, a sudden deluge of torrential water nearly knocked me senseless. The current swept me off my feet and I managed to scream, "Glen!" before going under the murky torrent. The rain must have started from that monster of a cloud haunting the sky. I'd been right about the riverbed, too, it had simply taken some time for the river to reach us.

Flipping, twisting, and churning in the water only intensified my terror of drowning in the flood as I pushed with all I had to break through the surface. My face above the river, I swallowed as much air as my lungs could hold, snatching a glimpse of Glen, confusion and horror making up his expression as he launched into a sprint to keep up with us then back under I went. The current was strong and thick with desert residue; I could tell from all the wet sand and cacti scraping my body.

Fighting once again for my life, I drove the water out of my way, cracking the shell of liquid. The river wasn't as ferocious as before, but I still battled for breath while the water struck my face with blinding mud. I was able to see two heads in front of me bobbing helplessly in the torrent and, looking past Caine and Raine, spied a winding path the water was rushing down.

"Lyn!" I spun madly to Glen who shot across the sand above me, desperately keeping pace with the current. He yelled something else, but I was pulled down yet again.

I could feel my resistance fading, see the black dots flicker before my eyes. I'd heard drowning was a peaceful way to die... "Bam!" My body smashed into rocks that fired me past the surface. I flailed then slammed back down, water biting my skin. Now we were surging through the channel.

The rapids moved so fast it created a shallower flow, allowing for air to enter my lungs. Good, I thought sadistically, grimacing as another rock slashed my side, we won't drown at least. Sweeping down a steep incline, I caught sight of either Caine or Raine crashing brutally into one of the gully's walls. His or her head wobbled then disappeared under the flood. Sudden panic ensued and I dug in, getting nowhere. Someone was going to die if they couldn't get their nose above water.

A flash to my right told me Glen, who might be our only saving grace, was doing the thing that would cut any chance of rescue. I tried to scream, but silt filled my mouth, chocking me, forcing me to watch him register the head going under then go diving in after them. He never came back up.

I spilled over another dip in the gorge and tumbled, dragging across sharp rocks, shifting into another slide. The end of this one looked even worse; water tore down the ravine and encountered an immediate hairpin turn where half of it washed over the wall and the rest went streaming on through to the right. It was a hellish amusement ride where you knew there was absolutely nothing you could do to stop from killing yourself; Strapped down with no way out.

Not able to do anything but anticipate the inevitable, I set my sights on the wave sweeping over the rise. To be thrown out was a possible wager for survival, but then again, what if I landed in something more horrid than the river? A dicey plan indeed, but it was the only one that had a chance to work. I threw aside my doubt and began pumping for all I was worth, picking up speed in hopes of being thrown out of the gully. My body collided with something that made my limbs recoil in shock and pain. Caine's drenched head burst from under water and without thinking I grabbed him and started kicking harder, revitalized with a goal of survival. Here it comes...

I felt like I was soaring through the air one moment, all fears and terrors wiped away, and the next I was plowing into the sand, gallons of dirty water washing over me. No movement was possible; my body throbbed and pulsed with each ragged breath. I coughed up some liquid, blinked the rest out of my stinging eyes, and squeezed Caine's hand. A sputter then he spit water and sucked in air, sodden hair plastered over his face.

There was another crash and Caine and I were both pounded farther into the ground by two other bodies. After a bunch of hacking and dripping water, the pressure ceased, people rolling off us. I looked to my left, seeing Glen, dirty and struggling for air. Someone's coughing never stopped, but the gagging intensified. Twisting, I figured out it was Raine, choking. With rapid scrambling, I staggered toward her convulsing body and heaved on her chest.

"Raine," I rasped, "Come on, breathe!" I hoped I wasn't hurting her as water drizzled past her lips. That was good, right?

More retching and she suddenly flipped to one side and vomited up mud. I let out my held air, the world spinning before my eyes. Water kept washing up over the side, soaking us, and I feared the waves would soon pull us back in. My limbs quaking, I got a hold on Raine and started dragging her away from the surf. Every movement I made brought on the shakes more and more, pain consuming my worn muscles.

When I figured she was far enough from the raging liquid, I staggered back for Glen who fought with all he had to get Caine moving, both of them getting mauled by waves from the flood. I dropped to my knees and gripped Caine, tremors worsening, but allowing him to be towed from danger with Glen's help. While pulling Caine, I noticed a nasty gash on Glen's hand. It bled profusely, turning Caine's shirt red even though ~~know~~ Glen kept trying to hide it. We let go of Caine as another round of hacking over came ~~he and Raine,~~ Raine and him and I snatched Glen's arm, smearing blood.

"What did you do?" I demanded, holding on when he attempted to jerk away.

"I hit a few rocks when I dove in." He yanked again and I released. "Nothing to worry about."

I narrowed my eyes.

"Have you looked at yourself?" Glen gestured to me. "At Raine or Caine? You three were in longer than I was."

Glancing just over my legs, I skimmed the red oozing out of multiple nicks and cuts. "They don't hurt."

"Then stop worrying," Caine said, finally having got the water out of his lungs. "And don't you even say 'I told you so'."

I wasn't going to. Yet. Still feeling the pitter-patter of drops, I believed the waves were reaching us even at our distance. I glanced up and more water pelted me in the face. The rain had finally arrived. I turned from the inky cloud above me to the raging river behind. If the downpour kept coming then the water would keep rising, flooding. That meant we could not stop running. Looking at the shape everyone was in, I didn't think we could start.

"We can't stay here," I told them, "We have to move. The rain's not letting up."

"Lyn, have you looked around?" Caine was in a fine state about it. Figures, though. It's not like I get a thank you for saving *his* life. "Raine can barely breathe, Glen's bleeding all over the place, and I-"

"Need to *help me move.*" It was time for his tone to end. We had been at each other's neck *Threats* long enough.

I went to scoop Raine up, but Caine got to her first. "You wouldn't make it five steps without dropping her. Go make sure Glen doesn't run dry."

One look at his eyes was all I needed; with a quick dash I was at Glen's side. His wrist was bleeding something awful no matter how he applied pressure to prevent it.

"Come on, Glen, don't tell me Caine's going to have to stitch you up, too." I got a faint smile from him, but the blood coloring his hand and shirt made worry overtake it much *Too* to quick. The dirt certainly wasn't helping keep infection out.

"Here." I gripped his arm, trying not to wince as the tacky feel of gore played across my fingers. "Let the rain clean it."

I watched red trickle in rivulets for a moment then Glen took my face in his hands, making me look at him. "Lyn, don't bother with me. Like you said, we've got to keep going."

I cast one more glance at his cut, but nodded anyway. We hunkered down, pushing against the storm, tiny raindrops feeling like teeth to our beat-up skin. Caine was ahead, carrying Raine when Glen and I caught up with him, relentless downpour twirling the sand to uneven footholds and forcing us to spend the rest of our energy.

The hunger was gaining. I could feel my stomach eating away at my muscles; sense the shaking in my limbs not only from the water, but starvation that threatened to bring me to my limit. We lost the rest of our food in the flood so if we had a chance for nourishment we had to hunt. What was there to hunt, though? I sighed, blinking away water droplets. Even if we managed to catch something in this wasteland there was no way to cook with the rain. Surely there was an end to it, I thought, the hot desert sun would come out and dry our soaked bodies, revive our spirit.

Lost in my thoughts, I never noticed Glen trip in front of me. I stumbled and plowed straight into his back, throwing us both to the ground. It was pitiful because not only could I not muster the strength to say sorry, but I had no shot at moving. The fight had left me, drained away with the river.

"Glen?" Caine's footsteps dragged to us, but Glen's words stopped them.

"It's okay, Caine, I've got her." Glen shifted and his arms soon lifted me.

"Hold up, Glen, you can't carry her the way you're bleeding like that."

Hugging me to his chest, I felt Glen press forward, past Caine. "What do you want me to do? If we stay, we drown, so I'll take my chances with Lyn. You make sure Raine makes it alright."

Caine must have seen the hard truth to Glen's words because I heard no more from him. Glen's shirt smelt metallic and I wondered how badly the wound was oozing if the rain hadn't washed away the scent. He was shaking too; I felt the faint spasms jarring me as we walked. Why was I letting him do this? Why couldn't I do anything about it?

Exhaustion and beating rain took me under before I could even figure out what to say...

Ch. 41 Nearly There

The city. All my senses were on edge. People flew by, knocking me around, inflicting pain while I searched for my building.

"Lyn!" My name called sent an earthquake rumbling through the whole place. Suffocation loomed above my head as rubble flung itself toward me.

Screaming, I hurdled whatever the quake stirred up, desperate to make it to my door. I arrived, threw the door open, and dashed inside, but the horrors awaiting me were much worse than those before. I froze, facing two identical men and moving shadows behind them. Backing away from golden stares, I found myself trapped. One look at the men's faces and that maniac grin spread across their features. A signal and all the darkness lurking behind them surged forward, consuming me until all I could see was a single pair of yellow eyes.

Upon waking, I realized I could not breathe. My lungs burned as I sucked down air, feeling as though the world's supply had run dry. I tasted the unmistakable flavor of blood and remembered my face was pressed against Glen's chest. It was *his* blood, not mine, that choked me.

"Lyn?" I knew I had to get a hold of myself. Glen was in a lot worse shape than I.

"I-I'm fine," I stuttered, shakily pulling back so I could see his face. "You're still bleeding?"

Glen looked terribly pale; blue eyes the only color to his face. His shirt was stained with red and filthy mud that the rain hadn't washed away. Glen's hair was all over the place, wavy and very dark, like it was still damp, despite the sun's searing rays. I noticed the way he avoided my gaze when he answered.

"It's quit... How bad was the dream?"

Not taking my eyes off his wound of bubbly crimson, I said, "Rough."

It was about all I could say without loosing it. "Caine and Raine. Are they around?"

Glen carefully set me on my feet and I was steady, not thinking about my nightmare. "They're close. Searching for food."

The mention of something to eat sent my gut into frenzy; I could feel the acid gnawing away at my insides, craving nourishment. A movement in the corner of my eye drew my attention. It was a snake. Food.

"They won't have to search much longer," I said, stumbling from Glen. "I see our meal."

He snatched my wrist before I could take another step. "Lyn, that's death waiting to happen. One bite from that thing and you're gone."

"We're gone anyway if we can't scrounge up some food." I yanked, but he never let go. "Help me and I won't die."

"Throw, Raine!"

Glen and I jumped, spinning in time to see Raine's dagger flying straight for the serpent. The blade buried in the sand right beside it and set the reptile on the defensive. It whipped its deadly head around to face Caine and Raine just out of its reach, both of them alarmed to find it focused on their faces. The snake struck out once at them, missing by less than an inch. I shook Glen off and made a dive for it, knowing it was either distract it or Caine and Raine were going to be bitten.

The serpent writhed in my hands and I became aware that my feeble fingers on it alone would do nothing to stop it from twisting to sink its fangs into me. I couldn't do anything, but hope to make the process slower, pray for help. Its scales cut into my flesh and I screamed when it jerked, hissing, teeth barely missing my arm.

Feet suddenly appeared by the snake's head, switching its interest from my body.

"Let go when we say!" Caine's shout came from the pair of feet skipping to dodge the reptile's attacks.

"I can't! It'll kill me," I wailed, feeling its tail coil around my leg, pressure becoming more and more painful.

"Let go!"

Gritting my teeth and putting every ounce of common sense I had out of my mind, I released the thrashing serpent. My body was immediately wrenched back by strong hands, just in time for me to see what the inside of a snake's mouth looked like. I swore I could feel little drops of poison dotting my face before the reptile slumped to the ground. Raine had stabbed the place my grip was as Glen pulled me away, butchering the snake and saving me a trip to the hereafter.

"Man, don't you hate it when it takes more energy to get the food than you get from eating it?" Caine crushed the reptile's head with his foot to make sure it had no chance of coming back. "Thanks for saving our skin, Lyn. I guess even experts miss sometimes."

The snake was terrible really, but to us, it was delectable. Sure the occasional scale or bone interrupted your chewing and the meat itself was tough and wiry, but it was food, and it sated the awful famine in our bellies. Caine had insisted he be the one to fool with the thing so none of us objected. Spotting the mangled skin in his hands, I now understood why.

"What do you think *that's* going to help you with?" I had to say something. The boy wasn't just going to get away scotch-free.

"Money."

Caine saw my confused look and explained further, a charmer's grin sneaking its way on his lips. "You ever heard of snakeskin belts?"

"Yes, and that's clearly not one of them."

"It is." He picked up a smooth cactus limb and wrapped the hide around it. "Just not finished."

I snarled seeing the limp, bloody thing draped over the branch. "You know you're going to be the one carrying that."

Caine looked at me. "I know."

"Then pick it up and let's get moving." Glen trudged past us with Raine who wrinkled her nose at the skin.

I curled my fingers, feeling the slight pain where my grip on the serpent had nicked me. My destination drew ever closer as we set out again, watching as the sprawling city grew larger and larger...

Ch. 42 San Francisco, California

*H*ere we were, the city of San Francisco in all its splendor and glory. The grand sight took my breath away and sent my heart soaring right over the lofty buildings and ocean of blue beyond.

"I've never seen anything so big," Raine stated, clearly in awe. "I finally know why Dad never came back. It seems so much better here."

"Come on, Raine." Caine danced over to her. "You'd rather be with your old folks than with us?"

She pushed him away, face screwed up in repulsion. "Ugh, Caine you stink!"

"She's right," Glen commented. "I can smell you from here."

"It's that gross snake skin he's carried for a day," I grumbled, flashing him a glare.

"Look," Caine began, unwinding the dried skin from the limb; "I'll hang the stuff on my belt so you guys won't have to see it."

He tossed the stick down. "It's that that stinks so bad."

"How considerate of you," I mumbled sarcastically.

Caine ignored me, finished rolling the scaly thing, and secured it to his pant's strap. "Don't worry. Soon as I sell this, I'll start making money the good old-fashioned way again. Besides," he grinned, indicating his appearance, "What better disguise than a trader, right?"

"We're not here to pick people's pockets, Caine," Glen said. "Lyn's our first priority."

Caine dismissed his concern with a wave of his hand. "That don't mean I can't have a little fun on the side."

"Don't go crazy. We've gotten ourselves in enough trouble as it is." I turned toward the city entrance. "I think we could have a hard time dodging messes in this place."

"If you don't make them then you don't have to avoid them."

I watched Caine waltz on by, obviously more excited about going in than me. Focus, I told myself, that's all I need to do.

The sights were surreal. Never had I seen so many vehicles, buggies, and buildings. The smells were new and intoxicating. Fumes from the industry were sharp while scents of food lingered in my nose making me ravenous. The sounds were sudden, nothing like blown leaves or rushing water, but they came robustly, setting me on edge even more.

Focus? Yeah right. It was easier said than done, but I ripped my eyes away from enticing delicacies, determined not to be swept up in it all. One glance at the others told me I wasn't alone in not being able to concentrate.

As we sauntered deeper into the city, I saw Raine look at every little thing, brown doe eyes centering on something then brushing over the rest around it. Caine was in his element; he tracked every movement with that dark russet gaze. I could almost see his mind picking out which person or place would offer up the best spoils. It was Glen I worried about. He, like me, had been raised with a great deal of land, never confined in the city. Glen was tense (much as he tried to hide it) and carried himself in a way that invoked apprehension.

There was too much going on in this place, I thought, dodging yet another group of ~~passerby~~ passers by. We'd been searching for nearly half an hour and nothing, not even a sign hinted we might be close.

"Well would you look at this?" Caine's voice got my attention and I glanced over to find him holding a newspaper, skimming the print on it.

"Where did you pick that up?" I asked, shuffling so I could read it.

"The trash. And before you ask why, let's just say it's the best way to learn some information without someone telling you."

Another trick he must have gathered from hard city living.

"Bad news for us, huh?"

"Terrible. Really terrible." Glen answered Caine. Apparently last to read the report, I finally made it click.

Indian Reservation Massacre. By pure willpower, I read what little I could underneath the headline. *Natives killed outside borders by what reports believe to be a massive group of murderers.* Dead. The people who had saved my life, provided us with a place of respite, were gone.

"I can't believe it." My hand instinctively went to my scar.

"Maybe we won't be visiting every week or so." Caine stated what we had discussed after leaving the

Natives. I had felt like we would never see them again. Looked like I was right.

"There was nothing we could have done," Glen reasoned, pulling back from the paper. "There isn't anything about a store in it so we're going to have to search the hard way."

I nodded away the shock, dismissing my thoughts of who the *murderers* could be. "So we split. It'll go faster that way."

A quick glance at Raine nearly made me second-guess myself, but I figured she was seasoned enough after all she'd been through with us.

"We'll have to," Glen confirmed, exchanging glances with me. "We can meet back here in an hour and swap information. Surely one of us will have some luck."

"That all?" Caine questioned, impatient arrogance hardly concealed in his features.

"Be careful," I added, locking eyes with him.

"You worried?"

"About you? Yes."

Caine smiled, shaking his head. "Don't be. Worrying about yourself should keep you occupied enough, Lyn."

He split with a wink and twist of his lips, easily melting into the crowd. I shook my head, sighing. Seeing Raine beside me, that same anxiety on her face, I bent down, letting her focus on me.

"You'll be okay, won't you?"

She gave me that sweet smile of hers I loved so much. "No one will ever notice I'm there."

"That's my girl." I squeezed her and off Raine went, disappearing with no trouble at all. Standing, I turned to face Glen; he was the last to go.

"I have a bad feeling about all this," I said. "This whole splitting up deal could turn out terribly."

Glen managed to grin. "It's going to be fine. You always have a bad feeling about something."

He was parting from me, too.

"You don't understand..." I trailed off thinking it was now or never. His handsome face looked confused, wanting me to spit out the rest of my sentence. Finally, I centered my gaze with his.

"It's you... I think I love you, Glen."

I saw that flicker of surprise cross his eyes then he smiled, heightening those good looks. "I know."

He moved in close; I never quit staring at him, too stunned to, really.

"But," the boy continued while my eyes traveled from his sapphire blues to those smirking lips. Glen encircled my waist with an arm; his other hand cupped my cheek, rough thumb tracing my jawline. He leaned down, lips ghosting across mine as he whispered, "I love you more," then crashed his mouth against mine.

The initial shock robbed me of my air and balance. I wound my arms around his neck to keep from buckling, deepening the kiss. Grit and sweat mixed with the salty sea breeze and scents of the city. The taste was so *male.*

Feeling Glen's hot hand at my hip loosen, I became aware of his easing away and the distance was enough to wrench my heart in two. I dove back into the boy's warm, dusty skin, heard his sharp intake of breath when my fingers tousled his streaked hair.

"Lyn."

I stopped my advance upon his warning murmur. Heat lit up my face when our gazes locked and goose bumps shimmered down my arms when Glen slid his hands into mine.

"Stay safe for me."

I was speechless, still having trouble keeping my heart under control, but I clutched his calloused palm as we drifted farther apart, knowing we couldn't stay.

"See you soon."

Not releasing until the very fingertips, I was as reluctant as he when we let go. I walked toward the bowels of the great city, but turned once more to catch that striking smile and blue-eyed glint aimed my way. All I could do was smile back and hope for the best.

My head pounded with thoughts as I hunted for my store. The newspaper still fiddled with my mind, begging for attention, but I was afraid of what I might figure out. *Merchants* irked me. I tried every way possible to think of what it would look like, but that only got me one heck of a headache so I turned to the fact every person I trusted was somewhere in this metropolis. Caine was probably ripping as many people off as he could, not even sparing a glance for my store; it would be too much of a bother for him. I could only hope Raine was being smart about her moves. Sure she was little, but any small girl was vulnerable, no matter what she'd been through. Then there was Glen.

My fingers found my lips, recalling the kiss. I had wanted it, but... I still couldn't bring myself to think it all real. The shock, even now, sent my chest thudding faster. I pushed the memory to the back of my mind for now.

Pausing to clear my head, I caught the scent of food wafting through the air. My mouth gushed when I inhaled the savory smell of meat and I turned to a shop located close to a corner I was standing on. The cook beckoned people to come buy his goods, boasting about how delectable they tasted. I longed to go gather with them, maybe sneak a bite or two and fill the gaping hole in my abdomen...

Who was I kidding? I'd be spotted in a second with my luck. Forcing my zeal to get something in my stomach into place, I slipped down a short alley, figuring it was likely around time for everyone to meet up again. My reflection in one of the dirty windows stopped me. I shifted to where I could see my face and body, distorted by the glass but visible. Looking at myself it was no wonder I'd not have any luck stealing food. My face was drawn and thin, not to mention smeared with mud. My eyes were tired and a dark sea green, nothing to help my sunburned complexion from our trek through the desert. The blonde in my hair was barely discernible from all the tangles and filth in it and the untidiness continued to my clothes that were grubby with muck. No doubt my smell was enough to keep anyone at bay.

I closed my eyes and turned away. What did I expect, some beautiful girl with perfect features? After everything I had been through, that was impossible. I ambled on down the alley, pausing at the end out of habit to make sure the coast was clear. Scanning the crowd, my gaze fell on a little girl skirting the masses, yelling someone's name. My name. It was Raine.

I stepped out of my cover and waved so she'd see me. As soon as Raine spotted me, she quit calling and busted to my position, knocking a few people around in the process.

"Lyn!" She buried her face into my stomach, sobbing. I stroked her curls, trying to be a comfort, but anxious to know what had gotten her so upset.

I noticed we were drawing some unwanted attention. Patting her back, I eased her into the narrow lane I had hidden in.

"Raine, you've got to calm down," I whispered, glancing everywhere to make sure no overly suspicious bodies were watching. "What happened? Why aren't you at the square?"

Raine pulled herself together as best she could and looked at me through her tears. "I couldn't... Caine, he-" she faltered, leaving me more vexed than before.

"What, Raine? Spit it out!" I was having a hard time keeping my voice down.

"Arrested," she whispered.

It felt like the city caved in on me, trapping my terrors inside.

"What about Glen?" I asked, thinking I couldn't loose him now. Not after...

"I thought he'd be with you." Raine shook her head, words spilling out in a panic. "I was walking by a fruit stand and snatched an apple when they weren't looking. I took off and the next thing I knew, there went Caine slipping through a big crowd. He was being chased and all I did was stand there and watch!"

There would have been nothing she could've done. I soothed her, urging Raine to finish the tale.

"I saw a bunch of police after him then the people stopped Caine... They shouted 'thief!', handed him over. They beat Caine, Lyn, then dragged him away! His face was bruised and there was blood all over his clothes..."

I clutched her tighter, feeling the shock myself. This city was not ours. Caine had gotten in too deep already; who knew where Glen was.

"I'm going after him."

I jumped a bit out of surprise when Raine said that. Giving us distance, I looked her full in the face. "Raine, listen to me. You can't go to prison and fight those cops. You want to get beaten and dragged away, too?"

I had hit a tender spot, but she shook it off, staring hard at me. "I won't. I have to go, Lyn, I owe Caine that."

"You don't owe him anything."

"Please, Lyn."

I bit my tongue, mulling it over in my head. What choice did I have? Someone had to get him out so I figured Raine had the best chances. Am I crazy? Still, one look at Raine and I knew I couldn't change her mind.

"Come back safe, okay?"

She nodded fiercely, battling tears, and hugged me one more time before I let her go. What had I done?

I rambled through the streets, thoughts clashing at an all time high. The horrifying understanding that I would never see the people I cared about again overwhelmed my mind. The thoughts actually hurt, but nothing I did would shake them so they attacked, rolling my head and crushing any resistance I could muster.

Caine had made the same mistake his parents did; the boy's arrogance had helped Caine into the water, but left him stranded to drown in his own cheek. I kept picturing myself running to the square and seeing the bodies dangling from nooses, Caine's neck in one of them. If he were hanged because of stealing, where did that leave Raine?

Every time I weighed the reality of what I let her do, torrents of guilt struck me. I imagined all the hoodlums lurking in the alleyways, ready to jump some helpless girl, the police with their guns and clubs. What if Raine was beaten like Caine or shot at? The nasty smiles of street vendors surfaced. Raine was only a piece in their hungry games. She'd be dead before the day was over.

Glen had never shown up; the memory of his avid kiss burned in my head. My last remembrance of he~~~~ and his lovely smile was when we departed

him

from each other. It felt like my heart would split open when I fought the idea of not seeing Glen's beautiful blues and handsome face again.

Through the fog in my mind I found a deserted bench and staggered to it, knowing my legs were not going to hold up any longer. I plopped down on the stone and covered my face with my hands. Hot tears of despair flowed over my fingers as I cried, giving up on it all. I knew people were looking, but I didn't care; I was finished.

So this is how I'm going to go out, I thought. No heroic death by battling, no natural calamity to leave me beaten while the life bled out of me, but *I* would cause my end. What was I doing? A few bad decisions always came with dangerous consequences; I had been brave enough to take on the worst of those so far. My whole purpose for coming to this hell was to find my uncle's store and my mother with it. Now I was here and I was just giving up?

I crunched the inside of my mouth until the sharp flavor of blood touched my tongue. The pain held back the rest of my sorry tears. I had made it, sacrificed everyone to get where I was. Clawing at my eyes, I looked up and read the impossible letters across the street. *Merchants.*

Ch. 43 This Is It

The feeling of defeat was engulfed by awe. I stumbled toward the store, *my* store. People were jostled and buggy horses were pulled to a rude stop as I crossed in a trance. More than a few choice words were thrown my way, but all that mattered was opening *Merchant's* door.

I trudged up the stone steps, placed my trembling hand on the knob, and entered after a deep breath for my nerves. The inside was quaint and rather pleasing to the eye with neatly stocked shelves and wooden inlays throughout. Exotic fumes mixed with scents of leather and herbs as I surveyed the interior expecting more crowd. Where were the owners?

Almost as soon as the question popped in my head, a woman waltzed into my sight, reading something in her hands. I held my breath when she skidded to a halt, taken by surprise at my presence. Spinning to face her, I found I mesmerized the woman. She forced me to pause and stare, too.

The woman had lovely blonde hair and blue eyes with dark lashes framing them. Her high cheekbones illustrated attractive features and she was clothed in a sharp-looking dress that showed a shapely figure. She seemed so familiar... My reflection in the glass took me back and I realized the woman reminded me of myself.

Just as the thought crossed my mind, a movement in the corner of my eye tore me from it. I swiveled to witness a towering man rise up from behind a wooden counter. A scream of panic escaped my lips when his physical appearance registered and my eyes sought something I could use as a weapon. I lunged for a decorative blade displayed in one of the windows, knowing it would likely do me no good. Yellow eyes, tall body tanned and rippling with muscle. My father. The Boss. How had he gotten here? I started back peddling, shaking my head in total disbelief. The man arrived before me, hunted me down? It wasn't possible, it couldn't be.

My back hit the windowsill as the ground began to rumble, rough at first then violently. I didn't want to, *really* didn't want to, but I ripped my eyes off of him and looked outside. The knife dropped from my grasp. Nothing could have prepared me for what I saw. Chaos ensued the streets. People ran like mad, buildings caught fire, and bodies fell, their corpses crushed under whatever created the quake. Dust obscured most of my vision, but forms rushed through it, savages on demon-possessed horses, murdering whoever was in their path. I had never seen anything like the horrors taking place in front of my eyes.

My chances of running were slim, but I still made for the door.

"Wait!" The woman called. I stopped, not because of her plea, but to avoid the savages tearing through my escape.

I swung around, glaring at the man behind the counter. How had he signaled them so quickly? The woman shrieked, terrified as I was at the sight rampaging inside and out. A loose vase wobbled from high on its perch and fell, shattering on her beautiful blonde head. She dropped in an instant, screams ceasing with her. My focus was on the unfathomable sight strutting through the doorway.

In the lead was a great, able-bodied beast of a man, bearskin cloak stirred by brewing wind and dust and his strapping body dappled with the blood of recent kills. Awfully familiar faces flanked him. Lieutenant broke out, assuming the right-hand position, elegant clothing marred by dirt and stained with red. Dev swept up to the left; he caught my attention, grinned wolfishly and winked at me, gray eyes gleaming under his orange mess of hair. Razor appeared like a deadly shadow, covered in gore, not one drop of it his. The man adjusted his twin blades when he saw me looking, turning them so I could clearly see the spotless metal.

The leader had stopped. His followers still filed in behind, but never took a step past where he stood, giving the man godly presence. Skimming over their faces, looking anywhere but at him, made me feel like I was back at the fort. I became more thrown each time I picked out someone I knew.

The Mexican brothers from the cockfights, Juan and Julio, had the crazed bloodlust all over their faces. Morin clutched a pistol in his only hand, ready for slaughter. Ossy, round and repulsive as ever, was caked in blood, smiling. The sight of Eggy, nearly took my breath. She was supposed to be dead. I felt strangely betrayed, knowing she must have led them right to me.

Everything save for distant screams of victims and galloping horses was silent. Time seemed to slow to a crawl as my gaze traveled up from the leader's boots, to his broad chest, delayed recognition almost rendering me too sick to look him in the face. I stopped at the cruel mouth, catching sight of that unmistakable scar, a startling flaw to his tanned skin, and traced it up the right side of the man's face. My heart hammered out a warning for me to calm down as I was overtaken by his golden eyes. If the Devil ever expressed his anger in a look, this man bore it; death was etched into his hard features. I knew he was ready to kill, just waiting for the right moment.

I looked at the man in the doorway, leader of this wicked pack of murders, my father. I looked at the man behind the counter, and oh my god. TWINS!

Made in the USA
Lexington, KY
23 August 2013